ON WINGS OF BLOOD

BLOODWING ACADEMY, BOOK 1

BRIAR BOLEYN

For more information, email: author@briarboleyn.com

Cover Design by Ank Book Designs

Interior Illustrations & Map by New Ink Book Services

Product Page Art by Wicked Smart Designs

Proofreading by Fake Plastic Stars

Flourish Art by Polina K, Emmie Norfolk, Gordon Johnson (GDJ)

CONTENTS

CONNECT WITH BRIAR

Sign up for my newsletter! Stay caught up on my latest new releases, giveaways, and other bookish treats: www.briarboleyn.com

Find me on Instagram at: https://www.instagram.com/briarboleynauthor/

I love getting notes from readers: author@briarboleyn.com

To my Street Team, the Rose Court. You will never know how much I appreciate you all.

And to my little sister, for being the first reader of this book.
You always give me the best book recommendations!

A NOTE ABOUT TRIGGER WARNINGS

Bloodwing Academy is a dark fantasy romance series with bully vibes. The series deals with topics which some readers may understandably find triggering.

A trigger and content warnings list may be found on the next page.

Please keep in mind that reading the trigger warnings list will spoil certain plot elements.

Avoid reading the trigger warnings list if you do not have any triggers and do not wish to know specific details about the plot in advance.

TRIGGER WARNING LIST

Abduction

Assault

Blood & Gore

Blood Play

Bullying

Child Abuse

Death

Dubious Consent

Emotional Manipulation

Graphic Violence

Injury/Threat to Animals

Mental Health Issues

Murder

Non-Consensual Mind Control

Non-Consensual Blood Feeding

Physical Abuse

Power Imbalance

Psychological Abuse

Sexual Assault (Threat of)

Strong Sexual Tension

Substance Abuse

Suicidal Ideation

Torture

BOOK 1

PRELUDE

PROLOGUE

I think I was drunk. Drunk on power, drunk on her blood.

I believed she'd forgive me. She'd forgive me because she had to. We were bound, her and I.

What was spoken would be forever unbroken. Wasn't that what the old man had said? *What was bound could not be unbound.*

I hadn't done anything wrong, I told myself. I'd just taken things to their logical conclusion.

I wasn't going to take pleasure from this. I was hungry. I *needed* her.

All right, maybe there would be a little pleasure. But it would be for both of us. Not me alone.

I stepped towards her, looked into her eyes, and for a moment, I hesitated.

I could feel the emptiness gnawing at me. The bloodlust was always there, lurking beneath the surface. When it came to her, I'd somehow managed to keep it at bay.

She didn't look at me like a thrall would have. Like I was something to be feared–or worshiped. She never had.

No, what was in her eyes right now was something else entirely.

Pure hate.

She'd trusted me. Even if she wouldn't admit it.

Now I'd destroyed that.

She was looking back at me like she had that first day. As if I wasn't a man, but merely a monster.

Still, the pull was too strong. I couldn't let her simply walk away from it. From me.

The first taste of her blood hit me like a drug. Sweet and rich and powerful.

She was everything I'd been craving. More. I drank more deeply. Her blood was like nothing I'd ever tasted. She was perfect. Instead of being sated, my hunger roared to life with a vengeance.

I felt her body tense, felt the slight tremble as she tried to pull away, but I ignored it. In time she'd grow used to this. She had to. This was our way.

Then my fangs were ripped from her neck without warning.

The ground around us erupted.

Minutes later, as the dust settled and she turned towards me slowly, my bite marks still fresh upon her neck, I knew the truth.

She was in more danger now than ever before.

And she'd never forgive me for what I had done.

CHAPTER I

MEDRA

*A*utumntide
  Ten Months Earlier

The leaves were turning color when he found me. The last vestiges of summer were fleeing as my imprisonment began.

I had died destroying a corrupt god in my own world. I had sacrificed to save the ones I loved. I had gone willingly to my end. I had gone with no regrets.

And I had expected the end to stay the end.

Fate was cruel.

I took my first gasping breath, feeling my soul fluttering violently about within my body, as if uncertain it had a true place there, before finally settling uncomfortably, as if unwillingly accepting we were stuck here together.

But where was here? This was not my world. This was not Aercanum. I could sense that from the very air. It reeked with the tinge of iron and ash. Blood and death.

With a groan, I shifted my weight, the movement sending ripples of pain down my back. Something was pinning my legs down.

I stirred again and, this time, glanced downwards. A chill ran through me. Not some-*thing*. Some*one*. Someone dead lay atop me, weighing me down.

I took a deep breath to steady myself. But that only made it worse as the scent of decay filled my nostrils more strongly. I gagged.

My ears pricked at a faint sound.

Then came another.

I strained to decipher the muffled murmurs. Footsteps marched against hard ground. People were coming.

I sat up and pushed at the heavy body that had fallen over my legs, struggling to free myself. Should I call for help? Or hope they'd pass by without seeing me?

The voices were growing closer.

Abruptly, a figure appeared on the edge of my vision, bouncing up the mounds of bodies like a large weasel.

It was a man. Small and wiry. He had a smirk upon his lips, revealing a row of ratlike yellowed teeth.

I lay still, hoping he would think me just another dead body on the heap.

But it was too late. He must have caught my movement before I'd seen him. With a quick rattish leap, he was on top of me, pinning me down.

I could smell the stink of his rancid breath as he lowered his face to mine and sniffed long and deep.

"Barnabas!"

The voice cracked the air like a whip. Loud. Deep. Commanding.

The man sitting astride me froze, his face torn in indecision.

"Yes, Master?" His voice became like the slithering of serpents. Odious and simpering.

"What have you found?"

An intake of breath. The man's face was very close to my ear. He inhaled again, drawing in my scent as if it held the fragrance of a rare wine.

And then, to my horror, his tongue snaked out. Red and foul-smelling, the twisting flesh approached my neck.

"Barnabas." The voice was sharper. "I asked you a question and I expect a swift response."

The tongue slid back into the rat man's mouth. I saw the look of disappointment in his eyes as he begrudgingly responded, "This one's alive."

A pause. "Impossible. All the others were dead. The place has been on fire for days."

There was a glint in the man named Barnabas's eyes I didn't like.

I held my breath as we looked back at one another. Then he smiled.

"Even so, she's alive, milord. And she smells"—he sniffed the air again like a hungry mongrel, and I flinched—"*exquisite.*"

He lowered his mouth to my neck again, and I shouted, raising my hands to push him away as I saw the glint of sharp teeth.

"Get off her," the other man—the lord—growled. His voice was predatory, threatening. I struggled to get a sense of how old he was. Younger than Barnabas, I thought. "Not a taste. Not another sniff. That's an order. Bring her to me. Now."

Barnabas whined so quietly only I could hear, like a dog fighting against its master's chain.

"Just a small taste. Just a little taste, pretty one," he whispered. "You smell so good. Better than anything I've ever had. When he has you, he won't let you go. I'll never get another chance at you again."

His lips parted and two sharp canine teeth appeared, sharp and elongated. Larger than I had ever seen on a man—or a woman, for that matter. He barred them like a wolf might do with fangs and began to lower his face to my neck.

Panic surged. I flailed, lifting my arms up to hit him. He shocked me with his speed and strength, forcing my arms back down almost instantly.

I was weaker than I'd been. From my arrival or the ordeal that preceded it, I wasn't sure which.

I kept struggling against him and felt his frustration as he tried to keep me pinned.

His face loomed over my neck. His teeth were so close. I shut my eyes, my entire body tensing for the inevitable attack.

Instead, there was a soft crunching sound.

I felt a wetness on my face and opened my eyes.

Barnabas's body was still on top of me. But his head was gone.

Letting out a gasp of horror, I sat up and shoved his corpse off me, glancing to the side to see his decapitated head rolling down the mound of bodies, a bolt embedded in his skull.

I wiped my arm across my face, trying to clean off the vermin's blood.

Which was when I realized I was very inconveniently naked.

"Get up. Come down here."

I gritted my teeth. It seemed I was about to exchange one captor for another. And this one didn't sound the sniveling sort.

"I'd much rather prefer to stay here," I called. "Be on your way. I require no aid."

There was silence for a moment. Then I heard a burst of voices. The man was not alone. My words had evidently shocked the group of people who surrounded him.

"Silence." The voices below fell silent. "It was not a request," the voice came again. "But if you decline to do my bidding for a second time, I'll gladly have one of my men carry you down."

I rose slowly to my feet and heard gasps from below, whether at the sight of Barnabas's blood dripping down me or the shock of a woman's naked flesh–who can say. They were mostly men, so likely the latter.

I lifted my hand to shield my eyes from the hazy sun which had half-peeked out from behind the clouds. Focusing my eyes, I saw a line of soldiers–some standing, others on horseback. All wore a distinctive style of red and black armor.

A man sat at the front on a black steed. He held a crossbow in his hands. I eyed the weapon with interest. It must have been a powerful bow indeed to decapitate with a single shot.

Then I looked up at the man's face and all thoughts of the bow left my mind.

He was striking. All sharp angles and pale skin. Lethal and alluring.

He was also much younger than I'd expected. Closer to my own age.

This man had saved my life. Killed one of his own men to protect me.

But as I saw the arrogant expression painting his handsome features, the cruel twist of his thin lips, I felt no gratitude.

Golden-blond hair framed a sharp jawline. He had a lean, elegant build, all muscular grace. Nevertheless, there was something about him that made me think he had been a frail and skinny boy once.

One of his features stood out from the others. His aquiline, hawkish nose. It was out of place. Too pointed, too large. Too less-than-perfect. But if anything, it made him look even more aristocratic, enhancing his haughty expression. It complemented the fine angles of his cheekbones and jaw and added to his wolfish air.

Some might even have called him unattractive. He certainly wasn't my type. I preferred a bulkier build. Darker hair. Still, I couldn't deny there was something about him. A sense of barely coiled power and dangerous cunning that simmered beneath the surface of his facade of tight control.

As I stumbled down the mountain of rotting corpses, he slid off his horse. Holding the crossbow in his left hand, he strode towards me. He carried himself like someone unused to having his authority questioned.

Piercing gray eyes glinted and I felt myself being assessed from head to toe. His eyes lingered slowly on every inch of my flesh, stripping away all of my modesty.

He took a step closer towards me, sniffing the air in a way that reminded me unbearably of Barnabas. I caught the scent of green apples wafting off him, just before I snapped and backed away from him. Later, I would wonder about that. He smelled fresh. Nothing like Barnabas or the rancid corpses.

Still, I couldn't bear that gaze raking over me any longer.

"Take a good, long look, why don't you?" I tossed my long hair over one shoulder and was disconcerted to feel it fall on bare skin. "I assure you, it's the last one you'll ever get."

One brave soldier hooted with laughter somewhere down the line. I grinned towards the soldiers, daring them to laugh again.

A glare from their young commander silenced them all in an instant.

The young man sneered. "I was trying to understand Barnabas's strange fascination. You smell absolutely revolting. But then, I suppose lying on a pile of corpses tends to do that to one."

He turned to one of the soldiers. "Get her some clothes." He snapped his fingers. "No, on second thought, give her your cloak. Take it off. Now."

I saw the soldier's eyes widen. "But, my lord, my prince," the man whispered, glancing at me surreptitiously. "You saw what she is. Her hair... She bears the mark..."

A prince, was he? He was certainly haughty-looking enough to be one.

"I know what she is," the commander responded. "Better than you do, I have no doubt. Now give her your fucking cloak. We're taking her back with us."

Hurriedly, the soldier unfastened his cloak and tossed it over to me. I caught it gratefully, trying to ignore the look in his eyes. Fear or revulsion, I couldn't quite tell.

"Prince or not, you're quite mistaken if you think I'm going anywhere with you," I declared as I accepted the cloak and wrapped it around me. "Thank you for the cloak, but I'll find my own way home from this place."

Part of that was true, at least. This wasn't home. I doubted I'd ever get back there again. But I could leave this hellhole into which I'd fallen.

A moment later I found myself wishing I hadn't spoken.

The young commander had mounted his horse. Now he turned to look down at me disdainfully. His nose, I noticed, was not only hawk-like but crooked, as if it had been broken before, perhaps more than once.

There was something about him that made me unable to look away. His eyes locked with mine in a silent challenge.

"If only the decision was yours to make. It isn't. But if you plan to make this difficult..."
He gestured to another soldier. "Find her proper clothes. Then bind her."

And they did.

We rode towards a city, a strange procession of soldiers, horses, and me, staggering in front of the commander's horse, my wrists chained together as I trod over uneven ground.

I could feel the prince's eyes on me, sense his cold amusement each time I tripped and stumbled.

I'd already developed a seething hatred for my new captor, but I managed not to turn my head and look up. Not once.

Eventually though, he spoke.

"Where do you come from?"

I ignored him.

"I asked you a question. Clearly you didn't belong in that place. So where do you come from? What were you doing there?"

I heard the snap of a whip and flinched.

"Don't make me ask again."

I bit my lip to keep the hysterical rise of laughter inside. Would this man truly *whip* me? I, who had until recently, been a princess of Camelot and a royal fae.

I might as well reply, I thought. Not with the truth though, of course.

"I don't know," I lied.

I wasn't about to tell him I'd dropped in from another world after destroying my own grandfather, who may or may not have been the closest thing my world had to a god. And besides, whatever I'd used to accomplish that feat, I was pretty sure hadn't managed to come along with me.

I hadn't wanted to fully acknowledge it before, but the truth was... I felt weaker. Oddly empty. Dare I say it? Mortal.

Still, there was obviously something about me that had drawn these soldiers' attention. They had said I was different. What was it that marked me out?

"Why are you taking me with you? Do you always accost innocent women you find on the road?"

He was silent for a moment. "You speak as if you don't know who I am. What were you doing in that place?"

"I got lost," I said blithely. "And I don't. Know who you are, I mean. Should I? Know you? I mean, besides knowing you're an asshole?"

He grunted as if annoyed, but didn't raise the whip.

"It's unbelievable to me that you can truly be so ignorant. But then, I suppose you'll find out everything you need to know soon enough," he said cryptically. Then, "Oh, fuck," I heard him mutter.

I looked up to see a soldier jogging towards us. He was of a small, frail build and wore round wire frames lined with glass on his face. Spectacles. I had seen some of the nobles back home wear them before. I gazed at him with curiosity and he stared right back at me, as if completely agog.

"My prince," he gasped. "I was told you had found..." He eyed me. "Found a woman of interest."

"I suppose you could say that," the prince drawled. "She's not that interesting, Lucius. Quite dull, in fact."

I ignored the jab.

"But... her hair," the soldier called Lucius wheezed. "The color. It's incredible. Absolutely incredible, my lord."

That again? So it *was* my hair. I touched a hand to my head. I'd been told my fae mother had vibrant purple tresses. Not that I'd ever seen her hair. She had died giving birth to me.

In comparison, my hair seemed to have settled into a dull, rusty red.

More than once I'd thought of carrots when I looked at myself in the mirror at night. Right now, the curls were tangled and bushy. My fingers tugged at them but it was pointless. I needed a brush, a comb. And a hot bath. At the thought of being clean and warm, a slight moan escaped my lips.

"Prince Drakharrow, do you have any idea what this means?" Lucius whispered loudly. I had begun to think of him as a kind of secretary. He was certainly toadying up enough to be one. "You must take her before the court. Why, she might even be..."

"We'll wait to speak of it," the prince-commander interrupted. "I've already sent a messenger ahead of us," he admitted, almost begrudgingly.

There was a tension in his voice that told me he knew very well what the other man meant. He just didn't want to acknowledge it. Not yet. Why? What was it about me?

"Excellent news, my lord. Excellent. I knew I could count upon your wisdom." I felt the toadying little secretary's eyes drilling into me. "I can only imagine the stir this will cause. Just look at her, my prince–her hair is truly... well, *red*."

"Yes, I can see that, Lucius," Prince Drakharrow snapped. "I have eyes. Red hair. It is indeed red. Well, we're bringing her back with us. The court will investigate the meaning of her appearance and settle the matter. It's all very tedious. Now we must return early without finishing our investigation into the matter of the village. But what can we do? I live to serve." I could almost hear his eyes rolling in annoyance.

"Pardon me. Am I boring you?" I hissed, turning to look back at him. I yanked on my chains. "I suppose this is just an ordinary day for you. Leading people around in chains."

He ignored me.

"Very well. As you say, my lord," the secretary-soldier said hastily, also ignoring my outburst but shooting me a shocked glance. "It is a true honor to be in your company as you return with such a very prestigious captive."

"I'm not a fucking *captive*," I snarled, spinning about to face the man.

The secretary gasped and backed away, tripping on a rock and nearly toppling over in the process.

Behind me, Drakharrow snickered. The first sign he might be something resembling a human that I'd seen. I looked back at him and glared.

"Do try to keep your footing, Lucius," the young lord drawled. "She's just another blightborn, not a unicorn."

"Indeed not! She may be far more important than any mythological creature of legend," Lucius squeaked as he stretched out his hands to regain his balance. "Though of course, there is a connection between..."

"This conversation is growing tedious. Look." The blond man pointed ahead. "We're nearing the city. The matter will be settled soon."

Lucius scuttled away, still muttering excitedly to himself.

I looked ahead to where he was indicating and drew in my breath. We had come to the top of a high rolling hill. Below us lay a city.

I had come from a castle which floated in the sky. I had used powerful magics to bring it down to earth and kill the ones who dwelled within it.

Already that seemed so long ago. So impossible.

Yet despite the wonders I had witnessed, I could honestly say I had seen nothing quite like what lay before us.

The city itself was built on a smaller scale than I had expected, but nevertheless looked grand and affluent. It lay affixed to the edge of a dark and restless ocean, where tumultuous waters splashed against white sands. Beyond the edge of the city limits, three enormous iron bridges stretched out, leading towards three rocky islands.

On the first island, perched like a white nest on a dark cliff, lay a structure built from bright, gleaming stone. It glistened upwards like a luminous pearl against the roiling gray waves and rapidly dimming sky. Soaring narrow spires filled its center while slender, graceful columns rose around the structure.

On the second island, a castle of deep onyx-colored towers and arches twisted skywards in shapes and at angles which should have been impossible, reminding me of the sharp, pointed fangs of a great stone beast.

The third and final island held the largest building of all and one which I suspected might be the oldest. Looking as if it had arisen from a jumbled mix of eras and styles, it resembled a castle or a great fortress. The structure sprawled like the web of a spider, spiraling outwards from a cluster of six towers, each of a different material and design. The only thing which provided any sense of continuity to the building, whatever it might be, was its color. All of the materials that had been used were of a dark crimson shade, nearly black.

I schooled my features carefully, trying not to disclose my impressions. If my captor could play at boredom, so could I.

"What is it?" I asked, trying to sound careless. "What is the name of that town ahead?"

"Town?" I caught the note of annoyance in his voice. "That is no mere town."

I shrugged. "City, then. What does it matter?"

"What does it matter?"

To my shock, I heard him dismounting behind me. In another moment, he was at my elbow, marching by my side.

"That, girl, is no town, but the capital city of Sangratha." I could feel his eyes on my face. "Honestly, if you are a spy for the borderlands, you're the worst one I've ever seen. How could anyone not know of Veilmar?"

"Oh? And you catch a lot of spies, do you?" I looked him up and down, letting my eyes linger on his black cloak and impeccable armor. "You don't look the sort to get your hands dirty."

"You don't know anything about me, as we've already determined," he retorted.

I tilted my head. "I know you're noble. That you're used to giving orders, not following them. That you're used to people doing your bidding–instead of you having to work to get what you want. I'd say I know enough."

He was silent.

"That man you killed. Barnabas," I ventured. "There was something strange about him."

He snorted.

"I mean, beyond the obvious," I snapped. "His teeth. They were... elongated. I think he was going to... bite me."

The pale-haired prince burst into laughter. "Do you now?"

"I don't see what's so funny about..." I started to say. Then I stopped.

He was smirking down at me coldly–smiling, if you can call it that, for the first time. With his lips parted slightly, I could see that his incisors were even longer than Barnabas's had been, and they narrowed into sharp, delicate points.

"Fangs," I said hollowly. "You have fangs."

He sneered. "Don't tell me you haven't heard of highbloods where you come from or I really will wonder if you fell from the sky. Or perhaps hit your head too hard against a rock." He narrowed his eyes. "Or have drunk a little too much?" A hand darted out and he tapped me on the side of the head, hard.

"Ow! I haven't had anything to drink, you fool," I exclaimed.

"I'm the fool but you're the one with naught in your head." He shook his head.

"I read a passage in a book once..." I began.

"Oh, you can read? I'm speechless."

I ignored him. "It spoke of creatures with sharp teeth that drank blood. They could not go out under the light of day. They attacked at night, sucking their victims dry. They led long lives." I snuck a look at him, hoping beyond hope that he'd tell me the book was mistaken.

"Well, three out of five isn't bad," he remarked. "We can walk in the light, as you can well see." He pointed upwards at the fading evening sun, which had come out from behind the clouds. "We lead long lives."

"But you... drink people?" I stared at him, trying to keep the horror from my tone. "You drink blood?"

He smiled, cruelly and slowly. "We are vampires. It's what we do."

"So you're what? Taking me back to your people to be drained?"

He stretched his arms over his head and I tried to keep my eyes off the muscles rippling beneath the dark cloak. "Perhaps. Who knows what they'll do with you? It's an honor to be drained, you know."

I couldn't tell if he was joking. Somehow I doubted it. "You're a monster."

He smirked. "Stop, you're hurting my feelings, blightborn."

"Don't pretend you have any," I snapped.

"You're right. They're a weakness, so I won't."

"Why do you need to take me anywhere? Why not leave me alone where you found me?"

His lips twisted. "On a heap of dead bodies? I should have thought we were doing you a favor."

I raised my wrists. "Ah, yes, if only all men were as courteous as you," I said sarcastically, clanging the metal chains together. "I'm quite killed with kindness."

His mouth twitched. "Many women would beg to be in your position. Perhaps not while walking on quite such a dusty road..."

"I don't wish to hear of your disgusting sexual exploits," I said, making a face of disgust. "Save your bragging for your men. They won't care if you tell tall tales about the women you tie to your bed."

"I have no need to make up stories," he snapped, sounding irked.

I tossed my hair over my shoulder but said nothing.

I could feel him staring at the red tresses for a moment. Finally, he said, "You asked why we're taking you with us? Well, you heard what Lucius said."

"That it's because of my hair? A rather stupid reason."

He snorted. "I agree."

I glanced at him. "You do? Well, then... Let me go."

"Unfortunately, there's more to it than my preference in hair color. I might think your rust-colored locks unsightly," he said snidely. "But it's not about my personal preference."

"Thank the stars for that," I said under my breath. "I have no wish for you to find me desirable. *My lord.*" I let the last two words drip with sarcasm.

He ignored me.

After a moment or two, I had to ask. "Fine. What else then? Besides my hair? You said I was a blightborn. What does that mean?"

He glanced at me. "All mortals are blightborn. You clearly aren't a vampire. But there are... differences. You aren't an ordinary mortal. Your ears for one. They're unusual."

I touched a finger to the tip of one ear, feeling the point. I looked at his. "Yours are round."

"All of ours our round," he said, gesturing to the soldiers in front of us. "I've never seen pointed ears like yours. They stand out."

"Is that all? So I was born with red hair and odd ears! And that's a reason to kidnap me?" I said, my voice beginning to raise.

"There's more," he said slowly, his eyes holding mine. He looked up and down my body and despite myself, I felt my cheeks turning red. "Other aspects of your appearance."

I bristled. "Like what?"

"Besides, I didn't kidnap you," he said, turning around to mount his horse once more. Apparently this conversation was at an end. "You were never *yours* in the first place."

My jaw dropped. "I beg your pardon?"

"You belong to Sangratha. You belong to any highblood who sees fit to take you. As Lucius said, it's an honor to be noticed by one of the Blessed Blood." He smiled, his lips tight. "You *should* be honored."

Sangratha. Apparently it was the name of this land.

Part of me longed to ask this so-called prince other questions. Such as his name. Or the meaning of the places that lay ahead of us on the three islands. What were they? Were we going there?

But I decided our hostile banter had gone on long enough. I licked my lips, already chapped from hours of walking without water or respite, and walked on in silence.

As we skirted around the edge of the city of Veilmar, soon enough it became clear where our real course lay.

The island in the center of the three. The castle of onyx stone.

CHAPTER 2

MEDRA

The castle was called the Black Keep. A rather uninspired name.

I heard the men whispering around me, speaking the words almost as if they were holy. Soldiers marched past to line up in formation and made sure to give me a wide berth, casting only curious glances my way.

Behind me, the prince rode calmly. Clearly he was not intimidated by the sight of the massive fortress we were approaching. He'd been here before.

We passed over the black iron bridge. I could feel it swaying slightly beneath us. Under our feet lay the open sea, rolling and churning as if it were angry at our presence.

Ahead of us, a gate stood open and beyond that, the doors leading into the keep.

One by one, the soldiers took up places on either side of the doors, until finally, it was just myself and the prince in the center of a long aisle of his followers. A quiet descended over the troops as we entered the courtyard.

Lucius stepped forward, bowing low. "I shall announce you to the hall, Prince Drakharrow."

The other man nodded. "Keep it brief. Skip the titles. Everyone in there knows me already, Lucius. The only time I'm called 'prince' is outside of Bloodwing, after all. It's a stupid formality."

Lucius blanched a little. "But... protocol dictates..."

The prince suddenly snarled, his teeth biting forward and clamping down. Beside him, I gasped and flinched.

Lucius stumbled backwards. "The most meager of titles, my prince. The barest," he promised.

The secretary hurried ahead of us.

The prince's hand gripped my arm. "I'll take the chains off now. Don't get any ideas. There's nowhere to run."

I didn't reply, simply watched as he took a key from his pocket and unlocked my bindings.

As soon as I was free, he began to stalk towards the keep.

"Are you all vampires?" I hurried to keep up with him. I was tall for a woman, but he was much taller. He took long strides. "The soldiers, too?"

"Not all but some of them," he answered. "Lucius is, if that's what you're wondering. You should be silent now. You won't like what happens if you aren't."

"I'm surprised you don't wish to keep me on your leash, my lord," I muttered under my breath. "Like your *other* women."

He didn't take the bait.

As we passed through the huge ornate iron doors into the blackstone keep, our feet touched white marble floors. I glanced down at myself. My feet were bare and dirty. I wore trousers and a tunic a soldier close to my size had reluctantly donated. The cloak around my shoulders suddenly felt like a much-needed shield and I pulled it tight, resisting the urge to raise the hood over my tangled hair.

I sniffed myself gingerly, then wished I hadn't.

I stank like a rotting corpse.

We stepped into the heart of the chamber.

Above us, thousands of candles glowed in iron candelabras hung high overhead.

A vast platform stretched out at the far side of the room. A line of people stood upon it, mostly dressed in red or black. Many of their garments were trimmed with silver or gold. They looked regal and powerful.

A man sat in their center on an elegant chair of carved stone, striking in clothes of crimson velvet. There was no crown upon his head. Still, I was reminded of the throne room of the Rose Court back home.

Below the platform, the vast room was packed to the brim with a massive crowd. As we entered, the throng parted, letting us pass through the center.

Hushed murmurs rose from around us. I listened to the subdued chatter, catching a few insults cast my way.

Let them look. Let them stare. I had no intention of remaining in this place long.

I kept my head up, striving to match the prince's stride step for step, even though it meant taking two steps for each of his.

Abruptly, I was pulled to a halt.

I yelped before I could stop myself as a hand gripped my hair and yanked so hard I fell to my knees on the floor. A woman looked down at me, her face gloating as she wrapped her fingers around strands of the hair she had ripped from my head.

Instantly, the prince was by my side, snarling even more ferally than he had done at Lucius back in the courtyard. His cloak swept around me like a bat's wings as he pulled me to my feet.

"Hands off," he growled. "No one touches her."

His voice echoed loudly off the stone walls.

A hush descended over the crowd. I glanced at the raised dais. The people standing on it were observing us intently. No one seemed interested in intervening.

The woman who had yanked my hair was well-dressed. Gold rings covered her hands and rubies hung from her ears. For a moment, she looked taken aback. Then her expression turned peevish.

"A few strands of hair. I didn't harm her," she protested. "We all know the stories. You can't keep her all to yourself, my prince."

I watched as she tried to summon an obsequious smile and failed spectacularly.

I glared at her, furious. "Bitch," I whispered as I shook myself off.

"Give them to me. The hairs." The prince held out his hand to the woman. His voice was cold. "Now."

Muttering under her breath, the woman stretched her hand out and I saw some long strands of red disappear into his palm.

I watched as the prince pocketed my hair. I wondered what he'd do with them. Tie them to his bed as a keepsake perhaps? I would have snickered if the thought wasn't so abhorrent.

I looked around at the people gaping at me as if I were a menagerie animal and bared my teeth. The chattering resumed, even more loudly than before, but I didn't care.

I might not have fangs like they did, but that didn't mean I couldn't pretend to be the most dangerous thing they'd ever seen.

They were pathetic, I decided, staring at me. What did I have that they so badly wanted, anyhow? Why had the prince brought me here? Was it simply my hair?

Then I thought of Barnabas and my heart sank. Not hair.

Blood.

We reached the raised platform a few steps behind Lucius. The small man dropped to his knees on the red velvet carpet that spread out around the dais and began to rapidly intone, his voice carrying easily across the vast hall.

"Lords and ladies of the Blessed Blood, allow me to present one who is familiar to us all–the Scarlet Warden of the Red Keep, High Prince of Sangratha, Bloodlord of the Pure..."

The titles kept coming. On and on.

For a moment, the prince stood by my side, his teeth gritted. Then, abruptly, he leaned forward and delivered a swift kick to Lucius's ankle.

There was a yelp.

The secretary continued at a much quicker pace than before, "With absolutely no further adieu, I present Prince Blake Drakharrow, my lords and ladies."

A brief pause. "And by his side, stands a... female... most unusual for a blightborn."

I suppressed a snort.

"An unpolished treasure found amidst the muck and mire." Lucius seemed to be refinding his flow. "Saved by the Black Prince from the edge of death and despair."

I coughed loudly, and cast a pointed look at the prince who was still staring straight ahead like a statue. It was true that this man, Blake Drakharrow, had shot one of his own men to save me. But after chaining me like a beast, I wasn't planning to offer him a thank you anytime soon.

"You all see this creature's rare qualities," Lucius declared pompously to the crowd, gesturing to me. "Here she is, to be presented to the court, by my high and honorable lord, Prince Blake Drakharrow..."

"Yes, you've said that part once already," Blake interrupted. "That's quite enough, Lucius."

Lucius scurried off to one side before he could be kicked again.

For a moment, I felt sorry for him. Until I remembered he was also a vampire.

Blake's hand gripped my wrist, pulling me abruptly forward. He raised his voice so it carried throughout the hall.

"We found this woman in the burned out village just outside of Veilmar." Not for the first time, I wondered what had happened to that village. At first, I had assumed its devastation had been Blake's doing. Now I wondered if that was the case. "There should have been no one left alive, but somehow there she was. You can see for yourself her strange traits." He lifted a hand laconically to gesture at me, then dropped it with a shrug, as if he were already bored of looking at me. "I thought it best to bring her before you and the Council."

Oh, he did, did he? And just who is this Council? So very hastily assembled. The hall is full. All here for you, my pretty.

I jumped, my wrist suddenly twisting in Blake's grasp.

It was a woman's voice. Low and melodic. And inside my own head.

Who are you? Who said that? I demanded.

You should never have allowed yourself to be taken. Really, girl, have you no pride? the woman's voice chided.

Pride? I have plenty of pride. Pride didn't arm me. Pride didn't give me a blade with which to slit his throat, I retorted.

Ah, but you wished to. That is something at least. Good. Hold on to that. Hold on to your rage.

There was something imperious about the woman's tone, despite her bloodthirsty nature.

Who the hell are you? I demanded again. *Get out of my head.*

You're right. We should cease this chatter and listen. You must see what these people want with you. There was a pause and I could almost picture the unseen woman tapping her finger against her well-formed chin. *From the look of it, they aren't complete and utter savages. They possess a sense of decorum. And taste.*

Taste? Is that what you call it? They drink blood. I felt hysteria bubbling up in my throat and quickly suppressed it. *Decorum? Is that what you'd call it when they chain me up and rip my hair out?*

There was no reply. The woman's voice was gone.

If it had ever been anything except my imagination in the first place.

A chill went through me.

Perhaps that was it. Perhaps I *was* dead. Perhaps I was in some twisted afterlife. Insanity might have been part and parcel with death. Maybe I was going insane. If that was the case, I hoped the madness would descend quickly and that I'd soon have no thoughts left in my mind at all.

But in the meantime, I looked at the people standing and staring down at me from the platform. And I stared right back.

My eyes went from one to the other, keeping my lips pressed together. Did I look hostile? Threatening? I hoped so.

Because they certainly did.

The man seated on the black stone chair leaned forward slightly. His eyes were a deep, unsettling red and he held a staff topped with a gleaming, scarlet gem. I looked away from him quickly, unnerved by his expression. He eyed me with the same keen interest one might give to a horse or some other piece of livestock one contemplates purchasing.

Next my eyes fell on the man to his left. He was younger, clad in black leather armor accented in gold. His eyes weren't gray like Blake's though; they were a pale blue, but shaped the same. In fact, he resembled Blake in many ways, though his build was a little shorter and stockier.

I glanced at Blake, who still held me by the wrist, then back again. Yes, the two might have been cousins. Even brothers.

A movement caught my eye. A young woman had folded and unfolded her arms restlessly. She stood further down the row of nobles. She was lovely, with pink lips and shimmering pale blonde hair. Her gown was a cascade of sheer violet over black silk. A diadem of silver embedded with purple gems sat on her brow. She tapped her foot as if impatient or annoyed, yet when she caught me staring, she looked back at me. There was something in her gaze beyond mere curiosity or even hostility. I saw naked hate. And past that, perhaps something like fear.

There was more to all of this. More to these strange and foreign people in this strange and foreign land. I scanned the line of noble folk. A thread of commonality stretched between all of the figures on the dais, linking them together.

Their hair, I realized. If hair was what made me stand out, it was what united all of them.

From the man seated in the chair to the younger man beside him to the woman looking at me with such cold fury. While their skin tones were a range of shades, they were unified by the lightness of their hair. Hues ranging from silvery white to golden blonde to silvery gray. Not a glimpse of brown or black or even red amongst them.

I cast my gaze out over the crowd and it was the same. While there had been some chestnut, brown, and black colored hair amongst the soldiers who had escorted me, I saw no glimmer of any shade beyond snowy pale or faint gold in this hall.

I looked at the man on the black chair, his hair as white as freshly fallen snow, cut to shoulder-length, sleek and straight, framing a bearded face, hard and cold.

The younger man beside him had hair of ashy blond, cropped short in a military style that emphasized the strong, angular lines of his face.

I glanced at the man by my side, the man Lucius had named Blake Drakharrow. His hair hung around his face, nearly chin-length. The strands were very pale gold. Blond in some lights, almost white in others.

I stood out amongst these people like a flaming coal.

Just barely I resisted the impulse to touch a hand to my head self-consciously.

I glanced away, avoiding the feeling, and my eyes rested on a girl I had not noticed before.

A child.

No more than nine or ten, she sat on the edge of the platform. Her long blonde hair had been braided with red ribbons and a few rebellious strands had escaped to fall in a frame around her pale, porcelain face. Now she slouched forward, her chin resting heavily in her hands, propped up by slender arms. Looking bored and disinterested in the proceedings, she kicked her feet absently against the dais.

I nearly smiled, watching her. I wondered who she could be. Someone important enough to be included amongst the powerful people on the platform but not important enough to be made to stand beside them. Or perhaps they had given up trying to make her stand nicely. Children were children anywhere. Even among vampires.

The man seated on the black chair was rising.

He held his staff as a symbol of strength, not as a crutch like a truly elderly man might. I got the sense of an ancient power. He loomed over the whole assembly like a dark shadow and something about the way he looked down at me made me weak in the knees. Not in a good way.

Blake's hand gripped my wrist more tightly. To hurt me or to steady me, I wasn't sure which.

Either way it worked. I stood up a little straighter, lifted my chin a little higher.

"A rare find indeed," the older man agreed, as he stepped to the edge of the platform. "You were right to bring her to us, Blake." His eyes honed in on mine, glowing faintly. "What is your name, child? Where do you come from?"

I had the impression he was doing his best to speak kindly. Yet I knew beyond a doubt there was nothing truly *kind* about this man.

Nevertheless, a warmth flooded through me and I found my lips parting before I could stop myself.

"My name is Medra Pendragon, my lord."

A wave of murmurs spread through the crowd. I did my best to ignore them.

"As for where I come from..." I cleared my throat. "You would not believe me if I told you."

Another ripple went through the crowd and I saw the older man frown as if I had said something inadvertently defiant.

"You have no knowledge of Sangratha? Of the Thralldom?"

I shook my head. "I don't even know what those words mean."

Though "thralldom" was pretty clear. I disliked the implications. Was this vampire kingdom based entirely upon slavery or some form of it?

"All I ask, my lord," I said, continuing onwards as carefully as I could. "Is for your forbearance and mercy. I may have been found in your land, yes, but I had no intention of being here. I did not mean to trespass. I wish only to return home."

The man was silent for a long moment.

Then, "Tell me, Medra Pendragon, how does one find oneself in a strange land as you did? And having no knowledge of how you found yourself here, how could you possibly return home? Where *is* home?"

I opened my mouth, then closed it again. He was right. I had no idea how to traverse worlds as I had apparently done purely by accident. I had been snatched somehow from the jaws of death but not by my doing or my choice.

"Your silence speaks volumes. You do not speak of your home. Therefore, are you a spy?"

"I've forgotten it," I blurted out. "I've forgotten my home. If I'm a spy, I've forgotten that, too. But I know I don't belong here."

"How convenient," the man said softly. "And yet perhaps this is precisely where you belong. Now tell me, what other dangerous information have you forgotten?"

I lifted my chin. "I said I've lost my memories. Not that I mean you any harm. There's no need for you all to be so suspicious. Why do you stare at me? Because of my hair? Red hair is not so rare where I come from. I remember that much. Is this realm so weak that you see me as a threat?"

The room erupted with noise.

"Silence!" the other man on the platform, the one who resembled Blake, bellowed. "We will have order here or the hall shall be cleared."

Quiet descended immediately. Around me people shifted uncomfortably, no one daring to look up at the man on the platform.

"If I may, Lord Drakharrow."

It was the young woman in the violet dress. She stepped forward, her hands clasped modestly together.

So, the man who would deal my fate was related to Blake Drakharrow. Was this his father?

"Miss Pansera." Lord Drakharrow smiled indulgently. "Do you have wisdom to impart to the court?"

The young woman gave a simpering smile. "To believe I had any wisdom to impart to *you*, Lord Drakharrow, would be the utmost presumption."

A titter of laughter came from the crowd. But the laughter was gentle. She was one of them, after all.

The young woman took a small step forward, her eyes coming to rest on me.

"No, no wisdom, my lord. Simply anger."

"Anger, Miss Pansera?" Lord Drakharrow's eyebrows rose.

"Anger at this creature."

I bristled.

"At this female's defiance," she continued. "Anger at her disrespect for your house, for this court, for our sacred traditions."

"I know nothing about your traditions," I said loudly. "And I meant no disrespect."

The young woman's face took on an expression of disgust. "Even now she speaks to me as if she had a place here. As if she had a right to speak among the Pure of Blood. But she was found on a heap of dirt. She reeks of the grave and I cannot help but hope you send her back to it, my lord. You do not deserve to be spoken to with such disdain."

Lord Drakharrow tilted his head thoughtfully. "What of the marks she bears, Miss Pansera? Would you have me kill her or allow her to depart despite that?"

The girl in the violet gown shrugged. "What does it matter if she bears a rider's marks when there is nothing to ride?"

I glanced quickly at the prince, confused by the words, but he would not meet my eyes. His lips were pressed together in a thin line. Was he displeased with Miss Pansera's speech? Or was he simply annoyed at having to be there at all?

Miss Pansera was stepping back demurely, taking up her place amongst the other nobles on the platform, her head bowed respectfully.

But though her head was tilted downwards, her eyes remained on me.

It was clear she wanted Lord Drakharrow to kill me here today. What had I done to make her my enemy? Or was it simply that I was not a vampire?

"Regan Pansera speaks true," Lord Drakharrow admitted to the crowd. "There have not been dragons in our lands in more than one hundred years."

My heart leaped at the word. Dragons.

"The last riders died out long before that." Lord Drakharrow scanned the crowd. "And we—the Chosen, the Pure, the Blessed Blood—are sadly the weaker for it. Are we not?"

A subdued murmur of agreement.

He raised his voice a little. "This girl, wherever she really comes from, bears the unmistakable marks of a rider. See the color of her hair. The pointed tips of her ears. Look at how her fingers and toes are elongated, just as the riders of old."

I glanced down at my hands self-consciously, curling them into fists. But my feet were bare. There was nothing I could do to hide them. All around me, everyone stared and murmured.

Beads of sweat prickled the back of my neck. I tried to remain calm. My hands and feet were like any fae's back in Aercanum. Elongated? I was half-fae, so I supposed they were. More than a full human's. There was nothing unusual about that where I came from.

"Her build," Lord Drakharrow continued, raising both hands and then lowering them to gesture to my body. "A lean, streamlined physique, optimized for balance and agility." He eyed me. "Her bones. Were we to conduct experiments, no doubt we would find them to be denser, reinforced. Reducing her risk of injury from maneuvers and impacts."

I swallowed hard. "Experiments" sounded ominous.

"I have no idea what you are even talking about," I announced. "The only thing I've ever ridden is a horse. Certainly not a dragon."

The crowd laughed. At me. Not with me as they had done with the perfect Miss Pansera.

"Do they not have dragons where you come from, Miss Pendragon?" Lord Drakharrow inquired. "Your name would suggest they do. What land is this you hail from? I would very much like to visit it one day."

I shook my head. "It's a name, nothing more. I cannot even recall the name of my land," I lied. "Perhaps there were dragons there once, long ago, but no one alive has ever seen them. Not where I come from. It's just a name."

It was, in fact, the name of kings and queens. The Pendragons were an ancient line. And thanks to my mother's poor choice of men, I was a part of it through my father's side.

Poor choice? Or careful plotting?

The voice in my head was back again.

Get out, I hissed at her. *You have no right to be here.*

A tinkling laugh. *You have no idea how wrong you are.*

But she was silent after that.

"I see." A thin smile. Lord Drakharrow thought I was lying through my teeth. "Well, *this* land did have dragons, Medra Pendragon. They were not simply names. They existed. And they had riders."

"And you think... what? That I'm one of them?" I stared up at him in disbelief. "You've already established there are no dragons anymore, right? So why does it matter?" I glanced at Regan Pansera, as if expecting commiseration—after all, we agreed about this, didn't we? But her eyes remained dagger-like.

"It was an ancient lineage," Lord Drakharrow was musing. "And your appearance, here, today could be seen as almost prophetic..."

"If I may, Lord Drakharrow." A woman's voice. Soft but regal. She stood on the other side of the platform, draped in red silk. She looked older than most of the nobles around her—though not as old as Lord Drakharrow. "As you know, House Avari prided itself on our dragon riders. This girl's appearance might be nothing. Or..." She hesitated, stealing a quick glance down at me. I got the impression this was a woman of great authority and power—but not as much power as Lord Drakharrow wielded. I sensed she would defer to him.

"Yes, Lady Avari?" Lord Drakharrow pressed. "Or?"

The older silver haired woman bit her lip. "Or it might be an omen. A sign from the Bloodmaiden herself."

A stir went through the hall.

A heavyset man in silver brocade stepped forward, his steel armored boots clanking against the platform. "House Mortis concurs with House Avari. The girl's arrival should not be underestimated. She is significant. She must not be permitted to leave."

"Interesting," Lord Drakharrow mused. "And the options as you see them, Lord Mortis, are?"

Lord Mortis glared down at me, his face stern. "Test her blood. Either offer her to the goddess should her blood be worthy or destroy her as if she never were. Or..."

Lord Drakharrow's eyebrows rose again. "Or? Is there yet a third option? Fascinating."

"Or mate with her," Lord Mortis growled. I flinched. "Preserve the rider's bloodline now that it has been found. The riders were all lost. Her blood seems..." He hesitated. I suspected he did not wish to use the word "pure" to describe me. "Strong," he settled on. "Her features are distinct. Prominent. That bodes well."

He stepped back amongst the other nobles on the dais.

Evidently those standing up on the platform were the ultimate elite. I saw nods of agreement from some of the lords and ladies around him. But to what part of what he'd just said? The part about killing me? Or offering my blood to some goddess?

Or perhaps worst of all—mating with me. Who was to do the honor? Lord Drakharrow?

A shudder went through me. No. Decidedly no.

I started eyeing the tall arched glass windows that lined the walls of the hall. How fast could I get to one? Would they be quick enough to stop me? If I did manage to dive through one would I fall onto a cobblestone walkway? Or sharp rocks along the cliffside? Or the turbulent waves below?

Best case scenario, I decided, I'd be cut and bleeding from the broken window and forced to swim out to sea as Blake's archers shot at me.

"A mating," Lord Drakharrow murmured. He raised a hand to his chin, stroking his silver beard. "Binding her to us. Continuing the lineage. Strengthening it. I cannot deny, it is an interesting idea."

He looked down at where I stood. "Of course, by rights only one man should be bound to her."

A stir went through the audience.

I looked around at the nobles, my face flushing hot with anger. "I wouldn't mind having a say in all of this, Lord Drakharrow."

"Oh? But you do not get a say, Medra Pendragon. Perhaps it has not been clear to you yet, but People of the Pure Blood stand here deciding your fate and your fate has come very close to death today."

I let out a hiss between my teeth. "But it won't be death, will it?"

He smiled, his fangs dropping, lethal and white. I flinched. "No?"

I shook my head, purposely making my hair fly out around my head in a curly cloud. I heard gasps as the mane of red fluttered in the air, then settled against my shoulders.

This was about my survival now. And to my surprise, I found I did wish to survive. I was not dead. I had not died. I rather wanted to keep it that way. At least, for now.

"No," I said emphatically. "I'm too valuable to be killed. You've all decided that already. As Lady Avari already mentioned, I could be an omen." What was it he'd already said?

That I had a dragon rider's physique. "Look at me. I'm a Pendragon. The *only* Pendragon. For all you know, the power lies in my blood. Maybe I can bring back the dragons."

A wave of gasps went up around me.

Had I really just said that?

Mentally, I shrugged. Who cared? I wasn't actually going to do it. I knew that, but they didn't need to. Perhaps I'd started off on the wrong foot. I should have been bluffing all along. Evidently the only thing these people recognized and respected was power as brutal as their own.

I was buying myself time. Time to get in amongst these coldblooded, fanged monsters. Time to find a weapon and cut some pureblood vampire throats, then escape with not just my life but perhaps a little bit more. Maybe some coin to get me out of this cursed kingdom. Maybe a map. Maybe a ship.

"Getting a memory or two back, are we now?" Lord Drakharrow's smile was slit-like, predatory.

"Maybe," I said blasély. "Who knows what I'll remember given enough time? It could be something useful."

"Perhaps the goddess sent her. Perhaps she's a gift from the Bloodmaiden," a woman near me whispered to her neighbor excitedly.

Lord Drakharrow's eyes shot towards her and the woman squeaked, then fell silent.

But it was too late. I smiled triumphantly. He couldn't kill me now. Not now that hope was spreading.

"Very well, Medra Pendragon," Lord Drakharrow said slowly. "Live you shall. But in bondage to the Pure, as are all blightborn. Such is your debt. Your value lives in your blood and your blood must be shared."

I took a step backward, my face falling, and tried to wrench my hand away from Blake's grasp. But the bastard held tight, jerking me back beside him with a savage twist.

Lord Drakharrow smiled at us. "You see? Already you are bound to my nephew. He found you. He saved you. You owe him a debt of life. A debt that can never be repaid."

"He *stole* me! He chained me, dragged me here," I protested heatedly. "I owe him nothing. What I wish for is to be free."

"Freedom within the Thralldom is of the purest sort," Lord Drakharrow assured me. I felt a prickle of unease go down my spine. "Bondage is freedom. The sooner you accept that, the happier you'll be."

He rose to his feet suddenly. "Today your life changes. Medra Pendragon, today you take up your place in the Thralldom. Today I lift you up from the murk and mire. I name you Dragon Rider of Sangratha. Let the one who found you be your guide in this new world."

Blake's hand jerked around mine. "Uncle..."

"Silence, Nephew." Lord Drakharrow warned. "I honor you both, here in this hall today. Make no mistake about it."

The vampire lord waved a hand and I felt power go through me, winding itself around me like an icy ribbon.

There was a sharp pulling sensation and I found my hand not simply being gripped by Blake's but actually clasping his back as if I wanted to.

There came the sound of tearing flesh.

I screamed, my eyes darting downward.

My wrist had been torn open. Blood dripped onto the marble floor beneath.

But not just mine. Blake's wrist was pressed against my own, and it was bleeding, too.

Lord Drakharrow was smiling down at us, his red eyes glowing.

"Let it be known that this bond is unbreakable, as enduring as the strength of our realm. By my will and the power of our ancient rites, Blake Drakharrow and Medra Pendragon are now bound together in fate and duty, forever unyielding, irrevocably united. As the dragon flies and the blood endures, so shall your destinies be intertwined. Your bond is forged. Through fire and shadows, you shall be one. What is spoken is unbroken. What is bound cannot be unbound."

I gasped aloud as our linked hands flew above our heads. Our blood, mixed together, trickled down my arm, warm and sticky.

Lord Drakharrow flicked his wrist and our hands dropped.

I let go of Blake's as fast as I could, stepping away from him as if I'd been branded.

Which I had.

I looked at my wrist. Already the gash was healing. But a mark remained. A teardrop shape. Bright red like a drop of blood. I rubbed at it and it stayed in place, even as the pain faded.

"This is but the first step in your binding," Lord Drakharrow said, watching me as I took in the mark. "Blood is the beginning just as blood is the end. Blood will have blood. Your essence has not been shared completely. The mark is the first stage."

I glanced around and suddenly realized how still the hall had become. Many of the vampires around me were licking their lips. Some were sniffing the air hungrily like Barnabas had.

I shivered. They smelled me. Smelled my blood. And they hungered for it.

I glanced at Blake, expecting to see the same bloodlust on his face. But to my surprise, he was as stoic as before. If anything, his jaw was clenched a little tighter, his lips pressed together even harder. He refused to meet my gaze.

"Medra Pendragon is hereby declared the Second Betrothed Consort of Prince Blake Drakharrow," Lord Drakharrow was decreeing to the crowd. "She is not to be touched. If she is fed upon, there will be slaughter. All in this hall have been warned."

The vampire's voice was cold. Yet for once, I was grateful for the power that lay behind it. Only a fool would have messed with that terrifying old man. I hoped none of the people licking their lips at the sight of my wet blood would be that stupid.

Then it dawned on me. The word he had used.

Second Betrothed.

Who was the first?

Then our eyes met.

A trickle of blood ran down her chin where she had bitten her lip clean through in silent fury. As I watched, she lifted a hand and wiped away the red streak, never taking her eyes from my face.

There was no doubt in my mind who Blake Drakharrow's First Betrothed was.

Regan Pansera.

CHAPTER 3

MEDRA

B lake Drakharrow strode down the stone hall ahead of me.

He had let go of my hand as soon as his uncle had finished speaking. Evidently he had decided I wasn't a flight risk at this point.

He'd spoken a few words with his uncle in private then stormed back out of the Keep, gesturing for me to follow.

He'd led the way back into the courtyard where he'd gestured to a soldier to give me a horse, then mounted his own.

We had ridden, not to some other part of the large castle complex as I had expected, but back over the iron bridge and to the mainland. From there, we turned, crossing the iron bridge that led to the sprawling castle of onyx on the third island.

Only when we arrived at the outskirts of the place and Blake dismounted, did I do the same. I marched towards him, determined not to be silent any longer.

"Where are we and what the fuck just happened back there?"

He looked up from his horse slowly. "Foul mouth you have."

"You haven't heard anything yet," I said sweetly. "Please don't tell me you took all of that bullshit seriously."

"I did. I do." He paused. His jaw twitched with tension. "And yes, we are."

I spoke through clenched teeth. "We are what?"

"You know exactly what. Betrothed." He raised one perfectly shaped white brow. "I can tell you're excited. I'm not surprised. Most women would be."

"Excited?" I exploded, ignoring his ill-fated attempt at humor. "When and if I wed, I'll choose my mate. He won't be chosen for me by some..."

"What?" Blake turned on me, his gray eyes suddenly clouded with wrath. "By the most powerful vampire in the Thralldom? Do you have any idea, any clue at all what just happened back there?"

"Why don't you enlighten me? It's obvious you're dying to."

"You were just elevated beyond the mundane."

I snorted with laughter. "Is that what you'd call it?"

His eyes narrowed. "Do you have any idea how many blightborn women would literally kill to be in your place right now? I found you on a pile of corpses." He sniffed the air with his hawkish nose, and his aristocratic features twisted in disgust. "You still reek of them."

I crossed my arms self-consciously. He was right. That didn't mean he wasn't also a bastard for saying so.

"I haven't exactly had a chance to take a bath. Someone was dragging me around in chains, as you'll recall," I pointed out.

"Well, you'll have all of the perfumed baths you want now. But there's far more to the bargain."

"More than being chained to you for the rest of our lives? That is what those words meant, right?" I hesitated, then added, "And I'm not the only one, am I?"

"Oh, you noticed Regan, did you? She looked delighted, didn't she?" He shrugged. "Don't worry about her. I'll see to it that she falls in line."

"I won't worry," I said. "Because I don't share. And I'm not your mate, no matter what your uncle or anyone else announced."

"Keep telling yourself that. But you felt the binding. You had no choice. Neither did I. Do you really think I'd have *chosen* this?" He looked me up and down, then shook his head. "You're beneath me in every possible way. Whoever you are, whatever you are."

I snarled, surprising myself. "Good to hear. Because you won't be touching me at any point. Let's get that straight. You certainly won't be *breeding* with me."

"I have no plans to touch you if you were the last woman in the Thralldom," he snapped back, looking just as furious. "But if I did..."

"Yes, yes, I should feel ever so honored, ever so grateful. Is that what you like to tell yourself as a woman lies beneath you? You think to yourself how *honored* she must feel? Gods, you're a piece of work." I shook my head. "I almost feel sorry for Regan."

He narrowed his eyes. "Regan is thrilled to be my future consort. She doesn't need your pity."

"Right. I'm sure. So, what now?" I changed the subject abruptly. "Where are we?"

"Ah, yes, your second question. If you're finished trying to convince yourself you aren't bound to me..."

"I'm not, never will be."

"Whatever. This–" He gestured around us. "Is Bloodwing Academy."

I wrinkled my nose. "What?"

"An academy. A school. They do have those where you come from, don't they?"

I glared at him. "I believe I've heard the words once or twice."

"Good. I daresay it's too much to hope you can read and write, too, and aren't secretly some swine herder's daughter."

I smirked, trying not to let him get to me. "You have no idea." I frowned. "Why does it matter though?"

"Because this is the school you'll be attending. Beginning tomorrow."

My jaw dropped. "What?"

"It's the most exclusive institution in Sangratha. You should be..."

"Honored," I supplied. "Funny how I'm not though."

He started walking towards an arched stone walkway.

"Where are you going?" I demanded, running to catch up.

"I thought I'd show you a few important things. Like where your room will be. Where you'll eat. And where you should be tomorrow morning when the bells ring to summon you to the first day of class."

"Oh, really? And where will you be during all of this?"

"I'm a third year student," he began. "So I'll be..."

I couldn't help it. I burst out laughing. "You? You're a student here? Aren't you a hundred years old? I thought you were a vampire prince."

He glared at me. "I'm closer to your age than you might think. And I may be a prince of my house, but even princes attend the Academy. Nobles from around the kingdom send their sons and daughters to Bloodwing. It's not like a school for mortal children, like you may be thinking. This is a school for..." He searched for the right word. "Forging us into who we'll be as adults. Establishing us as the most powerful elite of Sangratha. We are the kingdom's future rulers, after all."

I eyed him up and down, taking in his lean, well-muscled frame. "You look pretty adult to me already."

"Was that an accidental compliment, Pendragon?"

I made a sour face. "Absolutely not."

But it was his turn to smirk. "In any case, we spend three or four years at the Academy, depending on our specialty."

"Specialty?"

He paused along the stone corridor, his face impatient. "By the Bloodmaiden. Fine. Let's get this over with. I keep forgetting how completely ignorant you are."

I ignored the insult. After all, it sounded like these were things I needed to know.

"There are many highblood houses in Sangratha," he continued. "But four have always run the kingdom and it is these four which lead the school. Each one represents an ancient vampire bloodline. House Drakharrow–that's my house. House Avari. House Orphos."

"And House Mortis," I supplied.

When he looked surprised, I shrugged. "I listened."

"Fine. You know one miniscule piece of information about my world. Good for you."

What an ass. "What about Regan? Her last name isn't any of those four. But she was still standing up there with your uncle on the dais."

"She's a Pansera. Regan comes from a very noble house though it's not one of the ruling four. Here at the Academy, she falls under House Drakharrow. All of the nobles, regardless of their surnames, are aligned with one of the four houses and can trace their lineage back to one of the four bloodlines, however distantly."

"So you and Regan are related?" I snickered. "Strange customs you have."

He rolled his eyes. "Our betrothal was arranged for us when we were children. You wouldn't understand. Look, just try not to look any more foolish than you already do. You'll be embarrassing me enough already. It's bad enough you're linked to us now."

"How about you don't tell me what to do?"

He crossed his arms and took a step towards me. I held my ground. "You'd better get used to it, Pendragon. I'm the house leader. You answer to me. In every way."

I crossed my arms, mirroring him, and refusing to back away. "We'll see about that."

He chose to ignore me and continued his speech. "As I was saying, Bloodwing Academy is grouped by the four houses. And within each house are squads."

"Squads?"

"Units of up to fifty. You won't have to worry about them in your first year. It's a military tradition. In times of war, it meant that our generals were always prepared and ready with young leaders and support staff at hand to replace any who fell."

"And do you battle a great deal, your kingdom?" I asked, genuinely curious.

"You'll learn about that in your classes," he said, dismissively. "Now, within each squad are representatives from four subclasses. The highest ranking are warriors—usually vampire nobility but there have been rare exceptions. Beneath us are the support structure. Healers, alchemists, apothecaries. Those are self-explanatory. I assume you know what healers are."

When he looked at me as if I might be an idiot, I rolled my eyes.

"Great. Next are strategists. Very important. They're selected for their logic and foresight. They can visualize battles, help plan attacks, that kind of thing. The last class are scouts. They're also supposed to be able to use magic, but not all of them are mages. True arcanists are harder and harder to find."

"And where do I fit in?"

He snorted. "You don't. You're a fifth class. One that's extinct." He eyed me up and down. "Or at least, they were until today."

"I don't understand any of this. There are no dragons to ride so why the hell do I have to go to your stupid school?" I demanded.

"You'd have to take that up with my uncle, but it's what he wants. You're to join Regan and I."

He glared at me from gray eyes that were suddenly stormy. "You're the last person who belongs at this school as far as I'm concerned. You haven't even earned your way here like some of the other blightborn mortals. But what Viktor Drakharrow wants, he always gets. So I wouldn't suggest challenging him. Not unless you want to be drained faster than you can snap out a smart-mouthed comment."

He looked at me and shook his head contemptuously. "I don't know what kind of a curriculum they'll come up with for you exactly, but if I had to guess, I'd say you'll learn some of everything. Everything but healing, I suppose. Riders used to be second only to warriors. But that was when they had dragons." He shrugged. "So, you're right. You're pretty useless. I don't suppose you can fight?"

"Oh, I've got plenty of fight." I clenched my hands into fists, itching to let one fly.

He laughed in derision. "Sure. But do you have any skills?"

I said nothing, deciding that was just one of those things he'd have to find out for himself.

He shrugged. "Tomorrow I'll have Regan show you around. She'll show you the ropes."

I nearly choked. "Regan? The girl in the purple dress who looked like she wanted to stab my eyes out?"

He chuckled. "She'll do what I tell her. Don't worry, you'll see. She wants to please my uncle. You need each other. You'll be best friends in no time."

"I highly doubt that," I muttered.

But maybe I could hope. It wouldn't be so bad to have a friend in this horrid place.

Though I sincerely doubted the girl who thought I'd just stolen her mate from her–or at least planned to make her share him–was about to turn into my bosom buddy.

It seemed as if talking time was over.

Blake had resumed his long strides down the stone corridor. I followed him, refusing to ask that he slow down, forcing myself to keep up with his ridiculous pace.

He hurried me through the halls with furtive glances around the corners, as if he were worried someone might see us together.

From time to time, someone would shuffle past us–a fellow student with their arms full of books or a teacher holding a stack of parchment. If they dared to make eye contact, Blake would glare at them until they hurried on their way as fast as they could.

As our hasty tour continued, I caught a glimpse of the refectory. A huge stone hall with rows of wooden tables and benches.

"You'll eat there," Blake said briefly, before forcing us down another hall.

"What about you?" It was a jest, but to my surprise he paused.

"I can eat. We don't just drink blood, you know."

"I *don't* know," I pointed out. "I don't know anything about you monsters."

"You might want to stop thinking of us as monsters and try to see us as the rest of Sangratha does," he said, narrowing his eyes.

"And what's that? As gods? Heroes?"

He smirked. "Something along those lines."

"I don't understand," I snapped. "Don't you feed on your own people? You call us all blightborn and yet you need us, don't you? Where else do you get your blood from?"

He bristled. "You have no idea what our traditions are or how we feed. Some are..." He trailed off, then shook his head. "You know what? Never mind. I'm done trying to educate you."

"Some are what?" I demanded. "I'm interested. Truly."

"Sure you are. But you see, Pendragon, I've just realized something my dear Uncle Viktor forgot." He smiled coldly and suddenly leaned towards me, so close that he was inches from my face. I could smell him again. The hint of green apples. The bastard was a vampire yet he somehow smelled like an orchard. It made no sense.

"What's that?" I asked, my blood growing chill. I resisted the urge to take a step back.

"This school takes care of its own–and only its own. You're right. You aren't one of us and you never will be. I have nothing to worry about. You won't have time to shame me, because Bloodwing culls the weak. I doubt you'll make it through a single term here. No matter how much help you get, you'll fail and die and all I'll have to do is stand back and watch. You're worried about us having to mate? You think I'd actually pollute my bloodline with yours?" He tipped his head back and laughed. "Tomorrow you'll start to understand. But in the meantime–" He flipped a hand up and pointed. "Here's your door."

Before I could gather my thoughts to say a single word in retort, he was gone. Sweeping around the corner and out of sight, his black cloak whipping behind him like fucking bat wings.

I stared at the door he'd left me in front of. Heavy dark oak with an iron handle in the shape of a teardrop. Like the mark on my wrist.

For a moment, I hesitated, wondering if I was supposed to knock.

Then I squared my shoulders and lifted my hand, pushing the door open.

A blast of sound erupted from the room as the door squeaked on its hinges.

I flinched but forced myself to keep going, entering the noisy space and looking about.

While the stone hallway had been shadowy and dark, lit only by a few candles every few paces, this room was large, with cavernous high ceilings. The space burst with warmth and light. Countless candles glowed in iron sconces on the walls and hung from elaborate candelabras. The flickering light played off the deep sapphire blue hangings that were draped from the walls and which framed the tall arched windows that lined two broad walls. Diamond-shaped panes revealed a view of the sea and the setting sun outside.

Comfy plush armchairs, upholstered in midnight blue and silver tones, were arranged in cozy-looking clusters around the room. Thick, luxurious rugs covered the stone floors, their patterns a swirl of pale grays and blues.

A huge fire crackled in an enormous hearth, its mantle covered with stacks of books and dusty candlesticks dripping with melted wax. Another wall of the room was lined with bookshelves, where expensive-looking tomes stood alongside dusty scrolls.

In the center of the space stood a large, round table covered with parchment, quills, and inkpots.

Everywhere there were students.

Sitting in the cozy chairs reading, hunched around the table with their quills frantically scribbling, or lounging on couches around the fire chattering.

As I stepped fully inside the room, the conversations began to halt.

For the second time that day, every head in the room seemed to turn towards me.

My heart was pounding. I kept moving forward, my footsteps echoing on the stone in the sudden stillness.

I cursed silently. Just where the hell was I supposed to go from here?

"Medra! Medra Pendragon! Up here!"

My head jerked up as my name was called. A dark-haired girl stood high above on a stone staircase. As I looked up, she leaned over the balustrade and waved down at me.

She was petite and slender, with long silky black hair that had been meticulously woven into a perfect braid which hung down her back and was tied with a blue ribbon. She wore black-rimmed spectacles that made her dark brown eyes look slightly owlish. Her expression was calm and serene, as if she were unaware of the stir my appearance was causing below.

"Come on up," she called. "I'll show you around."

The girl wore a black cloak around her shoulders like Blake had, and beneath it a blue pullover sweater over a knee-length gray skirt There was something scholarly about her. I wondered which of the classes that Blake had mentioned she fit into.

I mounted the stairs towards her slowly, taking in the crest on the lapel of her cloak. Four intertwined dragons, stitched in gold, forced a circular sigil. There were words written around the edges.

"Sanguis et Flamma Floreant," I read aloud.

"It's the Bloodwing crest and motto," the girl explained. There was an intensity to her that suggested a thoughtful and determined mind. "It means 'Let blood and flame flourish.' It's written in Classical Sangrathan. I suppose you're not familiar with it."

I was, but I let her continue. What she called Classical Sangrathan was simply the Old Tongue in Aercanum.

She touched a finger to the crest gently. "All of your clothes will be emblazoned with it. It's to mark all of the First Years. We don't have a house motto or crest yet, you see."

"I thought I was House Drakharrow," I said, flushing slightly.

The girl gave me a reassuring smile. "Not yet. You're not an official consort yet, though you are betrothed and for all intents and purposes, that's what you'll be considered. I know, it's complicated. None of us have been selected by houses, though we may have allegiances and ties to a certain house. That would be an honor though. House Drakharrow is a very powerful house with a very strong leader."

I managed to suppress the comment that rose to my lips as I thought of Viktor Drakharrow and his nephew.

"It must be very overwhelming," she said sympathetically, misinterpreting my expression. "Come, I'll try to explain more. Let me show you to your room."

She started walking along the stone balcony and for the first time I noticed it almost encircled the room below. There were four passages leading off it. I followed the girl down one and then watched as she pushed another door open and gestured.

"This will be your room." She stood back so I could step past her and I peered inside.

To my relief, the room was small but cozy... and there was only one bed. No bunking up with any of my fellow Bloodwing students. Thank the gods for that.

The room was nestled in an upper level of the tower, so some of the walls of the room were curved.

In the center stood a large four-poster bed of dark wood, draped in heavy, velvet curtains of deep blue. At the foot of the bed rested a large wooden trunk. Somewhere to put the belongings I didn't possess.

On the far side of the room stood a tall wardrobe of dark oak, the handles shaped like coiled dragon tails.

Three tall, arched windows looked out over the churning sea below, where waves crashed against the rocky cliffs. Near the windows stood a small wooden desk, just large enough for scribbling or studying.

It was simple but seemed comfortable enough. I supposed I should be thankful it wasn't a cell in the Black Keep dungeon.

"I'm Florence, by the way. Florence Shen. I'm one of the wardens for the First Year dormitory."

I eyed her cautiously. "Wardens?"

She laughed. "Don't worry. It's not as severe as it sounds. You're not in prison. It just means I help to shepherd new students around and to answer their questions."

I tried not to look too skeptical. After all, to me this was a prison. Though Florence certainly looked very pleased to be here.

"So you aren't a new student?" I asked.

"No, I am. But I've been here over part of the summer. My mother is one of the librarians. I'm more familiar with the school than most students, especially most blightborn. That's probably why they selected me."

"Then you aren't a vampire?" The next instant I felt like an idiot. "Of course, you aren't. Your hair."

She smiled. "Exactly. And no, I'm not. Though there are halfborns. I don't believe we have any in our cohort this year. None of the students in our dormitory are highbloods. Eventually, the best of us will be selected into one of the four houses and that's when we'll choose a specialty and eventually be assigned to squads."

I stared at her. "And you... want that to happen? You want to be part of a vampire house?"

"It's the highest honor in Sangratha," she said simply. "Just being here at Bloodwing is beyond my wildest dreams. It's a huge honor for my family. I mean, it's just my mother and I, but she's completely over the moon."

The girl seemed nice. She also seemed helpful.

She did not seem stark raving mad. But I supposed looks could be deceiving.

I decided telling her how completely absolutely insane her excitement seemed to me wouldn't be the best idea at the moment.

Not until I'd gotten to know her better.

With a sinking heart I realized something.

"No bath," I said, my voice sounding hollow with disappointment, even to me.

Florence perked up. "You actually have your own private bathing room just through here."

She pointed to a door I'd mistaken for a closet and I sighed in relief.

"Hot water?" I asked hopefully.

She nodded. "That's one of the nice things about being at Bloodwing. You don't even need to call upon a servant to fetch it. We have real copper plumbing. They've had it here for centuries. Highbloods are extraordinary. They really think of everything." She beamed.

"Everything that can benefit themselves, I'm sure," I couldn't help but say.

She looked a little taken aback.

"Anyhow, thanks for showing me around," I said quickly. "How did you know who I was?"

She gestured and I looked down at my hair.

"Oh. Right. I guess I stand out like a sore thumb now."

"A little. I mean, not in a bad way," she said hastily. "But you are fairly easy to spot."

"And all of the other students, down in the..."

"The common room," Florence provided. "We all share that space." I appreciated how she made sure to emphasize "all."

"Right. Down in the common room. They didn't look very pleased to see me."

"Well..." Florence chewed her lip as if buying the time to formulate a diplomatic response. "This all happened very fast. For you, I mean. Many students spend years preparing themselves before applying to Bloodwing. Most are never accepted."

"So everyone is just dying to be here?"

Her eyes widened. "Oh, no. I wouldn't say that." She glanced back into the hall then lowered her voice. "Every year there are a few who don't wish to come. Some students had no choice."

"What do you mean?" I said, narrowing my eyes. "They were forced to come here?"

"Some would have been taken by force if they refused the summons, yes," she confirmed reluctantly. "But their families would have been compensated, I'm sure. Sangratha does not believe in wasting precious talent."

"And what if they or their families resisted?" I pressed. "What then?"

She shook her head. "I'm not sure. I don't think it happens very often." She looked almost hopeful.

"Right," I muttered. "I'm sure the vampires were very gentle with the ones who didn't want to come."

But Florence either didn't hear me or was pretending she didn't. She'd crossed the room and now I watched as she flung open the doors of the wardrobe.

"As you can see, most of your clothes have been prepared. Not everything you need is here yet, but you should be able to find suitable attire for tomorrow's first day of class," she said with pride as she indicated a wardrobe filled with an assortment of clothes.

I saw cloaks, boots, tunics, dresses, trousers, and even a gown or two. Everything I could see bore the Bloodwing crest. It seemed I would be wearing the vampire school's brand daily.

"Is there anything particular I need to wear tomorrow?" I asked, figuring it couldn't hurt. I didn't want to show up to a riding lesson in a short skirt, after all.

Florence shook her head. "Tomorrow's Orientation Day. We'll attend a few classes, and then there will be a welcome speech from the headmaster at the end of the day. You can wear anything you please. I don't have your schedule yet, but it should be delivered here in the morning."

She stifled a yawn. "Pardon me, Medra. It's getting late and it's been a long day. If you don't need anything else, I think I'll turn in."

I thought of how my day had begun. Had it even been properly morning when I found myself on that heap of corpses? And now look at how it was ending.

At least there would be a bath.

"Of course," I said quickly. "Thank you for showing me around. Do you mind if I tag along with you tomorrow? This school seems huge and I haven't quite gotten my bearings yet."

"You'd have been welcome to," Florence said, beaming again. "But you won't need my guidance. I've been informed that Regan Pansera herself is coming to pick you up in the morning and help you get through the first day of class. What an honor! She's a very popular student. Being seen with her will be a huge boon."

I planted a weak smile on my face. "Yes. Indeed."

When Florence was gone, I flopped down on my new blue-velvet bed.

None of this felt real.

If I accepted that this was real, then it meant I was alive. I was betrothed. I was a hostage of vampires. And I was a student.

I gave a snort of laughter. I wasn't sure which one of those things was more ridiculous.

I had never attended school. There were schools back home, in my city of Camelot, of course. But as a royal, I'd only had private tutors.

As for marriage? Back in Camelot, I'd been too young for it to even be talked about. Not to mention the fact that my kingdom had been in the midst of a war. But I had no doubt I'd have been permitted to choose my own partner, my own path.

I wondered if the war had ended with my death.

I tried to imagine my family back in Aercanum. My aunt, Morgan, and her husband, Draven. Had my uncle, Kaye, become king? What were they doing right now? Did they miss me?

I sat up abruptly, shoving aside the painful ache in my chest.

There was no point in thinking about the family I'd left behind. I knew I'd never see any of them again.

I breathed in deeply, then coughed. Florence Shen had been too polite to mention how badly I stank.

No more melancholy thoughts. There was a bathing chamber and I planned to use it.

The tub was black marble and slippery as hell. But when it was full and I'd successfully managed to get into it without breaking my neck, I sighed with bliss as the hot water soaked into my tired body.

I closed my eyes, running through the events of the day one more time.

I was in a new world.

Somehow, I didn't think there would be any going back to Aercanum, as much as I longed to return.

Was that the price I had paid? I'd gained a new life but been forced to give up my old one. And everyone and everything I'd loved was in the past.

I was sure many people would kill for a second chance like the one I'd received. But I couldn't say I was completely grateful.

Not when I considered the world where I'd wound up.

A world where vampires weren't just the stuff of legend.

No, Blake Drakharrow was an absolute ass. But he was absolutely flesh and blood.

He and his ilk were horrible. But I couldn't deny how powerful they seemed to be.

This entire world seemed to cater to them. Florence seemed ready to almost worship them. She was happy to be here and she thought nothing of the fact that the vampires might have involuntarily conscripted mortals to be here.

I'd forgotten to ask Florence about the burned out village where Blake had found me. What had happened to it? Why did no one seem to care?

I thought of what the highblood vampires had said about me. That I had the markings of a rider. A dragon rider.

Now that might be the most ludicrous part of all of this. They'd betrothed me to one of their princes because my blood was clearly valuable. And yet they had no actual dragons. Nothing for me to ride. So what was the point?

Unless there was more to my blood than I knew. More than they'd said.

But without another dragon rider to ask, I had no idea how I was going to find out.

I wondered what the dragon riders had been like. What had they been capable of? What had their dragons been like?

And most importantly, why had they all died out?

Of course, there was always the chance this was a mistake. The traits the vampires saw as marking me as a rider in this world, simply marked me as half-fae in Aercanum. Did that mean any fae from Aercanum would be considered a dragon rider here in Sangratha?

Or did it mean I was a fraud? Not someone with rider blood at all?

I supposed it didn't really matter. Even if I wasn't what they thought I was, how would they ever find out? There were no dragons to test me with.

All I had to do was try to fit in. Do as I was told. Go to my classes. Pretend I was a docile little lamb like Florence.

All the while, I'd be scheming to find a way out of here.

There was no point simply diving out a window. I needed to know my enemy first. If I'd been given a second chance at life, well, then I guessed I should make the best of it and actually try to form a real life once I left here. And that meant finding out more about this land and its people. There had to be other kingdoms. Maybe somewhere in the world was a place without vampires.

A place I could be free.

My eyes were closing. It was time to acknowledge how exhausted I really was.

In Aercanum, I'd spent every ounce of power I'd had before imploding like a star.

Then I'd woken up here, drained and tired. I'd been forced to march for miles before standing in a hall of judgment only to be led on a school tour.

It was time to rest.

I pulled myself out of the marble tub before I could fall asleep and accidentally drown, wrapped myself in one of the huge fluffy towels that were stacked on a small table, and shuffled back into the bedroom.

Dressing myself in a soft blue cotton nightset, I climbed up onto the bed.

The ceiling had been painted a rich dark blue and an overlay of little silver stars had been added to it. It was lovely, really. And totally unexpected in this place.

I stared up at it for a while, thinking about my next move and yawning repeatedly.

I was hungry. But the thought of braving the common room or making my way all the way back to the refectory was not appealing. I decided I could make it until morning. More motivation to get up on time. Speaking of which...

I fumbled around the bedside table until I found a timepiece and set it for six. That should be early enough.

Then I lay back on the bed, not even bothering to pull back the covers, and let my eyes fall closed for the last time that day.

CHAPTER 4

MEDRA

The timepiece let out a shrill piercing scream and I lurched out of bed cursing and flailing.

As my eyes slowly opened, I groaned. Running my fingers through my hair, I grimaced, then yanked my hands free. I'd forgotten to brush my hair out before falling asleep after my bath and now it was in knots.

Walking over to a mirror on the wall, I peered at my reflection. Excellent. My hair was as unkempt as a bird's nest. Not the look I was going for.

Grabbing a brush, I tried to tame the curls but it was no use. I'd have to wash my hair again that night and detangle it with one of the bottles of oil I'd seen in the bathroom. If I wasn't too tired again, that was.

In the meantime, I had two choices. I could go around today looking as if a crow might land on my head to nest anytime. Or I could put my hair back and show off my pointed ears.

Either way, I'd probably be getting a lot of stares.

I went with twisting my hair into a loose knot. That way it was off my face and hopefully the curls looked as if I'd intended them to be wild, rather than them being so completely by accident. Plus, this way my ears were covered if I tucked some hair over just so.

Next up was clothes. I yanked open the wardrobe and quickly selected a gray wool pullover sweater and fitted black trousers that had a little give to them. I had no idea what sorts of classes I'd been enrolled in, but I figured it made the most sense to wear clothes I could move around in easily. Just in case.

A pair of high brown leather boots came next. I laced them up quickly, just as my stomach started to rumble.

"I know, I know," I muttered. "Soon. I promise."

There was a tapping at the door and I jerked up. "Who is it?"

When there was no answer, I marched to the door and pulled it open.

Regan Pansera stood outside. She'd been tapping her foot impatiently but stopped as soon as she saw me.

For a brief moment, her face was a mask of emotions I couldn't quite read. Then her eyes met mine and she smiled warmly.

"Medra," she crooned. "So good to see you again. I'm glad your warden told you to be ready. I'll take you down to the refectory for breakfast."

I swallowed. Regan Pansera was the epitome of elegance. She may have been the most beautiful woman I'd ever seen.

Her silver-blonde hair had been styled to flow in soft waves and shimmered with a metallic sheen, as if there were truly metal in it. The early morning light brought out the warm, honeyed undertones of her rich complexion, a radiant caramel with a subtle glow. She wore a dark fitted dress of deep red that cut off just above the knee. Black polished boots with a high heel finished her ensemble.

There were words embroidered in black thread on the collar of her dress.

Sanguine Vinciti.

She followed my gaze and touched a finger to the embroidery with a look of pride. "Bound by blood. The motto of House Drakharrow."

I nodded and stepped out into the hallway. She led the way and I followed her in silence, unsure of the right thing to say.

But I didn't need to worry. When we reached the outer corridor, she spoke up again.

"I think we got off on the wrong foot yesterday," Regan said, glancing at me as we walked side by side. "I hope we can start fresh. After all, we're both betrothed to the same man. We're to be fellow consorts. That's practically like sisters."

I choked on the air I'd just breathed. Now, I decided, was not the best time to tell Regan she was welcome to keep Blake Drakharrow all to herself.

I forced a smile. "I'd like that. To start again, I mean. I hope you know that I mean you no harm."

"Of course, you don't," she said soothingly. "What harm could you do to a vampire, anyhow? I wasn't threatened by you. Not in the least. To tell you the truth, I was worried for Blake. His uncle can be so hard on him at times. I wasn't sure if Viktor was going to be happy Blake had brought you back or furious. I'm so glad everything worked out."

I stole a curious glance at her. She really did seem different this morning. Much more serene and happy. Was Blake right and she'd simply accepted the new order of things? I watched as she tucked a gleaming lock of hair behind her ear.

"So," I said, not really wanting to keep talking about Blake but also secretly dying to ask. "Is it common for men to have two wives around here?"

"Not always. There are many couples, especially among blightborn. Among vampires, especially highbloods, triads are considered the strongest formation for family alliances." She looked at me and smiled slightly. "I knew Blake and I would likely be joined by another consort. I just didn't think we'd be assigned one so soon. Or in such a very unexpected and public fashion."

Well, that I could understand and even empathize with.

"Yes, it was... quite a shock to me as well," I said, as tactfully as I could. Then I thought of something. "Are the consorts always women? Two women and a man, I mean?"

Regan shook her head. "Oh, no. There are all sorts of trios. Sometimes two men and a woman. Sometimes three men. It depends on the leader of the triad. Their tastes and preferences. At least," she corrected herself. "It usually does." She bit her lip. "Oh, I'm so sorry. I didn't mean..."

I shook my head. "That's all right. I understand."

So, I wasn't to Blake's taste or preference, was I?

I debated feeling sorry for the bastard and then went with decidedly not. So he didn't get to select his second consort himself and was stuck with me, who he already clearly despised. Cry me a river. At least he wouldn't be stuck with me for very long.

I considered asking Regan more questions about the intimate workings of these triads, then decided I didn't want to know. It was totally irrelevant. I wouldn't be getting intimate with either of them. Especially not Blake. At this point, Regan was honestly looking more appealing–if my tastes had swung to women, which as far as I knew, they didn't.

The hallways were bustling this morning. Regan was waving and greeting students as we passed. I saw many look at her in awe, then sneak a covert glance at me. She seemed to be deflecting attention away from me, which was a welcome benefit of being her new friend.

After pausing to briefly embrace a tall girl dressed all in black named Gretchen, Regan continued speaking. "So, we'll head into the refectory and get you some breakfast. I'll introduce you to everyone in our group. And then I'll get you to your first class. Speaking of which, here's a copy of your schedule."

She passed me a scroll covered with neat black script and I scanned it.

9:30 - History of Sangratha

10:30 - Restoration

12:00 - Lunch

1:00 - Advanced Weaponry

2:00 - Introduction to Bloodwing Libraries

4:00 - Commencement Address

Regan peered over my shoulder. "Oooh, History of Sangratha. All First Years have to take it. Restoration should be interesting, too. Professor Rodriguez teaches that. Make sure to ask him about the history of healing dragons. Fascinating stuff."

I eyed Regan in surprise. I hadn't taken her for a history buff.

She tossed her hair over her shoulder and smiled. "I make sure to excel in all of my classes. It's our duty to House Drakharrow."

I hoped my face didn't reveal how vomity I felt as I smiled back at her.

We reached the refectory—a sweeping, vaulted hall that exuded grandeur. High, ribbed ceilings rose dramatically over our heads, supported by a series of stone columns that marched down the length of the room. Light filtered in through rows of large, arched windows set high in the walls.

Outside, I glimpsed tall trees filled with crisp autumn leaves in hues of yellow, orange, and red.

Stepping into the refectory, a roar of student voices flowed over me along with the clatter of cutlery and dishes and, in the distant background, the sound of the wind rustling through dry leaves and the waves on the sea. If it wasn't for the vampires, I decided in that instant, Bloodwing Academy might have been, well, beautiful.

The walls of the hall were furnished with dark tapestries. Two large ones hung on each wall to my right and two my left, each emblazoned with a different motto.

I read each one.

"Ex Sanguine, Unitas." From blood, unity.

"Ex Sanguine, Virtus." From blood, strength.

"Ex Sanguine, Legatum." From blood, legacy.

"Ex Sanguine, Potentia." From blood, power.

At the far end of the hall was a massive tapestry of gold and red featuring the Bloodwing crest, alongside four smaller ones that I assumed depicted the symbols of the four houses and their crests. I couldn't make out their details from this distance.

But it wasn't what was on the walls that most concerned me at that moment. I sniffed hungrily and my stomach rumbled so loudly that Regan laughed.

Long, heavy wooden tables stretched across each side of the room, with a wide aisle in between. Each one was heaped with a lavish spread of food. I spotted platters of crisp bacon, buttery fried potatoes, and golden sausages alongside trays of fluffy eggs, and bowls filled to the brim with muffins, scones, and tarts. Alongside the hot foods sat trays of brightly colored fruit. Deep-red pomegranates, glistening green grapes, and piles of ripe plums were placed beside plates of crusty fresh bread. And those were only the foods I recognized. Many I had never seen before in my life. I watched as a girl picked up a slice of a strange fruit. It was bright red with small black seeds. As she took a bite, the juice ran down her chin.

Large silver pitchers of fresh juices had been placed along the tables. To my relief, I saw many students holding steaming cups of a familiar dark brown brew.

"Thank the Bloodmaiden for kava," Regan said from beside me. She raised her eyebrows. "Would you like a cup?"

"Kava? Is that what you call it? We use another word for it where I'm from. But yes, I do. Absolutely. I'd kill for some... kava." The word sounded strange on my tongue at first, but I knew I'd get used to it quickly with the amount I planned to drink. I wondered if I could brew my own kava back in my room.

Regan was weaving her way through the large room, obviously with a clear destination in mind.

"Let me introduce you to everyone," she said as she finally stopped at a table that was nearly full of students. "This is where you'll be sitting. With the very finest of House Drakharrow."

I looked down and my eyes connected with a pair of gray ones, steely and challenging.

For a moment, Blake Drakharrow's expression was pure disdain. Then a camouflage of indifference took over.

I waited expectantly for him to pat the seat next to him and smile up at Regan. Maybe even put on a display of affection solely for my benefit.

But instead, he just lowered his head back to his food and ignored us.

"Well, you've already met our brilliant leader, Blake," Regan said brightly.

"Not the leader yet," quipped a boy with dark blond hair and a mouthful of eggs.

Regan frowned. "No jesting, Theo." She looked at me. "Theo is Blake's cousin. He thinks he can get away with shows of blatant disrespect."

Theo clutched his heart dramatically. "Disrespect? Me? Say it isn't so. Will my beloved cousin banish me?" He looked down the table expectantly at Blake, but there was a mocking grin on his handsome face. I could see the family resemblance. But where Blake's features were lean and dangerous, Theo's were more filled out and, dare I say it, almost pleasant.

Blake's only response was to toss a muffin at Theo's head. It bounced off and landed on the floor.

I pitied the servants who had to clean up after all of the food fights these entitled highbloods must have.

Theo howled with laughter. "You cut me to the quick, good cuz. Wounded! I am wounded, I say."

"If only I'd wounded you in the mouth," Blake muttered.

I felt my lips twitch but quickly quelled them.

Theo stood up and bowed elegantly in my direction. "I nearly forgot myself, dear lady. Theo Drakharrow at your service. Courtier to the Black Prince himself. Beloved by all."

Regan snorted. "He gives himself too much credit. We barely tolerate him."

"He is a rogue and a rascal," growled a tall, ebony-skinned young man from a little further down the table. He nodded at me, his gaze thoughtful and intense. His silvery-blond hair was cut short and swept to one side.

"That's Coregon Phiri," Regan said, introducing us. "One of Blake's closest friends."

Coregan was a large young man. In contrast to Theo, there was a quiet confidence and authority to him that suggested he didn't need to be sarcastic or loud to get things done.

"To his great discredit," Theo chirped.

"Hush up, Theo. Who's doing these introductions? Me or you?" Regan complained.

Unfortunately, Theo took this as an invitation. He gasped dramatically. "Me? Take over? You had only to say the word!"

Blake's cousin leaped onto a chair and began to point. "Quinn Riley, say how-do-you-do." A girl with pale skin and long silver hair styled in three braids down her back lifted a hand. "And on Quinn's left you have Visha Vaidya. Watch out for this one, lords and ladies. She's a fighter."

A young woman with a rich, warm brown skin tone that contrasted beautifully with her short, silvery-white hair glared at Theo murderously. Her violet eyes were sharp and piercing as she looked at me. She managed to force a smile, but to me it felt more like a challenge than a greeting.

Theo was hooting at the young woman's expression. "Visha's family used to have the best dragon riders in Sangratha. I'm sure she'd like to conduct all sorts of nasty little experiments on you if she could," Theo explained. "Of course, most would involve draining you of all your blood." He looked back and forth between us, still grinning, as if he'd like to see us fight.

I crossed my arms, suddenly uncomfortably reminded that these weren't just my fellow students. They were vampires.

"Any of these pitchers filled with warm blood? Or do you take yours cold in the mornings?" I asked Theo conversationally.

"I prefer my red on ice, actually," Theo said seriously. "The fresher the better. Why? Are you offering a little taste?"

My eyes must have widened a little because he burst out laughing.

The entire table suddenly shook. Blake rose to his feet, his hands still in position from where he had slammed them down.

"Enough," he growled.

He walked away from us all without another word.

"Tsk, tsk," Theo said, watching his cousin disappear out of the refectory. "Who got his dark and billowy cloak all in a twist?" He whistled. "Methinks it was you, Medra Pendragon." He winked at me.

"Me?" I said blankly.

"Theo dared to joke about drinking you," Coregon explained, in his deep bass voice. "But such is forbidden. We all heard Viktor's decree."

"Blake doesn't like to share, you see. You're his. But of course, I would never lay a hand on you." Theo put a hand on his heart. "Or a tooth, for that matter. Swear to the Bloodmaiden."

"Just who or what is this Bloodmaiden?" I muttered, a little grumpy at being reminded that Blake Drakharrow believed I was his chattel.

"Here, sit down and eat," Theo offered. He slid down the bench and I eagerly accepted the spot, grabbing a plate and beginning to fill it.

As I suppressed a moan of delight and filled my mouth with another piece of sausage, I looked up to see Quinn Riley staring at me.

"Quite the appetite you have there," she said, with a snicker.

I swallowed my bite. "Unfortunately dinner was not provided when I arrived last night," I said coldly. "But even so, I always have a healthy appetite."

"I like a woman who can eat," Theo said approvingly. His grin widened. "Who am I kidding? I like a man who can eat just as much. Probably better." He cackled at his own joke and Coregon rolled his eyes.

"Oh dear!" Regan groaned from across the table. She stood up, grabbing napkins and brushing at the front of her dress. "I've just soaked myself in kava. Theo, be a dear and tell Medra all about the four houses." She looked at me anxiously. "I'm so sorry. I'll just go and change my clothes. I'll be back in a few minutes to take you to class. Wait for me here, all right?"

I nodded in between a mouth stuffed with two pieces of bacon.

Had Regan Pansera actually apologized to me? The girl really had changed overnight. Either she was genuine or she wanted to stay in Viktor Drakharrow's good graces.

"Only too happy to oblige, dear Miss Pansera." Theo gave a mock salute.

When Regan was gone, I looked at Theo expectantly. "Four houses?"

"Once more, I have been cast in a pivotal role," Theo mused. "Is it the historian I am to be? What a weight lies upon my shoulders." He tapped a finger to his chin. "Where to begin?"

Before I could say anything, he leaped to his feet, jumped onto the bench, and cleared his throat.

"The four royal houses of Sangratha," he intoned loudly. "A historical summary delivered by Theo Drakharrow to Medra Pendragon, this first day of Autumntide term."

Some of the students at the other tables looked up, startled.

"Quiet down, Theo," Quinn hissed. "You're not in a lecture hall! You're embarrassing us. Again."

Theo put a finger to his lips and whispered down to me, "Well, we wouldn't want that, would we, Medra?"

I couldn't help it. I smirked back at him. Theo Drakharrow was incorrigible and I was loving every moment of it. "Nope."

"False alarm," Theo called, waving his hands. "This tutoring session is only meant for one. Exclusive session. Back to your breakfasts, you cads, you knaves. Away with you."

The other students seemed to be used to Theo's outbursts. They were already doing as he suggested and going back to their own conversations.

I reached for a muffin covered with chunks of cinnamon and brown sugar and studied Theo. "You're really a Drakharrow?"

Theo puffed up. "Who says I'm a bastard?"

"I didn't..." I said quickly. Though I'd already noticed he had hair a shade or two darker than the other students at the table.

"A bastard I may be," he said. "But I was born on the right side of the blankets." He grinned. "Aye, a Drakharrow I am and proudly so. Why do you ask?"

"You're nothing like your cousin," I said bluntly. Abruptly I thought of something and my eyes widened. "Are you Viktor's son?"

Theo shook his head. "No, no. My mother is our esteemable uncle's youngest sister. Marcus and Blake's father takes precedence in the family order. Dear Uncle Viktor has no progeny. None that we know of."

"Marcus?" I inquired. "Who is he?"

"Blake's elder brother. You probably saw him yesterday, standing at Viktor's shoulder in the great hall yesterday. The kindest term for him is lackey." He shook his head. "Ah, what a merry time that impromptu soiree was."

I grimaced. "Merry. Indeed."

"Marcus graduated Bloodwing last spring," Theo explained.

"And now Blake is... house leader?"

"Not quite." Coregon's quiet voice interrupted. "House leaders must fight for their place. It has to be earned. It's not an inherited spot."

"That's right," Theo said. "As it stands, House Drakharrow has no leader at Bloodwing yet. One will be chosen by the end of the Autumntide Term. Everyone assumes Blake will get it, of course. But there are a few students within House Drakharrow who may decide to compete for the spot." He winked at Coregon. "Like yourself, old chap."

Coregon shook his head. "Blake can have it. Too much trouble managing this lot."

Theo pouted. "No duels? How dull." He looked around the table. "None of the others who might just have it in them to challenge Blake are at our table. Regan probably made sure of that when she did the inviting."

"What about the other houses?" I asked.

Theo nodded towards a table across the aisle from ours. "There's a house leader right there. Kage Tanaka. He's the leader of House Avari."

I stole a glance. A striking, tall young man with golden-hued skin sat at the head of a long table. "But his last name..."

"He's an Avari on his mother's side," Coregon explained. "He chose not to take the Avari surname. At least, not yet. He's proud of his father's lineage."

I stole another look at Kage Tanaka. The Avari leader looked... intense. Dressed in a tailored black uniform trimmed with silver braid, he exuded authority, dominating the group of students around him. As he spoke rapidly, his dark eyes narrowed in focus. I got the impression no one would dare to interrupt whatever he was saying.

Kage's uniform was inscribed with an insignia I assumed was that of House Avari. A silver dragon holding a crescent moon.

I squinted, trying to read the inscription written around the crest.

"*Luna sanguinea surgit*," Theo provided as he saw my gaze. "Blood moon rises. Oh, look, there's another one. Catherine of House Mortis."

He pointed at a beautiful girl with alabaster skin and white hair braided into a coronet who was striding down the row of tables, tossing a plum in the air and catching it again and again with effortless grace. She wore a short, white, high-collared dress paired with red, leather boots.

Behind her, two young women followed closely, both dark haired and beautiful. One had ebony skin and was dressed all in white. Her long hair fell in long narrow braids. The other had porcelain skin, chin-length hair, and was dressed all in red. The two women's hands were entwined.

The three women seemed to move as a unit.

I lowered my voice, "Are those her... consorts?"

Coregon made a choking sound while across the table Quinn snickered again.

"Her consorts?" Theo shook his head. "No, they're her thralls."

I sputtered. "Thralls? What does that mean?"

"It means she just had them for breakfast," Quinn muttered from across the table. "By the Bloodmaid, this blightborn girl really knows nothing."

Theo ignored her. "It means they're blood-bonded. It's not as crass as Quinn is trying to make out. But if you're asking if they're all lovers, too, then the answer is yes, most likely."

"Not as crass?" I managed to say. "But they're her, what? Slaves?"

Theo shrugged. "I mean, in a way, yes. But it's not as if they're being tortured. The feeding process can actually be rather pleasurable."

I didn't want to hear it. "So you mean they're willing? They weren't coerced? They volunteered for this?"

Theo exchanged a look with Quinn and Coregon. "Uh, well. Almost. Not exactly."

"Thralls means they're enthralled," Quinn said, practically giggling at my stupidity. "She has them under her thrall. They love her. They *want* her to feed from them."

"That's disgusting," I said, angrily. "You can't just do that to people."

Quinn's expression turned nasty. "But we can and we do. And they're just grateful it's not worse."

"What does that mean?" I demanded.

Coregon cleared his throat. "Traditionally, vampires have been more forceful in their hunt for blood sources."

"He means we used to kill those we drank," Theo explained. "But now we usually...don't."

"Usually?" I spat.

He shrugged. "Some people prefer the old way. It's not against the law to hunt blightborn, but most have moved beyond it. Veilmar is a safe city. The blightborn are protected. My Uncle Viktor has recently begun to promote a culture of restraint. He believes curbing our bloodlust, saving it, storing it, makes us more powerful."

I didn't even want to know what Viktor was *storing* the bloodlust of vampires for.

"And there's nothing wrong with that," Quinn retorted, as if I'd offended her. "What do you think your precious betrothed prefers?" She bared her teeth at me and I flinched. "Don't you think he's taken his share of blightborn lives? Hunted and killed to feed?"

"Blake does come from a very traditional branch of the family," Theo agreed, though I thought he looked a little uncomfortable. He shifted on the bench and looked around the refectory. "In any case, I think that's it for our house leaders. I don't see Lysander anywhere. He's the leader of House Orphos. His sister, Lunaya, may be in some of your classes. A very sweet girl."

I got the impression he was eager to change the subject.

"The weirdo house," Quinn muttered across the table. She stood up. "Well, I'm off." She glanced down at me, then shook her head as if there was no point saying good-bye politely.

I waited until she was out of earshot, then asked, "What did she mean by that? About House Orphos?"

Theo waved a hand. "Oh, you know. House Orphos has a reputation. They're rather... enigmatic."

"He means they're useless," Coregon added. "Weak."

"They're generally considered to be the least powerful house, yes," Theo admitted. "Though Lysander could change that impression with time. It wasn't always so. There's always one house that's generally considered weaker."

Coregon was rising to his feet. "Well, good luck today, Medra."

"Thanks," I said with surprise, checking the clock high up on the wall. It was only five minutes to nine. Classes didn't begin until nine-thirty. "You're off, too?"

He exchanged a glance with Theo. "I like to be early. There's some prep work I have to see to. I'm helping one of the professors."

Around us, the refectory was emptying out. But Theo didn't look concerned at all. He was helping himself to another plate of fried potatoes.

"So who did you drink from this morning, Theo?" I asked politely, watching him.

He paused with his fork midway to his mouth. "You know, we don't need to feed all the time. And we don't need to kill when we feed. As I've said, some choose to do so, but many don't. It's generally looked down upon these days as overly brutal. Bad form. You get the idea." He chewed a potato, then added, "Besides, most of us use the servants. We highbloods make sure to have a few on hand. If worse comes to worse, we just grab a First Year."

I blanched and Theo burst out laughing.

"That was a joke," he said.

"Very funny. Ha ha," I muttered.

"Well, here comes Regan." Theo pushed back his plate and stood up. "Guess we should be heading to class."

All around us, the hall had cleared out, except for a few servants who were scurrying about carrying dirty dishes and scrubbing the tables.

"Goodness, what a trek that was," Regan said breathlessly. She was dressed impeccably in a lilac wool sweater and a silky matching skirt. "I think I'll take some kava to go. Theo, you're such a dear for minding Medra."

Theo bowed. "Anything for you, Regan." He looked at me. "Well, good-bye, Medra. Don't do anything I wouldn't do." He winked one last time and then was gone.

CHAPTER 5

MEDRA

"That boy." Regan took a sip from the mug she'd just filled. "He'll be the death of Blake with all of his ridiculous antics. I think I'll carry this as we walk. Very carefully, of course." She laughed as if she'd said something funny and I forced a smile, trying not to think about vampires and blood.

We went slowly down the corridor, with Regan taking careful sips from her drink. She seemed preoccupied.

That was all right with me as my mind was busy considering all that I'd learned.

Blake was still an ass. But Theo could grow on me. Coregon was a neutral. He seemed to be trying to give me a fair chance, which was more than I could say for Visha or Quinn.

Quinn was a bitch, but maybe we'd warm up to each other eventually. Visha had left too quickly for me to get much of a read on her.

Were these people really my future friends? The students I'd be spending the most time with?

I glanced at Regan. Her silver hair swayed gently as she walked. She'd called us practically sisters. Was that what we were going to be?

I'd never had a sister. I was an only child.

Having a sister might have been nice. But I wasn't sure I wanted one who was also a vampire.

I gave myself a little shake. It didn't matter. Because these people weren't my family and I couldn't start thinking of them that way even for a second. I couldn't let my guard down, no matter how nice they were to me.

They used people. They fed from them. I wasn't quite sure how the enthrallment process worked but it sure didn't sound as if it was voluntary. It might have been a superior alternative to death, but it was still essentially... well, slavery. Wasn't it?

The halls around us were quiet. I checked my timepiece. Nine-fifteen. We still had plenty of time.

"So," I said, tentatively. "History of Sangratha, right?"

Regan looked over at me and smiled encouragingly. "That's right. It's just around this corner."

I couldn't help feeling a little relieved to hear that. This might have been a vampire school but I still didn't want to be late. What would Florence say, after all?

I expected to see students lined up in the hallway but when we turned the corner and Regan led me over to a wooden door, there was no one outside.

"Well, you'd better go inside. Everyone is probably in there already, choosing their desks," Regan said, brightly. "Unless you want me to stay with you? I don't have class until ten this morning."

"No, that's all right," I said, hurriedly. "I'll be fine."

She smiled reassuringly at me and then, to my shock, leaned in and gave me a peck on the cheek.

"You'll do great. Don't forget what I said. Ask Professor Rodriguez about dragon healers when you get to Restoration. I won't be around to take you to that class, but you should be able to find your own way. Ask one of the other First Years to help you. If they're clueless, find a warden or a Second Year. I'll see you at lunch, okay?"

I nodded. "Thanks for all of your help, Regan."

Her expression softened. "Like I said, consorts have to help one another. See you later... Sister."

I watched her walk away. I wasn't quite ready to call her sister yet, but I could admit I might have been wrong in my initial judgment. She'd obviously been having a bad day yesterday. But she'd been protecting Blake. Doing what she'd been trained to do.

She was willing to give me a chance when it came down to it. I had to be grateful for that.

I pushed the door open to History of Sangratha, expecting to hear a familiar buzz of noise like there'd been in the First Year common room.

But to my surprise, the room was silent. You could have heard a quill drop.

My breath caught as I scanned the room, taking in the dozen or more rows of students, each one already seated and scribbling notes on parchment. There must have been at least a hundred students or more in the class.

As I pulled the door shut behind me, the scribbling stopped and every pair of eyes fixed on me where I stood, hesitating, just inside the doorway.

I suppressed a groan. This was getting to be a habit.

Tiers of polished wood desks and seats curved around the lecture hall. In the center of the room, a woman stood behind an oak lectern on a raised platform, her hands resting on its edge. Her skin was a deep brown hue that contrasted sharply with the white streaks running through her long, dark hair, which had been pulled back into a severe bun.

The professor's lips were pressed into a thin line. A muscle in her jaw twitched as she stepped out from behind her lectern. She leaned against a carved, wooden cane, walking with a heavy limp. The cane tapped rhythmically against the stone floor as she came to the edge of the lecture stage.

"Miss Pendragon, I presume," she said coldly. "How nice of you to finally join us." She pointed up at the clock that hung on the wall behind the row of blackboards. "Only twenty minutes late."

Neat and precisely handwritten notes were already up on one of the boards. Those must have been what the students had been hard at work copying. At the top I caught sight of the professor's name, underlined for emphasis: Professor Amina Hassan.

I swallowed hard. "I beg your pardon, Professor Hassan. My timetable said class didn't begin until nine-thirty. I thought I was early."

My mind jumped to Regan. I wondered if I'd inadvertently made her late for her own class. Had she mixed up her timetable, too? If so, hopefully her professor would be less strict than mine was.

"There's no excuse for a lack of punctuality," the professor said, smacking the floor with her cane loudly. "Perhaps you believe that because you are allied with House Drakharrow, you do not have to respect the rules of this institution. Or your blightborn instructors."

I gaped. "I'm mortal, too, you know."

She sneered. "Yes. Of rider's blood. How very special."

My face flushed. "I didn't ask to be here."

Instantly I knew it had been the wrong thing to say.

The professor's eyes narrowed. "You shouldn't be here at all, Miss Pendragon. You haven't earned your place like they have." She indicated the many students sitting in the rows of seats, all watching us with fascination.

I noticed Florence in the second row. She had scooted over and was not-so-subtly patting the seat beside her.

I looked around the room slowly. "Half of these students are vampires, aren't they? Did they earn their place or are they just here because of their family ties? And of the mortal students, how many of them wanted to be here and how many of them were brought forcibly?"

If one could have heard a pin drop when I walked in, now the silence was truly oppressive.

I saw many of the vampire students snarling silently in my direction and tried not to flinch as rows of sharp teeth came into view.

The silence went on for so long that I thought the professor was about to ask me to leave. Or perhaps she was thinking of the best way to punish me.

Finally, Professor Hassan spoke. "What a fascinating point, Miss Pendragon. But the way in which Bloodwing students are selected is a topic we will not be taking up in this class. However, you are always welcome to meet with Headmaster Kim to discuss your concerns. Now, if you have quite finished disrupting this class, please take your seat."

I hurried over to Florence's row and sat down next to her. Guiltily, I eyed her quill and parchment. I hadn't even thought to bring my own. Regan hadn't mentioned school supplies to me.

Even though I was probably humiliating her just by my presence, Florence kindly slid a piece of parchment and extra quill over to me with a quick smile.

I tried to smile back, but the truth was, I was rattled. My first class wasn't off to a great start.

Professor Hassan had resumed her place at the lectern. "Miss Pendragon is evidently well-informed about many aspects of Sangrathan history and culture, despite her claim to being only a recent arrival in our land. Let's test her knowledge, shall we?"

Laughter broke out around me.

"For someone who has been so elevated by one of our esteemed houses, Miss Pendragon appears to show considerable disdain for those of the Pure Blood," Professor Hassan continued. "But I'm sure she'd be happy to answer some basic questions." She strode over to the blackboard and raised her hand as if poised to write. "Miss Pendragon, please tell the class why vampires drink blood."

"Why do vampires drink blood? I..." I stuttered. I'd wondered the same thing that morning but still wasn't sure I had a grasp on the answer. "To survive," I settled on.

Professor Hassan's hand dropped. "To survive? What an imprecise response. I require food to survive, water to live. But what do those substances *do* for me exactly?"

When I said nothing, she sniffed.

Beside me, Florence's hand shot into the air.

"Yes, Miss Shen?"

"Blood does help vampires to survive as Medra... I mean, Miss Pendragon... already mentioned. But more specifically, it enables them to recharge their unique abilities."

"Good, Miss Shen. And what are some of those abilities?"

"Oh, there are ever so many," Florence gushed. "They heal faster than us blightborn do and they can recover from much more serious wounds. They have heightened senses, including sight, smell, and hearing. They can move much more quickly. Their speed has even been mistaken for invisibility or flight. Vampires can go days without taking a blood meal, but doing so grants them superior strength, helps maintain their healing, and supplements their other powers."

"Other powers such as?" Professor Hassan prompted. "Someone other than Miss Shen, perhaps?"

A boy sitting further down the row on Florence's side put his hand up then nervously started to lower it.

"Yes, Mister...?" Professor Hassan said. "Do you have an answer for us?"

The young man licked his lips. He was brown-haired with a short, stocky build and seemed tense with nervous energy. His wide, expressive eyes darted about the classroom.

"Sharma, Professor. Naveen Sharma. Well..." He ran his hands through his already-messy hair, as if trying to buy time. But this only resulted in his hair standing up in every direction making him resemble a spiky hedgehog. Behind him, I heard some students snickering.

"Perhaps you'd like to stand up, Mr. Sharma," the professor suggested, sounding impatient. "It might help you to focus better."

Naveen jumped up, scattering his parchment and quill onto the floor. "Um, of course. Well, everyone knows that vampires can create thralls."

"Then that hardly bears stating, does it, Mr. Sharma?" Professor Hassan said drolly.

Naveen colored. "Uh, right. Well, each of the four houses also have their own special abilities. Though some of these require years of training before they can be fully utilized. One thing they all share though is the ability to sense emotions through blood. When a vampire is fully mature, they can manipulate others' feelings in this way."

Naveen sank back down suddenly as if he'd run out of steam.

"Thank you, Mr. Sharma." Professor Hassan looked around the room. "And of course, this is why it is so essential for the houses to keep their bloodlines pure." Her eyes found mine. "So that these extraordinary powers are not diluted. Except when necessary, in very rare cases."

My blood flared hot. She meant me. Well, Professor Hassan didn't have to worry. I wasn't going to dilute the blood of her precious vampire overlords.

Though her pronouncement did make me wonder just how often blightborns bred with vampires. Obviously it was unusual.

"This is why," the professor continued. "Service to a highblood is an honor, not a sacrifice. As is the tithing system as well as conscription."

My hand shot up. "Wait," I said, not waiting to be called on. "You're saying mortals should be glad to give up their blood but not only do they have to do that but they have to *pay* the vampires to live here? And accept military conscription?"

The room broke out into an angry chatter.

"Quiet down," Professor Hassan said loudly. "Settle down."

"I don't understand... They're using you but you speak of them as if they're gods or something," I said in disbelief. "What is wrong with you people?"

The room quieted around us as Professor Hassan and I stared at one another.

"Well, class, I'd say Miss Pendragon has truly proven her ignorance this morning, wouldn't you?" the professor finally said.

Laughter erupted around me, harsh and bitter. But I caught some students staring at me curiously, too. I wondered how many blightborn students were in this class and how many of them had thought similar things from time to time without ever daring to say it aloud.

I snuck a peek down my row. Florence wasn't laughing, neither was Naveen. But their faces were quiet and respectful. It was obvious they didn't want to get off on the wrong foot with this formidable teacher.

"Look up at the board, Miss Pendragon," the professor commanded. "Tell me what you see."

I glanced at the blackboard, at the notes the students had been copying down when I'd first walked in.

"The Great Famine," I read aloud. "The Blight of Shadows. The Dragon Cataclysm."

"Very good. Terrifying-sounding terms, wouldn't you agree? Have you ever lived through a famine, Miss Pendragon?"

I shook my head slowly.

"Neither have I. Neither has anyone in this class. Thanks to the highbloods," Professor Hassan said. "Yet our histories tell us that thousands of years ago, the worst famine the world had ever seen swept through the land, causing starvation and despair. Families abandoned children to die, unable to provide for them. Still other families resorted to *eating* their own children."

I shuddered.

"Then, one exceptionally powerful woman stepped forward. Some say she was a human. Others say a vampire. Still many more say she was not of this world at all but a goddess or the daughter of a god who had lived among us in mortal form. Unable to bear the sight of so much suffering, she spilled her blood upon the earth and having done so, she encouraged her mortal family to drink from it. They were nourished from her blood as she died and thus the first vampires were born. In the midst of the famine, a new race arose. They had no need for food or water. They could survive only upon blood, for days or months or even years if needed. The Bloodmaiden, as she came to be called, had saved her family. And her family continued her lifesaving work by creating an incredible elixir derived from their own blood. They distributed this elixir to many of their mortal neighbors, turning them into the Pure and saving countless lives. And so it continued. Many were spared in this way. But of course, not all could live. With the survival of the strong, came a culling of the weak. A tribute was required so that some could endure the famine while others sadly perished. A tribute made in blood. Weak mortals paid the price willingly, even eagerly, so that their fathers or mothers or sisters or brothers or children could be saved and become stronger, while they gave up their lives to feed others."

I shuddered again. What she described was still a kind of terrible cannibalism. No less worse than eating one's own child.

"But this was all long before our time. It was not the first time, however, that mortals were saved by highbloods. Centuries later came the Blight of Shadows. A deadly illness that ravaged the mortal world and caused people to turn into mindless, nightmarish creatures known as the Shadowed. These creatures thrived in darkness, preying upon others. Entire cities were turned into wastelands. By this time, mortals and highbloods coexisted. Those of the Blessed Blood would not stand for this. In a coordinated effort, they utilized their inherent resistance to the plague and their superior strength, and eradicated the Shadowed, reclaiming lands that had been lost and saving mortals from extinction for a second time. From this time forward, mortals willingly recognized their inferiority and took on the name we are still known by today–the blightborn."

"But perhaps this is still not enough to convince you of the virtue of those of Blessed Blood?" Professor Hassan questioned me. "A hundred years later there came the Cataclysm. Malevolent creatures swarmed Sangratha, bringing with them legions of monstrous creatures. Among them were the dragons–massive, fire-breathing beasts that answered to no one. The dragons ruled the skies and terrorized the land. They were almost unstoppable, laying waste to entire cities. But a few highbloods saw these creatures' worth, their potential. They found individuals with a rare affinity–the ability to bond to dragons. They honed these ones into the race that came to be known as riders. Together with the riders, the highbloods led the armies of the vampire and mortal realms in a great war, vanquishing the dark forces that threatened Sangratha and sealing away the terrors."

The room had grown very still. I didn't dare look around. I knew what I'd find. Everyone's eyes on me once again.

"We mortals accept our inferiority, Miss Pendragon," Professor Hassan said softly. "Because there is no other choice. The truth is plain to see. The Pure of Blood *are* superior. We live only thanks to their benevolence. They have saved us time and time again. We owe them not just our allegiance, our loyalty, our blood–but *everything*."

I said nothing. I refused to agree with her. In my heart, I believed she was wrong.

There were two sides to every story. And what she had just spewed was carefully written historical bullshit.

To the victors went the spoils. Wasn't that the saying back in Aercanum? And the victors also wrote the histories, didn't they? Obviously the vampires wanted to come off as the saviors of the world. It was all propaganda. Propaganda that most of Sangratha had accepted as the truth.

The fact that I would have to sit here for weeks on end and listen to this drivel being taught as fact was what really infuriated me. I looked over at Florence, wondering if she had grown up hearing lectures like this.

"Sadly, our time is up," Professor Hassan announced. "My apologies to the class for the time we lost educating Miss Pendragon instead of moving onto new topics. Thank you all for your patience this morning."

Around me, students rose to their feet, gathering satchels and supplies.

I started to pass back my unused parchment to Florence and thank her for the assistance but my words were cut short.

"Miss Pendragon." Professor Hassan's brusque voice cut across the room. "A moment, if you will."

Florence brushed past me. "We'll wait for you outside," she whispered.

I nodded, seeing Naveen walking beside her. He smiled briefly at me, then quickly darted from the room. I supposed he was a First Year student in our dormitory, too. Or perhaps another warden.

Professor Hassan waited to speak until the room had almost emptied out.

"Tardiness is unacceptable at Bloodwing and in my class, Miss Pendragon," she sternly informed me, glaring down from the lecture stage.

"I understand completely," I said quickly. "Miss Pansera escorted me to class but we were both under the mistaken impression that it began..."

"Miss Pansera? Miss Regan Pansera was your guide this morning?" the professor asked sharply.

I nodded. "She's Blake's other consort."

The teacher's eyebrows rose. "I am fully aware of that. What an honor to have Miss Pansera as your escort. An honor I doubt you truly appreciate."

"I can appreciate kindness whatever the source," I said, trying to keep my temper.

She frowned. "Very well. I'll be lenient with you this time, Miss Pendragon. Because of your esteemed guide. Miss Pansera had only your best interests in mind. But do not be late again. Should you be tardy a second time, there will be a penalty."

"I understand."

I hurried out of the lecture hall before she could change her mind.

Florence squeaked as she spotted me. "Medra! What happened this morning?"

"I guess there was an error on my timetable," I explained with a frustrated sigh. "Regan and I thought the class didn't begin until nine-thirty."

"Oh, dear," Florence said. "I hope she got to her own class all right."

"So do I," I replied.

"What's next on your schedule, ladies?" Naveen Sharma sidled up beside us. He had flattened his hair down, but a few strands still stuck out on the sides. The boy was even shorter than I'd realized. He only came up to Florence's shoulder. He was built differently, too.

He caught me staring at him and grinned as I blushed. "Never seen a dwarf before, have you?"

"A...what?"

"Naveen is blightborn but he's also dwarven," Florence explained. "His people live underground."

My eyes widened. "That's incredible."

"The dwarves are amazing builders. They construct entire cities beneath the earth. They're also notorious for their scouting skills," Florence said.

"Bloodwing must be very different compared to where you're from," I said.

Naveen nodded. "It's certainly brighter." He pointed to my schedule and I remembered his original question.

"I have Restoration next," I said, glancing at my schedule. "Then lunch, I hope."

"There's a lunch break after the next class," Naveen assured me. "I have Restoration next, too."

"So do I," Florence said. "Although, Medra, I'm surprised..."

But whatever she'd been about to say was cut short when Naveen elbowed her in a friendly way.

"Of course, you're in Restoration. Florence here is a brilliant student, you know. She has her pick of specialties," Naveen explained to me. "She's smart enough to be a strategist or a healer. Now she needs to pick between the two. Unless they approve her for both."

"I didn't know that," I said, raising my eyebrows. "But I'm not surprised to hear it. So is that why she's a warden? She made it sound like it was because her mother..."

"Was a librarian," Naveen finished. "Ha! No, that had nothing to do with it. You're too modest, Florence."

"Well, I'm not about to go around bragging about myself, Naveen," Florence said, blushing madly. "Or telling people I have two specialties."

"That's why I'm here to do it for you," Naveen said, grinning at me.

"Are you two...?" I looked between the two of them, suddenly wondering if there was more to this playful banter.

"Oh, no," Florence said, her eyes widening. "We've been friends since we were children. Naveen is like my brother. There's a dwarven stairwell to his city near the town I grew up in and we would visit each other. I met him at a market day when his people came above ground to sell some dwarven wares. Mostly gold, of course."

"I'm single," Naveen said, putting his hands up. "I had a girlfriend back home but being accepted to Bloodwing... Well, that kind of put a damper on things. Long distance and all that."

I nodded sympathetically, as if I understood, deciding not to say anything about my own limited experiences with the opposite sex.

"Goodness!" Florence exclaimed. "We have to get to Restoration. Now."

I looked around and noticed the hallway around us had emptied out.

"We have five minutes to get to the south tower," Florence sputtered, already almost sprinting away from us. "Hurry!"

CHAPTER 6

MEDRA

O f course, after the hell that History of Sangratha had been, my life wouldn't have been complete without running into Blake Drakharrow on the way to Restoration.

As we half-walked, half-ran down the halls towards class, I nearly collided with a tall figure emerging around a corner from the shadows.

The breath was knocked out of me. As I gasped and tried to regain my footing, strong hands gripped me by the shoulders and yanked me upright.

I felt a jolt as my eyes connected with a pair of gray, steely ones, then Blake's hands dropped away swiftly.

"Oh. Pendragon. It's you." Blake couldn't manage to keep the disgust from his voice.

I stared up at him, letting myself get a better look than I had that morning in the refectory. He wore a black, tailored suit that fit him impeccably, accentuating his tall, lean frame, the jacket hugging his broad shoulders and chest, tapering in at the waist to hint at his muscular, subtly defined torso.

"See something you like?" Quinn neared, stepping out from behind Blake as he pushed a lock of sleek pale blond hair off his forehead.

Coregon Phiri had appeared behind the pair, too, along with some other students. He nodded to me briefly.

I rolled my eyes. "Hell no. Just trying to get to class on time."

Quinn laughed nastily. "I hear you got off on the wrong foot with Professor Hassan."

"I asked some pointed questions about vampires that I guess she didn't appreciate," I said, with a shrug.

"The mortals worship us," Quinn said, studying her nails. They had been sharpened to points and painted bright red. "And soon you will, too. Good thing you're about to get *schooled*." She said the last part in an annoying, sing-songy voice that set my blood boiling.

"I have to get to my next class," I snapped, looking at Blake. "I suppose you and your little gang had better get a move on, too."

Blake smiled lazily. "Good idea. Best not be late again, Pendragon."

I didn't reply, just moved around the corner and past him before I could tell him to fuck off in front of his little group of sycophants. I suspected Regan wouldn't like that and since she'd been decent to me that morning, I decided I'd resist. For now.

We arrived at Restoration class in the nick of time. I slid into a row beside Naveen and Florence, then eyed the short, sturdy young man. "So what's your specialty, Naveen?"

"Oh, I'm hoping to become a scout," he said with a grin. "Most dwarves wind up specializing as scouts. And all potential scouts have to take a basic healing course." He grimaced. "Can't stand the sight of blood though."

For some reason this struck me as hilarious considering we were attending a vampire academy. I giggled.

He smiled back. "I know, I know. Ironic, right? I'd make a terrible vampire. Or a thrall."

The smile fell from my face. "I don't know why anyone would *want* to be..."

"Good morning, class!" The classroom door slammed shut as a man in dark emerald robes swept in.

"Since I'm a new face to all of you First Years, here's a quick introduction. My name is Professor Gabriel Rodriguez and I believe this is the most important class you'll take at the academy your entire year."

He dropped a worn leather satchel onto his desk with a soft thud, then shrugged off his robe and tossed it over the nearby chair. Underneath, he was wearing a threadbare brown vest that looked as if it had seen better days. His trousers were patched in more places than I could count. Yet despite his roguish appearance, he had a presence no less imposing than Professor Hassan's, maybe even more so. Rodriguez had the kind of quiet confidence that made you feel like he could handle anything.

Honestly, he wasn't bad to look at either. For a teacher, anyhow. His dark hair was all tousled in a way that almost looked intentional, unlike Naveen's. It stood out against his warm, olive-toned skin. And yet his face was lined, a little more than it should have been for someone his age. And he had this exhausted look to him, as if he was fighting off sleep but pretending he was fine.

I frowned. Professor Rodriguez was a walking contradiction.

Still, I sat up a little straighter, wanting to make a good first impression on this second blightborn professor.

Rodriguez leaned back against the desk and crossed his arms. "Now, what can you tell me about the healing arts?"

Beside me, Florence raised her hand slowly.

"Miss Shen?" I was impressed that he knew Florence's name already. But then, she seemed to have something of an established reputation at Bloodwing.

"The healing arts are key to the sustainability of Sangratha," Florence announced confidently.

"Very good. I'd quite agree. How so? Elaborate."

"In two ways," Florence said, picking up steam. "Healers and alchemists may be placed within military squads, supporting those in defensive positions and protecting the realm. Secondly, they serve in key roles within highblood households. Every household needs at least one healer."

"Very good," Professor Rodriguez replied. "Now look around the room if you haven't already done so."

I looked around and saw my fellow students doing the same thing.

"No vampires," I blurted out before I could help myself. I covered my mouth in embarrassment.

"Correct. Vampires can self-heal, but they rarely possess the aptitudes required to heal others—with the exception of some thralls. Nor do their magical abilities align with the healing arts or alchemy—again, except in some rare cases." The professor eyed me with curiosity. "You must be Miss Pendragon. As a consort to Blake Drakharrow, you'll have a high-ranking position within a triad unit as well as within the Drakharrow House." He frowned. "I'm actually surprised to find you here, Miss Pendragon."

"It was on my timetable," I said, flustered.

The teacher shrugged. "Well, I suppose someone thought you could use the basic training. Though if you don't have an aptitude for healing this may prove to be a difficult or even futile course for you. And, of course, only the most skilled students here will move into the next level of the class in Wintermark term."

I wasn't sure if it was because he made it sound almost like a challenge or if it was because I was determined to redeem myself after my lackluster experience in Professor Hassan's class, but I found myself blurting something out yet again.

"Perhaps I was put in this course because I have rider blood, sir? I've heard the history of healers and dragon riders is fascinating. Can you tell us a little about it?"

The room fell absolutely still. On either side of me, I felt Florence and Naveen stiffen. All of the blood seemed to have drained from Professor Rodriguez's face.

"Who told you to ask me that?" the professor demanded, standing up to his full height.

"I... No one," I stuttered. "It just seemed like an interesting topic."

Professor Rodriguez eyed me coldly. "From what I'm given to understand, you're new to Bloodwing and to Sangratha. You know nothing of our history. Someone told you to ask that question. I want to know who it was."

I stayed silent. But inside, I was wondering why the hell Regan thought this would be an interesting topic. Surely this would pay off for me somehow.

I hoped.

"Everyone in this room—with the exception of Miss Pendragon—is here because you've been selected for your aptitude in the art of restoration and alchemy or because your specialty is one adjacent to this, in which knowledge of basic healing techniques will be essential." Professor Rodriguez's eyes swept across Naveen, Florence, and I. "Therefore, most of you, if not all of you, are well aware of the subject matter that Miss Pendragon has inquired about. You also know why it's a sore subject with me."

I shrank into myself, cheeks hot with humiliation. "I'm sorry, Professor..."

"It's too late for that, Miss Pendragon," he snapped. "You asked a question and I'll provide you with the answer. Even if you already know it, which I suspect you do."

I had no idea what he was talking about. But I also knew there was no way to persuade him of that. At least, not right now.

"More than a century ago, when dragons were fading from this world, my great-great-grandmother, Isabella Rodriguez, gained renown as a healer. She was famed for not only her skill and inventiveness, but for her compassion." Rodriguez had begun to pace back and forth across the front of the lecture hall. "Towards the end of her career, when Isabella should have been safe in her retirement, settling down after a long life of helping others and aiding Sangratha, she was sent on a dangerous mission. One of the last dragons had lost its rider and lay dying. Now, as you all know, dragons were resistant to external healing, especially when their bond with their rider had been severed. They were notorious for refusing help from outsiders. And their response to interference could be... savage. Despite knowing all of this, my great-great-grandmother's resolve was unwavering. She went to the dragon's lair, fully aware that the odds were against her."

He paused, his dark eyes scanning the class. "And she failed. Of course, she failed. It was a suicide mission. The dragon, grief-stricken and distrustful, rejected Isabella's attempt at healing and scorched her to death instead. Healing, like everything, has its limits. And when it comes to dragons and their riders, the limits are more clearly defined. Yet the highbloods have never been willing to accept those limits."

I glanced at Florence and saw she was biting her lip nervously. Was Professor Rodriguez crossing a line? A treasonous one?

I got the feeling Rodriguez and Hassan must not have been the best of friends despite being on the same faculty.

"Dragons were more valuable to the realm than healers," the teacher went on. "Healers were expendable. And so countless healers were sent to try to save the dragons. So many that their names have been lost to history. Conveniently so. My great-great-grandmother's name was remembered because my family honored her legacy and her sacrifice. But many were forgotten. Or if they were remembered, it was only as failures in the eyes of the highbloods. Healers, you see, could not save the dragons. The last dragon died out. And so did the riders. Until now."

He met my eyes, his own rich, brown ones cool with mistrust.

"Stay behind after class, Miss Pendragon. I'll have a few tasks for you to be carried out over the lunch hour."

I took a deep breath and nodded.

He had to punish me. Part of me even understood why. I had forced him to publicly recount a family legacy that must have been incredibly painful. One which clearly still cast a long shadow over Professor Rodriguez's life's work.

The professor moved on to the course objectives, briefly explaining how healers fit into the broader context of the vampire military in their support roles. He sketched out the basic anatomy and physiology of vampires versus mortals, highlighting their key differences and similarities. I scribbled notes as fast as I could, trying to keep up with Florence, who was making neat, shorthand notes on her parchment–clearly this was familiar territory to her already–and Naveen who wasn't taking any notes at all, just listening intently as if he were memorizing everything Professor Rodriguez said.

By the time class finished, Professor Rodriguez was telling us to look forward to brewing our first alchemical potion next time.

"Don't forget, you'll need to bring a cauldron, vials, and mixing tools to the next class," he reminded everyone. "You can store them here in the storeroom after that. Of course, you'll need to make sure they're maintained and kept in clean condition."

For the first time that day, I heard loud bells chiming as the clock on the wall sounded twelve o'clock.

"Wish they'd done that this morning," I muttered under my breath as I packed up my quill and parchment and passed them to Florence, swearing silently to myself that I'd pack a proper bag full of supplies tomorrow.

"What do you mean?" Florence asked in surprise.

"Do you mean the bells?" Naveen asked, raising his dark brows. "They did ring this morning. They ring between every class and announce mealtimes."

I stared at them blankly. "I didn't hear them."

Florence frowned. "That's odd."

I rubbed my eyes, feeling a headache coming on. It had been brewing all morning, I realized, I just had kept pushing the pain away. "Maybe I was too distracted. Regan had just introduced me to all of these students from House Drakharrow..."

Florence nodded and looked relieved. "That's probably it. You'll get used to hearing the bells and now that you know what they're for, you won't be late again."

She glanced at Professor Rodriguez. "I guess you'll be missing lunch."

"Yes," I said hollowly. "Who needs food? I'm only mortal after all."

"I'll try to grab something for you in the refectory," she offered. "Which class do you have after lunch?"

I yanked my schedule out of my bag and showed it to her.

Her face fell as she scanned it. "Oh. You're in a combat class after lunch. Advanced Weaponry. Strategists and healers don't usually require combat training. Naveen will, as a scout, but his combat class is a completely different one." She perked up. "But we'll see you in the library at two o'clock. I'll bring you something then."

I tried not to groan, thinking of how I'd have to trek through the school on my own and get through a combat class on a stomach that was starting to feel very, very empty.

I forced a smile. "That's really nice of you, Florence. Thank you."

"Of course! We First Years have to stick together." She beamed.

I was just grateful she hadn't decided to shun me after the taboo questions I'd asked in our first two classes. Florence was most definitely the kind of student Quinn Riley had in mind when she said most students worshiped the highbloods.

Despite this, I found myself genuinely liking the studious dark-haired girl. Just because she admired vampires didn't mean she wasn't also a good person.

The sound of Professor Rodriguez clearing his throat loudly brought me back to reality.

"Miss Pendragon, if you'd wrap up the chatter, I have some tasks for you."

Florence and Naveen quickly left the classroom while I remained.

"You'll be spending your lunch hour here, Miss Pendragon," Professor Rodriguez said with deceptive pleasantness. "Your entire lunch hour."

I stared back at him, taking in his features. His richly warm complexion paired well with his large, hazel eyes. His dark hair had a natural wave to it and was slightly ruffled, giving him a rugged appearance. The lines of his face were strong. Well-defined jaw. High cheekbones. There was pride and resilience there. A demeanor that brooked no argument.

If I hadn't just accidentally made him my enemy, I'd probably have liked Professor Rodriguez.

"I think we got off on the wrong foot, Professor," I said, trying to keep my tone as respectful as possible. "I wasn't trying to bring up a painful subject."

"Unless you're going to tell me who told you to raise that painful subject, Miss Pendragon, you can keep your apologies to yourself." He ran a hand through his hair. "But I don't think you need to tell me."

I looked at him in surprise. "Oh, no?"

He shook his head. "You're betrothed to arguably the most powerful young man in this school. Not to mention one of the most entitled. It seems Blake Drakharrow's demeanor has already rubbed off on you."

My jaw fell open. "I only got to Sangratha yesterday. I only met Blake yesterday. And believe me, I don't want to be his betrothed. I hate him as much as you seem to."

"I don't hate any of my students, Miss Pendragon," Rodriguez corrected me. "And of course, I respect the Drakharrows. They're an ancient and respected house." But there was a blaze in his eyes that told me otherwise. "But pardon me if I fail to see how being intimately connected to such a powerful house is somehow to your detriment."

"Because I don't even want to be here," I sputtered. "You think I *want* to be here? At this school? In your class? Mixing with blood-sucking vampires?"

Professor Rodriguez stared at me. "I don't know what you and your chum Viktor Drakharrow are up to, Miss Pendragon. But there's clearly something at play. Some dark scheme. You arrived only yesterday, or so you say, and yet you've been given a position most girls at this school would murder for. You seem determined to pretend you're just another student. But you're not. If the signs are being read right, and looking at your physique, I think they are–" He ran his eyes up and down my body and I felt my cheeks redden. Would I ever get used to that kind of scrutiny? "Then you certainly do have rider blood. A great deal of it. If Viktor Drakharrow found you and put you in Bloodwing…"

"I had the vast misfortune to be found by Blake Drakharrow not his uncle, thank you very much," I spat.

"Viktor has always refused to believe the dragons were really gone. That the highbloods had truly lost so much power. Now it seems he has an ace up his sleeve. You." Rodriguez's hazel eyes stared at me intensely.

"But there are no dragons," I protested. "That's what you and everyone else has already said."

"How do I know that's the truth? How do any of us know?" Rodriguez's voice was soft, but he shocked me to the core. "I just believe what I'm told. Like all of the other blightborn sheep."

I stared at him. "You think Viktor Drakharrow has a dragon?"

"I didn't say that, did I? But I do know he has a rider. That's half of a very powerful, very deadly equation. You're playing with fire, Miss Pendragon. And I think you're likely to get burned. If you don't wind up burning up this entire school and all of us with you."

He slammed a stack of books down on the desk. "That's what I aim to prevent."

"What do you mean?" I asked, still feeling stunned.

"After you've spent the first half of the lunch hour cleaning up the storage room, you can spend the second half reading up on the history of dragons. At the end of this term, you'll be turning in a fifty-page essay on the subject." He smirked. "Oh, and I expect the subject of healing dragons and their riders to comprise a significant portion."

"You can't do this," I protested. "I need to eat before afternoon classes."

"I can do whatever I want, Miss Pendragon," he growled back. "If you have any complaints, take them up with Blake Drakharrow. Either he's your ally or your enemy. I suppose we'll see which it is. Regardless, I'm well within my rights as your professor to keep you here every lunch hour for the entire rest of the school year if I choose to. So you'd best buckle up."

I clenched my jaw but said nothing.

He started striding towards the door.

"Hey! Where are you going?"

Professor Rodriguez paused, then looked back and smiled. "I'm going to eat lunch. And when I get back at one o'clock, you'd better have made significant progress on that storage room and on that stack of books."

CHAPTER 7

MEDRA

I was sticky and sweaty by the time one o'clock rolled around. I didn't want to risk leaving the Restoration classroom too early and invoking Rodriguez's wrath but I also didn't plan on being late for my first Advanced Weaponry class.

I'd lost not only my chance to eat lunch but also a chance to track down Regan Pansera and put a few questions to her. Despite her claims to want me to have the best first day possible, it was turning out to be a disaster.

I'd been late for my first class, made a spectacle of myself in my second, and now had at least one teacher as an enemy.

Rodriguez's suspicion of Viktor Drakharrow and his apparent dislike for Blake seemed a little strange for Sangratha and for a professor. I would have thought he'd be currying the Drakharrows' favor just like everyone else at the school. But instead, Rodriguez seemed to have almost as many qualms about highbloods as I did.

I supposed there was a fine line between being critical of parts of highblood history–like the sacrifice of healers for a pointless cause–and actual treason. Still, considering how intense Viktor Drakharrow had seemed, I wouldn't have thought Rodriguez would want to be so public about airing his grievances.

I'd gotten so involved in cleaning up the storage room–the place really was a mess, with dust covering everything, and it was strangely satisfying to get things orderly–that I'd almost forgotten about my second task. By the time I'd snatched up one of the books in the stack, it was a quarter-to-one and I was nearly out of time.

I flipped open the first few pages and scanned as much as I could.

When five minutes had passed, I bailed. Deciding I could get more reading done later, I scooped up the stack of books and took them with me.

As I stepped out of the Restoration classroom, I realized I had absolutely no idea where to go next.

I stood there, heart sinking and panic setting in, as a rush of students began to flow through the hall around me.

"Medra!"

I looked down the hall and saw a hand frantically waving. Florence.

"Come with me," she said breathlessly, running up and grabbing my arm with one hand while shoving a muffin towards me with her other. "You have just enough time to get down to the training courtyard."

I stuffed the muffin in my mouth–some sort of nut and berry combination, not my favorite but better than nothing–as she pulled me along the corridors.

By the time we got down to the entrance to the courtyard, I was panting and so was Florence.

"Florence, you're going to be late for your own class," I moaned as I looked up at a clock on the wall.

"I have a prep period. I'm helping my mother get ready for the library session with the First Years." She chewed her lip as if indecisive.

"What is it?" I asked.

"Medra, I think there must have been a mistake with your timetable." The words came out in a rush. "Advanced Weaponry is a third or fourth year class. And it can get...dangerous."

"Dangerous?"

"It's normally only for vampires," Florence said. Her expression was truly worried. "It'll be full of highbloods. I should have said something when I saw your timetable, but I've never heard of a mistake like that being made."

"Maybe they put me in it because I'm a rider?" I said slowly.

"I don't know," Florence said. "But maybe you should..."

Just then the bells sounded.

A group of laughing students pushed past us. Visha Vaidya's violet eyes honed in on me as she strode by. Trailing behind her were Quinn Riley and Coregon Phiri. Only the dark-skinned young man greeted me as he moved past us. Quinn simply ignored me.

Last but not least, a few steps behind for once, sauntered Blake Drakharrow.

He shot me an odd look but for once kept his mouth shut. I didn't know whether to be grateful or not. Just this once, his input on my situation might have been useful.

But it was too late. I wasn't about to beg him for help.

Florence and I watched Blake head towards a rack of weapons lined up on one side of the courtyard. He picked up a hefty-looking halberd and started going through practiced motions.

"Those weapons look brutal, Medra," Florence said, chewing her lip. "At least in Basic Combat you're learning hand-to-hand techniques. And the scouts use lighter weapons like daggers and bows. Not greatswords and halberds."

You're not exactly a novice when it comes to weapons, my dear. Are you going to let your friend in on your little secret?

I gasped and jumped backwards. The woman's voice was back in my head.

Get the fuck out, I'm trying to think, I hissed furiously.

Florence was looking at me oddly.

"You know what, Florence," I said slowly. "I'm going to go in. I think the highbloods might be in for a surprise. You might be, too. I'm not a total novice at this. I've had a little bit of training. Back home." I decided to keep it vague.

Florence nodded. "If you're sure." She squeezed my arm. "I bet you'll be great. I'll see you in the library later." She grabbed my armful of books before I could stop her. "I'll put these in your room."

I shot her a grateful look. "Right. The library. Thanks, Florence."

I took a deep breath and stepped into the courtyard.

Blake Drakharrow had slung his vicious-looking halberd over his shoulder–rather a cocky thing to do with such a sharp weapon–and was standing addressing the class.

Oh, gods, I thought, suddenly panicked. Please tell me Blake isn't the fucking instructor.

I walked up and stood at the back of the group of highbloods cautiously, trying to hide myself behind them.

"Professor Sankara is delayed so I'll be supervising the class for now," Blake said, his deep voice carrying across the courtyard. He looked around at the students sternly. "No bullshit. I mean it. It's the first day. Just get started. Everyone knows what to do."

We did?

Everyone around me was nodding. The group broke up. Some students already had equipped themselves with their weapons of choice. They started pairing up. Others stood alone, solo drilling.

I walked slowly over to the weapons rack and looked at the options.

"Pick it up, bitch."

I whirled around.

Visha Vaidya was standing behind me, swinging a steel-tipped spear. "I said pick it up."

She glanced around, then took a step towards me. "You aren't even supposed to be here, you know that?" Her eyes were lit up gleefully.

"Regan messed with my timetable," I guessed. "And all of you were in on it."

Visha smiled nastily. "You made it this far. But it remains to be seen whether you make it out of this courtyard."

I looked around, wondering if this was what was supposed to happen.

There were no teachers. Blake was on the far side of the courtyard sparring with Coregon. Their halberds flashed in the afternoon sunlight. They moved so quickly I could hardly keep track of who was who. They paused and Blake glanced over at where I stood. He looked back and forth between Visha and I, then turned his back.

So. No help from that direction then. Not that I'd really expected any.

"Fine," I said, taking a deep breath. "I'll spar with you. Did you think I wouldn't?"

"What I think is that you've never sparred with anyone in your life," Visha said, her pretty face distorted by a nasty sneer. "Or picked up a sword. Look at those pretty, delicate hands."

I bit my tongue and decided not to tell her how very wrong she was. Let her find out on my terms.

Fae hands healed quickly. Much like vampires, I supposed. A useful trait. My hands might not be covered in blisters but they were more calloused than Visha could tell. What was more, my hands knew their way around a weapon or two.

I picked up one of the sleek, wooden shafts, balancing it between my hands and feeling the cool, smooth wood beneath my fingertips. It was lighter than I'd expected. I gave it a cautious twirl.

It felt right in my hands.

Visha was marching away. I followed her as she led the way to a sparring arena that had been cordoned off with thick, sturdy ropes attached to wooden posts.

A few other students paused what they were doing and glanced over at us curiously. But that was all I had time to notice. Because the moment I stepped into the ring, Visha lunged at me with lightning speed.

I barely had time to react. My spear came up just in time to deflect her strike.

The impact of Visha's spear clashing into my own jolted my arms. I staggered back against the ropes but managed to keep my footing

Visha gnashed her teeth, stepped back, then reengaged, striking at me again and again, each blow coming faster and harder than the last.

Fuck but she was fast. My eyes could barely follow her but somehow my arms kept up, raising and blocking with my spear again and again.

Still, it was clear I was on the defensive. I wasn't sure how long I could keep up the relentless pace. Visha's assault kept shoving me back against the ropes over and over until I was gasping.

I had to admit, part of me had believed I'd be able to take her. Easily. I might not have been a vampire, but I'd been trained by one of the best fae instructors in Aercanum. With a pang of sorrow, my mind slipped back to my mentor, Odessa. She'd not only trained me in combat; she'd been my friend. In some ways, Odessa was the closest thing to a mother I'd ever had.

She'd died protecting me.

But Odessa was gone. I was alone. I was here. And I was no longer the best pupil Odessa had ever seen. Because Visha would have given her a run for her money.

I'd been cocky to even think I could compete in this class. I felt a wave of panic spread over me. I should have listened to Florence and left when I'd had the chance.

Visha's spear spun through the air and swept low, catching me behind the knees and knocking me off my feet.

I went sprawling back into the dirt, the breath nearly knocked out of me.

I jumped back up just in time to miss her spear as it dove into the ground where my head had just been.

Visha's eyes gleamed with triumph.

Rightly so.

I was losing and she knew it. It was just a matter of time.

My heart was pounding. If I hadn't picked myself up out of the dirt, would Visa Vaidya really have speared me through the skull with the entire combat class watching? With Blake Drakharrow standing right across the courtyard?

For all I knew, this was the kind of behavior they allowed at Bloodwing. Hell, they probably encouraged it.

Are you done feeling sorry for yourself?

I flinched as the imperious woman's voice echoed through my head.

Now is not a great time, I muttered internally as I slapped Visha's latest blow away with my spear in the nick of time.

Are you really going to let this girl make a fool of you? Vampire or not, you are of royal blood.

Well, I didn't think I had a lot of choice, I snapped.

Visha moved towards me at a blinding speed and I jumped out of the way just in time, rolling across the dirt.

"Yeah," the girl crowed. "Get in the dirt where you belong, Pendragon."

You have the blood of kings and queens in your veins, girl, the woman's voice challenged. *You may not be what those creatures are, but you're more.*

More? I used to be more. I have nothing now. My powers are gone. Or can't you sense that from wherever the hell in my head you lurk?

Once this was over, if I made it out of this courtyard alive, I would really have to re-consider the idea that I was going mad, I decided.

Was that the kind of thing healers here could help with? Somehow I doubted it. I pictured trying to explain to Professor Rodriguez that there was a woman's voice in my head...and it wasn't mine. I doubted that would go well.

You think you're bereft. But I'm here, aren't I?

Oh, yes, I responded sarcastically. *And a great help you've been. Interrupting me at the very worst of times.*

But there was no response. Perhaps I'd finally been rude enough to frighten her away.

I managed to catch a glimpse at the edge of the roped off area. A number of students had come over to watch the fight. I saw Blake's face among them. He wasn't cheering for Visha like some of the other vampire students were doing. His face was a blank slate.

But his eyes followed me. Not Visha. Me.

The knowledge that he was watching me, judging me, probably hoping that I'd fail suddenly gave me the second wind I needed. I felt a rush of energy breaking through my fatigue and pushing me onwards.

Something shifted.

No, I wasn't a vampire. I could never match Visha for speed. I had come through my journey between worlds emptied of the fae powers I'd only just begun to learn how to access in Aercanum.

I had my body but only that. Nothing else was the same.

But standing there, on the matted earth with sunlight streaming down on us, I felt a fiery warmth spread through my veins. I took a deep breath and my heartbeat steadied. My senses sharpened.

Every detail suddenly seemed to stand out vividly, in a way it hadn't just a few moments before.

The sheen of sweat on Visha's brow. The way she was panting between blows. She was tiring, I saw with shock. I might not have been winning but I was certainly making her work for her victory.

The whistle of our spears cutting through the air suddenly filled my ears like screams.

The uneven texture of the ground beneath my boots sharpened.

I had something. Something even that monster Viktor Drakharrow had recognized. There might not have been dragons, but I had a dragon rider's build.

I had instincts to guide me. I just had to figure out how the hell to access them. In time, with practice, maybe my reflexes and agility could make me more skilled than most mortals. Maybe even skilled enough to beat a vampire.

My body flipped to the side as Visha came at me again, changing direction so quickly that I caught a look of shock in the other girl's eyes.

No, I didn't possess vampire speed. But my limbs were slightly longer than Visha's–than any student at Bloodwing. I might not have speed but I had something. Endurance. The very fact that Visha was starting to tire proved that, didn't it?

Visha thrust her spear against mine and our weapons collided, my teeth practically rattling in my head at the impact. My back was up against the ropes again. I could feel the harsh lines cutting into the fabric of my tunic and digging into my skin.

The highblood students around us were jeering and laughing. Some were shouting taunts, others placing bets on how much longer it would take for me to be defeated.

But when I looked, Blake was no longer among them. He wasn't across the courtyard either. So much for supervising.

I adjusted my grip on the spear, my stance becoming more balanced, more tightly grounded. I dug my feet into the dirt, preparing myself.

As Visha swung her spear in a wide arc, aiming at my side, I reacted as quickly as I could–ducking low and spinning away with a grace that surprised even myself.

The shift in the battle was subtle at first.

A well-timed parry here. A quicker step there.

I started to anticipate Visha's strikes, counter them with great precision.

The tables were turning.

I drove Visha back with a series of rapid, controlled thrusts.

And then, I saw my opening and took it and, shocking even myself, with a swift, powerful strike I knocked Visha's spear right out of her hands, sending it clattering to the ground.

I leveled my spear at the other girl's chest. "Yield."

She glared at me, her eyes filled with venom.

But she had to know there was no choice.

Without a word, she turned away, her expression twisting with anger and humiliation.

I wasn't sure what I'd expected. Applause from my fellow students? Not fucking likely.

But as I turned my back and moved towards the ropes, I felt the thrill of victory mingled with relief.

I'd just started to duck under the ropes when I caught a twitch of movement in the corner of my eye.

Then Visha was on me, yanking me back by the collar of my shirt.

For a second, I gagged, the fabric of the tunic tight around my neck, choking me.

Then I was crashing down, my back slamming into the hard dirt of the courtyard.

Visha was a whirlwind. She landed on my chest, straddling me, all sharp edges and ruthless speed. Her fists connected with my face, then my ribs. I tried to shift onto my side and shove her off but it was too late. Her knee collided with my stomach.

Nausea swept through me as I felt ribs pop and break.

But another part of me was already fighting back, instincts charged.

Visha was still laughing as I drove my fist into her jaw. Her head swung to the side, but not fast enough for me to miss the look of shock in her eyes.

She recovered quicker than I'd expected, her eyes narrowing in cold fury. Without warning, she grabbed a fistful of dirt from the ground beside us and shoved it into my face, rubbing it into my eyes and my mouth.

The gritty soil stung my eyes, blinding me momentarily, and Visha took full advantage. She grabbed the back of my head and smashed it back down again and again.

I screamed in anger. With a burst of strength, I shoved her off, and rolled to the side.

I crouched there, palms flat in the dirt, spitting out mud and squinting.

I felt like an animal. Like I'd been reduced to less than vampire, less than fae, less than mortal.

I was trembling with rage. Tears of anger were running down my face.

I'd fought a fae god, but even then I wasn't sure I'd felt this much hate. That fight had been cold. Brutal, yes, but not dirty.

Visha came at me again, sharp nails outstretched, clearly aiming for my face.

I dodged and rolled, feeling the rush of air as she missed me by inches, and kicked out at her shins.

With a cry she dropped to her knees. I scrambled, intending to get past her but she was too fast for me. Her hand reached out, yanking me by the hair so hard I gasped.

She pulled me down beside her and punched me squarely in the nose. I heard a sharp crack and blood sprayed into my eyes.

Instantly, Visha's fangs flared like white pearls and for a moment she hovered over me, eyes wide and dilated. She sniffed the air hungrily and I held my breath, expecting her to lose herself in a frenzy at any moment.

Then, as if with great effort, she shook her head and snarled. "You didn't think you were actually going to get out of here, did you, bitch?"

She reached down to her side and I saw a flash of silver. A knife.

Visha still had me by the hair. Now she lowered her lips closer to my face. "You look good in the dirt. It's where you belong."

I started to lift my head, intending to smash her in the face with it.

"That's enough, ladies. Break it up." The voice carried over the crowd, deep and resonant.

For a moment, Visha's hand stayed poised over me. Then the knife disappeared into her palm.

"I said break it up. Get off her, Visha. Now. Or you'll be packing your bags before nightfall. She beat you. Fair and square. I saw it all. But you decided you were done playing fair."

I turned my head to see who was speaking.

An extremely tall man with dark ebony skin had appeared on the outskirts of the crowd of students. There was a noble air to his attractive face. His silver hair was tightly curled and closely cropped to his head. A gold ring hung from one ear. He stood tall with his legs spread and his arms folded over a broad, heavily muscled chest. Our instructor, I presumed.

Blake stood beside him. If I hadn't known better, I might have thought the expression on the highblood's face was one of worry. Was he afraid he'd be getting into trouble for what he'd allowed to transpire?

Visha hissed. "Combat isn't about playing *nice*, Professor."

"No, but it's the first day of class and I'm not ready for our first murder," the teacher said calmly.

I flinched.

The man sighed. "You cheated, Visha. There. Is that blunt enough for you? Get up."

Visha slowly stood.

"This isn't over," she murmured as she looked down at me.

"You've got that right." I spit out a mouthful of dirt and tried to ignore the smirk on her face.

"Give her your hand, Visha," the man instructed. "Someday soon you'll be fighting not just your fellow students, but ones from visiting academies. Show some fucking grace."

Visha looked furious. She glanced once at the blood still trickling from my nose, then did as he said, holding her hand out.

"No fucking way am I taking that thing," I said, heaving myself to my feet on my own.

I groaned and clutched my chest. I was pretty sure something was broken. A rib. Maybe two.

"Pendragon, to me. Everyone else, clear out and get back to work," the instructor snapped. "There's half an hour of class left and I expect to see you use it."

I walked stiffly over to the ropes as Visha slunk away across the courtyard.

I could feel Blake there, standing beside the instructor, so I was trying not to show how much I hurt. But there was blood running down my face from my nose and into my mouth. I was panting and covered with dirt. And my chest ached everytime I breathed. I was pretty sure it was obvious.

Gingerly, I took up a position a safe distance away from Blake. I still wasn't sure what effect the sight of my blood had on him. Would he lose control like Visha almost had?

"So, this is the already-infamous Medra Pendragon," the instructor said, stepping forward as I came out from under the ropes. He gripped me by the arm and helped me down the rest of the way. "I'm Sebastian Sankara, your professor."

"Glad you were able to make it," I said, with not a little bitterness.

"Yes, well, you were the one out of place." Professor Sankara touched a hand to his chin. "I've just checked the roster and you aren't on it, Miss Pendragon. You weren't supposed to be here. This class is for advanced students who have attended Bloodwing for at least one year."

I closed my eyes for a moment. "I'm not surprised to hear that, Professor. Being at the wrong place at the wrong time is basically how my entire day has been going." I opened my eyes and looked over at Blake, but the bastard's face was unreadable.

I took a deep breath then winced as my ribs twisted painfully. "I'm sorry for disrupting your class, Professor. It was listed on my timetable so I showed up. I'll have to sort out where I'm actually supposed to be."

"Yes, I think a meeting with the headmaster is certainly in order," Sankara agreed. "But that wasn't the only reason I wanted to speak with you."

Belatedly I realized something. Unlike my first two professors that day, Professor Sankara *was* a vampire. I caught glimpses of his razor sharp fangs appearing and disappearing as he spoke. I'd been so distracted it had taken me this long just to notice.

"Miss Pendragon? Did you hear what I said? This class is exclusively for vampires."

I sighed. "Right. I guess I should have figured that out."

I reached down to grab my spear from where it had fallen out of the ring so I could carry it back to the rack. Bad idea. I suppressed a groan.

"At least, it usually is exclusively for vampires," Sankara went on. "Exceptions have been made."

My head shot up. "Excuse me?"

Professor Sankara was looking at me thoughtfully. "You showed admirable skill with a spear in your duel with Miss Vaidya. Most students wouldn't have dared to go toe to toe with her. Or with any vampire, for that matter."

My heart thudded. So he'd been watching us for a while. This professor seemed more personable than the other vampires I'd encountered. But he'd seen Visha grab me by the hair *after* I'd already won our first round. And he hadn't seen fit to intervene. He'd waited and watched to see what would happen. And let Visha kick the shit out of me until he deemed it had gone far enough.

I lifted my chin. "Well, I guess that's another reason I wasn't meant to be in this place. I *do* dare."

"Or it's the very reason you belong here," Professor Sankara replied. "You're clearly not unschooled. Who taught you how to fight?"

"I had a tutor," I said slowly. "Back where I come from. She taught me everything I know about combat."

"She must have been a very impressive woman," Sankara said. "I'd like to meet her."

"She's dead," I said shortly.

Blake's head jerked up. Our eyes met. His gray ones honed into me.

I looked away. "Do the students really kill each other here?" I asked.

"At Bloodwing?" Sankara nodded. "Sometimes. It's a ruthless world, Miss Pendragon. The school reflects that. The students here have to be the very best to get here in the first place. But once they're here, that's just the start of it. You have to earn your place at Bloodwing every day. The highbloods who are your friends now might be your worst enemy a few years down the road. Some of our most ferocious wars have been fought between houses. And if you can't keep your place, well…" He shrugged. "Someone might decide to take it from you."

"That's horrible," I said.

"None of you are children," he replied. "These–" He gestured around him, with a pointed look at Blake. "Are the future leaders of Sangratha. We need them to be strong."

"Strong and merciless," I said bitterly.

"Strong enough to protect this land and all the people in it, including the weak," Sankara replied. "But you–you're not weak, Miss Pendragon. Visha made a mistake when she assumed you were, didn't she?"

"I wound up flat on my back in the dirt," I said. "So pardon me if I'm surprised you think so."

Sankara smiled slightly. "What I saw was a fighter with promise. I don't think you're in the wrong place. I think you're in the right one."

"What?" Blake and I spoke in unison.

I glared at him, but he was looking at Sankara.

"But, Professor, that's impossible. This is an exclusive class, just like you said. She can't be here. It's for vampires. Highbloods only. The elite. She's not one of us." Blake glanced at me, looking me up and down. "Besides, look at her. If she's in this state after half a class…"

He let the words hang there. They shouldn't have stung as badly as they did. What did I care if Blake thought I was a failure?

Sankara rubbed his chin. "The elite, eh, Drakharrow? Yet from what I just saw, Pendragon has the potential to be as talented a fighter as…" He paused. "Well, who knows. Maybe even you."

"Me?" Blake bristled. "I doubt that." He frowned. "You know I respect you, Professor, but…"

"But what, Drakharrow?" The professor's voice was suddenly dangerously cool. "You're a student in this class. You were in charge. Were you really going to let Visha Vaidya stab your consort in full sight of the entire class? You could have intervened sooner than you did. So why didn't you? Why did you wait for me to do something?"

I looked back and forth between the two men in confusion. What did Sankara mean? Blake hadn't intervened at all.

Blake glanced at me. "As you saw, sir, Pendragon handled herself. Better than I could have expected. I thought it was more fair to at least give her a chance to prove herself."

I scoffed. "You're fucking unbelievable. Was that a backhanded compliment?"

"It sounds to me like you're saying she might deserve to be here, Drakharrow," Sankara observed with a small smile. "In any case, there's certainly precedent for it."

"Precedent?" I asked.

"Dragon riders used to have their own advanced combat classes," Sankara explained. "They were the warriors of the skies, after all."

"Did they fight alongside vampires...?" I asked, curious despite myself. "Did they train with them?"

"Absolutely. They had to. In fact, that's something I'll be mentioning to the headmaster when I speak to him about you later on. You're the only rider in the school and that means your curriculum should be as unique as you are. I'm not sure much thought was put into it based on what you've said."

"I was in History of Sangratha and Restoration before this," I said.

Sankara raised a brow. "Everyone has to take History with Professor Hassan. But Restoration? I'm not sure how much practical value that will hold for you. Another mistake on your schedule perhaps."

"Perhaps," I said, glaring at Blake again. "Today has just been full of those."

"Bloodmaiden! Look at the time. We'd better get you to a healer." Sankara glanced at me as I wiped away blood from my nose. "Not all of the students here are as restrained as my older cohort here. So you'll need an escort. What class are you supposed to have next?"

"Introduction to Bloodwing Libraries," I said. "At least, that's what my timetable says. I'm not sure it's correct."

The professor nodded. "That sounds right. All First Years have a general orientation to the libraries. But I'm not sure you're going to make it. You might have to catch up later. I want you to head to the Drakharrow House healer first. After that, see if there's time before Headmaster Kim's Commencement Address is scheduled to begin in the Dragon

Court." He glanced at Blake. "I assume I can trust you to show Pendragon the way to your house healer with no trouble?"

"No trouble at all, Sir," Blake said. He looked at me coldly. "I'll take her now."

CHAPTER 8

MEDRA

"**I**'m not a fucking parcel," I snapped, as Professor Sankara walked off to speak with another student. "Just tell me where the healer is and I'll find them. No need for us to spend any more time in one another's company."

"The professor said to take you, so I'm taking you," Blake said stiffly. "Unless you truly want to wander the halls for hours aimlessly, hoping you find your way there on your own."

"Asshole," I muttered. "Fine. Lead on."

He looked me up and down, then shook his head. "Visha sure got her claws into you."

I knew I must look filthy. Not to mention my nose wouldn't stop bleeding. I tilted my head up and pinched the bridge of my nose, trying to stop the bleeding as I followed Blake out into the corridor.

A group of giggling students were passing by. Vampires, from the look of them. When they saw me they stopped babbling, their mouths opening and fangs protruding.

"What the fuck?" I muttered.

Blake gripped my arm, firmly but not painfully. "They're First Years. Let's move." To them he snapped, "Get a grip."

"Get off me," I demanded, knowing it was useless.

Blake ignored me as I'd known he would. His pale features bore the same expression of frosty indifference I'd come to expect.

We moved through the halls. My nose still dripped faintly with blood. I kept a hand pressed to it, trying to stop the flow, finally resorting to wiping it covertly on my dirt-covered sleeve. I was already filthy. What were a few more bloodstains?

Every few steps, I glanced at Blake, wondering how he could stand to be this close to me with the scent of my blood in the air. Why wasn't he reacting like Barnabas or Visha or even those First Years had?

We rounded a corner and suddenly came face to face with a group of students. They braked to a halt as they caught sight of Blake.

Walking behind the rest of his group came Kage Tanaka, the leader of House Avari who I'd seen in the refectory that morning.

I eyed him with interest. He stood tall, posture straight and commanding. His shock of white-blond hair was gathered into a neat queue at the back of his head, while the sides had been shaved close. Just above the collar of his black, silver trimmed uniform, I glimpsed the inked curve of a crescent moon curling along the side of its neck, dark lines stark against his skin.

His dark brown eyes flicked to mine with an intensity that seemed to take in everything, missing nothing.

Just like with Blake, there was a danger to Kage that was palpable. Simmering just beneath the surface. Coiled tight and ready to strike.

A student in front of me hissed and licked her lips.

Maybe the scent of blood was nothing to Blake. But these students were reacting to it, their nostrils flaring, their teeth snapping.

I moved to take a step back, but Blake's grip on my arm held me in place.

"Well, well," said a boy with spiked pale hair, stepping forward so he was directly in front of Blake and I. "Looks like someone's having a little nosebleed."

He gave me a look that seemed meant to be flirtatious. "Maybe I could help clean that up."

"Get the fuck away from her, Kiernan," Blake snarled. He glanced at Kage. "Call off your dogs, Tanaka. Or I'll put them in line for you."

Kage Tanaka shrugged slowly. His uniform fit him like a second skin, hugging the lean muscular lines of his body. He said nothing to the boy Blake had called Kiernan.

My body tensed. I could feel myself preparing for another fight.

Kiernan grinned. Then he darted forward.

Before he could even touch me, Blake moved, so quickly I could hardly see what happened next.

Then the boy was flying backwards. His back hit the stone wall and he slid to the floor, his hands clutching his neck. He stared up at us, eyes bulging. His mouth moved but no sounds came out.

"What the hell, Drakharrow? It was just a joke," one of the girls at the front of the group said angrily. She moved to help Kiernan up.

"Do I look like I'm laughing?" Blake growled, his voice low and dangerous. His gray eyes were as sharp as a blade. I could feel his anger. It radiated off his body, barely restrained.

He moved forward, pulling me along with him, and the group of House Avari students parted quickly.

As we walked past Kage Tanaka, Blake nodded tersely.

Kage smiled slightly.

"Let's keep moving," Blake muttered, his tone flat. We turned the next corner and he released a slow breath and ran his free hand through his hair.

"What the hell was that about?" I hissed.

"No one can touch you," he said shortly. "Don't worry about it."

"Don't worry about it?" I laughed nervously. "That boy was about to... what? Drink me? Lick me? He only stopped because you punched him in the throat. Is this how it is for the blightborn? Every time I cut my finger, do I have to worry I'll be swarmed?"

Blake glanced around us. "First Years have less restraint about feeding. But they're supposed to keep their instincts in check and feed regularly to prevent a loss of control. That's part of learning to be a highblood."

"Funny, I'm not feeling reassured," I muttered.

"They're losing control for a reason." He took a deep breath. "Because of your blood in particular. You're not just any blightborn."

I was silent for a moment. "You mean it's because of my rider blood?"

"Something like that. None of us have known any other riders. But if this is how they smelled..." His voice trailed off. He eyed me, his eyes finally lingering on the blood crusted around my nose, coating my hand, my sleeve.

"Then what?" I demanded. "I'm so delectable none of you can resist me?"

In an instant, a solid weight had slammed into me and my back was pressed up against a wall.

My heart was pounding. I struggled feebly against Blake as his body held me in place but he was hard as a rock and just as stubborn. I tried to lift a knee to kick out at him, but he'd spread my legs, positioning himself between them.

"It's not a fucking joke." Blake's voice was raspy in my ear.

A shiver raced down my spine.

"You need to take this seriously," he breathed. "Or you won't last a week here."

"And you'd care if I didn't?" I gave a laugh that came out sounding braver than I felt. "Please. Don't pretend you care if I live or die."

He didn't move.

His body was solid. A warm mass pressed against me. If I breathed in, I knew exactly what I'd smell. Green apples. A faint hint of mint. Something underlying it all, like the pages of an old book. I hated that I knew all of that about him. It seemed so... intimate.

Intimacy with Blake Drakharrow was the last thing I wanted.

"What are you doing?" I hissed. "Get off me. Or is this it? You're going to feed from me now?"

"I'm not..." His voice sounded strangled. Like it was taking everything he had not to do exactly like I'd said.

He stepped away from me and I let out a breath.

"I'm not permitted to feed from you. Our bond isn't strong enough. And unlike some, I actually believe in honoring the laws of the Bloodmaiden."

I smirked. "Good." I started to turn away.

"Our bond isn't strong enough for me to feed from you..." he added. "*Yet*." He sneered. "Let's go."

I'd missed the library session, which was arguably the only class I'd really been looking forward to.

I'd been curious to meet Florence's mother and see what she was like. Hopefully Librarian Shen wouldn't mind if I came by at another time to learn the ropes.

Not that I thought I'd need a lot of help. The castle in Camelot had a huge library. I hadn't spent a great deal of time there but I knew the basics.

Blake had taken me straight into enemy territory when he'd brought me to the healer. House Drakharrow had its own separate area in the castle complex. A huge tower housed all of the Drakharrow students. Not just the highbloods, but also the students who had already passed First Year and been selected into House Drakharrow.

I still wasn't sure how all of that worked, but the thought of actually living in the same tower as Blake next year was disconcerting.

Already I couldn't wait to get back to the First Year tower where I could retreat to my safe, cozy little room and simply be alone.

After getting me to the Drakharrow infirmary, Blake had disappeared. A surprisingly nice young woman who had said she was a healer's apprentice had led me to a bed and examined me. Then she'd called one of the official healers over and together they'd consulted on my treatment.

Apparently, House Drakharrow made a point of keeping at least one healer arcanist on staff at all times. Which is why when I left the infirmary, not only was my broken nose set and no longer bleeding, but my ribs were already rapidly healing.

I'd have to return again the next day for a follow-up, but they'd released me in time to get to the headmaster's Commencement Address.

As I left the infirmary, Blake was nowhere to be seen. Apparently now that I was no longer actively bleeding, I didn't require an escort.

All of the students in the halls were heading the same way, so I simply followed them.

When we reached the Dragon Court, I drew in my breath.

I wasn't sure what I'd been expecting exactly. But... not this.

A covered walkway formed a square around a central, wide courtyard open to the sky. The walkway was lined with tall, pillared arches that framed the view of the courtyard, where bright green grass was visible.

As I walked out of the cloisters, the courtyard stretched wide, surrounded by towering stone walls covered in creeping vines just beginning to blaze red and gold. Trees lining the sides of the courtyard were lit up in autumn splendor. Fiery red and orange leaves carpeted the stone beneath my feet, crunching as I walked.

But it was what lay in the center of the courtyard that took my breath away.

A massive ring of stone dragons loomed over the gathering crowd like ancient watchers. Each one was at least two stories tall. Their rough, weathered scales caught the warm amber light of the late afternoon sun overhead. Shadows spilled from the immense forms, casting eerie shapes that danced over the faces of the assembled students.

There were four in total, arranged in a perfect circle, their enormous wings unfurled so that the tips of each wing overlapped seamlessly with that of its neighbors.

Each dragon was a different color. One black. One gold. One ivory. And one red.

The black dragon was carved from a deep basalt. Its stone surface was a dark, glossy black that absorbed the light. Its eyes were deep-set and narrow, with an almost menacing intensity. The dragon's jaws had been carved slightly open, revealing serrated teeth that looked sharp enough to cut.

The gold dragon had been shaped from a lustrous warm marble. Golden veins ran through it, making it shine and glimmer in the light. The dragon's face was regal and commanding. Its nostrils were delicately flared, its mouth curved into a slight, knowing smirk.

The white dragon was sculpted from alabaster. Its smooth, creamy white surface lent it a soft, ethereal quality. The white dragon's face bore a tranquil expression. I had an impression of quiet strength and serene beauty.

The red dragon was on the farthest side of the court. Carved from red sandstone, it had the roughest, most unpolished look of the four. The red dragon's eyes were narrow and sharp. Its nostrils flared aggressively. I swallowed as I looked into its ancient carved face, so full of passion and fire and rage.

A hand touched my shoulder and I jumped.

"Medra, what happened to you?"

I turned to see Florence and Naveen. They were staring at me in shocked horror.

I looked down at myself, remembering. My body might have been rapidly healing but my clothes were still in a sorry state, coated with dirt and blood.

I flushed self-consciously. "Uh, combat class." I looked around, then leaned in. "I had to see a healer," I admitted, my voice low.

Florence put a hand to her mouth. "So that's why you missed the library session."

I nodded, suddenly tired. "Please tell your mother how sorry I am. Maybe I can catch up another time?"

Florence pushed her spectacles up her nose and nodded. "I'll show you everything you need to know on our day off. Don't worry about it for now."

Naveen was still staring at my clothing. "Who did that to you?"

"Oh, it's nothing," I said, trying to be nonchalant. "You should see the other girl."

"She?" Florence's eyes were wide.

I nodded. "Visha Vaidya."

Naveen and Florence exchanged glances.

"But you were at her table this morning," Florence said slowly. "I thought..."

"I thought so, too," I said hollowly. "I don't think anything was what I thought."

Naveen shook his head sympathetically. "At least the day is almost over. Come stand with us? I think the headmaster is about to begin."

I followed them over to an empty spot on the grass.

A podium had been set up on a platform in between the gold and white dragons and a man was stepping up to it.

I had already heard his name mentioned once before. Headmaster Kim.

I wondered what sort of a man he was. Powerful, I assumed, if he had been appointed headmaster of the top school in the kingdom.

The headmaster wore dark robes of a rich and heavy fabric, embossed in red with the Bloodwing school insignia. His features were formidable and commanding, with a high, broad forehead and deep-set, dark and narrow eyes that moved amongst the crowd, piercing through us one after another.

The crowd began to settle down. I looked around me as we waited, already seeing some familiar faces from the classes that morning.

Then I spotted Regan. Across the courtyard, standing in the shadow of the black dragon. She was flanked by Visha and Quinn.

Our eyes met and she smiled, then raised a hand to give a little wave. My jaw clenched. I curled my hands into fists by my side.

Theo and Coregan stood nearby her, but their eyes were fixed on the headmaster. Blake was nowhere to be seen.

I forced my gaze away from Regan. I'd have to deal with that problem later.

A hush had fallen over the crowd. The only sound now was the whisper of the leaves.

"Welcome to another term at Bloodwing." Headmaster Kim's voice resonated across the courtyard, dripping with gravitas and not sounding particularly welcoming at all. "I'm sure most of you are familiar with my face by now, but for those who are new, my name is Kim Min-jun and I have the great honor of being headmaster of Bloodwing Academy. Now, let us begin."

He paused and the silence seemed to deepen. "You are here not by chance, but by design. This academy is a forge where the future leaders and warriors of Sangratha are shaped. Our purpose is clear: to create those who will defend this realm from its enemies, both within and without. You are the sword's edge of Sangratha."

He paused, his gaze sweeping over us.

"First Years," he intoned. "Whether you will become part of that sword's edge remains to be seen. You have been chosen to join our ranks at an academy where only the most determined will prevail. If you falter, make no mistake. You will be discarded. Hard work and punctuality are no longer optional. They are requirements. Respect is not negotiable. It is absolute. Deviations from Bloodwing's high standards will result in swift punishment. Mediocrity will not be tolerated here."

I stood taller, a little shaken, but refusing to let his words intimidate me.

"To the blightborn students in our midst," Headmaster Kim continued, his tone shifting slightly. I caught an edge of disdain. "Your presence here is a privilege. You are here to serve. And you will bow to the authority of your betters in all things. Any failures to demonstrate the proper deference will be met with severe consequences."

A pause followed as he surveyed his audience.

"But for those who excel," he continued, his tone softening ever so slightly. "There will be rewards. Attendance at the Wintermark Ball will be granted to those who show exceptional performance in Term One. And for those of you who survive your first year, there will be other privileges, such as access to Veilmar on weekends. These are privileges to be earned, not given. They are reserved for those who can prove themselves exceptional."

His eyes locked onto us with a steely gaze. "Bloodwing demands excellence. It will draw excellence from you like fangs draw blood."

A titter of nervous laughter rose from the crowd, but only, I noticed, from the high-bloods. None of the mortals were laughing.

Headmaster Kim smiled thinly. "So, strive to be the best or face the consequences. Sangratha is no place for the weak or unworthy. If you cannot meet these expectations, you will find yourself cast out."

I glanced at Florence. Did he mean cast out from Bloodwing? Or from the kingdom itself?

But the dark-haired girl was staring straight ahead, her lips tight. I looked around at the other blightborn students. They looked as nervous as she did. And these were students who were already supposed to be the best of the best. They had fought just to get here. I was here by random chance. So how should I feel?

As the headmaster continued speaking, I felt a prickle of unease across the back of my neck. It wasn't metaphorical. The sensation was palpable. A cold, invasive pressure bearing down upon me like a vise. With effort, I managed to turn my head. Sure enough, Regan Pansera was smirking at me from across the crowd.

My limbs gave a sudden jerk. Florence turned to look at me but my lips were frozen shut.

I took a step back, then another. I bumped into a student and they snapped at me, but I couldn't even apologize.

My body was no longer under my own control.

CHAPTER 9

MEDRA

My feet moved without conscious volition as I turned around and walked towards the back of the crowd. The sea of students parted slightly to make way for me. I felt their strange looks. A low chatter was beginning as I stubbornly pushed my way to the edge of the crowd.

I approached the black stone dragon. Unable to even lift my head to look upwards, I could nevertheless feel its fierce visage gazing down upon me.

I moved around the statue to the back and stretched out my fingers. The rough texture of the stone scraped my skin as I started to climb, every movement propelled by a will that was not my own.

My body might not have been my own but my feelings were. And with every desperate grip and foothold, my sense of humiliation deepened, the weight of my predicament pressing down on my shoulders like a physical force.

The crowd's murmurs grew louder as more and more students began to notice my ascent up the dragon's back. Regan wouldn't permit me to move my head a muscle beyond where she wanted it, but I could still hear the snickers bubbling up from the sea of faces below me. My cheeks burned with shame as I climbed higher and higher.

The dragon's black basalt head loomed closer as I dug my fingers into its cold and unyielding surface. My hands were covered with scrapes from the rough stone and my fingertips were cracked and bleeding by the time I reached the top.

As I mounted the dragon's head, even Regan's unnatural control couldn't keep me from feeling a wave of nauseating vertigo. The entire courtyard was visible, a sprawling expanse of stone and students. Over the walls of the cloistered courtyard edges, I could see the open sea in the distance. A gust of wind suddenly swept over me and the pressure of it pushed me sideways. But I couldn't even gasp out the terror I felt as I scrambled to grip the stone tighter with my bleeding palms.

Now this is a truly ridiculous mess. Get down this instant. You're humiliating yourself. The woman's voice in my head sounded furious.

I would if I could, I said, hearing the echo of what I'd already said earlier that same day. *I would if I could.*

You can and you will. I command it. Whatever this girl is doing to you, it must cease.

Make it stop then. Use your power if you're so mighty, I shot back. *Don't you think I've tried? I don't even know what she's doing to me.*

There was a pause. *Some form of compulsion, that much is clear. A very precise kind as no one else seems affected. Powerful, too, as you're like putty in her palms.*

Thank you for that astute observation, I said drily. *Can you get me down or not?*

Another pause. *There's a way to counter it, certainly, but such spells take training. You could learn. But it would take time.*

I don't have time, I said, frustrated. *What spell?*

An anti-compulsion spell, of course. It's magic of a sort. Some form of coercion. Vampire-specific, I'd assume. She paused. *If they all possess this, I'm impressed. It's quite a handy skill to have.*

Handy? It's not handy. It's disgusting. No one should have the ability to do this.

I thought of the other blightborn students down below. If the highbloods could turn this power on them at any time, make them do whatever they wanted... It was too horrible to consider. It shouldn't be permitted. How could this be the way of things?

I felt a command from Regan's mind to mine go through me and dropped to my knees on the dragon's head, the rough texture scraping painfully against my skin.

My heart sank as I saw hundreds of eyes boring into me. I had the crowd's full attention now.

What would Regan make me do?

Before I had much time to wonder, a deep, guttural roar erupted from me.

I sounded like the world's most pathetic lion. Or dragon.

Laughter rippled through the crowd of gathered students. I saw highblood faces sneering up at me with derision, dismissing me as if I truly were an animal or something they might wipe off their shoes at the end of a day.

Headmaster Kim's voice cut through the cacophony of laughter with icy authority. He was not amused.

"Cease this at once," he commanded. "Whoever is doing this, I command you to stop. Medra Pendragon, you will get down from there this instant."

And then he was in my head right alongside Regan.

For a moment, I could feel their powers warring against each other. Two wills fighting for control over my body, Regan's and the headmaster's.

Then Regan withdrew. She was gone as quickly as she'd come, unseen and unannounced. The coward.

The headmaster was in control of my body now. The sheer power of his authority threatened to overwhelm me. I felt choked with it.

I'd been broken free from one bondage only to be trapped in another.

Slowly, I stood upright, my body tense and rigid.

Far down below, I saw Theo Drakharrow looking up at me with wide eyes. He'd moved closer to the edge of the crowd. As our gazes met, he gave a little shrug and mouthed the word "Sorry."

"Get down now, Medra Pendragon," the headmaster commanded again. He sounded impatient. "The Blood of the Pure compels you."

My body could not resist.

I leaped from the dragon's head onto the stones below.

CHAPTER 10

MEDRA

I woke up with a groan, my eyelids fluttering open.

Everything hurt.

I looked up at the ceiling overhead. It was familiar.

Dark blue with silver stars.

I was in my room.

I tried to push myself up but a hand settled on my chest, gently pushing me back down again.

"Not yet, Medra. Rest." Florence. Her voice was gentle.

I managed to turn my head and look at her. "What happened?"

She chewed her lip for a moment, thinking. Probably of how to tell me something bad in the nicest way possible.

"The healer just left," she said finally. "You're supposed to stay in bed, at least until tomorrow morning. They'll be around to check in on you at seven o'clock. Then, if they say you can get up, you're to go and see Headmaster Kim in his office at eight."

I groaned. "Wonderful."

Florence rose to her feet. "Are you in pain? Is it bad? The healer left a tea for you with some herbs for the pain. I can give you a dose, but it will make you drowsy."

I pushed myself up onto my elbows, ignoring Florence's look of worry. "What time is it?"

"It's just past ten. You've slept for almost six hours."

I felt as if I'd slept much longer than that. My body felt terrible. But considering I'd leaped off a giant statue, I felt better than I had any right to.

"Headmaster Kim wants to know who did this to you," Florence said carefully. "I told him I didn't know. But I'm sure he'll ask you again about it in the morning."

I nodded.

"Was it...?" Florence's voice trailed off.

Did she even want to know?

I met her dark brown eyes.

"Regan?" she breathed.

I tried to shrug but failed and instead slumped back onto the pillows. "I mean, I've never experienced anything like that before, but yeah, I'm pretty sure it was her. It felt like her. It felt... awful."

I sighed. "Look, Florence. I think you should go. You probably shouldn't even be here."

Florence's face shifted into confusion. "What do you mean?"

"I mean, it's clear Regan has it out for me. And she's a very powerful girl. You said so yourself. She doesn't exactly have my best interests at heart and she's popular at Bloodwing, right? So having her as my enemy is bound to be bad. If you're seen with me, she'll think we're friends..."

"We are friends," Florence said.

"No, we're not," I said firmly. "We don't have to be. It's not too late for you. Or for Naveen. You can just..."

"What? Run the other way?" Florence sounded put off. But that was okay. Better that she hate me now and be safe later.

"Not run exactly, but find other friends. You're a brilliant student. Naveen said you have a ton of potential. I don't think I'm the best person for you to be seen with."

Florence frowned. It was the first time I'd really seen her do it and it made her look surprisingly fierce.

"Medra, I'm not going anywhere. And neither is Naveen. I don't like bullies."

I shook my head wearily. "And yet, you live in Sangratha."

She was quiet for a minute. "That's true."

I eyed her curiously. "So you don't think everything here is perfect here after all?"

"Perfect?" She shook her head. "Nothing is ever perfect. Do you know what I had to do to get here?"

I shook my head. "Tell me."

"It was a fight. A struggle. My family and I grew up in a town near where Naveen lived, but when my father died, we moved to Veilmar. My mother was a librarian for a noble highblood family there. She couldn't afford to pay for a private tutor and the family refused to allow me to study with their own children. My mother taught me herself on her own time, even though she was usually exhausted. I studied the books she snuck out of the highbloods' library, knowing at any time she could face punishment for bringing them to me. When she applied for the position at Bloodwing and got it, the family didn't want her to leave. They insisted on keeping me as collateral so she'd be forced to come back to see me. Then they decided that I could eventually take her place. They could see that I had, well, potential..." Florence blushed. "And they knew it would be cheaper than hiring a new librarian, someone with formal training. They didn't want me to apply here, but I snuck out and I did it anyway. Once you've applied, you can't be kept from your examination. So there was nothing they could do once I'd made the preliminary cut."

She lifted her chin. "So I know a little bit about bullies–privileged ones at that."

"But I thought you revered the highbloods, Florence," I said, as gently as I could. "Including Regan."

She shook her head stubbornly. "They're not all like that. Most use their power for good. It's different, serving people who are superior when they really are."

I bit my tongue and said nothing. I wasn't ready to argue that point.

"But it's wrong for them to take advantage like Regan did, using thrallweave on you," Florence went on.

"Thrallweave? Is that what it's called?"

She nodded. "It's a powerful coercion ability. Only vampires have it, of course. It's a skill like any other. Some are naturally more powerful with it, but most need to train themselves before they can really use it well. Regan must have some natural ability. Her control over you seemed fairly tight."

"It certainly felt tight," I said bitterly. "So they all have this thrallweave. And they can use it on you–on any blightborn–at any time? And you think that's fair?"

"They can also use it on one another–and sometimes they do. Sure, some use it to bully, just like Regan did. But sometimes it can be used for good."

I couldn't imagine a scenario where that was possible but decided not to ask.

"Anyhow," Florence concluded. "Lord Drakharrow himself instructed that you were to attend this school. What Regan is doing goes against protocols. She's your fellow consort. You're supposed to work together."

I'd temporarily forgotten and wasn't thrilled at the reminder. Work together? Yeah, right.

"You'll need allies to get through Bloodwing and I'd be honored to be one of them," Florence said. "I'm sure Naveen will feel the same."

"It's too dangerous, Florence," I said, trying to shake my head. "You and Naveen could wind up being bullied by Regan or someone like her, or worse just for being friends with me. Maybe it's better if I fly solo. You don't want targets on your back."

"Blake Drakharrow wasn't in the Dragon Court today," Florence said thoughtfully. "I wonder what he'll do when he learns what Regan did."

"If he finds out," I pointed out. "Even if he does, I really don't think he'll care, Florence." I decided to be blunt. "Look, Blake has made it very clear that he didn't choose me and he doesn't want to be stuck with me. I'm pretty sure he'd have been just fine if I'd died jumping off that dragon statue today. Besides, he and Regan have been betrothed since they were children. Obviously his loyalty is going to be to her."

"I'm not so sure about that," Florence said, shaking her head slightly. "I've heard some things."

"He was there when Visha challenged me," I reminded her. "He didn't do anything to stop her."

"Yet Professor Sankara did show up eventually," she said. "Maybe Blake went and got him."

I groaned. She had a point but I didn't want to acknowledge it. Blake had vanished for at least a little while during my fight with Visha but who knows where he'd really gone. Maybe to drink from a thrall.

"Fine," I conceded. "Maybe. And maybe dragons are real. But oh, wait, they aren't."

Florence smiled gently. "You should rest. But from the sound of it, I think you'll be okay for your meeting with the headmaster in the morning." She moved over to the little nightstand next to the bed and began to pour out a draught of tea into a small porcelain cup. I smelled lavender and honey along with herbs I didn't recognize.

"I suppose I'm in trouble with the headmaster," I said. "He didn't seem thrilled with me climbing his dragon."

Florence gave me a sympathetic look. "I'm not sure why he wants to see you. Maybe he just wants to find out who did it."

"I can't believe this was only the first day of school," I grumbled.

"You did have a rough start. Hopefully the next one is calmer. Maybe I can show you the libraries after lunch? I have a spare, a period where I don't have a class. If you're free at the same time, we can meet up."

"That sounds great," I said enthusiastically. I frowned. "Hopefully I get a chance to eat lunch tomorrow. I wonder if I have Professor Rodriguez again."

"You'll definitely have to sort out your schedule," Florence agreed. "Hopefully you can do that with the headmaster first thing. Speaking of lunch, you missed that, but there's a dinner tray here for you. The healer wasn't sure if you'd wake up tonight or not, or if you'd be hungry, but…"

I sat up straight, ignoring the pain in my back and sides. My ribs had taken an unneeded second beating when I'd jumped from that dragon. "I'm ravenous. Where is it?"

Florence grinned and passed over a tray of food.

I breathed in deeply, spotting chunks of beef and potatoes sauteed in a creamy tomato sauce, buttered bread, a raisin scone, and a cup of pumpkin spice pudding.

"I'll leave you to eat your food and rest," Florence said. "But I'll keep an eye out for you at breakfast and lunch tomorrow."

"Sounds good," I said, from between a mouthful of buttery bread. "And Florence? Thank you. For everything."

When she'd left, I devoured the tray of food, then propped it on the nightstand and leaned back on my pillows.

My hair fluffed around my face in a bush of curls. I knew I should get up to bathe and brush it out, but I was too tired. Everything hurt. Maybe I could braid it in the morning.

I closed my eyes, preparing to sleep, then thought of something and they popped back open.

Hey, you. Lady in my head, I snapped. *Get out here. Or do you only come when you're not wanted and at the worst possible times?*

I waited.

I resent that. But the woman's tone was mild. *I come when you need me. I've only ever tried to help.*

You come when the very last thing I need is a distraction, I said with a sigh. *And to help? It's arguable whether you've ever helped.*

I've rallied you to help yourself, the woman said smoothly. *Sometimes we just need a little push.*

Speaking of push, I'd like to push you out of my head. How do we go about doing that exactly?

A pause.

I'm not sure. It's not so bad like this, is it?

I snorted. *Having a passenger in my own brain? Yes, I'd say that's bad. I'd prefer privacy.*

It's an interesting conundrum, the woman said thoughtfully. *And you can't say I never help. I helped you get here in the first place.*

Now it was my turn to pause. *What the hell does that mean?*

Tsk, tsk. Language. You're of royal blood.

I'm nothing anymore, I snapped. *Certainly not a princess. I think that much is very clear. And I should have been dead. I was supposed to be dead. Is that what you mean?*

Silence.

What did you do? How did you "help"? I persisted.

I'm not sure I quite like your tone. This certainly isn't the appreciative spirit with which I expected my gesture to be received.

I could practically feel her sulking. *So I was right. Do you mean you did this? You got me to this place somehow?*

I think the words you're looking for are "Did you really save me? How wonderful! I simply cannot believe my good fortune!"

I was quiet for a moment. *Maybe I wanted to die. Did you ever stop to think of that?*

Nonsense. The woman's tone was sharp. *Absolute nonsense. Why, you had barely even begun to exist. I wasn't about to let you be snuffed out so soon.*

You know, I said slowly. *You* know *about me. About what I was. You were in Aercanum with me.*

Back in Aercanum, I had been what you might call an unnatural child. Not only did I have a fae mother and a human father, but I was blessed or cursed, depending on how you looked at it, with accelerated growth. By the time I was a few weeks old, I was walking. A few months later and I was talking. So, the woman was right. I'd existed for only a short time.

Thanks for reminding me I'm a complete freak of nature, I added bitterly.

You're not a freak. You're beautiful, she scolded. *You're perfect. Never allow anyone to tell you differently.*

Mentally, I froze. *Just who are you exactly? And why are you so attached to me? You say you saved my life, but why? Why me? Why do all of this for me and why stick around?*

Perhaps you're just a very worthwhile young woman, she hedged. *However, you're certainly right that I don't provide my assistance to just anyone.*

I'm sure of that, I said wryly. *Give me a straight answer. Please.*

Another pause. *Well, I should think it was fairly obvious. In fact, I'm surprised you haven't figured it out by now.*

Yes? I prodded.

There's only one person who would ever go to this much trouble for you. I'm your mother.

CHAPTER II

MEDRA

The ghost of my dead mother is riding around in my head, I seethed, as I walked towards the headmaster's office.

Not dead, the woman corrected. *I'm talking to you right now, aren't I? Let's say... betwixt and between.*

Externally, I rolled my eyes. *So, half-dead.*

Orcades. That was her name. Orcades Le Fay. Then, Orcades Pendragon after she'd married my father, Arthur. I supposed I should start thinking of her that way.

Apparently, I was merely scattered when I died birthing you, Orcades continued. *But my soul hadn't fully departed Aercanum. When you died–well, when you were meant to die–I found you...*

And inserted yourself into my head, I said frostily.

A part of my soul lodged in you to keep you safe, she clarified. *I wasn't even doing it consciously. I was able to help you pass from one world to another, with your own soul and body still intact.* A pause. *I'm still not sure precisely how I did it. But it was a wondrous accomplishment. I doubt many have ever achieved something similar.*

I could practically feel her preening.

Couldn't you have picked my own world? I complained ungraciously. *Couldn't you have just brought me back there? Where my friends and family were?*

Well, no, if it was that easy, I would have. Think of your soul like a ball spinning out of control and straight into danger–into nothingness. I grabbed hold of you and, well, tossed you out of danger. But I didn't get a chance to look at exactly where you would land.

I was a spinning ball, I groaned. *I see. What a lovely way to think of your own daughter.*

Oh, pish posh. I could almost imagine her waving a perfectly manicured fae hand. *A ball, a flower. However you wish to imagine yourself, you were impossible to control. I'd never done this before, remember. I did what I could. I did my best.*

She had a point, I had to admit.

Fine. I mentally cleared my throat. *Well, in that case... Thank you. Though it would have been much better if you'd chosen a world without vampires,* I couldn't help adding.

Yes, I can see that, she said thoughtfully. *But of course, I had no idea there would be vampires here. Perhaps you should look at it as a fascinating challenge.*

A challenge? My eyes narrowed dangerously and a student coming towards me squeaked in alarm and jumped to the other side.

You'll survive and thrive. I have no doubt about it. Once you get your bearings. And once you make friends with that other girl–the powerful one.

Regan? I snorted derisively. *No, that's not going to happen.*

If you could win her over, she could be a powerful ally. And after all, you're going to be sharing a...

No, no, no. Let me stop you right there. There will be absolutely no sharing. No nothing. I thought of something. *Oh, gods. We need to get you out of my head. Soon.*

You're just realizing it, aren't you? She sounded sympathetic. *I promise I won't be present should anything happen between you and... well, anyone else. In a romantic way.*

I felt sick to my stomach. *You certainly won't be because we are ending this disturbing situation as soon as possible.*

She sighed. *Medra, you silly girl, I'm your mother. I have absolutely no interest in... Well, you know. Being a Peeping Tom. I'll simply be happy that you are happy. When that delightful time comes.*

I don't think we should speak about it anymore, I said. *Or ever again. Ever. Now tell me how to get you out.*

Well, I'm not really sure about that part. Perhaps there is no way.

I stopped in my tracks and a girl walking behind me ran into me.

There has to be a way, I hissed internally, after apologizing to the girl. *There is always a way. Haven't you proven that by bringing me back from the brink of death? And bringing part of your own soul with me? None of that is supposed to be possible. And yet here we are.*

Why not try it this way for a while? We could make a formidable team, she countered. *You would benefit from my wisdom.*

I'd rather benefit from it in another way. Preferably without you right here in my head, I said, clenching my jaw.

Oh, very well. She sighed forlornly. *Well, I suppose you could start by consulting some ancient books. Or some wise person.*

A book? A wise person? You sound as if you've been reading too many fairy tales. I could feel my panic mounting. *Are those really your only suggestions?*

Well, did you really expect me to have an answer for you? I've already said I don't even know if it's possible, she reminded me.

Beginning with books isn't a terrible idea, I said grudgingly.

Bloodwing was sure to have an impressive library. Maybe the answer was waiting for me there. Could it really be that easy?

I turned another corner, this one lined with arched windows overlooking the sea. It was a calm day. A warm autumn breeze blew in, smelling of brine.

This wasn't how I imagined meeting you, I said.

I suppose that makes two of us, Orcades replied. *But I'm glad I had the chance. Even if it's in this very strange way. Daughter.*

I was quiet for a moment. Not because I had nothing to say. But because suddenly tears were pricking the corners of my eyes.

She had died giving birth to me.

I could still remember the first time my mentor, Odessa, had told me what my mother's final words had been.

Orcades had called me the most beautiful thing she had ever seen. And considering that, as a high fae, her life had been incredibly long, I supposed that was saying something.

So am I, I said finally.

I stopped. There. I'd reached the headmaster's office. No one was outside.

I knocked on the door.

"Enter." I was surprised to hear a woman's voice.

I pushed open the heavy oak door and stepped inside. I'd entered an antechamber. The room was sparsely furnished and meticulously neat.

A pretty blightborn woman sat behind a mahogany desk. Her skin was dark brown and flawless, her lips painted a deep crimson. She was young, maybe only a few years older than me. Her eyes were calm, almost vacant, as if detached from her surroundings.

A pinprick of red on the side of her neck caught my eye. Then two tiny holes. Barely noticeable unless you were looking for it. Fang marks.

The realization hit me: the headmaster had fed from her. She wasn't just a school secretary. She was his thrall.

The young woman gestured to the door behind her. "He's expecting you. Go right in."

I nodded.

As I stepped forward, my gaze snagged on the far wall. It was lined with six painted portraits. Written above in gold letters was a sign that read "Bloodwing Board of Directors."

I scanned the names on the placards beneath the paintings quickly. Only one was familiar.

Natsumi Avari. Could this be Kage Tanaka's mother? Natsumi's long, white-blonde hair framed her face. She had dark, angular eyes–beautiful but stern. Her expression radiated a cold elegance, as though she saw every detail but was unimpressed by it all.

I turned away and opened the door to the headmaster's inner office.

Headmaster Kim sat behind a carved wooden desk. The four pedestals holding the desk up depicted, rather grotesquely in my opinion, four naked women, their faces frozen in ecstasy as they licked blood from their lips. The wood was dark and polished to a gleam.

"Miss Pendragon. Please, sit," Headmaster Kim commanded, his voice frosty. I felt the weight of his eyes on me as I complied, taking a seat in one of the two plain wooden chairs that had been arranged before the desk.

The headmaster, draped in dark robes trimmed with crimson, looked me over. I tried to appear nonchalant. But in truth, I was unsettled. The secretary. The carvings. These were some of the first blatant signs of vampirism I had seen within the school, and in the headmaster's office no less. I would have been lying if I didn't admit they frightened me. After all, yesterday this man had been in my head. Sure, he'd been trying to stop Regan and prevent me from making an utter fool of myself. That didn't change the fact he had invaded me as easily as she had.

The headmaster steepled his hands over the desk. "I understand you had quite an interesting first day at Bloodwing."

"You might say that," I replied. "I certainly made a fool of myself in more ways than one."

He surprised me by smiling slightly. "Would you like to tell me who was responsible for the mishaps?"

I remained silent.

"Surely you have some idea of who sabotaged your schedule," he encouraged. "Or at least who used thrallweave on you during the commencement address."

I met his eyes. "No. None at all." I shrugged and leaned back in my chair. "Besides, does it matter?"

He raised his eyebrows. "I'm surprised you don't want retribution."

"Oh, I didn't say that." I smiled coolly. "But isn't that the point of Bloodwing? To be ruthless? I paid attention to your speech. The way I see it is, whoever sabotaged me yesterday was doing exactly what you taught them to do."

"That's certainly one way of looking at it. What an interesting specimen you are, Miss Pendragon. Few blightborn see vampires so clearly upon their arrival here. Most have rather idealistic notions of what highblood life is like."

"I'm sure they do. But I didn't grow up idolizing vampires. So hopefully I can see you all for exactly what you really are," I said.

Headmaster Kim leaned forward. "And just what is that?"

We looked at one another.

"Powerful," I said at last.

Headmaster Kim opened his mouth but I never did find out just what he would have said, for at that same moment, the door behind me opened and Professor Sankara strode in, a vibrant purple silk robe swirling around him.

"Sorry I'm late, Headmaster." The tall dark man scratched his chin ruefully. "Not a naturally early riser, as you know." He looked over at me and smiled. "Miss Pendragon. Good to see you again."

I couldn't help smiling back. Sebastian Sankara was a vampire just like Headmaster Kim, yes. And yet, there was something that set them apart from each other.

Even though the combat teacher had watched Visha pummel me into the dirt just to see how far things would go, I found myself already on the verge of forgiving him. After all, Odessa had been a tough teacher, too. Not quite that brutal, but I had a feeling she'd have mostly approved of Sankara's methods.

Or was that just the twisted way of Bloodwing? The fact that such brutality between students was already becoming acceptable to me?

"Thank you for joining us, Sebastian. I understand you have some thoughts about Miss Pendragon's curriculum going forward," said Headmaster Kim.

"I do. Advanced Weaponry may have been put on Medra's timetable as a joke but there was nothing funny about how she beat Visha Vaidya in my class yesterday," Professor Sankara said bluntly. "She should be permitted to remain in the class."

Headmaster Kim's brows rose. "It's a second year class."

"It is. And you know how selective I am in admitting only the finest students. Highbloods only and only ones with the real potential to be warriors at that." Sankara glanced at me. I realized I hadn't seen Regan there yesterday. Did that mean she wasn't warrior material? Or was she simply in a different section? "But she's got something. Lord Drakharrow was right to send her here. I've never seen a finer blightborn fighter. With a spear or with her fists."

I gaped at him. A warm feeling spread in my stomach. I hadn't heard praise like that in a long time. Damn, it felt good.

"But she *is* blightborn," the headmaster insisted. "Not a highblood. Rules are rules."

"As I told Miss Pendragon yesterday, dragon riders used to train alongside highblood warriors. They had to. They'd be fighting side by side. Well, if we want this young woman to have a chance in hell of doing the same someday then we should help her excel in every way we can."

"Perhaps it escaped your notice, Sebastian," said the headmaster mildly. "But Miss Pendragon has no dragon. How could she possibly fight alongside highbloods?"

Sankara shrugged. "I didn't send her here. That was a decision far above my paygrade. But I doubt Miss Pendragon wishes to be useless. Dragonless or not, give her something to do. Something to aspire to." He looked at me. "You want to be able to fight alongside highbloods one day, don't you Medra?"

I stared back at him.

Fight alongside highbloods? No. Fight *against* highbloods? Absolutely fucking yes. And to do that, I needed to know what they knew. I needed to get as strong as I could.

I'd take any combat training they'd allow me to.

"Of course, I do," I lied. "Absolutely. Yes." I looked at the headmaster and tried to appear as doe-eyed and eager as I could. "Please, sir. I might not have a dragon. But I have a rider's blood. And my blood is yearning to fight. Make me an asset. Let me be a student Bloodwing can be proud of. After all, Lord Drakharrow himself sent me here. He obviously wants me to learn everything I can, right?"

If Headmaster Kim had been preparing to refuse, my mention of Lord Drakharrow seemed to do the trick.

He frowned. "Fine. Miss Pendragon may officially remain in Advanced Weaponry. But she'll need to complete the basic combat training with the other blightborn students as well. She's not excused from that."

"That's fine," Professor Sankara said quickly. "That class is light weapons and hand-to-hand combat. It'll be a good contrast. She should get all the practice she can." To me, he added, "You might be tired some days. You'll be getting a good workout. Two hours of combat class a day most days as the term goes on. Sometimes more when I keep you late. But you don't mind that, do you?"

I shook my head. "Not at all. I like going to bed exhausted. It means I've worked as hard as I could."

It was sort of true. The more exhausted I was, the less time I also had to feel sorry for myself. To miss the world I'd left behind. To think about the people I'd never see. I'd rather go to sleep bloody-nosed and dirty and worn out than lie there, sleepless and anxious, thinking about things I had no way of changing.

Or worse, conversing with my mother.

I'm still here, you know, she reminded me.

I ignored her.

Loud voices suddenly came from outside the room.

The door behind us banged open for a second time, this time with more force as it slammed against the wall. Professor Sankara and I both turned to see who had come in.

Professor Rodriguez stood in the doorframe, breathing hard, his worn leather satchel swinging haphazardly by his side. His dark hair was even messier than yesterday. It looked as if it hadn't seen a comb in a week. His trousers had, if anything, even more patches than the ones he had been wearing the day before. Rodriguez, I decided, needed to ask for a raise. Perhaps blightborn teachers weren't paid as well as highblood ones. Could that be it?

"Good morning, Gabriel. Was there something you urgently needed?" The headmaster's voice was cool. It was clear he was not impressed by the interruption.

"As I tried to tell your secretary, Headmaster, I have some input to give at this meeting as well," Professor Rodriguez snapped, apparently not put off by Headmaster Kim's lukewarm reception.

Rodriguez seemed to notice Professor Sankara seated beside me for the first time.

The two men's eyes met, just for a heartbeat, but something passed between them. Professor Rodriguez's fierce expression faltered for the briefest moment, a hint of color rising to his cheeks.

He cleared his throat. "Sorry, I didn't realize Sebastian was already here." Then he frowned. "But actually, no, if Sankara was invited then I'm not sure why I wasn't."

"Professor Sankara had relevant input to give regarding one of Miss Pendragon's classes," the headmaster replied, clearly trying to keep his temper. "As you can see, not all of Miss Pendragon's professors are present. Professor Hassan is notably absent. We are sorting out Miss Pendragon's curriculum this morning and I did not think every teacher at Bloodwing needed to be in attendance."

"As you should be," Rodriguez said. "Sorting it out, I mean. And that's where I come in. We all witnessed Pendragon's little debacle yesterday afternoon, didn't we? Or else heard of it."

I flushed. I had no doubt the whole school would be talking about it today and laughing in my face.

"Many students have thrallweave used on them inappropriately from time to time, Rodriguez." Headmaster Kim waved a hand dismissively. "A childish prank. If that's all this is about..."

"It's not," Rodriguez interrupted. "Though, from what I saw, it's a wonder Miss Pendragon didn't die. You got into her head, too, didn't you, Kim? Tried to stop whoever was using her? Told her to get down immediately? And then she jumped off the top of the dragon's head?"

Headmaster Kim said nothing.

"Just as I thought," Rodriguez said, sounding satisfied. "She's ridiculously susceptible. She's a danger to herself and to others. Do you really want your only dragon rider pupil killing herself because some jealous highblood student tells her to? I'm sure Viktor Drakharrow would love to hear that his nephew's consort died in her very first week of class."

I could see the headmaster beginning to bristle.

"And don't tell me there are no dragons so it doesn't matter," Rodriguez added before the headmaster could speak. "We all know Viktor..."

"Lord Drakharrow," the headmaster interrupted.

"Yes, yes. Lord Drakharrow. We all know Lord Drakharrow has a bee in his bonnet about getting the dragons back. He won't accept that they're gone forever. And now that this girl has appeared, he certainly won't take keenly to her being lost as soon as she's found." Rodriguez paused his tirade, still breathing hard. "Does he even know? Lord Drakharrow, I mean. That Miss Pendragon was gravely injured multiple times on her very first day?"

"She was not gravely injured in my class, Gabriel," Professor Sankara said, with a frown. "Some small injuries are typical for Advanced Weaponry." I thought of my broken ribs and nose but said nothing. "She held her own."

"Really, Sebastian?" Rodriguez raised a dark eyebrow. "I wasn't expecting denial from your quarter. From what I hear, Miss Pendragon's nose was broken and she had to be escorted through the halls by Blake Drakharrow lest the highblood first years swarm her and make her their feast."

"Blake Drakharrow is her betrothed. Who else would you have had escort her?" Sankara said, looking baffled.

Rodriguez glanced at me. He was the last person I'd expected to find as an ally. And yet... here he was. It was strange.

"How would you help me, Professor?" I asked, speaking up for the first time since his arrival. "I didn't think there was anything to do about the thrallweave."

"Ah, but that's where you're mistaken," Rodriguez said triumphantly. "Every spell has a counterspell. And thrallweave, though it's taken as innate vampire magic, is still a spell–though one frequently believed species-specific. It is, in fact, not species-specific. Non-highbloods can master thrallweave..."

"You're saying blightborn can work thrallweave?" the headmaster interrupted, his face credulous. "Impossible."

"Not impossible. With diligence and hard work it can be done. Though very few mortals have an aptitude for such magic, it's true," Rodriguez replied. "In fact, we used to teach such a class here. It was offered to highbloods and select blightborn. Secondary Level Thrallweave, I believe it was called."

"And I suppose you're one, are you, Gabriel?" Professor Sankara's interest seemed genuine. "Have you mastered thrallweave? How very impressive. But then, I'd expect nothing less from you."

Professor Rodriguez flushed a little just above his worn collar. "I haven't, no. Not really." I got the distinct impression he was lying. "But I do have experience with the opposite. Thrallguard."

"Thrallguard?" I burst out, unable to contain my excitement. "Is that what it sounds like?'

"It's a defense against thrallweave." He looked at the headmaster. "One which every dragon rider used to receive proficient training in."

"That was long ago," the headmaster said.

"True. But I'm sure Lord Drakharrow would like his pet rider–" I bristled but said nothing. "To receive every possible educational opportunity that the riders of old had," Rodriguez said.

"You're suggesting you train Miss Pendragon is this thrallguard spell?" the headmaster said. "Professor Sankara has just successfully argued that she should take his Advanced Weaponry class. With that plus her regular classes and study periods, I'm afraid Miss Pendragon will have enough on her plate."

"I'd be happy to add another class, Headmaster," I said quickly. "Maybe I could replace one of my other less suitable classes, like Restoration? Or I could go during lunchtime or after classes are finished. I'd put in the work. Whatever was needed. I swear I would."

"She sounds enthusiastic to me, Headmaster," Sankara said with a grin. "Little wonder. If there's a student out there so determined to do her harm that they had her climb one of the dragons during your speech, then who knows what they might try next? Perhaps Rodriguez is right and it's not such a bad idea. Just a little unusual."

"Unusual, yes, but I do have other pupils. She wouldn't be the first," Rodriguez said quickly.

"Your first and foremost duty is to teach the classes you've been assigned, Gabriel," the headmaster said coldly. "Not to facilitate your own side projects."

Rodriguez colored. "Of course. Which I do. But school rules stipulate a professor is allowed to hold private sessions. And I do this for a few select pupils. You might be surprised to know that so far, all have been highbloods."

I watched as Professor Sankara and the headmaster looked at one another.

"Not as surprised as you might think," the headmaster muttered finally.

"I suppose it makes sense that some of our elite students would want to be able to guard against the use of thrallweave," Sankara agreed. "After all, the most dangerous enemy a highblood can face is another highblood."

My heart was beating fast. It sounded as if this "thrallguard" was something only the most elite highblood students could afford to take private lessons in. And it also sounded like Professor Rodriguez was one of the only non-vampires who knew how to teach it. If not the only one in the entire school.

I wondered how he had wound up so skilled in thrallguard himself. But I wasn't about to ask. Not in front of Headmaster Kim.

"Paranoia," the headmaster said dismissively. "Highbloods rarely use thrallweave upon one another. Most of the time it doesn't have a high success rate."

"Yes, but when it does..." Sankara shrugged. "When the great houses have been at war with one another, having a highblood from another house under your power could be the tipping point between victory or defeat. Enthralled highbloods make powerful spies."

"As did thrallweaved riders," Rodriguez pointed out. "And Miss Pendragon is the only rider in existence. The only rider blood in Sangratha. What if one of the great houses tried to steal her away from Bloodwing? You know Lord Drakharrow has many enemies."

Headmaster Kim and Professor Sankara exchanged another look.

"That is true," the headmaster said finally. "Very well. You may train her in this art. I'll permit it."

I wanted to clap my hands together in glee but restrained myself. Learn how to block Regan and her coercive attacks? Yes, please. Perhaps, eventually, I could even figure out how to teach this skill to other students, like Florence and Naveen.

"Excellent. You're making the right decision. Miss Pendragon seems a quick study. I'm sure she'll catch on fast. And then she'll be much safer at Bloodwing. We want her to be competitive with the highblood students, after all, don't we?" Professor Rodriguez said confidently.

I raised an eyebrow at him. Was he really going to sing my praises after how furious he'd been at me just the day before? But it didn't matter. I was just grateful he'd shown up and made this offer.

Over the next half-hour, we finalized the rest of my timetable. Then Headmaster Kim rose to his feet. "I have a meeting with some of the board members in a few minutes. I'm afraid we'll have to wrap things up."

"Of course," Professor Sankara said. "Miss Pendragon, I'll see you at our next class."

He swept out of the room, his long purple robe trailing behind him.

"I'll escort Miss Pendragon to the refectory," Professor Rodriguez offered. "Breakfast is still being served. She can grab something before her next class and I'll set up a time to begin her training."

"I'll have an updated timetable delivered to you later this morning," Headmaster Kim told me as he hastened from the room.

I followed Professor Rodriguez out into the hall. Now that it was past eight-thirty, the corridors were bustling with students moving towards the refectory or heading towards class early.

"What was that in there?" I asked, after we'd taken a few steps away from the headmaster's office.

Rodriguez glanced at me. "What do you mean?"

"I mean..." I tried to say it in the right way. "You were furious at me yesterday. Suddenly you're showing up to save me? I don't understand."

He frowned. "I might object to you personally. That doesn't mean I wish you physical harm."

"How kind of you." I risked rolling my eyes. "Does that mean I still have to write that essay?"

He looked amused. "Yes."

"But you think what Regan did to me was wrong?"

"So it *was* Miss Pansera. Interesting. I figured as much."

"Shit," I muttered. "I didn't mean to say that."

He looked over at me. "Did you tell the headmaster?"

I shook my head. "Why bother? I highly doubt she'd get in trouble for it. She's a highblood, right? Do they even punish them?"

Now he really looked amused. "You've caught on pretty fast considering it's only your second day." He pursed his lips. "So Miss Pansera told you to ask me about dragons and healers, huh?"

"Shit," I said again. "Please don't say anything to anyone. Clearly you were already well aware she was a huge bitch. Look, I just want to move past this. If I have to do the essay and clean your storeroom, fine. I get it."

"You have to do the essay because it'll teach you things you ought to know. As for the storeroom..." Rodriguez ran his hands through his hair. "You might not have time for that now," he conceded. "We'll see. It already looks better than it did before, in any case."

"Do you really tutor other highbloods in how to guard against thrallweave?" I asked, curious.

"I do," he replied. "But not many know it's something I offer. So, few know to ask. And that's how I'd like to keep it. I'd prefer you not share the information."

"I understand." I hesitated, then added, "I really appreciate you offering to teach me. When she was in my head... It was horrible."

"It's a grotesque violation, that's what it is. It's something that should never be used. Especially by one student on another. But Bloodwing permits it. They look the other way when it's merely a blightborn student being humiliated." Rodriguez shook his head angrily. "Usually the highbloods keep themselves somewhat in check. But every year..." He paused as we passed a group of chattering First Years.

"Every year?" I prompted, once they were gone.

His face hardened. "Every year someone dies."

CHAPTER 12

MEDRA

It wasn't a total shock to me that highbloods sometimes killed blightborn students. Honestly, I was just kind of relieved to hear it wasn't on a daily basis.

But it did put into perspective how much worse it might have been the day before, when I'd jumped from the stone dragon. If I had died, it would have been a minor inconvenience. Not completely unexpected.

Professor Rodriguez left me at the entrance to the refectory. Quite a few students still remained, sitting at long tables, eating and chatting. I didn't see any of Blake and Regan's crew, which was good news for me.

I grabbed a mug of steaming kava, added three teaspoons of sugar and some cream, and then sat at the end of one of the tables, plucking food from the mostly-full platters of breakfast items.

There was no sign of Florence and Naveen. They were probably already heading to class.

This time, when the Bloodwing bells chimed, I was ready. Florence had told me there was a five minute warning bell before the start of each class. This time I was out in the hall and heading towards my History of Sangratha class before it even rang.

I'd memorized my new timetable but had it tucked into a pocket just in case. Today would be a little different in more ways than one. Headmaster Kim had left the Restoration and Alchemy class on my schedule for now, after Professor Rodriguez had told him it would be a good idea for me to learn the basics, though he doubted I'd show an aptitude for healing.

I thought he might be wrong, however. Alchemy, for instance, seemed more about mixing and brewing potions in the right quantities than about a natural talent or arcane ability.

True, I'd never baked a cake or mixed a recipe before in my life, but what child doesn't like pretending to make "potions" in the bathtub or out in the gardens with some mud? Alchemy seemed interesting and potentially fun. It was also linked to Herbalism, which was offered to more advanced students. I knew Florence wanted to take that class and I planned to stick with her as much as possible, so I was hoping I might be able to add it, too.

First Years only had four classes a day, but some courses alternated. After lunch today, I had Advanced Weaponry followed by my new class, Basic Combat for Blightborns. But some days I seemed to have Basic Combat or Advanced Weaponry without the other one. Instead I had a spare period that I was supposed to be using for research and study.

The first half of the day went by quickly. This time, I kept my head down in History of Sangratha. Quite literally. I focused on copying notes off the board as quickly as I could. Then, Florence and Naveen and I hurried to Restoration and Alchemy where Professor Rodriguez acted as if he hadn't bitten my head off the day before. Instead of making me stay for lunch to work on the storeroom, we made plans for my first thrallguard training session the next day.

Then, to my shock and relief, he let me leave to get something to eat–but only after reminding me that he expected to use all of my upcoming study periods and spare time to work on my dragon essay. That would have been well and good if I hadn't needed to use them for the even more pressing issue of getting my mother out of my head. Of course, I didn't mention that to him.

By the time I strode into Advanced Weaponry after lunch, I was feeling pretty good about how the day was going. I'd made it to the halfway point without anyone trying to murder me or lick blood off me and I hadn't seen Regan, Blake, or any of their ilk once.

That changed as I walked into Professor Sankara's class. The sky was overcast today. Just like the day before, the air in the courtyard was filled with the scent of sweat and metal.

Several students had arrived early. Some were sparring together in pairs, while others were practicing on wooden dummies or running drills with weapons in hand.

There was a loud grunt from the corner of the courtyard and my eyes flew to where Blake Drakharrow stood, steadily attacking a punching bag suspended from a thick iron chain.

He was shirtless. His lean, muscular frame was coated in a faint sheen of sweat as he worked. The bag swung with each savage blow he delivered, its surface denting from the force of his strikes. His pale gold hair clung to his forehead, giving him a wild, untamed appearance.

I swallowed hard. It was the first time I'd seen him shirtless. The first time I'd seen the black ink that marred his otherwise flawless pale skin. He'd been wearing high-collared shirts previous days, plus cloaks overtop those.

Now I saw that intricate tattoos covered his back, arms, and even snaked partway up his neck. Some of the markings were in Classical Sangrathan. Words I couldn't make out from this distance. But most were dragons. Their scales spread across his chest. Their claws raked down his arms as if ready to tear flesh.

As he jabbed out and rotated, another flash of ink caught my eye. My breath hitched. A full dragon was etched across his entire back, its wingspan stretching from shoulder to shoulder, its tail coiling down his spine, and its snarling head seeming to rise from the base of his neck.

I forced myself to look away.

I hated him, I reminded myself. He was arrogant and cruel. The embodiment of everything I despised about the world I was trapped in.

And yet... I snuck another glance. I couldn't seem to tear my eyes away from him.

His fists flew. Left hook. Right jab. Cracking against the leather bag with brutal force. The muscles in his arms tensed and released, tattoos rippling with every strike. He was favoring his left hand. But he fought well with both. The dragon wings on his back flared as he twisted, pounding with first one hand then the other.

I cursed inwardly as my gaze lingered on the ink sprawled over his skin.

Blake Drakharrow was beautiful in a way I didn't want to admit. In a way that made my blood simmer and my mind spin with confusion.

How could someone so vile be so compelling?

Blake suddenly stopped, his eyes flicking towards me before I could turn away. Our gazes locked and a slow smirk curled over his lips. My heart skipped a beat and for the first time I saw something in those pale, silver eyes. Awareness. Did he know the effect he was having on me?

As he moved to wipe the sweat from his brow with the back of his hand, I hastily turned away.

He was marked by something ancient and dangerous. Seeing him like that, bare and exposed, stirred something in me that I didn't want to feel. Made him seem more like me.

But he wasn't.

No matter how beautiful the man or how mesmerizing the dragon, Blake Drakharrow was still a monster.

I could never let myself forget that.

I spent the rest of Advanced Weaponry working with Professor Sankara one on one. At first, I had to list some of the skills I already possessed so he could get a better sense of where to start me.

Odessa had trained me extensively in traditional sword combat. I felt fairly proficient with longswords and short swords. We'd moved onto spears and polearms. My footwork was quick and precise and I could usually use speed and agility to outmaneuver my slower opponents.

"As you saw yesterday, that won't be enough here," Sankara said. "You're impressive for a mortal." Every time they called me "mortal" I was tempted to correct them. I was mortal. But only half. Still, what would be the point of explaining about the fae of Aercanum? They'd never believe me. "But here, your opponents won't be mortals. Vampires move faster, hit harder. For the next while, I want you to focus on speed and reflexes."

I thought of the way my body had seemed to come more alive, to quicken, as I was fighting Visha. But I said nothing, simply nodded. I had no idea if I could will that to happen again.

Sankara gestured towards a set of weighted practice weapons hanging on the wall nearby. "Take those. Practice your forms with double the weight you're used to. We'll see how quick you really are."

By the time Advanced Weaponry finished, I was a sweaty, dripping mess. But there was no time to go back to the First Year dormitory and bathe or even change. With only ten minutes before my next class, I had to hurry to get to Basic Combat for Blightborn. I made a mental note to bring a towel and extra set of clothes next time, so I could at least sneak into a bathroom and change.

Mercifully, Blake had stayed far away from me the entire class. Which was exactly how I wanted it. Our betrothal was meaningless to me–and it was clear it was just as meaningless to him. I also didn't want other students thinking it set me apart as special. Or worse, marked me as a target.

Being the only rider already did that, anyways.

Regan had yet to show up for a single Advanced Weaponry class. I was starting to wonder if it was on her schedule. Maybe she was exempt. Or maybe there were two time slots for the class being offered this term and she was in the other.

I was starting to think I'd never see her there and that was a relief.

If I could stay away from Blake and his bully friends, maybe I could make it through this term. Maybe Bloodwing could even be bearable. Dare I say it? Even enjoyable. The school itself was growing on me. I liked being tested, challenged. I liked learning new things every day. Oddly enough, I was more interested and invested in my lessons now than I'd ever been with my tutors back in Camelot.

Naveen was waiting in the hall outside the Basic Combat for Blightborns classroom.

Florence was not. She didn't have to take a combat class. At first I'd been surprised by this as one of her future career options was strategist. You would think a military strategist would have to be pretty familiar with combat.

But apparently a strategist's position was primarily theoretical. Florence would be valued more for her knowledge of historical battles and her ability to develop campaign plans. If she went with this path, in times of peace, she might be posted as an advisor to a noble highblood house. She'd coach them on security measures, defense tactics, and ways to help keep their forces strengthened in preparation for future conflicts. If it ever came to full-out war, she'd be safely stationed in a command post, issuing orders and adapting strategies in real time, but never actually out on the field.

Strategists could also become diplomats and become valuable go-betweens for the highblood houses or even as representatives of Sangratha to other lands.

"You look more excited for this class than you did for the others," I observed. Naveen was barely hiding a grin. He kept hopping up and down on both feet as he stood waiting.

"I am," he agreed. "I'm ready to move. I'm tired of sitting on a bench all day scribbling on parchment." He feigned a few jabs and I laughed. "I'm not like Florence. She loves keeping her nose in a book. I'm actually surprised she doesn't want to become a librarian like her mother. I'm sure Bloodwing would love to have her."

"That's a good point," I said, surprised I hadn't thought of it. "It would be a safer position, too, right? Librarians aren't really ever in danger."

Naveen gave a little shrug. "I mean, within the school library I've heard it can be cutthroat. Some of the librarians are vampires. But they usually aren't from very powerful houses. Still, that just means they're competitive when it comes to keeping the little power they do have. I've heard Professor Shen say the library is not for the faint of heart."

I snorted. "That's kind of funny. I've always thought of libraries as rather dull places. Peaceful and quiet, if anything."

"They sure seem that way," Naveen agreed. "Oh, look. The door's opening."

Sure enough, the classroom door now stood ajar and students were lining up and making their way inside.

We followed the others into a large open room. It resembled the courtyard we used in Advanced Weaponry in many ways, except this one was fully indoors with a stone ceiling.

"I've heard our instructor is a dwarf," Naveen told me, his voice low. "We can tolerate sunlight and we can build up an even greater tolerance, but it's more comfortable for us inside. Especially when you're, uh..." He broke off nervously.

"Yes, Mr. Sharma? Was there something you cared to share with the rest of the class?" a dry, female voice said from behind us.

I whirled around to see a short, sturdy-looking dwarven woman.

Our newest instructor had an impressively muscular build, with broad shoulders and thick forearms. Her gray hair was streaked with a few strands of dark brown and pulled into a ponytail. Her eyes were a striking shade of dark blue. A deep scar ran across her left eyebrow. She wore faded studded leather armor that had seen better days. It was clear she preferred functionality over appearance.

"Professor Stonefist," Naveen said, his voice weak. "I didn't see you there."

"No, you didn't, Sharma. And that could get you killed." The professor's voice was brusque.

I hid a smile. This woman was obviously the no-nonsense type. She reminded me of Odessa already.

The professor raised her voice so the entire class could hear her. "I'm Magda Stonefist and I'll be your instructor. You're here because you're a future scout or because you need to fulfill the basic combat class requirement. You're also here because you're mortal. You're blightborn. In other words, you're weak."

The class broke out in a stir of mutters.

"Well?" Magda demanded. "Aren't you?" She pointed to the hallway. "That's what *they* think you are. But weak doesn't mean useless. Weak doesn't mean expendable. That's what you can prove in this classroom. That's what you'll have to prove to me."

She scanned the room. "This class could just as easily have been called Basic Survival for Blightborn. Because ultimately, survival is what I'll be teaching you. Sangratha has been at peace for the last five years. If you can call it that." She muttered the last part under her breath so only Naveen and I heard it. "But times can change. Times can change fast."

I glanced at Naveen and he gave me a quick shrug, as if to say he didn't know what she was talking about.

"Don't consider this class optional. Don't consider it theoretical. This class could save your life." Professor Stonefist glanced at Naveen. Then her eyes swept over the rest of the group, pausing on the few dwarven students in our midst.

"Some of you have natural advantages," she acknowledged. "Dwarves were built for close-quarters combat. We have high endurance. I'll teach you dwarven students how to use that. The rest of you will learn how to fight smart. You're not here to learn how to look pretty with a sword. In fact, for many of you, a sword in your hand is the last thing you'll need. We'll use smaller weapons. Clubs, daggers, crossbows. We'll focus on swift, efficient strikes. Evasion will be our watchword. But sometimes a face-to-face fight can't be avoided. Hand to hand combat is dirty, messy, but sometimes it can be your only chance against someone stronger and better trained. You'll learn how to make the most of what little time you have to react. In future terms, we'll focus more on learning the art of stealth."

She started pacing back and forth. "Scouts have one of the most dangerous roles in a unit. They go ahead of their squad, into enemy territory, and often return with nothing but their lives. Some don't return at all. In the last civil war, between the four great houses..."

I turned to Naveen, my eyes wide. "War?" I mouthed.

"I'll tell you later," he mouthed back. Then he seemed to think better of it. "Ask Florence," he mouthed.

I tried to tune back into what Professor Stonefist was saying.

"If you're chosen to be a scout, your job isn't to fight. It's to move unseen, to gather information, and to survive long enough to report back with it. That means learning how to use your environment, how to disappear into the shadows, and how to remain silent even when it seems like everything around you is trying to find you."

Magda paused, her expression growing more serious. "Some of you may know I wasn't always an instructor at Bloodwing. Decades ago–yes, decades," she said drily, as some chatter went up from the class. "Vampires aren't the only long-lived race in Sangratha, as you should be aware. Decades ago, I was a scout in the last civil war between the great houses."

She looked over the class, her eyes dark with a faint challenge. "Some of you may have heard of me. They called me Grimblade."

Beside me Naveen gasped. A few other students in the courtyard did, too, clearly recognizing the name.

"But I thought..." Naveen stopped, his face reddening.

"You thought what, Mr. Sharma? Care to share that thought with the whole class?" Professor Stonefist barked.

Naveen shifted nervously. "I thought... I guess I thought Grimblade was a man," he said sheepishly.

There were some snickers. But I saw a few students nodding.

"You thought wrong, Sharma," Magda Stonefist said. But her voice was mild. "It won't be the first or the last time someone makes that mistake though. Some of the most famous scouts in Sangrathan history have been female. Many of them were also dwarves. All of you should be aware of that."

She strode forward into the center of the courtyard. "Now. Let's get started shall we?"

"Grimblade?" I whispered at Naveen.

His face was still red as a beet. "I'll tell you later."

"We'll be starting with the basics over the next few weeks," Professor Stonefist was announcing loudly. "Grappling, strikes, throws, disarming techniques. You'll learn how to make your movements count, and more importantly, how to stay on your feet when someone bigger or stronger comes at you."

She looked around at us. "When I was scouting in the Yavara Jungle, I survived because I knew how to use my surroundings. If you make it through this course, I also teach an advanced Concealment and Survival class where you'll learn how to disappear in plain sight, set up ambushes, and turn the environment into your weapon."

Naveen's eyes lit up. "Awesome," I heard him whisper.

"But first," Professor Stonefist continued. "We'll start simple. I want you to pair off, get into the rings, and show me what you've got. Knock your opponent down or pin them. I'll come by each of you, assessing your strengths and weaknesses."

I was about to ask Naveen if he wanted to pair up when Professor Stonefist marched up to us.

"Nope," she said, crossing her arms over her chest.

"Nope what?" I asked, confused.

She grinned. "Go find another partner, Pendragon. I can tell from the look on this lad's face that he wouldn't give you a fair match."

"Yes, I would," Naveen said hotly.

She raised her eyebrows. "Really? You'd be okay throwing your friend into the mud and slamming your fist into her face?"

That sounded remarkably similar to what had already happened to me yesterday but I said nothing.

Naveen blushed. "Well..."

I rolled my eyes. Naveen was clearly too much of a gentleman. Or maybe he just needed to learn what women could really do. In any case, I wanted a fair fight. Not someone I could beat one-handed.

"Go partner up with Aldric over there," Professor Stonefist instructed him. As Naveen walked away, she eyed me up and down. "And you. A rider, huh? Lean and slender. Those ears look pointy. Can you hear better with them than most people?"

"A little," I admitted. Fae did have better hearing than mortals. And I was half-fae.

"Good. Perhaps you'll wind up a scout since there are no dragons to ride. Wouldn't be the worst outcome for you." She scratched her chin. "You can pair up with Lace Ironstride over there. She's a Second Year student who usually helps me supervise the First Year class. She's more experienced, but I suspect you'll keep her on her toes."

I looked over to where a bold-looking dwarven girl was standing with her feet spread apart.

"Sounds good," I said, cracking my knuckles. "So the goal is...?"

"The goal is for one of you to be taken out. You can do that in a nice way or a not so nice way. Lace fights fair. Usually." Professor Stonefist grinned at me and I grinned back.

Lace was built like a boulder. She was at least a head shorter than me, but much more solid. Her strength was clear in the way she moved.

Still, a few minutes later, Lace was on her back. I'd pinned her in the dirt but I didn't rub her face in it like Visha had done. I also didn't punch her in the nose.

"Good match," I said, standing up and offering her my hand. I suspected Lace would be an even more challenging opponent the next time. She'd underestimated me a bit, but I was sure it wouldn't happen twice.

She took my hand and nodded as she jumped to her feet. "You're fast. I'm stronger, but speed can be a great asset, too."

"Speed is something that we dwarves always need to work on," Professor Stonefist said ruefully, approaching our ring. "You've got impressive speed," she said to me. "Quick reactions and agility are valuable in a fight. But don't forget, you need to be more than just fast. Strength and endurance are key, too."

I winced a little, thinking about how Visha had certainly proven that the day before.

Professor Stonefist walked around me, observing my posture and form. "In the next few classes, I want you to work on building up your strength and endurance. We'll focus on drills to increase your resilience. Strengthening your core and upper body will help you maintain control and get more power into your moves."

I nodded. "Understood."

The professor turned away. "Switch!" she bellowed. "Find a new partner. If I haven't come by to give you an assessment, I will do so before class ends. Or you'll stay late and wait. One or the other."

I quickly found a new partner. First up was a slender dark skinned mortal boy named Vaughn Sabino who nearly had me matched in speed for a few minutes. But I wound up pinning him face-up against a wall. He was gracious about losing and made me promise we could spar again the next class.

"I'm usually the fastest in the group," he said, with a grin, as I left the ring. "I'm looking forward to a challenge."

By the time class ended, I was sore and tired but happy. Basic Combat was different from Advanced Weaponry, but in a refreshing way. The class seemed much more at ease–with the professor but also with one another. Even though we'd arguably spent the last hour fighting and competing, it had been in a good natured way. I sensed a camaraderie already starting to develop.

Professor Stonefist was tough but she seemed fair. I appreciated that she was mortal. It was a nice change of pace to be amongst mortal students and not highbloods, even though I was a little worried I wouldn't have my mettle tested quite as much.

"So, what were you going to say when the professor interrupted us at the start of class?" I asked Naveen.

He flushed. "Oh. That. I was going to say that as we dwarves age, it's easier on our eyes to be indoors. Artificial lighting isn't as harsh as sunlight."

I laughed. "That's funny."

"Why?"

"Well, a long time ago, I read in a book that it was vampires who had a natural aversion to sunlight. But here it turns out it was dwarves not vampires."

Naveen smiled. "I'm not sure vampires are averse to anything. They don't have many natural weaknesses."

"What about each other?" I suggested.

Naveen nodded. "You make a good point."

"Tell me about that civil war Professor Stonefist mentioned. Who fought in it? What happened?"

Naveen held up his hands. "Look, I wasn't even alive then. You'd be better off asking Florence or taking out a book from the library." He paused. "Actually, I'm sure we'll learn more about it in History of Sangratha."

I didn't want to wait that long.

"But all you really need to know, I guess," Naveen continued. "Is that it involved the four houses. They split into factions. Two against two."

"Who was allied with House Drakharrow?"

Naveen scratched his head. "I'm pretty sure it was House Orphos. All I know for sure is that it was House Avari against House Drakharrow. The other two houses were strong but not as strong as those two."

"So House Mortis took House Avari's side?" I thought back to Catherine, the leader of House Mortis who I'd seen strolling through the refectory with her two thralls the day before.

"Right," Naveen said. "House Orphos was a little stronger then. But not by much. House Mortis and House Avari seemed to have the stronger alliance."

"But who won?" Then I guessed, "House Drakharrow must have."

"You're right. How did you know?"

"Lord Drakharrow." I scowled. "The Drakharrows seem to have the most power right now."

"They do," Naveen agreed. "Though they haven't always. But yes, Viktor Drakharrow basically rules Sangratha. The other houses defer to him. At least, they do for now. I suppose the professor was right and it is an uneasy peace in some ways."

"What happens to Bloodwing when the great houses fight? I mean, aren't we supposed to be neutral? I thought all of the highbloods had sons and daughters here."

Naveen sighed. "We are. Supposed to be. Honestly, you'd be better off asking Florence. She loves topics like this. But the long and short of it is... During the civil war, it was chaos. I think Bloodwing shut down. The school was supposed to be preparing students to stand on guard for the kingdom. But the truth is, like you've probably already guessed, it basically helps to fortify the four most powerful houses. That's why what happens in the school when it comes to house and squad selection is so important. It's an indication of what's to come in the outer world. The most powerful squads and the most powerful house inside of Bloodwing are usually reflective of the most powerful up-and-coming house. Or which house will maintain their power."

"Only three of the school houses have leaders," I said.

Naveen shrugged. "Right. But everyone knows Blake will wind up the leader of House Drakharrow at Bloodwing. He doesn't have any real challengers. Well, unless you count his friends. I suppose his cousin Theo could challenge him."

I shook my head. "Theo doesn't seem the type." I frowned, then amended, "But I don't know him very well."

"I'm exhausted," Naveen groaned. "But I'm also starving. I think my stomach is winning out." He raised his hands. "Don't tell me how bad I smell. I don't want to know."

I laughed. "You go on to the refectory. I get it. But I'm heading back to the dormitory for a bath and then to the library."

We split up, agreeing to meet in the common room later, unless we fell asleep first. For me, it felt like a very real possibility. Especially after I'd taken a bath and changed into fresh clothes. I eyed my comfortable bed with longing but then with a sigh, forced myself back out the door.

There was a new area of Bloodwing Academy I wanted to explore.

CHAPTER 13

MEDRA

The Bloodwing Library was a large, imposing building that extended across several floors. As I entered through the towering double doors, I paused, overwhelmed by the sheer size of the place.

Rows and rows of tall dark wood bookshelves lined a wide main aisle. Long wooden tables were interspersed among the rows, providing workspace for students. Crimson banners bearing the school and house mottos hung from the walls. On either side of the room, tall stained glass windows lined the walls, spilling their rainbow light onto the polished floors. The air was cooler here and tinged with the aromas of old parchment, leather bindings, dust, and melted candle wax.

I glanced upwards and gasped. An enchanted ceiling divided into four quadrants moved and swirled, like a living mural. I saw an elegant city with tall white towers, rolling hills leading into green forests, a ship at sea in the midst of a storm, and tall snow-capped mountains. Each scene must reflect somewhere in Sangratha. I imagined it was even more beautiful at night, when stars would twinkle above it all.

The central hearth on the far end of the main room crackled with a low fire. Nearby was a long wooden counter with a group of people standing behind it. Students were lined up over there. That must be the librarians' desk. I decided I'd start off by asking one of them for help.

If I couldn't find anything relevant to exorcizing ghosts from one's head, then I'd also brought one of the dragon books that Professor Rodriguez had lent me. I could always sit down and read that and try to get started on my essay.

Just as I'd begun walking down the main aisle, a figure emerged from the stacks to my right.

A woman, slender and petite, with dark eyes framed by wire-rimmed spectacles. She wore a cream-colored sweater with lace trim along the sleeves, tucked into a high-waisted skirt of dark blue, belted at the waist. Her long black hair was tied up in a messy knot at the nape of her neck, strands falling loose as if she'd been too engrossed in her reading to tuck them back. Her knot of hair was held in place with a quill that stuck out at a haphazard angle. A small ink stain smudged the cuff of one otherwise perfect cream sleeve.

She walked with her eyes glued to an open book she held in one hand, occasionally flipping a page with a frown of concentration. This was impressive, considering that she was pulling a wooden trolley behind her with her other hand—a trolley that was filled with precariously stacked books, which she must have been reshelving.

The woman seemed completely lost in whatever she was reading. Her brow furrowed as she muttered under her breath.

I cleared my throat and she jumped, blinking violently, as if shocked to find someone there.

"Oh, I didn't..." she began, looking flustered as she pushed her spectacles higher on her nose. "You're not lost, are you?" Her voice was soft. She had the air of someone who was always thinking about something else.

I smiled. Clearly this was Florence's mother, Librarian Shen.

"No, not lost. I was looking for..."

The peace of the library was shattered in an instant.

Boisterous laughter and loud footsteps came from behind me.

Florence's mother frowned and turned to see who had come in.

I turned, too, but I should have already known.

They were all wearing dark robes emblazoned with the Drakharrow house motto: *Sanguine Vinciti*. Bound by blood.

Visha was in the lead, with Quinn and Theo behind her.

Visha strode past me as if I wasn't even there, without a nod or acknowledgment of any kind. As she went by, she knocked against Florence's mother's trolley full of books. I couldn't tell if she'd done it by accident or on purpose, but either way, the impact sent several books tumbling to the ground with a soft thud, their covers splaying open.

Behind her, Quinn giggled. Then Visha reached her hand out lazily to purposefully smack another stack of books off the trolley. Quinn laughed as if this was hilarious, then went a step further and carelessly kicked some of the scattered books out of her path. I heard the leather bindings scrape against the stone floor and winced.

"Oh, girls..." Florence's mother exclaimed, wringing her hands together as she looked at the mess of books. "Please don't do that."

Visha and Quinn just ignored her and kept going.

Theo trailed behind them with a sheepish expression. He wouldn't meet my eye as he went past. But he must have seen the stricken look on Professor Shen's face because as his gaze fell on the scattered books, he paused, then bent down to pick a few of them up. As he handed them to Florence's mother, he glanced quickly at me and shrugged apologetically, as if trying to make amends for the rudeness of his companions.

But I wasn't about to let him off that easily. I glared at him and said nothing.

Putting his head down, Theo disappeared down the main aisle.

Florence's mother's shoulders sagged as she looked down at the remaining books on the floor. Her cheeks were flushed as she bent down and started picking up the volumes.

I crouched down quickly beside her. "Here. Let me help you with that. You're Florence's mother, aren't you?"

She looked up at me, startled. "I'm Jia Shen, yes. Who are you?"

"I'm Medra Pendragon," I said, smiling and putting out my hand. "It's nice to finally meet you. I've heard so much about you from Florence."

"Ah, yes," Jia said, pushing her glasses up the bridge of her nose again, and smiling slowly. "Florence mentioned she'd made your acquaintance."

"She's been very kind and helpful. I don't know how I would have made it through these first days without her, honestly," I said.

Jia Shen's smile grew a little. "That's my Florence."

"I'm so sorry about the books," I said, gesturing to the mess. "Are they always like that?"

Her face clouded. "It's all right. I'm rather used to it."

I was shocked. "But you shouldn't be. You're a Bloodwing librarian. How can they get away with it?"

"Oh, they don't do it to all of the librarians," she assured me. "Just the blightborn ones."

She rose to her feet with a groan and wedged a stack of heavy-looking books back onto the trolley. Then she bent down to pick up one of the books Quinn had viciously kicked. "Oh, dear. This one will have to be tended to." The spine of the book had split and some pages were sticking out.

"It's vandalism," I said hotly. "Not to mention incredibly rude. Those spoiled brats."

Jia eyed me nervously. "It's clear you're new here. Please, don't bother saying anything on my account."

"But you deserve to be treated with respect. I don't understand."

She shrugged. "Every year some of the students pick a teacher to target. I guess this year it's my turn."

I felt a chill go down my spine. "Has it just been students from House Drakharrow? Or are all of the highblood students treating you this way?"

She tilted her head. "Now that you mention it, it does seem to be mostly Drakharrow students." She sighed. "I wonder what I did to aggravate them."

I thought I knew.

"I think it's because of Florence," I confessed unhappily. "Because she dared to make friends with me, I mean. I tried to warn her..."

Jia held up a hand. "No. If what you say is true..." She looked me up and down. "Florence told me you're the rider. That you didn't even want to be here."

"That's true," I said slowly. "I was forced to come here."

"And forcibly betrothed to Blake Drakharrow, from what I understand." I nodded and she shook her head. "The highblood customs... Even when I think I'm used to them, they do something that reminds me I may never be."

"So, you don't... adore them all? Like Florence seems to?" I said curiously.

Jia looked around, as if not wanting to be overheard. "Florence will learn, in time. Just as I learned. But you need to keep something in mind here, Medra. None of us have a choice. We were born blightborn. Florence tells me you're new to Sangratha." She gave me a curious look that reminded me I needed to learn more about this world's geography. Just how large was Sangratha anyhow? "Well, if that's true, try to imagine what growing up here is like." She looked at me carefully. "You don't question the people who hold all of the power. To do so could be dangerous. For you or for your friends."

It was a warning, but a gentle one.

I nodded. "I understand." I bit my lip. "But now Florence is accidentally making enemies of the Drakharrows. I warned her she should stay away from me. Maybe you can talk to her..."

"No," Jia Shen said quietly. "I draw the line there. My daughter will choose her own friends. And if there are consequences for her choices... Well, that's how we all learn. I won't tell her who to associate with." She reached out a hand and touched my hair gently. "So red."

I flushed.

"It must be hard, standing out like that all the time," Jia said thoughtfully. "You're brave to be here."

"So is your daughter," I responded.

She smiled. "I could talk about my daughter's fine qualities all day. But you didn't come to the library simply to discuss Florence. What can I help you with?"

I had thought carefully about how to phrase my request. Jia Shen seemed very kind, but I didn't want to horrify her by telling her my secret the first time we met.

Wise decision, Orcades murmured.

Oh, you're still there, are you? I replied drily. She'd been quiet all day. *And here I thought my problem might have taken care of itself.*

Very funny. Those children need to be taken in hand. When I behaved in such a way as a girl, my Nurse didn't hesitate to whip me.

I cringed. *They're not exactly children. And that might be going too far.* Or was it? *But I agree. They're out of line.*

Little privileged bastards each and every one, Orcades said primly. *If I were back in my own body, I'd happily deal with them all for you.*

I grimaced. I could only imagine what she'd do if she were back in her high fae form. I'd been told my mother had once been a powerful general in my grandfather's army.

Florence's mother was looking at me expectantly.

"Um, I'm doing some research into a rather unusual topic," I blurted out. If only she knew just how unusual. "I'm hoping you can help me find some relevant information. Anything to do with curses, spells... Or, um, magic to do with souls."

"With souls?" Jia Shen looked thoughtful. "Soul magic? You must mean blood magic. We have a great many texts on blood magic here, of course."

"Does blood magic involve using souls...?"

"Necromancy does, of course. Blood magic can at times. And necromancy and blood magic are very interwoven. Although, bloodmancy is a House Drakharrow specialty, just as necromancy is often considered the purview of House Mortis." Jia looked at me expectantly. "You might consider consulting Blake Drakharrow on this topic..."

"No," I said firmly. "Absolutely not." I shook my head. "Sorry, Librarian Shen. I don't mean to be rude."

She seemed amused. "Oh, you're not being rude. And you may call me Jia. No, I understand. I suppose I just hoped that Mr. Drakharrow was kinder to you than to the average… Well, it doesn't matter." She looked at a nearby row. "I can find some materials for you. Enough to get you started. If you don't find what you're looking for, the library is sure to have more. You can always come back and find me another day."

"Wonderful," I said, feeling relieved. "Thank you so much for your help, Jia."

"Of course," she said, pausing as she began to pull the trolley towards the stack. "Though it would help if you gave me a little more detail on what you're looking for exactly. You mentioned curses. Has someone you know been cursed?"

"Well," I hedged. "Not cursed exactly."

Decidedly not, Orcades harrumphed. *I am not a curse. My presence is a gift.*

An unwanted gift, I said, through clenched teeth. *I'd have preferred a more typical mother-daughter chat.*

No one asked us what we wanted, my mother replied placidly. *That's life. I would have preferred not to die giving birth to you.*

I pressed my lips together. *Fair point.*

I knew it was a mother's prerogative to mention the pain she'd endured bringing a child into the world. And considering my mother had lost her life doing so, I decided she could complain all she wanted about the experience.

"Does necromancy involve harnessing the soul of someone who has died?" I asked Jia carefully.

"It can, absolutely. Necromancy is usually associated with raising the dead. House Mortis's armies were powerful because of the necromancers that traveled with them."

I cringed at the implication.

"But a soul can be even more powerful than a body," Jia continued.

"Did necromancers ever use souls in… bodies that weren't their own? The soul's, I mean?"

"I'm sure it's been done before, though I can't think of an example off the top of my head. My! What an interesting paper you must be writing," she said brightly, reminding me of Florence. "Is this for Restoration?"

"Yes, for Professor Rodriguez's class," I lied. "He has me doing some extra work for him."

That was entirely true. Just not the subject matter it concerned.

"Fascinating. There is always so much to learn, isn't there?"

I could think of topics I'd much rather read up on than necromancy, but I wasn't about to say that. I smiled in agreement as I followed her down the stack, careful not to knock the trolley where she had parked it at the end of the aisle.

A little while later, I sat alone at a table near the main aisle, armed with a stack of books with titles like *Blood Magic Unveiled*, *The Necromancer's Codex*, *Arcane Revenants*, *Bloodmancy for Beginners*, and, my personal favorite, *Soulbound Secrets: The Art of Making Friends and Influencing Spirits*.

That last one sounds promising, Orcades said, as I flipped through the books. *I like the sound of that.*

Aren't we already friends? I teased. *Or should I be worried?*

Oh, darling, Orcades replied. *You're my daughter and I love you, but you're sadly lacking in finesse when it comes to dealing with souls. That's all I'm saying.*

I bit my tongue and flipped the book open, trying to settle back into the hushed ambiance of the library.

But the silence was abruptly disturbed by a burst of laughter.

I glanced up from the book, my attention distracted by insistent, high-pitched giggles.

My heart sank as the source soon became clear.

Blake Drakharrow was walking up the center aisle. He was flanked by a girl who clung to his side, her arm draped possessively around his narrow waist.

Regan.

She giggled loudly again and I flinched as the grating sound echoed off the walls. Regan tossed her glossy silver hair around her shoulders. Her face was lit up with a smile that looked too practiced to me, as if she were putting on a show for anyone watching.

Blake's eyes met mine and he smirked, as if he were enjoying the spectacle he and Regan were making.

As they passed by my table, Regan turned her head slightly and shot me a glance that was icy and dismissive.

My cheeks flushed with irritation.

I tried to redirect my focus back to the books in front of me, but the disruption had left a sourness in the air.

For the next few minutes, I flipped angrily through book after book, trying to find something that didn't involve simply summoning a spirit or putting a soul into a cat or dog or another person but instead would get a soul out of someone. Preferably without killing them in the process. Or losing the soul.

But from everything I read, summoning a soul and even imbuing a soul into another living creature was one thing. But giving such a spell permanence was another. Usually the soul summoning only lasted a short time and when the soul faded away back out past the veil into wherever souls went, the creature it had inhabited usually didn't survive.

Well, that's disheartening, Orcades observed.

You can say that again. I closed the book glumly. *Did you ever stop and think that entering me might kill me in the process?*

I was trying to keep you alive. I had absolutely no idea what the outcome would be. You know that, she chided. But her voice was gentle.

I know, I admitted. *It's just... disturbing. To think this new life might not even last.*

I don't feel my soul slipping away, if that helps, she assured me. *Perhaps none of these books are quite relevant to our situation. Whatever magic bound us together in the first place was something beyond necromancy. Especially as we were bound by love, not simply a necromancer's selfish desire for power.*

Were we? I asked, feeling oddly embarrassed by her mention of the word.

Why, of course we were, she said stolidly. *A mother's love is the most powerful thing in the universe. Why, to think there was a time when I didn't even think I could* love you.

You didn't...?

I was interrupted by Theo Drakharrow slinking up beside my table.

His cloak was pushed back around his shoulders and his hands were shoved deep in his pockets.

He looked uncomfortable. Anxious.

Good. That was how he should feel.

I stared up at him. "What do you want?"

"Medra." He chuckled nervously. "Looks like you found the library. Got enough books there?"

"Is this where you distract me so Regan can pull some nasty prank behind my back?" I said coldly. "I'm not interested in another chat, Theo."

"Look, about all of that..." He paused and glanced over his shoulder. "I was doing Regan a favor, but I don't like how that all turned out. I just wanted you to know that."

"Yet you played along quite well. Helped Regan ensure I'd be late for Professor Hassan's class and get reamed out," I pointed out.

"Well, yes," he said lamely. "But..."

"And you sure didn't seem to have any interest in stopping her when she made me climb that fucking dragon and almost kill myself," I continued.

"I've always wanted to climb one of those things, you know," Theo said. "You looked amazing up there. For a moment, anyhow."

"You mean before or after I roared like a lion and then plummeted off?" I rolled my eyes.

"I thought you were roaring like a dragon." He tried to hide a grin but not before I saw it. "Well, before that, obviously." He scratched his head. "Look, I just wanted to say that I know we got off on the wrong foot, but we're going to be in the same house eventually. The same family."

"No. Hell no," I said firmly. "I'm opting out. But what a fucked up little family it is."

He grinned lopsidedly. "I won't deny that. Anyhow, I like you, Medra. I mean, you can try to opt out but you might find that more of a challenge then you think. And if you are stuck with us, then I think we could get along."

I didn't say anything. Because the truth was, I liked Theo, too. At least, a little bit. In another world, maybe we could have been friends.

"You keep terrible company, Theo," I said at last. "Your friends are bullies."

"They can be," he admitted. "But they're fun, too. Sometimes. You don't know them like I do. We grew up together, and each of them..."

"Let me guess. Each of them has a different sob story that explains why they turned out so mean and nasty?"

He snorted. "Well, basically... yes."

"No excuse," I said bluntly. "We all have a sob story. It doesn't mean we should treat other people like shit."

"You're right," he said, a little sadly. "But... it can be hard to stop them once they get going."

I shook my head. "What did you come over here for? Are we through?"

"I wanted to apologize. I mean, I do apologize."

I leaned back and crossed my arms. "Does that mean you won't go along with any of their future nasty little plans for me? Or is this just the first of many 'apologies'?"

Theo winced. "The first and the only, I hope." He looked at me expectantly. "I also wanted to invite you to a party."

I stared. "A party?"

"Right. Almost every night, we party on the beach down below the castle. We have a big bonfire, drink some wine. It's a good time all around. You should come one night. We can talk more. I'd really like that." He smiled encouragingly.

"I...don't think so, Theo," I said slowly, shocked that he was inviting me in the first place. "Does Regan know you're over here inviting me?"

He looked obstinate. "She doesn't need to know."

"What about Blake?" I prodded.

He said nothing.

"I see," I said slowly. "Well, I'm not sure how fun it would be for me to come and hang out where I'm not wanted. But thanks for the invitation. I'm sure we'll see each other around."

"Lots of people come. It's not just House Drakharrow," Theo said stubbornly. "Well... I'll keep an eye out for you." He leaned down and dropped his voice. "There's a staircase by the Advanced Weaponry courtyard. You take that all the way to the bottom. Then exit out onto the beach. From there you should be able to find us. Feel free to come by one night."

I nodded. "Sure. We'll see." But I knew I wouldn't be joining him.

As Theo walked away, I plonked my head down onto my pile of books with a groan.

I'd found nothing useful and it was past six o'clock. My stomach was growling. But I hadn't even opened Professor Rodriguez's book on dragons since that first day.

I told myself I'd at least get through a few chapters. And then dinner.

I wondered if snacks were allowed in the library. If so, I'd be able to get a lot more done next time. I could stay until midnight. But as I glanced around, I spotted a large sign in bold letters that read "Absolutely No Food or Drink!" Below it, in smaller letters, someone had scrawled, "Yes, That Means Even Highbloods. You Will Be Banned."

Somehow I doubted the sign would be enough to stop Blake and Regan's crew. I suddenly pitied the poor Bloodwing librarians, having to deal with all of the rich and privileged highblood students.

Hands slammed down on the table and I jumped.

"What the hell, Blake?" I said angrily as I glared up at him.

A grin slowly formed on his face in a way that made goosebumps form on my arms. "Just trying to keep you on your toes, Pendragon. Just checking if those rider reflexes are any good."

"You know they are." I tried to look more cocky than I felt. "Just go and ask Visha."

He laughed.

I glanced around. "Aren't you forgetting something? Like your accessory?"

"Accessory?" He looked at me blankly.

"Regan," I said pointedly. "Aren't you two attached at the hip?"

"Oh, you saw that, did you? She can't seem to get enough of me." He leaned down until his face was close to mine. "Jealous?"

I pushed my chair back so we were further apart and crossed my arms over my chest. "You wish. The sight of you makes me want to vomit. With or without your arm candy."

He leaned back against the table, then gestured to all of the books in front of me. "What are you reading about, anyhow?"

"Just researching ways to kill you," I said sweetly. "Vampire Murder Methodology 101."

He scowled. "You shouldn't joke about that."

"Why not?" I demanded. "Because only highbloods are allowed to murder blight-born?"

"No one's murdering anyone," he protested. "You need to lighten up."

I rolled my eyes. "Right. Because you'd have actually cared if Visha had stabbed me to death right in front of you. Or if Regan had killed me when I jumped off that stone dragon."

He narrowed his eyes. "You're exaggerating. You were fine. Besides, Professor Sankara showed up in time. As for Regan, the headmaster stopped her. She knew that would happen. It's not as if she..." He trailed off awkwardly.

I smiled. "Exactly. Don't bother denying that she would have loved to see me die yesterday."

He grabbed the book closest to me before I could stop him.

"Serpents of the Sky: A History of Dragons," he read aloud, before I could grab the book back. He sniggered. "What is this? Homework?"

"Professor Rodriguez gave it to me," I said coolly. "Now give it back."

He dropped the book onto the desk with a thud and stood up. "The only thing left of the dragons are those stone statues. So what's the point? They're ancient history."

"Then why am I here?" I said, meeting his gaze.

And in that moment, I realized I really did want an answer.

"Why am I here?" I repeated. "Why was I brought here?"

"To Bloodwing Academy?" He frowned, looking confused.

"To this world," I hissed. "To you." I shook my head. "Never mind. Never fucking mind. You know nothing. Just like everyone else."

He took a step away from the table, then paused. "You should be glad the dragons are gone," he said quietly. "You think we're bad? The highbloods? They were even more brutal."

I met his eyes steadily. "Maybe that's exactly what this place needed. Balance. Something to keep you in check."

He said nothing. Simply turned and walked away.

I went back to my book, *Serpents of the Sky*, this time more eagerly than before.

Brutal were they?

Suddenly I wanted to learn everything I could about the creatures Blake Drakharrow deemed worse than vampires.

BOOK 2

CHAPTER 14

BLAKE

A few days earlier...

I slammed the double doors open, hearing them crash against the walls with a satisfying bang.

"What did you just do?" I roared as I stalked towards the long table where my uncle and brother were already seated.

My brother rose to his feet, nervously glancing across the table at my uncle.

"Back the fuck off, Blake," Marcus said. "There's no need to act like a barbarian."

"A barbarian?" I seethed. "A barbarian? Yet you had no qualms about betrothing me to one today, Uncle. We know nothing about this girl or where she really comes from. For all we know, one of the other houses planted her there themselves."

I glared down at the ancient vampire who sat staring up at me calmly from eyes as red as blood.

Viktor Drakharrow led our house. Even before that, he had been a force to be reckoned with as my father's strongest and most brutal general.

"There is no way one of the other houses would have sat on a secret like that for so long. Or that they would have parted with that girl so easily. You always knew you'd be assigned a second consort," Viktor replied quietly. "You have a little..." He gestured to his face.

I wiped at my face, my cheeks flushing. There at the corner of my lips. A few spots of blood. I brushed them away.

"Feed in a frenzy, did we, Brother?" Marcus laughed. "How unlike you."

"Shut the fuck up, Marcus," I spat. "I'd been out on campaign for days. I was hungry."

"Of course you were," Viktor said soothingly. "And you deserved to feed. Just as we all do."

I'd grabbed a House Drakharrow thrall on my way into the Black Keep. There was a group of them always around, always available. Viktor made sure of that. I didn't like to use them, but this time I'd been desperate.

Of course, with Marcus around, they didn't last long. This one had been pretty, too. I doubted I'd see that poor woman again.

I settled into a seat further down the table and crossed my arms over my chest. I knew I was being petulant. I couldn't help it. This wasn't how I'd expected my day to go.

When I'd found the woman–Medra Pendragon–I'd thought she'd be a fine prize for my house, certainly. But my future bride? No. I hadn't anticipated Viktor's play. But I knew I should have.

"You both know there is nothing I wouldn't do to maintain House Drakharrow's ascendancy," Viktor said, leaning forward. "I know you may believe I acted rashly today, Blake. Perhaps you even fear I do not have your best interests at heart. Nothing could be further from the truth." He paused. "What you brought back–what you found–was the greatest gift you could have given to your house. Perhaps the most significant discovery made in the last century."

I caught Marcus scowling. The bastard was jealous. Good.

I took a deep breath, trying to quiet my anger. "You really think she's important?"

Viktor exchanged a glance with my brother. "I know we don't want her getting into the hands of our enemies, that's for certain. You heard what they said."

I frowned. "Lady Avari was itching to get near the girl."

Viktor nodded. "And Lord Mortis. You heard him. Now the question is, do you think either spoke the truth?"

I glanced at my brother then back at Viktor. "You think they wanted us to destroy her?"

"Lady Avari? Yes. Absolutely. She believed I would. But first she wanted to plant the idea of the girl being an omen in the minds of the others."

"So that when you killed her, they'd question the wisdom of your decision," I guessed. Viktor nodded.

"And Lord Mortis?"

"Perhaps he thought I would suggest we wed the rider girl to one of his younger sons as an experiment." My uncle smiled. "I doubt he was expecting me to do what I did."

"No," I said, glaring at him. "I doubt he expected you to use me as your pawn. But then, that's what we all are to you, aren't we, Viktor?"

Viktor frowned. "We all work for the good of our house."

"If you don't want the girl, I could take her off your hands, Brother," Marcus said with a leer. "That hair. It's quite unusual. I wouldn't mind wrapping my hands in it. Do you think she looks like blightborn women in other ways? Or is everything about her different? Right down to her..."

"She's mine," I snarled. "You'll keep your fucking hands off her."

"Oh, ho. The little lion cub doesn't want to share." Marcus laughed and put his hands up.

"Stop it, you two," my uncle said absent-mindedly, rubbing his temple.

"You could have wed her to Marcus. Why didn't you?" I demanded. Though if Pendragon thought I was bad, she'd have been in for a real shock with Marcus.

"I wouldn't have minded getting some of that rider pussy," Marcus agreed. "I could have made her beg for some highblood cock. And we wouldn't have had to wait so long to seal the bond either. I'd have made sure of that."

"Enough." My uncle slammed his hands down on the table. "Blake, you know I have other plans for Marcus. Once he has learned, that is, to show some *fucking restraint*." He practically screamed the last words.

My brother and I both flinched.

Marcus had already had two consorts.

But he'd killed one. They'd been sisters. Twins. Daughters from a minor house. Marcus had become obsessed with them and taken both to mate without my uncle's permission. He'd been... severely chastised. As had both women.

The surviving sister was back at Drakharrow Manor now, our family's main estate.

She hated my brother, of course, so their connection was weak. She brought him neither power nor honor. I doubted she'd defend him in a fight. She'd been a mistake.

Just like Medra Pendragon was for me.

I knew Viktor hoped to mate Marcus with either Catherine Mortis or, failing that, Lunaya Orphos.

But as Marcus had developed a bad reputation for recklessness and bloodshed, few wanted to risk their daughters. Even in exchange for a potentially powerful alliance with House Drakharrow.

"Lord Mortis will never allow Catherine to become Marcus's consort," I pointed out. "She's too valuable for that."

"Chances are she'll take her father's place as the head of House Mortis," Viktor agreed. "But nothing is set in stone. Still, Lunaya Orphos would be a fine second choice."

"The girl's not even right in the head," Marcus complained. "I don't want an idiot for a wife."

"I'd have thought that would make her perfect for you," I quipped.

Marcus snarled.

In truth, I'd have hated to see Lunaya Orphos forced to marry my brother. She'd always seemed like a sweet and quiet girl. The exact sort that Marcus would walk all over.

"Let's focus on the Pendragon girl," my uncle said. "You'll keep her on a short leash, Blake. The binding ritual in the Black Keep was but the first step. Still, the girl doesn't need to know that."

"We could have learned more about her and more quickly by sampling her ourselves," Marcus complained. "Why not bring her here now?"

"You really are an ignorant fuckwit, aren't you, Marcus?" I said, rolling my eyes.

"You're my heir, Marcus, but your brother is right," Viktor said, looking as if he were on the verge of losing his temper again. "Do you know so little about riders and their blood?"

Marcus gave a sullen shrug. "I don't know what you're talking about."

"Only one highblood can taste her and truly benefit from it," I said, leaning forward. "And it won't be you, Marcus."

"Blake is right. We don't want to dilute her power. The potential it has is too great to waste. If we're right that is. If she's really a rider." My uncle gazed out the nearby window. "If she is... Then she may give me the opportunity I've been looking for."

I looked at my uncle covertly. There were no dragons. And yet he refused to stop acting as if this girl's appearance actually meant something.

"Her blood will be useful at least," I conceded. "I don't see how she's important beyond that."

But I also knew my uncle had tricks up his sleeve that he would never tell us about.

"Why give Blake such powerful blood?" Marcus demanded. "Why not me, uncle?"

"Because it's a fucking double-edged sword, you big imbecile," I snapped.

My uncle looked at me. "You've paid more attention to your history lessons than Marcus has, I see."

I stood up. "I have. And I know just what you've done. Don't think I don't." Suddenly my fury welled up. "This would never have been allowed to happen if my father were alive."

Viktor rose from his seat. "You dare to say that to my face. When all I have ever done is try to hold this family together?"

"What you've done is tried to consolidate power. Hold this family together?" I gave a sharp barking laugh. I was taking a risk, speaking to him like this, and I knew it. Still, I couldn't seem to stop myself. "I'm not so sure about that. How is my dear mother doing, anyhow, Uncle? Have you had any word from her since she retreated to the Sanctum? Because I have not."

"When she chooses to speak to us, she will do so. I have no control over that, Blake," my uncle replied coldly.

The Bloodmaiden's Sanctum. Only a few women were ever granted access to the most sacred temple in Sangratha.

When my father had died, my mother had announced her intentions to retreat from the world for a time.

We hadn't seen her since.

She'd been one of the most powerful women in Sangratha. Now she was simply...gone.

"Speaking of family loyalty, Blake," my uncle said. "You need to get your pup on a leash."

"He means Aenia," Marcus said, sneering. "Get the little bitch in check or we'll have to put her down."

I felt myself exploding.

I couldn't even remember moving but suddenly I was across the room with my hands around my brother's throat.

"Don't you ever dare threaten our *sister* again, Marcus. Don't you dare."

"Let him go, Blake," my uncle commanded. "Drop him. Now."

I dropped him just as I'd been instructed to. Marcus fell to the floor gasping.

"You bastard," he choked out. "Fucking bastard."

"If you harm a hair on Aenia's head, there will be hell to pay when Mother returns," I warned Marcus.

"Enough, Blake," my uncle said. "You took responsibility for the girl."

"I haven't forgotten," I said sourly.

"Good. Then deal with her. Before she becomes an embarrassment to our family. Or worse, a menace."

I nodded tightly, and began to turn away.

"And as for Theo..." My uncle continued.

I stopped. "What about Theo?"

Theo Drakharrow was my aunt's son and my closest friend.

"I've heard some disturbing news about your cousin," Viktor said.

For a moment, my heart sank. Was Theo considering vying with me for the house leadership? I imagined having to kill my cousin. The thought filled me with revulsion and horror.

"I've heard Theo has been embarrassing House Drakharrow again. Engaging in...disturbing liaisons."

"Are you fucking kidding me right now?" I exclaimed. "Marcus literally kills his own consort, but you're worried about Theo embarrassing you because he likes to sometimes fuck other men? The other houses don't have a stick up their ass about it so why do you?"

"The other houses might condone such unnatural liaisons. We are not the other houses," Viktor said coldly.

"No," I spat. "We're certainly not."

House Orphos mandated that their house leader take a male and a female consort. Such triads were believed to make their leader stronger. House Mortis left such decisions to the individual. I knew Catherine Mortis preferred women, but suspected she'd be forced to take at least one male consort—at the very least, for breeding purposes. Still, that didn't mean anyone batted an eye to her penchant for running wild with women.

"Keep your cousin in line. Next thing you know he'll be pursuing his trysts with mortals," Viktor said coldly.

I took a deep breath, trying not to point out the miniscule distinction between the average blightborn who Viktor so evidently disdained and the dragon rider blightborn he'd so freely betrothed me to.

"Disgusting. Absolutely disgusting," Marcus agreed, but I could see him trying to hide a nasty grin. He was baiting me, hoping I'd snap again and draw Viktor's ire. "Absolutely no shame. No taste whatsoever."

"House Drakharrow rises above all other houses," Viktor lectured. "Do not forget this. We surpass them because we are more restrained. Because we are superior."

"You'd think we'd only mate with members of House Drakharrow then," I said coldly. "Like in the good old days."

"When sister married brother? Do not think I have not given it consideration," my uncle said, eying me with a frosty gaze. "Perhaps in the future, we will go back to those old ways, just as you suggest."

"If we're through here, I'd like to get back to Bloodwing," I said. "That is, if you have no further demands of me."

"Marcus can deal with Theo if you don't, Blake," Viktor said, not breaking his gaze. "But I don't think you'd like his methods."

Marcus cracked his knuckles. "A warning might be all our cousin needs. Let me do it my way."

"No," I said, clenching my jaw. "I'll deal with it. I'll take care of them both. Aenia and Theo. Leave them to me."

Viktor nodded. "Good. You're a good nephew, Blake. You both are. Together, this family will be the leaders this realm requires. Stay loyal by my side. Watch and learn."

I nodded. "Always, uncle."

I left the room, my heart beating fast.

Viktor was the most dangerous man I'd ever met, while Marcus was simply a menace.

Medra Pendragon had no idea what a close call she'd had. If she thought I was a monster, wait until she got to know my brother.

No, better that she never had the opportunity.

CHAPTER 15

MEDRA

Two Weeks Later

Bloodwing Academy was a beautiful enigma.

The more I wandered through its maze-like halls, the more I felt as if I were falling in love with the old castle's strange allure. Many of my fellow students were brutal, but there was somehow serenity here, too.

Passing through a corridor, I could glance out a tall, arched window and be greeted by the sight of the sea, wild and silver under an autumn sky.

On my way to class, I might pass through a courtyard filled with towering trees, like none I'd ever seen before in Aercanum, their branches twisted and ancient, creating canopies of gold and red against the sky. I'd already come to love walking beneath those trees, smelling the crisp air that carried the scent of damp earth, wood smoke, and fallen leaves, each step crunching pleasantly under my boots.

The castle's nooks and crannies seemed endless. But it was this very quality I was coming to adore. Though the academy's size was intimidating and I'd run across more than one fellow First Year looking lost and wild-eyed, I was starting to take an odd comfort in its labyrinthine nature. It was as if the building itself was inviting me to unravel its mysteries.

Two weeks had passed since my arrival in Sangratha. Two weeks since I'd become a student at Bloodwing.

I'd made some notes for my essay on dragons, but hadn't really started writing yet. Still, the more I learned about the ancient beasts, the more grateful I was that there were none left alive.

Dragons had a reputation for brutality. Left unchecked, they would kill and feed as voraciously as a highblood, if not more so. Their appetites were vast. Keeping dragons had been an expense only the most elite houses could maintain.

The relationship between dragons and their riders seemed precarious to me. The dragons were possessive and passionate about their riders. But they could also turn on them in an instant. The death of a rider was as likely to happen at the hands of their own dragon than another. Dragons were prickly creatures, easily offended, selfish and demanding.

The relationship between riders, dragons, and highbloods was similarly fraught. Riders tethered the dragons to the vampires. They were the only thing that had kept the dragons in check. When a rider fell, their dragon's loyalty to a highblood house could not be guaranteed until the dragon had agreed to bond with a new rider of the same house.

There were many stories of highblood houses having to fight and kill their own dragons that had gone berserk.

And still other stories of highblood houses that had fallen entirely because they'd been unable to overcome their own dragon's might. Those were my favorite.

As for my sessions with Professor Rodriguez in thrallguard, it turned out that learning how to block thrallweave was as exhausting as a combat class. If not more so.

"You've been granted the right to train in something most vampires themselves never master," Professor Rodriguez had explained at our first session. "Most highbloods assume the ability to block is innate. Some are capable of it, some are not."

His dark hair fell across his brow as he leaned forward, his eyes sharp and focused. "The art of thrallguard has ancient roots. Some historians claim the skill originated with mortals in the first place and not vampires at all. That's the most believable explanation to me."

I shifted in my chair, feeling anticipation and trepidation. "What do you mean?"

"Mortals have always had the most to fear from vampires, no?"

"I'd say so," I muttered.

He smiled slightly. "We're weaker in most ways. But even so, every mortal has the potential for magic, no matter how miniscule. At some point, a mortal developed their defenses and was able to block thrallweave."

"I expect the vampires didn't like that," I speculated.

"No," he agreed. "The mortal who first discovered how to block thrallweave may have been severely punished. But not before they passed on the skill to someone else."

"And eventually the vampires took credit for it entirely?" I suggested.

He nodded.

I suspected this was heresy. Something Rodriguez wouldn't dare to say to a highblood's face. But here he was, daring to say it to me.

"Eventually, vampires made the skill their own. Dragon riders were the only mortals permitted to learn it."

"Why?" I demanded, leaning forward. "Why them?"

"I should think it would be obvious. Because they held the key to the realm's most valuable weapon. A weapon that the highbloods themselves were never able to wield, to their perpetual frustration and fury. Dragons. A vampire could never control a dragon."

"But if a vampire could control a rider, they essentially had a way in," I guessed.

"Exactly. Now, you might think this would be an excellent thing. A way for a house to control a dragon via their rider. But the houses have long been in bloody competition with one another. So having a rider open to the coercion of other houses was a weakness. Imagine a rider soaring above on an incoming attack, only to be turned away because someone down below was powerful enough to enthrall them. So, long ago, it was agreed that those chosen to ride would be trained to shield their minds, in order to protect their mounts and their Houses." Rodriguez passed, watching me. "The mind is a delicate thing. Even vampires with all their power and skill can be vulnerable to thrallweave."

"How vulnerable?" I demanded. "Can it kill them?"

"It can kill a mortal, certainly. It's rare for a highblood to be able to kill another high-blood with thrallweave alone. But there are legends where it happens. Whether there's any truth to those stories..." He shrugged. "We're not here to practice thrallweave. We're here to protect your will. Thrallguard is a grueling skill to hone. There will be moments when you want to quit, when it feels like your mind is splintering from the strain. But you will endure."

"I will," I agreed, gritting my teeth.

Rodriguez looked amused. "You're eager to learn. That's understandable. I was as well."

I suddenly thought of something. "Did you attend Bloodwing, too? When you were young? Who taught you how to use thrallguard?"

He smiled pleasantly. "We aren't talking about me today. This is about you, Miss Pendragon."

Still, I wondered if he had, wondered if Rodriguez had been bullied by highbloods just like what was happening to me. That would explain why he'd worked to hone his ability in thrallguard.

"Unlike in a combat class, thrallguard is not about physical strength," Rodriguez went on. "It's about mental resilience which is, arguably, even more important. You need to be warned—the process can be...invasive."

I nodded, feeling a tremor of unease.

"I'm going to test your defenses today. The process isn't particularly gentle. But I'll try not to push you too far." He rose and stood in front of me. "We'll start now."

Before I could even formulate a reply, I felt it—a sharp, sudden pressure against my mind, like someone forcing open a door I hadn't realized I'd left unlocked.

Panic washed over me. Regan. It was happening again.

My thoughts scattered as I instinctively tried to pull away. I gripped the armrests of my chair and leaned as far back as I could get, as if hoping that would be enough to stop the sensation.

But Rodriguez didn't stop. He pushed again and a wave of focused energy brushed up against my memories from earlier that same day—eating breakfast in the refectory, walking down the hallway towards class.

My heart raced as I suddenly realized what he might find if he looked a little longer. I scrambled, desperately trying to erect barriers, but his presence slipped through the cracks like smoke.

The pressure grew more invasive, more threatening, and I felt panic rise within me.

He was going through my memories. So far he had only sifted through recent ones. I felt him pushing through my days at Bloodwing, felt him peering into my memory of standing atop the black stone dragon, felt him feeling my fear, my terror.

"You're letting me in too easily," Rodriguez said. His voice sounded as if it was coming from far away. "You have to push back. Your mind is your own. Guard it with your life."

"I thought I *was* pushing back," I said through clenched teeth.

He sighed and I felt the mental pressure ease, disappearing as suddenly as it had begun. "Blocking someone from entering your mind isn't like swinging a sword or using brute force. It's about control. Subtle, precise control over your own thoughts. Think of it as the gradual building of a fortress. But this fortress can't be made of rigid stone. It has to be adaptable, flexible. Eventually, it can become impenetrable."

That was what I wanted. To become a fortress.

I frowned, curling my fingers in my lap. "But how? How do I even start?"

Rodriguez's expression softened slightly as if he sensed my fear. "It's going to take time. We'll start with a tactic I first learned. It's called mental partitioning. You'll learn how to separate your mind into different layers, creating barriers between your surface thoughts–between the ones you're okay with others seeing...."

I winced. There wasn't really anything in my head I wanted a stranger to see.

He saw my expression and smiled slightly. "I know. But just think how much worse it could be if I were someone else." He let the suggestion hang there.

I nodded firmly. "Right. I understand. I don't want you to go easy on me."

"That's the spirit," he said with a small smile. "Anyhow, mental partitioning. Creating a barrier between your thoughts. The ones you don't mind revealing and the ones you need to keep hidden." He shrugged. "We all have those, right? Eventually I might let you see what I had for breakfast, too, Miss Pendragon."

He grinned and I smiled weakly.

I wasn't sure what I'd been expecting, but I hadn't anticipated it being this difficult. This... invasive. I could still feel the echo of Rodriguez's presence in my mind, a reminder of how easily he'd been able to slip past my weak defenses.

My non-existent defenses.

My stomach churned. What if this wasn't training? What if this was real? If it was someone trying to harm me or, worse, trying to force me to harm myself or someone else again? My mind flashed back to Regan, to how helpless and violated I'd felt.

A tremor of resentment flared through me. I knew Professor Rodriguez was doing this for my own good, but the potential he had to tear through my mind, to search for every vulnerable thought, left me feeling raw and exposed. I hated it. I hated how easily my weaknesses could be discovered, no matter how I tried to hide them.

Rodriguez had been waiting. When I nodded that I was ready to continue, he gestured for me to close my eyes.

"Imagine your mind as a space. An open field, let's say. Now start constructing layers. These will be the partitions. The first layer should hold nothing of importance. Your recent thoughts, trivial memories. These are the decoys. Eventually, I'll only sense what lays behind them if you want me to."

I closed my eyes, trying to picture my mind the way he described it. It felt strange, unnatural. But as I focused, I began to form a mental wall. It was thin, like a piece of paper, hardly a wall at all. But it was a start.

"Good," Rodriguez said. He was trying to be encouraging. "Now, I'm going to attempt to push past that first layer. When you feel me approaching, I want you to reinforce it. Don't just let me through."

I tensed up. There it was again. Like a soft knock against the edge of my mind. His presence was there, probing, but not forceful. Not yet. It was a gentle push, like someone testing the strength of a door.

I flinched, instinctively wanting to pull away, but instead I focused on my wall, adding another piece of parchment, then another. I imagined it thickening, reinforcing it with iron bars, holding it firm.

"That's it," Rodriguez said. "Keep building your wall. Feel the pressure. Don't let it crack."

The pressure increased slightly, but the wall held. My heart was pounding but I also felt a small bloom of pride.

Rodriguez spoke again. "Good. We'll stop there for today." He paused. "I could push your wall down if I tried, but I'm not going to do that."

My sense of pride plummeted. "Okay. Thank you...I guess?"

He nodded. "I'm not going to take it easy on you. But this is just the beginning. It takes time and practice. You'll need to learn to disguise the partitions. After all, if someone senses a wall, they'll know there's something behind it you don't want them to see."

"So what do I do?" I asked, opening my eyes, and feeling frustrated once more.

"You need to appear ordinary. Your thoughts should seem like an open book–but only the pages you want someone to read. Everything else should be hidden, masked by false thoughts." He paused, as if searching for the right words. "It's about constructing a new reality. A new you. A believable one. You'll need to practice disguising your true intentions. Sometimes, it's not just about stopping someone from entering your mind but about making them think there's nothing worth searching for in the first place."

This was another level of thrallweave's power I hadn't even considered before. Regan hadn't been interested in my memories. She'd just wanted to control me. But if she'd gone searching? There was no way I'd have been able to stop her.

Right now, I was an open book.

Just like all of the other blightborn students.

But I doubted any of them had come here from another world.

"I know what you're thinking," Rodriguez said, watching me. "We'll work on the compulsion aspect of thrallweave, too. That's what Miss Pansera used with such blunt force the other day. But let's start slow. Thrallguard training can be, well...intense."

My stomach tightened. This was more complex than I could have imagined. Yet deception was my forte, wasn't it? After all, I was here. They didn't know what I truly was, not who I truly was, not really.

"What do I do next time?"

"You'll start by practicing simple distractions. Next time we meet, I'll push harder, and you'll need to throw some false memories and thoughts in my path. Anything to divert attention. It's like leading someone down the wrong corridor in a maze." He paused. "But for now, let's just work on building that first layer. Keep it firm, focus on controlling what I see."

I nodded and stood up. I felt weak and shaky. And Rodriguez hadn't really even let loose on me. Not like he could have.

"This is going to take time," he said, leaning back in his chair. "But you have potential. I wouldn't have offered to teach you if I thought you didn't. Once you truly master this, no one will be able to touch your mind again. Unless you want them to."

I couldn't imagine ever wanting that. I nodded my thanks. But as I left the room, my mind was racing and the feeling of vulnerability lingered.

The more we practiced, the more of a chance Professor Rodriguez would have of seeing my most painful, private memories.

And if he got too close, if anyone did, I wasn't sure what would happen.

The following weeks were grueling. Professor Rodriguez didn't ease up. Each session, his attacks grew a little stronger and my wall fell over and over.

The only good thing was that he seemed to have forgotten about the essay I was supposed to be writing. Maybe he'd taken pity on me. Though I was sure it was temporary.

Some nights, after a particularly intense session, I'd lie awake, thinking about how easily Rodriguez could get into my mind. Or any other highblood, for that matter.

It was like my grandfather all over again. Reaching for me, grasping, taking from me what didn't belong to him. My memories. My life.

Eventually a night came where I was exhausted. But there was only so long I could stay inside.

Brooding and melancholic, I paced the First Year common room, trailing my finger along the window ledges.

Back in Camelot, I'd have gone for a ride with Odessa. I'd have galloped my horse hard, felt the wind in my hair. But here, I had no horse. Nowhere to go. So far as I knew, even the exits to Bloodwing were guarded. We weren't permitted to visit the city.

A spark of light down below the castle caught my eye. A fire, down on the beach.

Theo's party.

I glanced across the room at where Florence sat scribbling on parchment. Books lay open in a semi-circle all around her and she seemed to be reading from two or three simultaneously. Naveen had gone to bed already.

But I was restless. There was a fire in my blood tonight and I couldn't seem to quell it.

I glanced down at the bonfire again, then made up my mind.

CHAPTER 16

MEDRA

"This was a terrible idea," Florence moaned as she walked behind me across the sand.

We had no idea what students wore to these parties, but I'd made a point of finding some clothes that *weren't* branded with the school motto. Bad enough that I already wore it day in and day out in class.

I'd pulled the dress I was wearing out of the wardrobe in my room. The dresses and gowns seemed to be the only pieces of clothing that weren't stamped with "Sanguis et Flamma Floreant." The bodice was a tight-fitting corset, made of black leather that laced up the front with crimson thread. The sleeveless design left my arms bare. The skirt hit just above the knee and flowed out from my waist in soft, layered folds of black tulle. It was a little more sultry than I was used to, but it was also dark and broody...which fit my restless mood just fine this evening.

Florence, on the other hand, had chosen a look much more like her day-to-day one. She wore a white button-up shirt embroidered with the Bloodwing crest and a skirt of dark gray. Overtop, she'd pulled a dark blue cloak, even though the night was warm and she didn't need one.

She looked studious and, well, like a librarian. But I didn't tell her that. She was already being bold by coming out with me in the first place. If she was comfortable, that was all that mattered.

Not that either of us were actually comfortable. But as we'd gotten dressed, we'd drunk enough wine to make us temporarily brave.

The night was warm and muggy. The salty scent of the sea drifted on the breeze.

In the distance, we could see a large bonfire flickering, casting an orange glow over the sand as its light reflected off the crashing waves.

High above us, Bloodwing Academy loomed, the castle's towers silhouetted against the starry sky. Even from this distance, I could make out the tips of the stone statues, high above in the Dragon Court.

I tripped in the soft sand and let out a curse.

Bending down, I yanked off the boots I was wearing and dropped them in the sand, making a mental note of where I left them in relation to where we'd just come.

The sand was cool between my toes.

"Much better," I said with satisfaction.

Florence said nothing, just wrapped her cloak more tightly around herself.

"Are you cold?" I asked, feeling guilty. I'd had to convince her to come.

"I'm not sure I should have come," she said nervously. "Theo Drakharrow invited you, not me. I'm an uninvited guest."

"You're *my* guest," I said loyally. "If they don't want you there, we'll leave. But I don't think it's going to matter. Theo made it sound as if it was a big party every night on the beach." I shrugged. "Maybe they always invite a lot of blightborns."

Florence shook her head. "I don't know, Medra. Highbloods and blightborns don't usually, well, party together. We might work side by side and be close colleagues, but we don't really socialize except on special occasions."

I raised my eyebrows. "Well, maybe it's time that changed. Theo obviously thinks so."

"Theo is a bit of an outlier, even among his own group," Florence said, echoing my impression of him. "I just hope..." She trailed off.

"What?" I stopped walking. "You hope he isn't pranking us?"

She nodded, looking uncomfortable.

"Fair enough." I took a deep breath. "Maybe this was a bad idea. We can go back."

The wine we drank had left us nicely buzzed but now the effects were fading.

"No." Florence shook her head stubbornly. "Don't listen to me. I'm being silly. We should go. I should be honored that you thought of inviting me."

I laughed and put my arm through hers. "Now you're truly being silly. You're my friend. Who else would I invite? I would have invited Naveen, too, if he wasn't asleep already. I'm just glad you were brave enough to come along."

"Speaking of bravery..." Florence bent down and reached under her skirt.

"Florence!" I said in delight as she pulled out a metal flask. "You naughty girl."

"I had it strapped to my thigh," she said, giggling. "I read about a girl doing it in a book once."

"Just what kinds of books do you read for fun, Florence?" I opened the flask and took a swig, then sputtered. Rum. Strong stuff, too.

Florence took the flask back and downed some of the rum. Her eyes sparkled with mischief.

Better. Much better.

"Who knows what will happen tonight?" I said playfully. "Perhaps we'll find you a..." I paused. "Boy? Girl? I'm not sure what your preferences are. I never even thought to ask if you had a sweetheart already."

Even in the starlight, I could tell she was blushing wildly. "I'm not. I mean, I don't. I mean..." She took a breath. "I've never had a boyfriend. Not really. But boys. Men, I mean. I think I prefer men." She looked at me dubiously. "Though they are awfully stupid at times."

We both burst out laughing.

"Absolutely," I agreed. "But there's just something about them..."

We sighed and kept walking across the beach, still arm in arm.

"Maybe we'll find you a nice boy at this party," I suggested. "Someone sweet who loves books and loves to study. Someone whose favorite place is the library."

Florence snorted. "Fat chance we'll find someone like that here."

"Hey, he might have a little wild side. After all, it turns out, so do you." I nudged her playfully. "That wouldn't be such a bad thing, would it?" I tried to wink at her but ended up blinking both my eyelids instead. We burst out laughing.

"Just how strong was that rum?" I managed to finally say, once I'd gotten my laughter under control.

But Florence had halted and was looking ahead of us with a dubious expression.

We'd reached the edge of the party. The bonfire light shimmered over the sand. If we took another step forward, we'd be within the circle of its glow.

"I don't see any other blightborns," Florence whispered.

I followed her gaze.

The party seemed to be in full swing. I could hear music and saw some highblood students dancing near the flames. Others lounged on the sand, sipping from flasks or bottles of wine.

The crowd around the bonfire was almost entirely vampires.

I scanned the group quickly a second time and realized there were in fact a few other mortals besides Florence and I.

But they seemed to be thralls.

They sat in the laps of highbloods or lay beside them in the sand, their necks tilted back, exposing their throats to the waiting mouths of the vampires who held them close.

I watched a dark-haired girl tip her head back as a highblood boy sank his fangs into her neck. The scene was both strangely seductive and deeply disturbing. She didn't resist. In fact, she seemed almost blissful, her eyes half-closed as the highblood boy drank his fill from her veins.

Sickened yet fascinated, I watched as the vampire slowly pulled away from her, his lips stained red with blood. The thrall's head lolled to the side, a faint smile on her lips.

My stomach turned. This is what we were to the highbloods in the end. This is all we were. *Food.*

I needed to make sure I never forgot that.

Even if Florence and I weren't thralls, we were still mortals in a world dominated by these creatures.

I felt the weight of danger. The sense of being *prey.*

We'd been wrong to come here.

I suddenly thought of Florence being enraptured and subdued by one of the highbloods and a chill crept up my spine. Would she be flattered to be chosen? Would she be *willing*?

How did the thralls even sustain friendships with other blightborns when they were in such parasitic relationships with vampires? Were they looked down upon? Or envied? There were so many questions I hadn't thought to ask, so many things about this world I realized I still didn't know. I knew it was an honor to be a student at Bloodwing. Was it an honor to be a thrall?

Florence seemed frozen by my side. She had seen the thralls, too. "I think some of them are sellbloods," she whispered.

"What's that?"

"They're..."

"Medra!" There was a high-pitched hoot of laughter.

For a second, I thought it was Theo. *Hoped* it was Theo.

My heart sank as I saw who was coming across the sand towards us.

"Fuck," I muttered.

Regan Pansera moved towards us with the grace of a cat. She wore a slinky dress of some half-sheer red material that hugged her slender form. Her hair was up in a high, sleek ponytail. She lifted one hand gracefully to tuck back a wayward silver strand, never taking her eyes off us.

She was smiling. Like a cat that'd found a mouse.

"I had no idea you'd be here tonight," Regan preened. "Oh, look, you've brought another little blightborn girl with you. Who is your friend?"

"Regan, meet Florence Shen," I said stiffly. "Florence, this is Regan Pansera."

"I know who you are," Florence said softly. "Pleased to meet you, Regan."

I could feel Florence's anxiety, her discomfort, and was racked with guilt for having brought her here. Why had I thought this might be fun? I'd been bored and restless, so I'd thought, why not?

But Regan Pansera was the "why not?"

The only consolation I had was that I hadn't seen Blake anywhere in the crowd.

"Who are you talking to, Regan?"

Three more highblood girls lurched towards us, rather unsteady on their feet. Clearly they'd had a lot to drink already.

One of the girls had blood rimming her mouth. She looked at me drunkenly. "Are these your new thralls, Regan?"

"My thralls?" Regan laughed sharply. "I should think not. You know House Drakharrow keeps its own thralls. The cleanest, most refined blood we can find. I have no need to keep my own."

The implication was that our blood was polluted somehow. Not pure enough for Regan to drink. I gritted my teeth but said nothing. Debating whether my blood would taste good to a highblood was not an argument I had any intention of getting into.

"But a thrall can bring other conveniences," one of the other girls purred. "Other pleasures. It's so easy when you have one bound to you. Waiting for you in your room at the end of each day."

Regan tossed her head. "Yes, well, I have Blake, don't I? I don't need some commoner to keep me warm."

I felt an unexpected wave of distaste at the idea that Blake was the one keeping her warm. Did he wait for her in her room after school, waiting to peel her slinky dress off?

I shifted on my feet, curling my toes into the sand.

One of the girls suddenly clapped her hands over her mouth. "By the Bloodmaiden. That girl's hair is red."

"Yes, her hair is red," Regan said testily. "Don't be such a dimwit, Larissa."

"I'm not," the girl called Larissa protested. Her eyes narrowed to slits. "I just meant that if her hair is red then this must be your co-consort. I've seen her around of course." Larissa continued to address Regan, not me. Apparently I didn't even warrant a direct interaction. She grinned slyly at Regan. "What a blessing it must be to have her by your side. A real dragon rider."

"Oh, yes, it's a blessing all right," Regan agreed, her voice dripping with contempt. "She's everything I could have wanted in a fellow consort."

The other girls were looking me up and down. I felt like a cow at an auction house. But at least they weren't bothering Florence.

"She's pretty, Regan. I didn't realize how pretty she was," said one of the other two girls slowly. There was a glint in her eye. I got the impression none of these highblood girls actually liked Regan, even if they were part of her social circle. "Stunning, really. No wonder Lord Drakharrow paired her with Blake."

The girl reached out a hand as if to touch my hair.

I slapped it away.

She laughed as if this was hilarious. "Oooh, prickly little bitch, isn't she? Well, you'll put her in her place, won't you?"

"She has a lot to learn about her place in the world, that's certainly true." Regan narrowed her eyes at me.

"I can't believe they actually paired you and Blake with a blightborn. I mean, really, what was Lord Drakharrow thinking? To mate his own nephew to..." The girl looked around furtively and dropped her voice. "A fucking barbarian. I mean, is her blood even clean? Have you tasted it?"

"Of course, I haven't fucking tasted her, Gretchen," Regan snapped. "I already told you that. Neither has Blake. She's off-limits. For now."

I felt anger rising inside. There was no way in hell either of them were ever tasting me. Ever. I'd die first.

"Neither of you will be getting a taste," I snapped. "In your dreams. I didn't ask to be made your stupid consort or to be betrothed to your asshole fiance. And if you think things are going to go even one step further, you have another thing coming."

The girls all stared at me.

"By the Blessed Blood, she really is ignorant, isn't she?" one of the girls whispered finally. "Is she... you know?" She tapped a finger against her temple. "All there? No wonder she climbed that dragon on the first day."

They all snickered, even Regan.

"She's practically an imbecile," Regan announced. "You know I adore and honor Lord Drakharrow. He's practically family to me, after all." Regan gave a long-suffering sigh. "But I can't help but feel he made a terrible mistake. Medra's no match for me and she's certainly no match for poor Blake." She looked me up and down. "She's blightborn trash. That's what she is. Refuse Blake saved from a garbage heap. She has no idea what she's doing. I suppose she's just grateful for the free food."

The other girls burst out laughing.

I opened my mouth in a fury, barely struggling against the urge to slap Regan full in the face.

"Medra! There you are!" It was Theo. He pushed his way between the girls, a broad smile on his good-looking face. "I was wondering if you'd ever show up one of these nights."

"*You* invited her here?" Regan hissed, looking back and forth between Theo and I.

Florence was acting like if she stayed quiet enough everyone might just think she was invisible. I didn't blame her.

"You have a lot of nerve, Theo," said Regan.

"Of course, I do," he said flippantly. "I'm a Drakharrow, aren't I?" He turned to me and slipped his hand in my free arm. "Come along now, Medra. Come along now, Medra's friend. Be welcome, be welcome."

"I'll tell Blake about this," Regan hissed as Theo started to pull us away. "It's an outrage. This is a private party. I started these bonfire nights in the first place. It wasn't your place to invite anyone."

"Oh, shut the fuck up, Regan," Theo said, sounding bored. "Who do you think told me to invite her in the first place?"

Even though I knew it must be a lie, I almost laughed as Regan's jaw dropped open.

"You're lying," she whined, her voice rising an octave. "You're such a liar, Theo."

"And you're such a vapid bitch," Theo snapped. "I pity my cousin for having to breed with you someday."

He tugged us away from Regan's furious wailing and towards a large log that had been set up on the other side of the fire where two highbloods were sitting.

Theo made a shooing motion. "Go, go. Find some place else to sit. My friends need this seat. Move along, thank you."

To my amusement, the highbloods did exactly that, hurrying away and finding a new place in the sand, where they looked back at Theo nervously.

Theo pulled Florence and I down onto the log, arranging one of us on either side of him.

"There," he said with satisfaction. "That's much better, isn't it? Beautiful night. Beautiful fire." He let go of our arms and fished inside his shirt. "Beautiful night for..." He pulled out a small glass bottle of a swirling, shimmering liquid. "A bit of ambrosia?" He grinned wickedly.

I had no idea what was in the bottle, but I caught Florence staring wide-eyed at the contents.

"Is that Crimson Ambrosia?" Florence asked.

"What is it?" I leaned forward, curious.

"Don't try it, Medra," Florence said immediately. "It has a completely different effect on mortals than it does on highbloods."

"That's not quite true," Theo countered. "Have you ever tasted it?"

When Florence said nothing, he raised his eyebrows. "Well, I have and I've associated with blightborn who have. It can be very pleasurable for both species."

"I don't have to try it to know that it's highly addictive," Florence said quietly. "It causes euphoria in highbloods," she explained, looking at me. "But in mortals, the euphoria's effects are compounded. It can cause hallucinations and make you even more susceptible to thrallweave."

I shuddered. "No, thank you." I looked around us. "In fact, after that last unpleasant encounter, I think we should go. Right, Florence?"

Florence looked relieved. "Sure. I wouldn't mind going back now. It's getting late."

Theo looked back and forth between us with an incredulous expression. "What are you girls talking about? You just got here. The night is young. You can't leave." His face turned serious. "Look, I understand, okay? Regan got her claws into you before I saw you. She's not the most hospitable."

I laughed hollowly. "You could say that."

"But you can't run from her. That's exactly what she wants you to do."

I bristled. "I'm not running."

"Seeing you leave when you just got here will make Regan very happy," Theo countered. "Besides, she's just jealous of you, Medra."

"Jealous?" I sputtered. "Of what? She clearly hates me."

"Of course, she hates you," Theo said, grinning. "She hates anyone who she thinks is a threat. Actually, she hates most everyone so that's not quite true. But you, she definitely sees as a threat. You should be flattered."

"Her life seems pretty perfect so I don't see how I'm a threat." I shrugged. "She knows I don't want her boyfriend and he certainly wants nothing to do with me."

"Blake wants nothing to do with Regan either so it sounds like you're all in the same boat," Theo said.

I shook my head. "No, that can't be true."

Theo glanced around to see if anyone was nearby. "Look, she and Blake are on the rocks."

I eyed him skeptically. "No way. I saw them in the library the other day. They looked like the perfect happy couple." I glanced across the fire at where Regan still stood. She was surrounded by a different group of highblood students now. She had regained her poise and seemed to be animatedly telling a story. The entire group around her was laughing. "They seem perfect for each other, too."

Perfectly awful.

"I know exactly what you must have seen, but believe me, it's all bullshit," Theo said. "Blake plays along because he has to. His uncle wants him to. But it's just for show." Under his breath, he half-muttered, "He's fucking miserable most of the time."

I was a little shocked but refused to show it. I wasn't going to show a smidgen of pity for Blake Drakharrow. So his betrothal to the most beautiful and popular highblood girl in the school wasn't going so well? As if he couldn't get out of the situation if he actually wanted to.

"Regan can't handle rejection though. She thinks she can actually make Blake want her," Theo went on.

I shrugged. "Maybe it'll work. After all, they seem to have a lot in common. They're both full of themselves, bigoted, and cruel. The perfect match."

"You don't know Blake as well as you think you do, Medra. He's my cousin. I grew up with him," Theo said. He shook his head, a little sadly.

"Next you're going to tell me he's not that bad," I said, my temper flaring. "He's an asshole, Theo. And honestly, you're not that much better in my books. I really don't know why we came."

"You came because I'm so charming," Theo said, shooting a winsome smile at me. "And it's a good thing you did, because who else is going to tell you all of the things you need to know?" He looked around covertly. "Look, you could get killed here, Medra. Believe it or not, I don't want that. I don't think Blake does either."

I felt a prickle of unease. "What things do I need to know?"

"Like what it really means to have Regan as an enemy," Theo said, his voice low. "It changes everything. Consorts are supposed to..."

Florence rose to her feet.

"Florence?" I asked.

She took one step across the sand, then another.

I rose to my feet and looked down at Theo. "I guess we're leaving. We'll have to talk another time."

"Medra..." Theo was watching Florence, a look of alarm on his face.

I glanced back at my friend. Florence was walking at a steady pace. She hadn't spoken or looked back at me since standing up.

And she was walking straight towards the bonfire.

CHAPTER 17

MEDRA

"Florence! Stop!" I shouted.

I ran towards her and stood in front of her, putting my hands on her shoulders and pushing gently.

But it was like going up against a wall. A moving wall that just kept coming.

Florence was surprisingly strong. I stumbled as she collided with me.

For a moment, she met my eyes and I saw the confusion there.

Then her eyes clouded. She tried to pull out of my grasp and step around me.

"Theo!" I called. "A little help here."

He was by my side in an instant, looking at Florence, his normally easygoing features marred by worry.

"Fuck," he said. "Someone's thrallweaving her."

I glanced around. Regan was still on the other side of the fire. She had her hand over her mouth and was laughing as she watched me try to stop Florence.

"Regan, so help me, if this is you, I will fucking kill you," I shouted over to her.

She put up both hands and shrugged, as if to say, "Not me."

Some of the other highbloods around her were looking at Florence and I with curiosity, but most looked bored. Clearly they'd seen this kind of thing before. None of them seemed about to take the credit.

I gritted my teeth. "Who is it, Theo? Can you stop them?"

Theo was scanning the crowd. I followed his gaze.

There. Further back from the bonfire, a group of students were sprawled in the sand laughing hysterically.

One of them pointed at Florence and said something. Their laughter grew even louder.

"Who the fuck is doing it?" I hissed. "Which one? Can you stop them?"

Florence was a weight, pushing against me, trying to pull out of my grasp. I doubted she was this strong normally. The thrallweave must have been making her exert herself beyond her limits. I wasn't sure how much longer I'd be able to hold her.

Just as I had that thought, Florence lifted her hands and, clasping my wrists, started to dig her nails into my skin.

I yelped. Her fingernails were sharp and she wasn't holding back.

"Florence," I begged. "Please. Stop. This isn't you. You're hurting me."

But looking at her face was like looking at a ghost. Florence wasn't there. She was gone.

Was this what I had looked like when Regan had been controlling me?

I felt furious and helpless. How could this be allowed? If I let go of Florence, I knew whoever was doing this was going to make her walk straight towards the bonfire. Would they let her walk right in?

"It's someone from Kage Tanaka's crew," Theo whispered to me.

Sure enough, I caught sight of a familiar face. The boy with blond, spiked hair who had tried to grab me in the hallway when I was with Blake.

"Kiernan," I shouted, remembering his name. "Leave her the fuck alone, you big bullying asshole!"

Kiernan leered in our direction, then said something to his friends who laughed even harder.

Florence pushed me, catching me off guard, then darted to one side.

"Shit!"

I moved to grab her but she was fast. She darted towards the bonfire and I caught her at the last moment, my hands wrapping around her wrist just as she'd nearly reached the flames.

I didn't want to hurt her, but I held her as hard as I could, terrified she'd manage to break away again.

Then, as quickly as it had started, Florence collapsed to the sand.

She looked up at me, her eyes unclouded, her expression dazed. "What happened?"

I looked over at Kiernan. Theo stood in front of him, a furious expression on his face. He was clearly telling the other boy off. Kiernan didn't look repentant whatsoever. But at least he'd stopped.

"We need to get you out of here," I said shortly. I didn't want to tell her what she'd almost done. Not until we were away from these people. "Now."

I linked my arm through hers tightly and started marching across the sand.

"Was that... Was it real?" Florence whispered.

I glanced at her. Tears were streaming down her face and she was biting her lip.

I was going to fucking kill Kiernan, I decided.

"Hey, don't leave so soon!"

It was Kiernan again. The spiky-haired boy was blocking our path.

"The fun's just getting started. House Avari wants you to come party with us." He gestured back at his group of friends and I saw Kage Tanaka had joined them. The tall boy stood at the back, his arms folded over his chest, watching us silently.

Kiernan leaned in towards me. "I have a very special invitation from Kage himself. We hear Blake's not making you feel very welcome in House Drakharrow. Well, we'd like to change that. Bloodwing can be a *very* welcoming place. If you know the right people."

I'd just opened my mouth to speak when Florence broke free from my grasp. With a choked sob, she flew across the sand back towards the castle.

"You fucking bastard." I shoved Kiernan, hard.

I was shaking with anger.

I didn't know what I was going to do. Only that I had to do something.

Kiernan looked surprised. Then he grinned. "Oh, so you like it rough, do you? So do I." He reached for my wrist but I was quicker than him. I raised my hand and slapped him, hard across the face.

Instantly I realized it had been the wrong move. My wrists were bleeding from where Florence had scratched me. My hand left a trail of blood across Kiernan's face.

Kiernan's eyes lit up strangely. He sniffed, then reached a hand up and touched his cheek. When his finger came away wet, he lifted it towards his mouth.

A gleam formed in his eyes. My breath caught in my throat as I watched him pause, his nostrils flaring slightly as he scented my blood.

"Don't," I started to say, my hand already lifting again to grab at his wrist and stop him.

A shadow darted between me and Kiernan, knocking me backwards.

"I thought I told you to keep your fucking hands off her," Blake snarled. I hadn't even seen him arrive. He'd come out of nowhere. "*You are not to taste her. She is mine.*"

I flinched as the words hit me with a power I'd never felt before. Thrallweave. He was using it on Kiernan.

"Wipe it in the sand," Blake growled, his voice dripping with fury. "Now."

Kiernan hesitated, his hand halfway to his lips. There was a flicker of fear in his eyes.

Slowly, he lowered his hand, his fingers trembling a little as he bent down and wiped his hand in the sand beneath our feet.

The fire crackled behind us, sending sparks into the night air. The sounds of the party had faded away.

Blake still didn't move. His body remained like a wall between Kiernan and I. His back was rigid and tense.

"You were warned once before." Blake's voice cut through the night air like a knife. "This is the second time you've come near her. Do anything like this again and there won't be a third."

Kiernan clenched his jaw, clearly fighting the urge to retort.

Finally, the boy took a step back.

Blake turned around to face me.

For a moment, I stood frozen, my heart racing. I could feel the dangerous energy radiating off him.

"You shouldn't be here." His voice was cold. But there was something else there, too. Something dark. Something possessive.

I stiffened as I remembered the words he had used.

My jaw tightened, fury and confusion warring in me. "I didn't ask for your protection. I can take care of myself."

Blake stepped towards me, the heat of his presence suddenly stifling. "It's not protection, little dragon. It's a claim." His gray eyes darkened as they flicked down to my exposed neck, an unspoken reminder hanging between us. "You're mine. No one touches what belongs to me."

My skin prickled. With anger and something else. Something I couldn't admit, even to myself.

A finger tapped me on the shoulder and I jerked, whirling around.

Kiernan. The idiot was still standing there.

"Kage wants her to join us," he said sullenly, as if reminding us he was still there. "I was just delivering the message."

The air seemed to freeze.

Blake stiffened instantly, his body taut once more. Slowly, he looked towards where Kage Tanaka stood, surrounded by his highbloods, watching the scene unfold with an unreadable expression, arms still casually folded as though this was all part of some private game where only he and Blake knew the rules.

I watched as something crossed Blake's face. His stormy gray eyes narrowed. The air around us seemed to grow heavier.

Without a word, he moved. One moment he was standing in front of me and the next he had whirled around, crossing the space between him and Kiernan like a flash of lightning.

His hand shot out, gripping the other highblood by the throat.

Kiernan's eyes widened, his terror showing as his feet left the ground.

My breath caught in my throat. "Wait," I started to say.

But it was too late.

With one swift, merciless motion, Blake hurled the other highblood into the bonfire.

Kiernan's scream was swallowed by the roar of the flames in an instant, his body engulfed in heat. For a split second, the flames surged and the smell of burning flesh tainted the air. Then anything that had been Kiernan was gone. Turned to ash. Consumed by the fire, as if he had never existed at all.

My heart was pounding. I stood there, frozen, staring at the fire.

Blake moved to stand beside me and I glanced up at him. But he wasn't looking at me. His eyes were fixed on Kage.

I looked across the fire.

The other house leader didn't look the least bit upset at the way Blake had snuffed one of his followers out of existence. If anything, Tanaka looked impressed. He raised an eyebrow in silent acknowledgement, then turned away.

I felt sick. Kage was enjoying the chaos he had sparked. The tension between the two men was palpable. There was a long rivalry here and somehow I'd gotten stuck right in the middle of it.

This was worse than Regan.

Blake had just fucking killed for me.

Maybe the worst part of it was... For a moment, I'd liked it. He'd done what I'd wanted to do.

Blake remained rooted in place, staring at the place Kage had been standing, before finally shifting his gaze down to me.

I watched his eyes and for the first time noticed the unfocused glaze. He'd been drinking. He was drunk or at least halfway there.

His eyes lingered on me, moving from my face slowly down my body.

A slow, lazy smirk spread across his handsome face.

"You look good tonight, Pendragon." His voice was low, almost amused. "I think I've changed my mind. You should stay. Enjoy the party."

My pulse quickened. The casual way he spoke after what he'd just done made my skin crawl.

He took a step closer, his tall frame towering over me.

His hand moved, as if he was about to touch my waist.

Instinct flare, quicker than thought, and in a heartbeat I had a knife in my hand–drawn from my corset, from the hidden sheath between my breasts.

The cold steel was pressed against Blake's throat before his hand could reach me.

His eyes widened, ever so slightly, surprise flickering over his face.

Then his smirk widened. My heart sank.

But still, I leaned in, spitting the words with a venomous intensity. "I'll never be yours, Blake Drakharrow. Ever. If you're looking for a girl who will do what you want, you won't find her here. Remember that."

For a heartbeat, the world stood still around us. The fire crackled from afar, casting shadows across Blake's pale face. I spotted the curling swirls of his tattoos rising up from the open collar of the white shirt he wore and I tried not to think about that day I'd first seen them, the way he'd moved, the way his body had looked gleaming with the sheen of sweat. The way it might feel to run my hands over it.

Blake stared down at me, his expression unreadable.

I didn't know if I wanted him to talk or not. I didn't know what I wanted. And that was becoming a problem. A problem I could end–right here, right now. It would be so easy. For a moment, my breath hitched as I thought of sliding the blade across his throat.

Would the other highbloods kill me in an instant for daring to touch one of their own?

Silence was best, I decided. I pulled my knife away, sliding the blade back into my corset. Turning on my heel, I strode across the sand, away from the fire, away from the highbloods, away from Blake.

As the darkness swallowed me whole and I left him standing there alone, I didn't look back. Not once.

CHAPTER 18

MEDRA

As I stumbled across the sand in the dark, heading back towards where I'd left my boots, a shadow drifted out of the night.

I reached for my knife, heart pounding, waiting for the moonlight to illuminate the stranger.

"Medra? Is that you?"

I stopped, my heartbeat slowing. "Vaughn?"

It was Vaughn Sabino. The mortal boy who had nearly been my match in Basic Combat class the first day.

"What are you doing here?" I asked with surprise.

"Oh, you know." I caught him shrugging. "Out for a moonlight stroll. It's a beautiful night." Then he grinned mischievously.

My heart sank. "You're going to the party."

He nodded. "Theo invited me."

"Theo?" I shook my head. Just how many blightborns had Theo invited? "He invited me, too. Florence already left. Did you see her on your way down?"

He shook his head. "Why don't you come back with me?" he suggested. "I wouldn't mind some company."

I shook my head emphatically. "No. I'm not going back there." I hesitated. "To be honest, I wouldn't suggest you go either, Vaughn. It's all highbloods. The only mortals are..." I paused, trying to remember the word Florence had used. "Sellbloods?"

For a moment, his grin faltered slightly. Then he shrugged. "Sounds about right. I'm still going. Theo..." His voice trailed off. The moonlight wasn't bright enough for me to actually see him blushing but somehow I knew he was.

"Oh," I said at last. "So it's like that."

He shrugged sheepishly. "I mean, he's Theo Drakharrow. He's charming."

"He is," I agreed. I thought of how Theo had at least made Kiernan stop the thrallweave he was using on Florence. "Well, I suppose if you were going to fall for a highblood, you could do worse."

"Thanks," Vaughn replied, with a laugh. "I'm not sure I've fallen for him yet. But we'll see how things go. Are you all right to walk back alone?"

I thought of the knife between my breasts. I tilted my head. "After I beat you in class, you still actually have the nerve to ask that?"

Vaughn laughed. "See you there tomorrow, Medra."

I watched him disappear into the night. Should I have told him about what Blake had done to Kiernan? Would he still have gone?

Maybe Theo would tell him. I hoped Theo knew what he was doing...and that he'd keep Vaughn safe.

I strolled along the beach, walking closer to where the waves were crashing onto the shore.

I wanted to get back to Florence. But even after all that had transpired, I was still restless. I could practically feel the blood pounding in my veins. Longing for... what? Release?

For something. Something I couldn't pinpoint.

I trailed my feet in the water. The chill feel of it against my skin was cold and bracing. I kicked at a crashing wave and the spray splashed back onto my bare arms and calves.

A sound from up ahead made me freeze. I looked along the beach.

There was another figure coming towards me.

At first I thought it was just another student on their way to the party.

Then I realized this was a much smaller form.

A child.

My brow furrowed. Even shrouded in darkness I could tell this was a young girl. Small and slender. She couldn't have been more than nine or ten. Clearly she didn't belong to the chaotic party I'd just left behind.

"Are you all right?" I called out, my voice carrying over the waves. I quickened my pace a little.

A child shouldn't have been out here in the dead of night.

The girl didn't answer.

The moon came out from behind the cloud that had been partially hiding it and answered for her.

The girl was a vampire. Her telltale hair was braided into a white crown around her head.

As we neared one another, her pale face came into view. A thin trail of blood trickled down her chin, dark in the moonlight.

"Are you...hurt?" I asked, my voice laced with unease. But I already knew the answer.

She didn't reply. Instead, she raised a small hand to her face, wiping at the blood. Then she brought it to her mouth, licking her fingers with a practiced motion. Just like Kiernan had nearly done with my blood.

The girl's eyes locked onto mine with an eerie, unsettling calm. She smiled. What should have been the innocent smile of a child seemed far more sinister.

I knew this girl, I realized. I'd seen her that first day, sitting on the edge of the dais in the Black Keep, kicking her feet in boredom. Her presence on the dais meant she belonged to one of the four great houses.

My skin prickled, but I forced myself to remain composed. She was still just a child, I reminded myself. "You should get back home. Do you need me to go with you?"

The girl said nothing, just kept smiling that haunting smile as she drifted past.

I stood there, frozen in indecision for a moment, watching the small figure vanish into the darkness. If it had been a blightborn child, I wouldn't have let them go. But the girl...

She seemed like she could take care of herself. I turned away.

I'd just taken a few more steps forward when a soft whimper broke through the quiet. It came from the shadows, just beyond the waterline.

Another child.

My heart leaped into my throat, my body moving before my mind could even catch up. I sprinted towards the sound.

I scanned the darkness, looking for a child's shape. But there was nothing.

Then, in the dark, I found it. No more than the size of both my hands.

A small puppy, its fur matted with blood, lying in the sand. It was barely breathing. Its body trembled weakly as a soft whine escaped its throat.

I dropped to my knees beside it, my hands shaking as I carefully lifted up the limp form. The warmth of its blood stained my hands.

Horror flooded me as I realized who must have done this.

The girl.

"Hang on," I whispered to the little creature.

I held it close to my chest and it let out another faint whimper, its eyes dull with pain. My pulse raced as I turned back towards the castle and started to run.

In the light of the First Year common room, I could see that what I had rescued wasn't a dog like I'd first thought.

This creature looked as if a fox had mated with an owl.

It had a coat of reddish-orange fur, like the last of the autumn leaves, except for its chest which was a soft creamy white. The animal's eyes were wide and round. They seemed impossibly large for its small face, gleaming like gold in the firelight.

Now that I could see it more closely, the pup wasn't much bigger than a kitten. It lay where we had placed it on a soft blanket on top of a large footstool near the fire. The pup's huge bushy, red tail curled around it. As Florence crouched down on the floor next to it, the creature let out a small cry.

"It's a fluffin," Florence said softly, as she inspected the wounds. "A male, if I'm not mistaken."

"What is it exactly?" I leaned down. "Some kind of a dog?"

We were lucky. The common room was empty. Otherwise I wasn't sure what our fellow students might have thought of my bringing back a bleeding animal.

Florence had already been in her room by the time I'd returned. Part of me felt bad for banging on her door to wake her. But part of me thought letting her go to sleep without talking through what had happened that night would be worse.

"They're related to dogs, yes," she said, absent-mindedly, as she gently ran her fingers over the animal's tiny body. "This one is just a baby. Did you see the mother anywhere nearby?"

I shook my head. "It's that young then?"

"Yes. Just a few weeks old. Naveen had one when we were young, but he got it when the pup was older. They aren't supposed to be taken away from their litter when they're this young."

Naveen and Florence had grown up together. I'd forgotten. "So, he lived in Veilmar and had one of these?"

"No, that was before my mother and I came to Veilmar. When we lived closer to Naveen and his family in the country. Their dwarven settlement was underground, of course. Fluffins actually live underground. It's rare for one to be up on the surface."

Right. I remembered them talking about some sort of stairwell access to the underground city Naveen came from.

The idea of an entire race of people who dwelled below the surface was fascinating to me. I made a mental note to read up on dwarven culture. Right after I'd read up on fluffins. And dragons. And how to get my mother's soul out of my head.

And here I thought you'd forgotten about me, Orcades chided gently. *Not that I'm not content where I am.* A pause. *That betrothed of yours is certainly a forceful man. Handsome, too.*

No. Nope, I muttered internally. *We are* not *discussing that. Not right now. Possibly never.*

Oh, all right. She sighed. *But he would make a wonderful fae. Your grandfather would have loved him.*

I clenched my jaw. *That is not the glowing endorsement you seem to think it is, Mother.*

I know you killed him, but Gorlois le Fay had his good points once, she began.

I cut her off. I had recently discovered a way to silence her. It was one of the accidental benefits of what Professor Rodriguez had been teaching me. Compartmentalization.

My mind quiet again, I watched as a soft glow spread from Florence's hand, enveloping the creature, centering on its wound.

Fascinated, I watched as the wound closed slightly, but not entirely.

"A highblood did this." She looked up at me.

I nodded in confirmation. "I think so. Can you tell for certain by looking at the wounds?"

"Someone fed from him. He's lost a lot of blood. I can tell that much." She stroked the fluffin's fur. The creature's eyes were half-closed. "But then they also did this." She pointed to the long gash along the little pup's side. "Why?"

"I don't know, Florence." I shifted uncomfortably in my spot on the floor. "I sort of hoped you might have a guess."

She shook her head mutely. "So cruel. So pointless. And why feed on a pup? Highbloods don't normally use animals. It's considered beneath them."

I stayed silent as she reached for the kit she'd brought down from her room and pulled out clean bandages and a bottle of salve. Carefully, she applied the salve to the wound. The pup whimpered, its eyes flickering open again.

"I'm sorry, little one," Florence whispered. "I'll be as gentle as I can." She glanced up at me. "I can't heal it completely. I'm not that skilled. All I can do is stitch it and hope for the best."

I watched as she worked, stitching along the gash, the horrible wound oozing blood onto the salve.

The little pup stirred slightly, letting out another weak whimper, his wide, owl-like eyes flitting open then closing again.

"He's so little, so fragile," Florence said sadly, as she wrapped bandages snugly around the fluffin's torso. "I've done what I can but he's still feverish. Whoever attacked him did more damage than I can heal. The fever might come down on its own. But...it might not."

I crouched beside the fluffin pup, watching as he breathed shallowly. He seemed to be falling asleep.

"So what do we do?" I'd hoped Florence would have the wisdom I lacked. The magic solution. Something that would set everything to rights.

But when I looked into her dark eyes, I saw she felt as lost as I did.

She sat back on her heels. "We'll let it rest for tonight. But we might need help–real help–tomorrow." She hesitated. "One of the house healers would be best. Someone with more skill or stronger magic. If the fever doesn't break, if the wound gets infected, it could get worse."

The fluffin pup lay quietly, his small chest rising and falling gently. I pulled the blanket overtop, tucking it in around him. I thought again of the girl on the beach. I wasn't going to tell Florence about her. Not yet. She'd been through enough tonight already.

"We'll figure it out in the morning," I said quietly. I examined my friend. She looked exhausted and sad.

Florence slowly lifted her head and met my eyes. "I'm sorry."

"For what? You have nothing to be sorry for, Florence. I understand why you left."

"Yes, but I should have waited for you..."

"Stop." I raised my hand. "Please. I'm the one who should be apologizing. I should never have made you come. It was so stupid of me. This is exactly what I was afraid of–of you getting hurt because of me." I thought of Florence's mother, Jia, and the way the Drakharrow students were treating her. It all came back to me.

"Maybe you were right after all," Florence said, staring down at the floor.

I took a deep breath. "What do you mean?"

She looked at me. "I mean... maybe they are monsters."

I was shocked. "The highbloods?"

She nodded. "All my life..." She lifted her chin and gave a brittle laugh. "Can I tell you something, Medra? All my life I've wanted to be one."

"A highblood?"

She nodded. "They're strong. Beautiful. They all *belong*. We blightborn... We don't have that. Do you know what I mean?"

I wasn't sure I did, so I said nothing.

"We only belong in terms of how we relate to *them*. And that used to make me feel safe. Coming here made me feel safe. They wanted me. Our protectors wanted me. They saw value in me. Some day they might even need me." She gave a hollow laugh. "But tonight..."

Florence's worldview was changing. And that might be a good thing. But I didn't want her to go too far. Because her mother had been right. Florence's ideals, no matter how naive I might think them, did protect her. They were a comfort. And I didn't want her stripped of all that. Not in a single night. Not because of me.

"That boy. Kiernan. The one who did that to you. He's dead," I said quietly. "I thought you should know."

Her eyes widened. "What? Medra, what did you do?"

"Not me. Blake Drakharrow."

Her eyes widened. "Because of me?"

"Not just because of that," I hedged. I doubted Blake even knew what had happened to Florence. Or if it would have affected him one bit if he had known. No, he'd done what he'd done to Kiernan because someone had threatened *me*. His property. Not because he cared about either Florence or myself. "Kiernan threatened me after you left. Blake... He threw him into the fire."

Florence covered her mouth.

"Is that typical?" I still had no idea. "Do highbloods usually kill each other like that?"

"The rules are different for highbloods," Florence said slowly. "I'm starting to wonder if there even are rules for them at all. But if Kiernan did something to threaten you then I suppose Blake could easily argue that it was a challenge to House Drakharrow's honor and he'd been within his rights."

"Kage Tanaka was there, too. I think it had something to do with him."

Florence nodded. "There's a strong rivalry between those two. But they seem to keep it in check. At least, they did before this."

I decided not to point out we were only a few weeks into the start of term. There was plenty of time for things to go to hell.

"What happened to you was wrong, Florence. So wrong. I'm so sorry it happened tonight. I thought the party would be fun. I made a massive mistake." To my shock, I realized I was near tears. "You could have died."

Florence slid around the ottoman, careful not to disturb the sleeping pup. "Hey. Medra. It's all right." She put her arms around me and I leaned into the embrace, smelling the scent of the lavender salve she'd been using. She smelled calm and comforting. Peaceful. I squeezed her back gratefully.

When she pulled away, her face was solemn. "Besides, you already had it happen to you. You know what thrallweave is like. Having someone in your head like that... It's so violating. When I got back to the dormitory, the first thing I did was throw up."

"I don't blame you," I said, eying her sympathetically. "And you're right. It's a horrible violation."

"I'm glad Kiernan is dead," she said slowly. "Isn't that terrible? There must be something wrong with me."

"There is nothing wrong with you, Florence," I said firmly. "I'm glad he is, too. That wasn't the first encounter I had with him. He seemed like a nasty piece of work."

"But it's so final. He's just gone. Forever. Even he didn't deserve that. Did he?" She hiccuped and I realized she was trying to hold back sobs.

I slipped my arm around her shoulders. "You didn't do it. You didn't hurt him. Neither did I. It was out of our hands."

Was it true? I'd wanted to kill Kiernan, yes. But I hadn't done it. Blake had beaten me to it. I doubted he was sitting by the bonfire crying and wracked with guilt right now. No, he was probably drinking with Regan. Or doing other things.

"None of this was your fault," I repeated. "None of it. Kiernan knows the system better than either of us. He was a highblood. He knew what might happen. He acted like a bastard... and he paid the price."

"Maybe he paid the price Kage Tanaka should have paid," Florence suggested, saying exactly what I'd been thinking. "Didn't he say Kage sent him over?"

"You think he was what? Expendable? That Kage knew what was going to happen? That it was some kind of a test?"

Florence shrugged. "Maybe. I don't know how highbloods think. I'm realizing that more and more every day."

"But you grew up with them. In a highblood house, I mean..."

"I grew up *worshiping* them. Idolizing them. Adoring them. But it was always from afar. I didn't really see them up close that often. They had children my age, but we weren't friends. The family my mother served lived in, well, basically a palace. We lived in a little cottage on the grounds with the other servants. I would see the highblood family from time to time and they were so beautiful. They looked so noble. Then there were feast days and rites at the temples. We all worship them, Medra. I don't think you quite understand." She shook her head. "One day we'll go into Veilmar. Then maybe you'll get it."

"I'd like that," I said. "I want to understand. I really do. Sellbloods, for instance. You said there were some at the party? The ones being fed from?"

She nodded.

"What are they exactly?"

She colored. "They work at brothels. But not the kind you're thinking of," she said quickly. "Blood brothels. They sell their blood."

I stared at her. "Like thralls?" I didn't see the difference.

She shook her head. "No, they're not thralls. They're not under any kind of enthrallment for one. And they don't belong to a certain highblood or certain house. They might get some pleasure from the act. I'm not certain. Having your blood taken... Well, no one really claims it's painful. Not that I've heard."

I didn't want to think about how pleasurable it might or might not have been to have Blake Drakharrow suck my blood.

"So some people make their living this way?" I said. "Selling their blood?"

"Yes. It's the way some blightborn choose to live. But they're often looked down upon for it."

"What a surprise," I said with irony. "Seems to be the way with brothel workers. No matter what kind or where you are."

"Some sellbloods do both," she said hesitantly. "Sell their blood and their bodies, I mean. There are certain brothels that cater to that."

I tilted my head thoughtfully. "If they're selling to highbloods then I'm not sure why they'd be looked down upon. I thought serving a vampire was the highest honor. No matter how you served."

"You're right, but... that's just how it is," Florence said lamely. "They're often despised. The lowest of the low. Blightborns treat them poorly and highbloods don't really treat them any better. Their work can be dangerous. They're more vulnerable."

She looked at me and shook her head abruptly. "How can you be so strong, Medra?"

"What do you mean?" I asked in surprise.

"Tonight. With everything that happened. You saw Kiernan get killed. You saw what he did to me and you didn't just stand there—you acted. Which is more than I did for you when Regan was thrallweaving you in the Dragon Court. You've already been through so much and look at you, you're barely rattled."

"Believe me, I am. But on the inside." But I knew what she meant. I tried to think of how to explain. "You don't want to be like me, Florence. Trust me."

She frowned. "What do you mean?"

"I mean, I'm like this for a reason. I'd rather be like you."

She gave me a disbelieving smile.

"It's true," I insisted. "You're so..." I searched for the right word. There were many I might have used. Honorable. Kind. Naive. Idealistic. "Good," I settled on. "You have a good heart."

"You do, too," she said immediately. "I've seen it. You've been kind to me. Kind to Naveen."

"But I'm not kind. Not nice. Not really. I never have been. Even as a child. I've never viewed the world as a good place. I've never really believed that good would triumph over evil or that people are naturally good at heart." And it was certainly even harder to believe in those things here in Sangratha. "I'm a pessimist, I guess," I finished awkwardly. "I'm always inclined to think the worst of people, not the best."

Florence was staring at me. I wanted to look away from those soft, gentle eyes but I didn't.

"Medra," she said. "Sometimes the problem is that we don't see ourselves the way others do. Look at what you did tonight."

I frowned. "What do you mean?"

"I mean look at the fluffin. You found him on the beach. You could have left him there to die. So why didn't you? Because you hoped against hope that he would live. And why did you want that? Because you have a kind heart. Because you're a good person."

I didn't want to argue with her. I knew there was nothing good about me.

I tried to smile. "Maybe. Maybe there's hope for me yet."

"I know there is," she said firmly. "You're my friend, after all. And I have the best friends. You and Naveen."

But when I went to sleep that night, my dreams weren't filled with Florence or Naveen or the fluffin pup.

I saw only a man with piercing gray eyes standing in front of a blazing bonfire.

CHAPTER 19

MEDRA

The next day, Vaughn wasn't in Basic Combat with Naveen and I. I wondered about it, but then decided he'd probably had a much later night than I had. I wondered if he'd tried Theo's ambrosia.

When Naveen and I came out of our last class, Florence was waiting in the hall. She looked frantic.

"What is it?" I asked in alarm.

"The pup," she whispered. "His fever is higher. He's worse, not better. And there's nothing else I can think of to do."

"Would your mother...?"

But Florence was already shaking her head. "This isn't one of her areas of expertise. All she could do is point us towards more resources. But we don't have time to sit around reading books."

"So you're saying the pup is going to die?" I said slowly.

She took a deep breath. "What I'm saying is we need to get it to a real healer. If we take it to the First Year infirmary, we'll get into trouble."

"There are house healers," Naveen said, looking at me. "You already saw one."

I understood what they were suggesting. "You want me to take the fluffin to the House Drakharrow healer."

Florence shook her head. She looked miserable. "You can't do that. You're not allowed in the House Drakharrow tower without Blake. Not yet. You'd have to go to Blake first and ask him to do it."

"Beg him, you mean? Ask him for a favor?" I clenched my jaw and felt like screaming. The fluffin pup was only in this mess in the first place because of the cruelty of a highblood girl. And now Florence and Naveen wanted me to go and ask another highblood for help.

We'd put the pup in Florence's room last night. I thought of how small he'd looked curled up on his makeshift bed, just a little ball of red fur. Was he dreaming of his mother? His brothers and sisters? He'd probably never see any of them again.

"You don't have to do it, Medra. I know you don't want to be beholden to him," Florence said softly.

She and Naveen were both watching me. We'd told Naveen what had happened this morning. He'd been shocked, and upset he hadn't gone with us. I think he felt guilty about not being there to protect Florence. Not that he'd have been able to do anything.

I exhaled. "No, it's all right. I'm being stupid. I'll do it. I'll go and talk to him." I lifted the leather satchel that held my school books up onto my shoulder. "If I can find him, I mean. I don't have another Advanced Weaponry class until the day after tomorrow."

"Maybe we'll run into him in the refectory," Florence said. "But I can't go and look. I have another class right now."

"I could come with you in an hour, but I have to turn in a paper first," Naveen said. "The class is on the other side of campus."

I shook my head. "It's fine. I can go and look now. This was my last class of the day. If he's not there, I'll check the library."

This wasn't how I wanted to spend my afternoon, hunting down Blake Drakharrow. I couldn't even ask any of his friends for help. I knew exactly what they'd do–laugh in my face. Well, maybe not Coregon or Theo.

I was supposed to be working on my paper on dragons and searching more of the books Florence's mother had found for me on blood magic and souls.

I hadn't really read much more about dragons–and fortunately, Professor Rodriguez hadn't asked. We'd been too focused on my thrallguard training. I knew the history was fascinating, but it also seemed like a far less pressing topic than getting Orcades out of my head. Now both things would have to wait yet again.

I moved through the hallways, passing groups of chattering, laughing students. It was almost the end of the day and a steady crowd of people were making their way to the refectory. The vast stone hall was a favorite place for students to hang out at the end of each day as they waited for dinner. Snacks and refreshments were always left out on a large buffet table on one side of the room.

When I reached the refectory, I stood in the hallway near one of the open stone arches, scanning the room. I spotted Quinn and Coregon at the House Drakharrow table with some other Drakharrow students, but I didn't see Blake or Theo anywhere.

I'd decided I'd ask Theo if I saw him first. He was more approachable than Blake. If I had to owe a favor to someone, I'd much rather it be him.

With a sigh, I decided to check the library next. I took my favorite route through the massive castle. The one that led through the Dragon Court. It was the end of autumn and the leaves had mostly fallen now, but there was still something refreshing about passing through the open air and through the grove of trees that encircled the stone dragon statues.

Some afternoons, I'd taken to sitting under one of the trees with Naveen and Florence and studying. Even though it was a beautiful space, it was usually deserted. As winter approached, it would soon be too cold for us to go there.

As I neared the courtyard, a figure entered the passage ahead of me.

My heart sped up.

Blake.

I hadn't seen his face, but I didn't need to. I recognized his walk. That ridiculously arrogant swagger.

I didn't say anything, just started to follow him down the hall. Where was he heading?

As it turned out, he was heading to the same place I was–the Dragon Court.

I'd let us converge there. Then I'd approach him.

But when we reached the courtyard, I hung back, waiting in the shadows of the cloisters while he strode into the court and stood in the middle between the four stone dragons.

He stood there for a moment, with his head down. For a second, I wondered if he might be praying. But to what? Highbloods all worshiped something called the Bloodmaiden. I still wasn't entirely sure what she was. Some sort of a goddess, I'd assumed.

Blake glanced up and looked around the courtyard. I was supposed to be approaching him, but instead, I found myself ducking. As I crouched down, my foot hit a pebble and there was a small clatter.

I held my breath.

"Come out, Pendragon," Blake called. "I know you're there."

I sighed and stood up slowly, brushing the dust off the black fitted trousers I wore and pulling down my gray sweater emblazoned with the school crest.

I walked over to where he stood waiting in the middle of the court.

There was a tightness in my throat as I approached him. He wasn't even looking at me, but rather, at one of the dragons.

Blake was all hard angles. Sharp and tense. Even now, the muscles in his jaw were clenched, as if he were on the verge of an attack. A predator about to spring.

Then he turned his head and looked down his hawkish nose at me, tilting his head upwards in the haughty way I'd grown accustomed to and the tightness in my throat became a lump.

He wasn't perfect. But there was something about him that had become unbearable for me to look upon–and yet just as unable to look away.

A shocking urge seized me to touch that jaw, to trace the angles of those aristocratic cheekbones, and to stop, right there, in the center, with a finger pressed to those beautiful lips. The only soft thing about him.

I wondered what his mouth would feel like. Rough or tender, soft or firm?

The lips twisted arrogantly. "Reduced to stalking me now, are we, Pendragon?"

I cleared my throat. "You wish." I needed to work on my comebacks. But he'd caught me off-guard.

"You've come to thank me for last night then, I suppose. There's no need to grovel, but I will accept it if you must." He gestured to the stone floor in front of him. "Supplicate yourself if you're so inclined."

For a split second, I froze, imagining going down on my knees for Blake Drakharrow. Putting my hands on the front of his trousers and unfastening the buttons one by one as he looked down at me, his fingers tangled in my curly hair as I drew out his length and ran my hands over it.

A wet heat grew between my legs. The lump was back.

I choked it down and forced a laugh. "In your dreams, Drakharrow. Maybe that's what all the nice little highblood girls do for you, but I'm not one of them. Or have you forgotten?"

His gaze raked over me and I felt my cheeks burn. "Oh, I hadn't forgotten."

He took a step towards me and I stepped back instinctively. He smiled. "I'm not going to hurt you, Pendragon. I would have thought last night had proved that."

"You mean because you killed someone?" I scowled. "That wasn't for me."

He cocked an eyebrow. "Wasn't it?"

I shook my head. "You did that for yourself. For your messed up sense of honor. For whatever is between you and Kage Tanaka."

"Right," he said drily. "It had nothing to do with protecting you. Nothing at all." He rolled his eyes. "Tell yourself whatever you want, blightborn. I did you a favor."

This wasn't going the way it was supposed to go. I felt a pang of guilt. What would Florence say? What would she tell me to say next?

"Fine," I blurted out. "Thank you. All right? Satisfied now?"

His eyes roamed over me. "Never."

Now it was my turn to roll my eyes. "Whatever. That's not what I'm here for."

"No? Well, I suppose you want me to guess what you're really doing, since you won't admit you were following me. Perhaps you're here to admire the dragons."

"They are incredible," I admitted, looking up at the huge stone statues. "So lifelike."

He glanced at me as if he couldn't believe we were agreeing on something. "Yes." He took a step towards the gold dragon. "They were all modeled after real ones, you know."

"Specific dragons, you mean?"

He nodded. "This was Molindra. A Luminthar. She rode for House Orphos."

"A Luminthar? That was a breed?"

He eyed me. "Aren't you supposed to know this? I thought you'd been assigned an essay on the topic."

I crossed my arms over my chest. "How would you even know that?"

His lips curled mockingly. "I have my ways. Got into some trouble with Rodriguez, did you?" He shook his head. "Rodriguez. Such a hard ass. Anyhow, yes. It was a breed. Each of the four houses specialized in breeding a particular type of dragon. For House Orphos, it was the Luminthars. They drew strength from the sun and were famous for their aural attacks. They could sow fear in their enemies or inspire their allies. For House Mortis it was the Silvraynes. That one was Alabryss." He pointed to the dragon sculpted of smooth, white alabaster stone. "She could breathe ice."

"What about the black dragon?" I asked.

I was treading on dangerous ground, the longer I stayed here. And yet... Blake's face became so animated when he spoke. Clearly this was a topic he was passionate about.

He laughed. "You mean the one you mounted?"

I flushed. "You don't have to make it sound so..."

He waved a hand. "Fine. But if you'd have done that in real life, he'd have scorched you. His name was Nyxaris. He rode for House Avari. He was a Duskdrake. They were ferocious in battle."

I looked at the black dragon's serrated teeth and menacing eyes and shuddered. "So the red one was House Drakharrow's?"

Blake stepped towards the red stone dragon and put a hand against the rough, unpolished sandstone. "Vorago. He was an Inferni. The Inferni flew for House Drakharrow, yes."

"And what was special about them?"

He shrugged. "They were fucking indestructible. At least, when it came to attacks from other dragons."

"What does that mean?"

"It means their weakness was themselves. They were volatile. Unreliable. Breeding them was a danger all in itself. House Drakharrow lost more dragons and dragon riders than any of the other houses." He looked me over. "They were prideful, stubborn, and hard to control. Sound familiar?"

I flushed. "I'm surprised House Drakharrow wanted them."

"We wanted them because they were the best. They were the fastest of the four breeds. When they were ridden by well-trained riders, their attacks could be the most powerful of any breed. Once a rider bonded successfully with an Inferni, they could draw on their mount's strength and even their courage. At least, so they say."

"So they say," I echoed.

I looked around me at the four statues, trying to imagine a time when these beasts actually flew through the skies. "Their appetites must have been huge."

He nodded. "Which is why only the four great houses could afford to own them."

"Own," I said bitterly. "Why must you try to own everything?"

He looked at me but said nothing.

I turned away and looked up at the red stone dragon. Vorago.

The dragon's eyes were the most aggressive of the four. Whoever had carved him had perfectly captured a sense of burning passion and rage.

"He doesn't want to be here," I said quietly.

"He wants to fly," Blake agreed. "He's angry that he can't. He's trapped here for another few centuries. Until the stone he's carved from finally crumbles and he falls to dust."

He stepped up beside me, looking up at the red dragon, but made no move to touch me. Still, I could feel him there, just a few inches away from my shoulder. I held very, very still.

"Why are you really here, Pendragon? Obviously you want something. What is it?"

I hesitated, then leaped. "When I left the party last night, I saw a girl on the beach. A young highblood girl."

He was close enough that I sensed him stiffen.

"She had clearly just fed," I continued.

He snorted. "You can tell when we've just fed now, can you, Pendragon?"

"There was blood on her lips," I said defensively. "And that isn't all. After she passed by, I heard a cry."

He glanced at me. "Was someone hurt?"

I was honestly shocked he'd even asked.

"Not someone exactly. An animal. Do you know what a fluffin is?"

He scoffed. "Everyone knows what a fluffin is. I probably had a stuffed one as a child."

I tried not to show my surprise. "Right. Well, there was a little fluffin pup there in the sand. It was bleeding out."

"Feeding doesn't usually kill, if that's what you're worried about, Pendragon." He was trying to sound bored. But I could tell he wasn't.

"It hadn't only been fed from," I snapped. "Someone had left it bleeding from a huge gash in its side. They'd done that to it and left it there. To die alone, in the dark. A little puppy." I looked at his profile, the angles of his pale face glowing in the late afternoons unlight. "I think it was the girl. She was only a child. No more than nine or ten."

"You probably thought you saw a highblood girl but in reality she was just some blightborn brat who snuck over somehow from the city," he said, waving a hand.

"She wasn't a stranger. She was definitely a highblood. I knew her," I persisted. "I saw her that first day when we came before your uncle. She was there, sitting on the dais."

He froze.

"You know who I'm talking about, don't you?" I glared at him. "Who is she?"

He turned to me slowly. "Does it matter?"

"Does it matter? She hurt an animal. An innocent creature. A baby." I shook my head. "But no, I guess it doesn't matter. I should have known you wouldn't care. It's just an animal to you, isn't it? After all, even highblood life is obviously meaningless to you."

He leaned towards me. "That highblood you're referring to would have liked nothing better than to sink his teeth into your pretty little throat. And do you think he would have stopped once he'd started?"

I refused to give an inch. "Who was the girl?" I demanded again. "It's obvious you know her. So why not tell me?"

He turned his head. "She's my younger sister. Aenia."

"Your...sister?" I was shocked. "I didn't know you had a sister."

"Yes, well, you don't really know a fucking thing about me, do you, Pendragon? Besides despising me, I mean."

"Fairly certain the feeling is mutual, Drakharrow." But I found I could hardly breathe. His sister?

He ran his hands through his hair. "Aenia shouldn't have been out there. She could have been hurt. It's not safe for her. I'll speak with her."

I stared at him. "And that's it? You're more worried about *her*?"

He glared at me. "Of course I'm worried about her. She's just a child. She's still learning our ways. She didn't know any better."

That didn't fit with the child I'd seen. She was young, yes, but she was lacking in innocence. There was something even more predatory about Aenia Drakharrow than there was about her older brother, and that was saying something.

"Fine. She's your sister. I can understand your being worried about her. If it's any consolation, I did ask her if she was all right. But she wouldn't answer me. She just walked away and... I didn't know if I should try to stop her." I drew a breath. "But Aenia wasn't the one hurt. The fluffin was."

He frowned. "I assumed it died after you found it."

"No, he didn't die. I took him back with me. To the First Year common room."

He shook his head. "Of course, you did, Pendragon. I'd expect nothing less." Yet there was something almost admiring in his gaze, as if he might not be entirely mocking me.

"Right, well, not all of us think animals are meaningless," I snapped. "Anyhow, I need your help."

"You have a strange way of asking for it," he replied.

I bit my tongue. "I was hoping I'd run into Theo instead."

He laughed out loud. "Is that your way of asking for help? Telling me you wish I was my cousin?"

"I only mean that I doubt Theo would have to be asked. He'd probably just offer."

"Offer what? I still don't even know what you're trying to say." But the corners of his mouth slid upward. He knew.

"For fuck's sake," I said through gritted teeth. "Will you take the fluffin to one of your house healers or not?"

He looked at me for a long moment, the corners of his mouth twitching as if he was going to laugh again.

If he did, I'd punch him in the face, I decided. No matter what he did to me after that, it would be worth it.

"Fine," he said.

"What?"

"I said 'fine.' I'll take the thing. Where is it?" He looked around as if I might have brought the fluffin with me.

"I... It's back in the First Year dormitory," I stuttered. "In Florence Shen's room. She stitched it up last night. But now he has a fever and it's getting higher. She doesn't think he's going to make it."

"Is it a he or an it?" Blake asked, looking amused again.

"It's a he. A male pup."

"Next you'll tell me you've named the thing." He shook his head.

"I haven't. But feel free. Consider it your reward for helping," I muttered.

"I'll come by the dormitory in one hour to collect it. I'll bring a basket to carry it in."

"Really?" I stared at him in disbelief. I tried to collect myself. "And you'll talk to your sister? I'm worried about her. Someone could get hurt. What if it had been a child?"

"Aenia wouldn't do that," he snapped, with surprising ferocity. "She'd never hurt a child. I said I'll talk to her."

I nodded. "Fine."

He spread his feet. "Well? What are you waiting for? That's what you came for. Go."

I shook my head at him in disbelief. What an arrogant self-important asshole. But I didn't dare say that aloud. If he wanted the entire Dragon Court to himself, he could have it.

I turned my back on him without another word and marched out of the courtyard, through the surrounding cloisters, and back into the hall leading to a row of classrooms. I'd get to the library another way.

But when I reached the empty hallway, I had a change of heart. I stopped, then turned around.

Staying close to the wall, I moved back towards the Dragon Court as quietly as I could.

Blake was still standing there. He glanced around, checking to make sure he was alone.

For a moment, his eyes scanned the spot where I stood, behind a pillar in the cloister and I thought he was going to call me out again. But his eyes moved past. He hadn't seen me.

He walked towards the red dragon and then past its huge flank. I couldn't see him for a moment. I stayed where I was, waiting for him to come back.

A moment passed. Then another.

I shifted my position, moving to a different pillar so I'd have a better view.

But there was no one there.

He must have gone behind it. I moved along the row of arched open windows carefully, expecting to see Blake standing in the grove of trees looking down at the sea at any moment.

The grove was empty.

There was no other way out of the Dragon Court besides the way I'd come and the walkway directly across from me, both of which I'd had a clear view of.

He'd disappeared.

CHAPTER 20

BLAKE

I'd had a fluffin as a child, but it hadn't been stuffed. It had been real. A snuffling little thing with a tail bigger than its entire body. Father had brought it back from a trip to a dwarven city. I must have been no more than eight years old.

I'd loved the creature. Taken it everywhere with me.

Not it.

Her.

Thistle. I'd named her Thistle.

She was a sweet little thing. Loyal to a fault.

She slept in my bed every night.

Marcus had laughed at me for that. He'd always been a bastard, even then.

Mother had chided him, but he hadn't stopped. He'd never stopped. He never would until someone stopped him. Someone he was actually afraid of.

I shifted the basket I carried to my other hand, trying not to jostle the little sleeping creature inside. I'd peered in once when I'd picked it up from the First Year common room. Pendragon hadn't been around, but her friend, Florence, had thanked me over and over again for helping.

It had been embarrassing, actually. I hadn't known what to say.

One would think I'd be used to accepting thanks and praise from blightborn.

Honestly? I'd been disappointed that *she* hadn't been there. I thought she'd be waiting, maybe with a look of gratitude on her ordinarily hostile freckled face. Now that would have been a refreshing change. Having her look at me with something besides hate for once.

Though I had to admit, I'd grown accustomed to that stubborn set to her jaw. To seeing her pointy chin lifted towards me, as if she might actually be able to injure me with it. I knew she wanted to.

Even her ridiculous hair had grown on me a little bit. Those red curls that seemed to always be tangled, like they had a mind of their own. Untameable, like she was. Wild and challenging, refusing to listen to anyone around her. Always determined to get the last word.

But when the sun caught it just right, like in the Dragon Court earlier today, it could turn those strands of orangey-red into flame. I'd found myself staring.

And that infuriated me.

Drakharrows didn't stare. We didn't gape. We didn't...

It didn't matter.

She was insufferable. Completely and utterly maddening.

Then there was the way she carried herself. Like she had something to prove. No, worse, like she had no doubt she belonged here. She didn't cower, she didn't grovel. She didn't suck up to us like so many of the blightborn did. She just... didn't care. She honestly didn't give a fuck. And that bothered me. It rubbed me the wrong way.

Every day, she got a little bit more under my skin.

That stubborn, defiant set to her jaw when she argued with me. I'd wanted to wipe that smug look off her face more times than I could count. It drove me crazy.

And yet, there was something about the blaze in her green eyes that made her impossible to ignore.

She stood up to me, which no one else dared to do, and by the Bloodmaiden, it was annoying. But at the same time, it was...impressive. And infuriatingly attractive.

Fine. It was fucking *hot*.

The fluffin made a whimpering noise and I paused, lifting the basket up so I could look inside. The pup wasn't in great shape, but he was still breathing. If I could get him to a house healer, he should be okay.

I walked a little faster. If someone saw me with this thing, it would be humiliating.

I set my lips in a hard line and when a First Year came around the corner, I stared down at them until I saw a tear trickle down their cheeks. They ran past me with a sob.

I grinned.

If only I could do that so easily with other highbloods. If I saw Kage Tanaka right now, I'd never live this down. Carrying a puppy through Bloodwing? He'd laugh me off the face of the earth.

And if I came across Regan... Fuck. That would be almost worse. She'd ask if it was for her. And what would I say then? There was no way I was giving the thing to her. The last pet she had she'd forgotten about and it had starved to death. The only person she ever took care of was herself.

I stalked down another corridor. I was nearing the House Drakharrow tower. Glancing around quickly to make sure no one was around, I shucked off my cloak and draped it over the woven cage, praying no one saw me like this.

Turning the next corner, I quickened my pace and headed up the winding stairs to the upper levels of the Drakharrow tower. At least no one from House Avari would see me now. Other houses weren't permitted to visit rival towers.

When I reached the Drakharrow infirmary doors, I paused and listened. It seemed quiet inside. Hopefully they had no patients. Unless Theo had done something stupid and fallen off a table in the refectory again.

I pushed open the heavy door and stepped inside.

One of the healers stood by a wooden table, sorting through dried herbs and glass vials. Good. She was the same one who'd helped me when Pendragon was injured a few weeks back. I knew her.

The woman looked up as she heard me enter, her brow furrowing as she saw the cloak dangling over the shape of the basket.

I cleared my throat and strode forward, yanking the cloak off the carrier.

"I have an injured fluffin," I said curtly, holding the basket up so she could see inside. "I want you to treat it."

The healer blinked, as if taken aback. "An animal?" Her gaze flicked back and forth between me and the cage.

"A fluffin is an animal, yes," I barked. "I believe I just said that. Can you heal it? Yes or no?"

I wasn't about to tell her how the wounds had been inflicted. If she thought I'd done it, fine.

"I..." She cleared her throat and smoothed the front of her apron. "Yes. Of course, my prince." Only the House Drakharrow servants bothered to call me that within the school.

But the fact that the healer was showing deference even though I'd brought an animal into the infirmary was a good sign.

I placed the woven carrier on the table. The fluffin pup stirred, his wide eyes fluttering open for a moment. The poor thing seemed too weak to do much else.

"Healer Ailith, I believe?"

She nodded.

"Ailith, I want you to keep this between us," I instructed. "No one else hears about it. You'll take care of the fluffin in your own chambers so no one else sees it. Understood?"

Her eyes widened a little but she nodded quickly.

Good. She wouldn't dare challenge me. Not a blightborn healer. I was used to being obeyed by the blightborn who served our house. This would be no different.

My jaw tightened. I looked down at the fluffin pup in silence.

Then, without thinking it through, I bent down and whispered through the wicker bars of the cage, "Be strong, all right? I'll be back."

I straightened up and caught the healer's raised eyebrow. But she quickly schooled her expression into a neutral one.

My cold demeanor snapped back into place. I nodded at her. "I expect this animal to receive the very best care and to thrive under your watch. Remember–this stays between us."

The healer gave me a measured look. She wasn't stupid, this one.

Good. I wanted her to save the animal, after all. I could only imagine what Pendragon would say if I couldn't manage that much.

"Of course, my lord," Healer Ailith murmured. "It will be done."

Without another word, I turned and left, resisting the urge to open the little cage and pick up the fluffin.

I'd check in on him tomorrow, I decided. Just to make sure he was still alive.

Not because I cared one way or the other, of course. But because House Drakharrow had standards to maintain. We needed to be obeyed in all things, no matter how trivial.

CHAPTER 21

MEDRA

"And so began the Era of Pretenders."

Professor Hassan's sharp voice cut through the air, the tap of her cane punctuating her words as she moved across the lecture platform. She paused to look out on where we sat, huddled in our seats. We'd all learned long ago that she preferred no interruptions during lectures.

"The monarchy, as you know, was abolished after the last king was deposed. Each of the four great highblood houses–House Avari, House Drakharrow, House Mortis, and House Orphos–believed they had the right to rule the kingdom. No single crown could claim authority over the others, however. And so each house set up their own royal courts, with their own princes and princesses of the Blessed Blood."

I kept my head down, scribbling notes on the parchment. The older woman had no patience for daydreamers or slackers, and she relished in cutting down students she deemed unworthy–as she'd done to me that first day.

"For a century," Hassan continued. "The kingdom was ruled by a regency–four regents, one from each house, appointed to rule Sangratha. This arrangement lasted a hundred years. The Era of Pretenders was relatively peaceful, and yet a facade. Each house continued to harbor ambitions of true sovereignty."

Professor Hassan paused, letting the words sink in. I leaned forward a little in my seat. All of this must have been old news to most of the other students, especially the highblood ones. But to me it was all fresh and I found myself actually interested.

"Then it all fell apart. Ten years of civil wars followed. The Dragon Wars. A bloody conflict that decimated the population." Her voice took on a hard edge. "We will discuss the alliances formed between houses in another class. At the start, the four houses fought each other. Towards the end, House Orphos gave its support to House Drakharrow while House Mortis pledged itself to House Avari. As you all know, it was during this war that the last of the dragons perished. The Dragon Wars were as catastrophic as they were inevitable."

My hand faltered for a moment and I paused my writing. Professor Hassan's loyalty to the highbloods had always been obvious. But she seemed in an especially patriotic mood today.

"When the war ended and the last dragon fell, the kingdom was shattered into four territories. Each house claimed control over its own chunk of the realm, no longer united, but merely coexisting."

"Then came the Peacebringer." Professor Hassan's tone softened slightly. "A highblood prince from House Drakharrow, the Peacebringer had grand ambitions of re-unification. He was not just a skilled diplomat, but bore the marks of the finest of leaders. He reunited the four houses and reestablished the regency, restoring order to the kingdom and bringing Sangratha back to a place of strength and power."

Professor Hassan leaned on her cane. "His death... came too soon and was the ultimate tragedy."

I wondered who this man had been. Someone from House Drakharrow... Did that mean he was related to Blake?

"When the Peacebringer died," Hassan continued. "His brother took his place as regent for House Drakharrow, and thus the kingdom has resumed a regency by four."

My heart was hammering. His brother? She had to mean Viktor Drakharrow.

I thought back to what I'd seen that first day at the Black Keep. Had there been four regents on that dais? A woman from House Avari and a nobleman from House Mortis had each spoken. I couldn't recall seeing anyone from House Orphos, but that didn't mean they hadn't been present.

Regardless, only one man had seemed to hold real power in that vast hall. Viktor Drakharrow.

If there was a regency by four, it seemed an unequal one. House Drakharrow clearly held the most power.

The bells rang, signaling the end of class.

Professor Hassan straightened up, her voice becoming brisk. "We'll continue this next week. Read the next chapter in your *Chronicles of Sangratha: An Official History* textbook. Be prepared to discuss the Peacebringer's reforms and how they continue to shape the kingdom."

Around me, Florence and Naveen rose and started to gather their things. I stayed seated, my mind churning. I'd thought of something else. This Peacebringer... Had he been Blake's father?

I packed my things slowly and followed Florence and Naveen out of the lecture hall.

They were already chattering as I caught up to them.

"Who was the Peacebringer?" I interrupted abruptly, my mind still on the lecture. "Was he Blake's father?"

Florence nodded.

I gave a sardonic laugh.

"What is it?" Naveen asked.

"It just seems kind of ridiculous that someone like Blake would have a father who was literally called the 'Peacebringer.'" I frowned. "Also, I had no idea Sangratha was ruled over by four regents. That first day, in the Black Keep, it seemed like only one person was in charge–Viktor Drakharrow."

Florence exchanged a look with Naveen. "You're not the first to think that."

"There's something going on," Naveen agreed. "I've heard the other houses are restless. Viktor took his brother's seat at the table but he has an oversized presence. I've heard the other houses don't like him."

"He acted more like a king than a regent the last time I saw him," I said. "But the other houses allow it, so maybe it's a delicate balance?"

Naveen shrugged. "I sure hope so. No one wants another Dragon War."

Florence punched him. "There are no dragons, you ninny. So they'd have to call it something else."

"The Dragonless War," Naveen deadpanned. We laughed.

I thought of a civil war between the four houses. What would happen to the three of us if something like that happened? "How did Blake's father die? What was his name?"

"Alexander Drakharrow," Florence said. "And that's the funny thing. No one really knows. At least, none of us blightborn."

"How can no one know how this Peacebringer guy died?" I asked in disbelief. "Wasn't he the most famous lord of the land? Wouldn't his death have been investigated?"

"You'd think so," she said thoughtfully. "But it happened when he was at home with his family. I've always thought it was some sort of an illness. Or something kind of embarrassing that they didn't want publicized. Like a freak accident." She looked up at the clock on the wall. "You have a spare now, right? Are you still coming to my Magical Foundations class?"

I nodded.

It was still strange to me how differently magic worked in this world. Back in Aercanum, my fae abilities had come almost effortlessly. There had been no real work involved in their conjuring. I was born fae and thus I was born with certain skills. It was hardly even magic at all. Just a part of who I was.

But here in Sangratha, magic worked very differently. Mortals could potentially wield it, for one. But few had the innate talent or discipline. Magic in Sangratha required discipline and precision. The finest spellcasters, alchemists, and arcanists were good not just because of intrinsic talent but because they'd put in the work. Spells were complex, requiring perfect timing and specific incantations. Mistakes could lead to embarrassing failures or catastrophic outcomes. Performing magic was physically exhausting and mentally draining. Which was why so few students at Bloodwing wound up as actual arcanists, even though they were highly valued. Especially ones who could perform elemental magic.

Of course, Florence had an interest in many disciplines. I'd lost track of all of the classes she was taking and the potential career options she had ahead of her. But it was clear that if she wanted to become an arcanist, the path was available to her.

When I'd arrived here, I'd been reborn as a blank slate. I'd felt the absence of my powers at first as a conspicuous gap. But now I hardly noticed their absence at all.

It was clear if I did ever want to wield any magic again, I'd be starting from scratch. Which was part of why Professor Rodriguez, who had become something of a faculty advisor, had instructed me to attend a class with Florence and have her instructor give me an assessment afterwards. I might have enough of an aptitude that would make taking some spellcasting classes worthwhile; I might not.

I had my own reasons for wanting to attend the class.

When we entered Magical Foundations and took our seats, I got my first look at Professor Elowyn Wispwood. I eyed her curiously as she set some books on her desk. Florence had told me the professor was a halfborn. A rare thing, a hybrid child born to a mortal and a high blood. In this case, Wispwood's mother was a blightborn. When it came to a mortal woman bearing a half-highblood offspring, usually such children didn't survive birth. When they did, they lacked the suite of vampire powers that highbloods possessed. They didn't require blood to survive, but neither did they live as long.

Professor Wispwood was tall and willowy with pale blonde hair that she kept in a smooth twist. But her hair was where her similarity to a highblood ended, so far as I could see.

Florence said Wispwood was absolutely obsessed with magic, often drifted off into daydreams during lectures, but was nevertheless whip sharp and incredibly astute when it came to evaluating her students. I could tell she was one of Florence's favorite professors.

I watched Professor Wispwood write on the board, her handwriting small and neat. How strange it must have been to live between two worlds. To look like a highblood but not be one.

Florence had told me it was unusual for halfborns to attend Bloodwing and even rarer for one to be a teacher. Like sellbloods, they had a tenuous place in Sangrathan society, with highbloods preferring to believe such unions between vampires and mortals never took place at all.

Had Professor Wispwood been accepted and welcomed by her vampire father? Or had he abandoned her and her mother?

The lecture began. Professor Wispwood moved gracefully across the platform as she spoke, a pastel rainbow skirt swirling around her long legs. Her voice was melodic. Soft, but poised. A few minutes into her lecture it was clear to me that she was obviously brilliant. She spoke effortlessly and passionately, without notes, constantly gesturing with her hands.

Florence had told me this class would be on the topic of magical conduits. I'd jumped at the chance to attend—and it wasn't long before I saw my opening.

"...And, of course, as we've discussed, conduits can be found in nature, in objects, or even in living things." Professor Wispwood traced a diagram she'd sketched on the board and gestured for us to copy it down. "In rare cases, a magical conduit can even be something as intangible as a soul."

My heart skipped a beat. This was coming closer than I could have hoped.

Professor Wispwood continued, "Souls are, of course, one of the most dangerous conduits to manipulate. Soul-binding magic is incredibly volatile. The risk is not only to the integrity of the soul being moved but also to the spellcaster."

My chest tightened. I glanced at Florence, who was furiously taking notes. After a pause, I forced my hand up.

Professor Wispwood's eyes flickered in my direction. "Yes?" Her tone was encouraging at least.

I hesitated for a moment. "What about magic that binds souls together? Where two souls exist in one body? Is that...possible?"

Florence shot me a curious glance, but I ignored it.

Professor Wispwood's brows furrowed thoughtfully. She leaned back against her desk, crossing her long legs in front of her. "Ah, soul-binding. That's a very specific and dangerous field of magic."

She tapped the piece of chalk she held against the desk and looked at us all doubtfully. "This is a rather advanced area to get into, but as Miss Pendragon has asked the question and it's a fascinating topic, I'll take a few minutes to answer it."

My heart sped up. Finally, someone who actually knew something.

"Soul-binding is dangerous because the very act of inviting another soul into your body puts you at great risk," she went on.

And what if the soul wasn't invited? I thought.

I can hear you, my mother said sweetly. *You forgot to mute me today.*

I'd been using my limited ability in thrallguard more regularly to silence our connection. I tried not to do it too often because I empathized with her position–being stuck in my head with nowhere to go and no one else to talk to but me. I'd probably have been a lot surlier and sullen than Orcades was, if our roles were reversed.

Hopefully we'll learn something useful that can help us both, I murmured internally. *Surely you want to be free?*

She didn't reply.

I wondered, belatedly, if she was afraid. Was there a chance she'd simply disappear into the ether if we managed to expel her? Would it be the end, the real end for her?

I quickly turned back to what Professor Wispwood was saying.

"When two souls occupy one body, the boundaries between them can blur, and often, the host risks losing their own sense of self entirely. This magic is therefore rarely practiced and for good reason."

My heart sank. That didn't sound optimistic.

Professor Wispwood paused, as if weighing her next words. "Historically, we know of instances when this magic was used long ago. It's rarely spoken of, but in the past, some highblood vampires would use soul-binding to extend their lives through unconventional means. In their desperation to live beyond the limitations of their bodies, some highbloods would perform a binding ritual with a blightborn. The blightborn would willingly take in the vampire's soul, allowing the vampire to live on through them. A way of cheating death, so to speak."

A murmur rippled through the class. I looked around me. Florence's Magical Foundations section was made up entirely of First Year blightborn students.

My stomach twisted as Professor Wispwood's words sunk in. I gripped my quill tightly.

"But it wasn't always willingly," Professor Wispwood continued. "Sometimes these rituals were performed unwillingly. There are even accounts of this magic being used on dragon riders."

My heart beat faster. I expected the professor to look right at me, but she was lost in her train of thought. If she'd remembered I had rider blood, she wasn't showing it. Or she thought it was irrelevant.

Even so, another murmur went through the room.

"Yes, dragon riders," she confirmed, nodding. "I mean, think of it. By binding their soul to a rider, a highblood hoped to be able to control a dragon directly. There was no other way to do it. The rider's bloodline, their connection to the dragon, would remain, but the vampire's soul would be in control. At least, that was the hope."

A cold shiver ran down my spine. What she was describing was nothing short of murder. Reading between the lines, it seemed obvious the vampire's soul purposely overrode the host's.

"The process was far from perfect," Professor Wispwood went on. "If the rider was not fully bonded to their dragon at the time the ritual was performed, and not only fully bonded but the dominant party in a very fragile, very complicated relationship, then the bond would rupture. The rider would die. Sometimes, the dragon would, too. It was a dangerous gamble, one that very few vampires succeeded in pulling off. Still, for some the risk was worth it."

The risk of being able to control a dragon and still possessing all of the power that came with being a highblood.

My thoughts were racing. I hadn't learned how to free myself from my mother's soul, but I had learned something else. Something much more terrifying. The longer Orcades' soul stayed within me, the more I risked losing control.

Professor Wispwood was trying to get back to the original topic of conduits. But I couldn't hold myself back.

My hand shot up, my mind unable to keep back the question.

"Was there a way for the dragon rider to fight back? To get the highblood's soul out of them? You said they were often unwilling after all."

Immediately a ripple of shocked whispers began to spread.

Florence looked at me in alarm, her eyes wide.

But if the question seemed borderline treasonous to Professor Wispwood, she gave no indication of it. Simply tilted her head thoughtfully, her eyes flashing with curiosity.

She raised her hand to silence the chatter in the room.

"That's an interesting question," she said, her tone calm. "If there was a way, it would have involved blood magic. Blood magic is powerful because it can break bonds that other magic cannot. As you're all aware, bloodmancy is the domain of House Drakharrow. But when it comes to blood magic and soul-bonding, I don't believe it's much practiced these days. I've never seen such incantations myself. Of course, that doesn't mean they don't exist."

My heart sank. This was what I already knew. It hadn't been a direct answer. It was the same as no answer at all.

Professor Wispwood walked briskly to the blackboard, clearly deciding to return to safer ground. "Now, let's return to the subject of magical conduits. Imbuing power into inanimate objects is another application of conduit magic. Weapons, jewelry, even everyday items can serve as vessels for magical energy, provided the spellwork is precise..."

But I barely heard the rest. My thoughts were spiraling, caught in the implications of all that I'd just learned. Blood magic. Soul-binding. Highbloods using mortals for their own twisted immortality. Dragon riders being harvested for their bodies, being used as vessels for someone else's consciousness...

Take deep breaths or you're going to keel over, Orcades said gently.

For once, I did as she said, forcing myself to breathe in and out.

Florence was giving me strange looks but to her credit she didn't stoop to whispers.

The class ended in a blur. The other students packed their things and filed out of the room.

I started wandering towards the door.

"Excuse me, Miss Pendragon," Professor Wispwood's voice called from the front, sharp but not unkind. "I believe you're due for an assessment."

Florence tugged on my sweater and brought me to a halt. She gave me an encouraging nod. "I'll wait for you in the hall. Good luck," she whispered, before heading out the door with the rest of the class.

When we were alone, Professor Wispwood beckoned me forward. "Let's get started, shall we?"

I walked slowly to the front of the room and watched as the professor pulled out a small box from one of her desk drawers. She placed it gently on the desk and flipped it open.

Leaning forward, I peered inside. Within the box were several objects—a polished stone, a small wooden bowl, and what looked like a shard of glass.

"Magic is not about raw talent, as you probably already know. It's a craft. A skill that requires practice, just like any other. But before we can begin teaching someone, we have to assess where their potential lies, what kind of magic responds to them."

She picked up the polished stone and handed it to me. "Hold this and focus. Try to channel your intent into it. The stone will react to your affinity for elemental magic, if you have one."

I did as she instructed, my fingers closing around the cool surface of the stone. I concentrated, trying to block out my racing thoughts, focusing on the weight of the stone in my hand. After a long moment, I felt... nothing.

Professor Wispwood frowned slightly. She took the stone back and placed it in a box. "No elemental affinity, then. Let's try something else."

Next came the bowl. Professor Wispwood filled it with water from a flask. "This test will reveal any aptitude for energy manipulation. Place your hands above the water and try to make it ripple. Focus your energy and your intent."

I hesitated, then placed my hands above the water and tried to focus. But my thoughts kept drifting. My mother's soul. The dragon riders. The way the professor had said they could be used and discarded. The idea of my soul being controlled...

"Enough."

I looked down.

The water remained inert.

Professor Wispwood frowned. "Very well. One last test." She held out the glass shard. "This shard is meant to reflect magical energy. Sometimes it shows colors, other times images or flashes of light. Focus and we'll see what it reveals."

I stared into the glass, my own reflection staring back at me, distorted slightly by the shard's uneven edges.

You'll never pass if you can't focus, my mother's voice chided. *Your professor reminds me of a tutor I once had. I was her prize pupil. It all seems so long ago now.*

It probably was long ago, I grumbled. *No doubt hundreds of years. And she's not my professor, she's Florence's. I'm just here for the test.*

"This is rather peculiar," Professor Wispwood murmured, interrupting my side-conversation.

She took the shard back, placing it carefully on her desk. She drummed her fingers lightly on the wood as she looked down at the three items. "You should have had some reaction to at least one of these objects."

I swallowed hard. "What does that mean?"

The professor picked up the shard and looked at it. "You clearly have some kind of magic running through you. Everyone does. But the usual tests are showing nothing conclusive." She tilted her head thoughtfully and scanned my face. "You have rider blood."

"So they tell me." I forced a weak smile.

"That may be part of the problem," Professor Wispwood murmured. "It's possible that's blocking or interfering with these tests. I can't say for certain where your abilities lie or if you even have any. You certainly don't have any clear aptitudes. We'd have to conduct more advanced tests to understand your full potential. For now, I'll have to put down that your assessment was inconclusive. Perhaps we can try it again next year."

I felt disappointment well up. I had hoped for some answer, some direction. Instead, this seemed like a step back. How could I even perform a ritual to undo a soul-binding if I had no magic to guide it?

Just as I turned to leave, Professor Wispwood spoke again, her tone more measured. "There is one historical case that comes to mind regarding your earlier question about expelling a soul."

My heart leaped. "Yes?"

"Centuries ago, a highblood forcibly bound his soul to a mortal mage. The mage, a skilled arcanist, found a way to separate their souls using a forbidden ritual. It worked, but at a heavy cost. The vampire's soul was destroyed. The mortal survived, but her mind was shattered. She lived the rest of her days in madness."

Professor Wispwood's eyes met mine, sharp and knowing yet kindly. "Blood magic is not a path to walk lightly. We're fortunate to have the four houses to guide us. A consultation with someone in House Drakharrow might be what you're looking for if you have any more questions on this subject. If you'd like a referral, there are some excellent students who might be willing to mentor you." She tapped a finger to her lips. "Of course, you wouldn't be able to assist in their spellcasting based on what your assessment just showed, but there's much you could learn from observation and I'm sure they could use an extra scribe."

"Thank you. I'll consider that, Professor Wispwood," I said quietly, and left the room.

You've been awfully quiet considering everything, I said inside my head as I walked down the hall.

Orcades was silent for a moment. *Well, I suppose it's simply that I have no wish to steal my daughter's life.*

I froze.

Next came a feeling of overwhelming relief.

Some part of me had secretly been worried. My mother had been a powerful, near-immortal fae princess, after all. Even in death she had managed to somehow survive and weave our fates together. If she had wanted to take over my body, could she have done it?

You are my child, she continued. *My love for you knows no bounds. I agree this situation does grow tedious. No child should be so constricted by a parent. Should I have found myself in your position, no doubt I would have chafed against it just as you do.*

I felt a lump in my throat. *So you do understand.*

She sighed. *I know you are not ungrateful, my dear one. I wish we could have gotten to know one another better under different circumstances. Ideally face to face. But I doubt that is ever to be. After this, I suspect I will leave this plane, once I am no longer bound in your vessel. In the end, perhaps that is for the best.*

She spoke so calmly of the finality of her own demise.

But I didn't want to lose her. Not completely.

There was a difference between not wanting to share my mind with my mother and not wanting her out of my life completely.

I'd be alone, without you, I said, reminding myself of a plaintive child.

You won't be alone, she said with tenderness. *Already you've made friends. You'll thrive like a rose, even in this dark place.* I could almost hear the smile in her voice. *You'll give these highbloods hell, I have no doubt.*

A pause.

There is something I have been meaning to mention, she said.

My heart sped up. *Yes?*

I may have inadvertently already made some...changes.

Changes? Changes to what? I clenched my jaw. *Changes to me?*

"How dare you show your face in these halls, blightborn bitch?"

A pair of hands roughly shoved me against the wall. I fell against it with a cry, my shoulder colliding painfully with the stone.

"What the fuck?" I exclaimed, trying to turn my head.

There was a flourish of black as their robe whipped about them, some laughter, and then whoever it had been was gone.

The voice had been a girl's. Not Regan's. Quinn's? Maybe.

I started to push myself up from the floor. I'd dropped my book bag and some of the textbooks had spilled out.

A strong, slender hand reached down and picked one of the books up.

I looked up. Blake stood there, a bored expression on his handsome face. He passed me the book but made no attempt to pick up the others.

Grimacing, I pushed myself to my feet and brushed my clothes off.

"Thanks," I said curtly, grabbing the book and shoving it into my satchel.

"You have such a winning way about you, Pendragon," he drawled. "No wonder you've made so many friends."

I gave him a fake smile and started turning away.

His hand grabbed my shoulder. Just for a moment. Long enough for me to stop. Long enough for me to feel the heat of his skin through the fabric of my sweater.

"What?" I demanded. "You're going to shove me against a wall, too?"

"Been there, done that. Too easy," he said, with a sneer.

He looked around us carefully. The hall had emptied out.

"I came to tell you," he said, lowering his voice. "The fluffin is with the healer."

The fluffin. I'd almost forgotten about the little thing.

"Good. That's...good. Thank you for telling me." I frowned. Had he sought me out just to tell me that?

"He'll have the best treatment. The healers in our tower are the finest."

"That's good to know," I said cautiously.

I was still shocked he'd complied, that he was doing this for me at all. Not to mention finding me just to update me on the pup's condition the very next day.

"What will you do with him? Once he's healed, I mean," he said.

I stared at him. He looked at me, cool and nonchalant. Maybe trying a little *too* hard to look nonchalant. What was he up to?

"I don't think Florence and I had thought that far ahead," I said slowly. "Maybe we could try to return it..."

"No," he said, cutting me off. "Its family will be gone by now. Besides, we have no idea how it got to the surface. It could have been running from a predator..."

"We? There's no 'we' here," I interrupted, my temper rising. "And we know how it got to the surface. It *was* running from a predator. From which it did not, in fact, escape. For all we know, your sister brought it above ground. Why can't we bring it back down?"

He frowned. "Aenia?"

He glanced around again, but we were still alone. He shook his head. "She wouldn't go below the surface. There's a passage on the island but it's been caved in for years." He ran his hands through his hair. "Maybe the fluffin fit through a crack in the rocks somehow, but I doubt there's any way she could have." Still, he looked uncertain.

"What was she even doing on this island in the first place? Doesn't she live in the Keep?"

He looked uncomfortable.

I shook my head in disbelief. "You don't even know how she got here, do you? She's a child. Is she just allowed to run around wherever she wants? Where's her mother?"

As soon as I said those words I knew I shouldn't have.

"That's none of your concern," he said coldly. "She's my sister, not yours."

"You're right. If she was mine, I'd be taking better care of her," I snapped. And making sure she didn't feed on helpless animals, I thought, but I didn't add that.

He gave me a cool look. "She's a highblood," he said, as if that was all that needed to be said.

Then he turned and walked away.

CHAPTER 22

MEDRA

I pushed at my mashed potatoes, my mind a million miles away from the refectory where I sat with Florence and Naveen.

"You're sulking, Medra. What's wrong?" Naveen teased. "Not enough butter on your mashed potatoes?"

I stuck out my tongue at him. "Oh, you know. Just thinking about how ignorant I am."

"Ignorant?" Florence looked puzzled. "You're not ignorant. You're not stupid, Medra."

"Not stupid, no," I agreed. "But ignorant, yes." I looked back and forth between them. "There's so much that I don't know. That you two do, just from having grown up here."

They'd never pushed to find out where I was from. When I'd explained that I'd lost my memories, that had seemed to be enough for them. They'd accepted it. They made a point of never asking me about my past. They didn't pry. Was that friendship? They were the first friends close to my own age I'd ever really had. I was incredibly grateful for them.

"Well, if you'd been listening instead of murdering your mashed potatoes," Naveen began. I looked down at my plate and saw that I'd pushed half the potatoes onto the table in my distracted state. "Then you'd have heard us talking about something you might be interested in."

I perked up. "Oh, really? And what's that?"

Florence glanced around, then lowered her voice. "The House Leader rite is coming up."

"What is up with everyone looking around to make sure they're not overheard lately?" I grumbled, but they'd grabbed my attention. "The House Leader thing? Is it some sort of a secret? I thought it was an open and shut selection. Blake is going to be the new House Leader for Drakharrow at Bloodwing, right?"

"Well, probably," Florence said slowly. "But there are a few rites throughout the year. Not just the House Leader one."

"When is the House Leader selection, anyhow?" I asked.

"We don't know. First Years don't get told much," Florence admitted. "It's always unexpected when it happens."

"I would have thought your mother would know," I said, a little surprised.

Florence shook her head. "She's not allowed to tell me anything about it. Though it's an open secret among most of the highblood students. They'll have a better idea than we do."

"There are two big events throughout the school year," Naveen explained. "One happens every year. One only happens if a House Leader position is open."

"I already know about the House Leader selection. What's the other one?" I asked, curious.

He exchanged a glance with Florence. "It's a game for the consorts."

I scrunched up my nose. "A game? Really? And I have to participate?"

"You're in it whether you want to be or not, Medra," Florence said quietly. "So is Regan."

"In fact, we were wondering if anyone had told you about it. A professor? Maybe Rodriguez?" Naveen looked at me inquiringly.

I shook my head. "No. Nothing. No one has mentioned it. Not until now."

"You must be wondering why we didn't mention it before," Florence said. "But non-highblood consorts are so rare... Honestly I keep forgetting that's why you're here. It's such a strange situation."

"You're telling me," I said bitterly. "So what's involved in this consort game thing exactly?"

"They call it a game but it's not a childish one. The Consort Games are basically a test to weed out the weak," Naveen said.

Considering I was the only non-highblood consort, that didn't sound good.

"The consorts are supposed to work together to succeed and survive," Florence added. "Right now, you're not officially a consort yet. Not until you pass the Games."

For a moment I considered trying to fail the Games on purpose. I didn't want to be an official consort. That sounded worse than whatever I already was.

Then I put my hands flat on the table. "Wait. What? Are you telling me I'm supposed to work with Regan? As in, these Games are actually dangerous?"

Florence bit her lip and nodded nervously. "I'm afraid so. Failure is not an option. Which is why I'd hoped that Regan had talked to you already." She looked miserable. "She's supposed to be your teammate."

"She hasn't said anything to me about it." I thought for a moment. "So we're supposed to work together for this? Regan and I? There's no other choice?"

"We don't know very much. In fact, that's basically the only thing my mother would tell me when I asked her about it again recently," Florence said. "But yes, you're supposed to be a team. You're supposed to prove you can cooperate. The point of a triad union is strength. The consorts are supposed to be able to cooperate to protect their archon."

"Archon?" I raised my eyebrows. "You mean Blake?"

"Blake, yes. Or Catherine. She's the archon of her triad. Or she will be. The archon can be male or female," Florence explained.

"This is ridiculous," I moaned, putting my chin on my hands. "There is no way I am ever going to..." I glanced at Naveen and saw he was blushing. "You know what I mean. I'm not going *through* with any of this so what's the point?"

"Medra, I know you hate Blake. And Regan is no better. But this isn't just about your preferences," Florence said wretchedly. "I simply don't see how you can defy Viktor Drakharrow, even if you wanted to. If it's any consolation, while I know you don't want to hear this, you're in an extremely powerful and privileged arrangement in many ways. One that many blightborn would envy. But since I know it's not about the status for you, keep in mind that this is about your very survival."

Naveen nodded. "That's what Florence and I are worried about. No matter what happens with Blake, you're a First Year. You've seen how they treat us. You're going to have to get through the Consort Games. Somehow."

I thought back to the day in the Black Keep. Slowly I raised my left wrist and tugged the sleeve of the gray sweater I wore down just enough that a mark appeared.

"Is that the mark from the bonding ceremony?" Florence asked softly, looking at the red teardrop shape.

"*Bondage* mark, more like it," I said bitterly. "I wish I could get rid of it. Scrub it off like it was ink."

Naveen's face was troubled. "But it's not ink, Medra. You're part of that triad now, no matter what."

"Do you think Regan has the same marking?" I asked, suddenly curious. I'd never thought of it before.

Florence shook her head. "No. What you have is something different. I've never seen it before. You said Viktor did it?"

I nodded. "He marked Blake, too. He said some words. Almost like an incantation." They'd also reminded me of a marriage.

What is spoken cannot be unbroken.

I shuddered, wondering what kind of magic had been involved. There had to be some way to undo it. It was a betrothal, I reminded myself. We weren't married. Yet. Viktor Drakharrow had said this was just the beginning. I refused to accept–refused to believe–that I had to stay linked to Blake or to Regan in any way.

Maybe killing Blake would break the bond, a nagging voice in my head said.

It wasn't such a terrible idea. It might wind up being the only way.

I thought of the fluffin. How Blake had been willing to take it to a healer. All right, then, the man had one miniscule redeeming quality. He didn't hate animals.

Especially not tiny, cute ones.

That wasn't enough to make him actually tolerable. Or worth not killing. Was it?

"You should ask Rodriguez about all of this," Naveen was saying.

"Professor Rodriguez?" I frowned. "You don't even take a class with him. I didn't think you knew him."

"Everyone knows Rodriguez. He has the biggest chip on his shoulder when it comes to highbloods and yet he's still a cornerstone of Bloodwing," Naveen said, grinning.

"Not to mention that he likes you, Medra," Florence said encouragingly.

"I'm not so sure about that," I said, with a grimace. "He tolerates me."

"He's giving you private lessons, isn't he?" she said, lowering her voice so no one else could hear. "That's going above and beyond, I'd say. He didn't have to do that."

She was right. I'd been an ass in his class, but he seemed to have forgiven me. He had insisted I be trained in thrallguard and he was patient with me in our lessons, if not exactly warm and friendly.

"He might be able to tell you if there have been any blightborn consorts. Even what they did to survive," Naveen said. "It's worth at least asking about."

"Maybe they just liked their fellow consort and actually worked together," I said. Deep down I knew that wouldn't be happening with Regan.

"The person who would really know the most is Professor Hassan. But I don't think you should approach her," Florence said regretfully. "She really doesn't like you."

"Not the biggest Professor Hassan fan," I acknowledged. "Though she is certainly knowledgeable."

"I think she'd be more likely to accuse you of trying to cheat than to give you any helpful information," Naveen said. "I wouldn't bother."

I nodded and pushed my plate away. "Well, no use putting it off." I rose from the table.

"Now?" Florence looked surprised. "You're going now?"

I shrugged. "May as well see if he's in his office."

When I got to Rodriguez's office, the door was ajar.

Usually I'd wait in the hallway if I arrived at one of our lessons early and he'd always come to the door of his office and beckon me in.

But now, when I peeked through the crack in the door, it looked as if the room was empty.

Rodriguez's tall shelves lined with books caught my eye. He had quite the collection. I knew his interests went beyond restoration magic. He knew a great deal about dragons. What else was he interested in?

Ignoring a slight twinge of guilt, I pushed the door open, then shut it behind me exactly as it had been—slightly ajar.

I was just waiting in his office, I told myself. I wasn't going to touch anything. I knew I shouldn't be in there, not without his permission. But desperation was gnawing at me.

I glanced around the room, taking in the dark wood bookshelves that lined the walls from floor to ceiling.

My gaze locked onto a row of books that seemed older than the others. They were at the top of one of the shelves in the far corner.

I was tall but not that tall. I'd need a rolling ladder just to reach them.

Fortunately, Professor Rodriguez had one built in alongside the shelves.

I grabbed it quickly and slid it over to the shelf. Climbing up, I scanned the books quickly, keeping my ears open for sounds from the hallway.

Some of the volumes were on dragons. Others were on blood magic. One book called *Blood Magic and the Serpents of Flame* caught my eye, but I kept scanning, hoping to find something more relevant to my immediate situation.

I had almost reached the end of the shelf and was running out of titles to read when I saw it.

The Dark Art of Eternal Bonds.

My fingers brushed the edges of the cover. I felt a cold tingle pass through my hand, as if the book itself might be aware of my intentions.

I froze for a moment, listening for any sounds from the hallway. But it was quiet.

Carefully, I lifted the book from the shelf and cracked open the cover. The parchment was brittle and as I flipped through the pages, the words at first made no sense. Just a jumble of letters, shifting and moving like smoke.

I blinked, feeling panic rise in my throat, but then, the text suddenly sharpened and became legible.

This was the right book. I could feel it.

My fingers flew to the table of contents, my eyes scanning the page. And there it was: "A Ritual to Undo the Binding of Souls." The words jumped out at me, like a beacon in the dark.

My hand hovered over the page, torn between ripping it out and shoving the whole book into my satchel.

"Find something interesting?"

My heart lurched and I almost dropped the book. I grabbed at the ladder before I could fall backwards, then turned my head.

Professor Rodriguez stood in the doorway, his hands shoved in a pair of shabby brown trousers.

"I'm sorry," I said automatically. "I didn't mean to intrude. I was just waiting for you to come back."

"You've got quite an eye for rare books." Rodriguez stepped further into the room. He was watching me closely, as if unsure I really knew what I'd found. "Few students can read Classical Sangrathan."

"I can't," I blurted. "Read it, I mean. I just thought the cover was beautiful."

I looked down at the cover, praying it was unique. I hadn't even glanced at it yet.

Fortunately, the book wasn't the dullest I'd seen. It was covered in deep, black leather, cracked with age but still rich and polished as if it had been well-cared for over centuries. Silver filigree was coiled around the edges, curling into patterns that resembled wisps of smoke. In the center of the cover was embedded a serpentine silver dragon. I touched it lightly with one finger, feeling its ridges.

"Yes, it's a beautiful book. And rare. Put it back." Rodriguez's voice was soft, but his eyes were hard.

I quickly did as he said, then climbed down the ladder.

"Now, did you need something, Miss Pendragon? I don't recall us having an appointment. Or were you simply snooping?" He dropped a stack of papers onto his desk with a thud and I jumped.

Yes, something was going on with Rodriguez, I decided. He was always on edge, but now he was practically on guard. What was going on with him that he was this suspicious? Or was it just the fact that I'd touched the book?

Part of me wanted to ask him about the ritual, but with his suspicious attitude, I decided I'd better not risk it right now.

"I need something," I said, walking up to the desk.

"And that something is?" He sank into the wooden chair behind his desk and leaned back.

Even with his misguided sense of fashion, Rodriguez was a handsome man. It wasn't the first time I'd thought so. With his dark hair and long legs he was exactly my type. Or he would have been, if I wasn't fairly certain he already had a crush on Professor Sankara.

Or the type I thought was my type before a certain crooked aristocratic nose forced its way into my nighttime dreams...

I forced the thought out of my head.

"I need help surviving the Consort Games," I said bluntly. "Why did you never tell me about them?"

Rodriguez looked up at me from dark eyes, with a considering expression. "Teachers aren't permitted to tell students about Bloodwing rites. Especially not that one."

"Well, I know it exists so it's not a big mystery. I even know when it will happen," I bluffed.

He raised his eyebrows. "Do you? That's interesting. I don't."

"It's always held after the Frostfire Festival, right?" I guessed.

The House Leader rite was happening first. Florence and Naveen had seemed certain of that. And we were too close to midwinter for the Consort Games to be squeezed in before the break. They'd have to take place sometime afterwards. Probably in the spring.

"That's traditionally when they happen. But who knows about this year?" He looked at me directly. "Things change. The unexpected happens. Just look at you, for example."

"Speaking of the unexpected, I understand the consorts are expected to work together." I glanced at the door. Rodriguez had already shut it behind him. "How am I supposed to survive these Games when Regan Pansera hates me?" I hissed.

"That's certainly a problem," he agreed. "For you. Not for me."

I groaned and sank down into the hard wooden chair he always left out for students. I knew better than to take him at his word.

Rodriguez was a hardass, yes, but he didn't hate me. He might not like me as much as Florence thought, but I doubted he actively was hoping I'd die.

At least, I hoped not.

"Professor," I wheedled. "Please."

He laughed. "Whining will get you absolutely nowhere, Pendragon."

I sighed. "Can you at least tell me if there have been any situations like this? Any precedents for consorts who can't or won't work together?"

"Oh, there have absolutely been situations like that," Rodriguez said. "But you won't want to hear about any of them."

My heart sank. "Why not?"

"Because when that happens, the consorts usually die. Male and male, female and female, male and female. Whatever the configuration."

"But it's not fair," I said, starting to get angry. "I don't have a choice. Regan won't work with me, even if I wanted to work with her."

"Have you tried asking her? Talking to her about it?" Rodriguez picked up a quill and began to twirl it.

"Not exactly," I grumbled.

"Try that first. You never know." He tossed the quill up in the air.

"Fine. I will," I said. "But let's be realistic here. She won't agree. Even if I beg, which I'm prepared to do. Is Viktor Drakharrow really going to let us both die in this game just because we can't work together?"

"Viktor Drakharrow is a very busy, very important man, who probably has no idea that Regan hates you," Rodriguez said. "And who is going to tell him?" He tilted his head. "You?"

"Maybe I could get a message to him," I said desperately. "Send him a letter. I don't know. Something."

"Or you could stand on your own two feet and figure this out."

"That's easy for you to say," I shot back. "Sitting safely behind your teacher's desk."

Rodriguez's face hardened. "It's not as safe as you might think. We're blightborn after all, Miss Pendragon."

"Speaking of which, is there a precedent for *that*? For a blightborn consort succeeding in this game, I mean?" I asked, leaning forward in my seat.

"Yes, but the consorts usually worked together in those cases. As far as I can remember." He gave me a look that was almost sympathetic. "Look, there's only one real way I'm going to be able to help you get through the games and you already know what it is."

"Practicing thrallguard."

He nodded. "Exactly. If Regan really hates you as much as you think, then she'll try to get to you. If she somehow survives and you don't..."

"Then she'll get exactly what she wants," I said hollowly.

And what I didn't. Blake Drakharrow.

"She hasn't tried to thrallweave you again, has she?"

I shook my head. Now that I thought about it, I wondered why she hadn't.

"Good. Blake probably warned her not to."

I laughed. "I seriously doubt that."

Rodriguez shrugged. "You never know. He probably doesn't want his uncle finding out you're in conflict with one another. It would reflect badly on him."

"Now that I can almost believe," I said with a sigh. "Well, thank you. Can we have another session soon please? Maybe we can even double them up?"

"I'm not sure I'll have time for that, but..." He must have caught my stricken expression. "Fine. We'll double them up sometimes. I'll have more time over the Wintermark break. Are you staying at Bloodwing for the festival? I assume so. You don't have any family in Sangratha, right?"

I shook my head. I hadn't thought about it. I supposed the school would be almost empty over the break. But that didn't bother me. I'd enjoy the quiet.

"I'll be here at Bloodwing, yes. And that would be great," I said with relief. "Thank you, Professor."

Out in the hall, I had only one thing to say.

So, is there something you want to tell me? I asked my mother.

She sighed. *I did try to tell you.*

No, you didn't, I argued. I thought back. *When?*

The other day, she reminded me. *In the hall. Just before we were so rudely interrupted.*

I tried to remember. *You said you made changes.* My heart sped up. *What kind of changes?*

Well, Classical Sangrathan for one. You can read it.

It's just the Old Tongue, I said immediately. *The ancient language of Aercanum.*

You were tutored in the Old Tongue, were you? Her tone was sardonic.

Well, no, I admitted. *Not that I can recall.*

I was. I grew up speaking it. Reading it. Classical Sangrathan is the Old Tongue, with a few slight variations. The text you found in your professor's office was a very old one. Older than your school mottos.

That's why it took me a moment to be able to understand it, I replied.

Yes. We were both... processing what you saw.

Will I still be able to read Classical Sangrathan when you're... gone? I asked.

I have no idea. That's an excellent question.

What other things have you done to me? I demanded. *What changes have you made?*

I haven't done anything intentionally. Consider this more like... spillage, she said.

Spillage? My back went up. *I do not like the sounds of that.*

I'm seeping into you, she said. Her voice was almost tired. *I try not to, but I can feel it happening. A little bit more every day.*

I thought for a moment. *Does it hurt? Is the same happening to you? Am I seeping into you, I mean?*

It doesn't hurt, no. Thank you for asking. Her voice was tender. *I'm not sure. It's hard to tell. You have far fewer life experiences than I do. Far fewer skills.*

Well, thanks, I said sarcastically. *No need to remind me.*

This could be a good thing, she said. *Maybe something of me will be useful to you. Like the Classical Sangrathan.*

She was right about that, I had to admit.

I think I've found the right ritual, I told her, the excitement I'd felt slowly returning. *You saw the text?*

I did. Thank you for letting me see it. But I think you're forgetting it's on a shelf in your professor's office. Rather out of reach for the moment.

For the moment, I said. *But now that I know where it is, we can get to it. I'll come up with a plan.*

Things were coming along. It wasn't hopeless. Not anymore. I'd get the book, even if I had to break in during the dead of night and steal it.

But I didn't think it had to come to that.

Professor Rodriguez had promised to give me extra lessons in thrallguard. Surely during one of those sessions I'd arrive early and the door would be open again.

Next time I'd go straight for the book, grab it, stash it in my satchel, then wait outside. He'd never even have to know. I could return the book as soon as the ritual was complete.

CHAPTER 23

MEDRA

V aughn showed up at class the next day. Not Basic Combat for Blightborn, where he hadn't been all week. No, this was the History of Sangratha which we all had in the mornings.

He entered the lecture hall quietly, avoiding eye contact with anyone.

But Naveen stood up immediately. "Vaughn," he shouted, waving his arms. "Over here. Come sit with us."

The tall, skinny boy was hunched over. He kept his head down as he walked slowly over to us.

As he approached, I could see why. My heart sank.

Vaughn's appearance was shocking. His left eye was bruised, fading into shades of purple and yellow. His right arm was in a sling. Obviously it had been broken.

"Vaughn," Florence whispered, her face horrified as he slid into our row next to her. "What happened to you?"

Vaughn stared down at the desk, his normally cheerful face drained. He fiddled with the edge of his sleeve with his left hand. "It's nothing. I had an accident."

"An accident?" Naveen's eyes were wide as he took in Vaughn's battered appearance. "An accident?" he repeated, his voice a mix of worry and disbelief. "That doesn't explain the black eye or the broken arm. What kind of an accident exactly?"

My heart was hammering. I thought back to the last night I'd seen Vaughn, on the beach near the bonfire party. Theo had invited him, he'd said. I'd never told Florence about that. There had seemed to be no need to.

Vaughn shifted uncomfortably, still not meeting our eyes. "I fell down. It's worse than it looks," he said quietly. "The healers... They were able to fix most of it." I knew better than most just how much the healers could fix and how rapidly. If this was how Vaughn still looked even after seeing a healer then it must have been ten times worse before.

"But there's some permanent damage." His face constricted. I saw how hard he was working to keep it together. "They're not sure..." He cleared his throat. "They're not sure if I'll still be able to be a scout. I might be expelled from Bloodwing if they won't let me switch to a strategist training path instead."

A wave of anger rushed through me. I'd seen this before. How highbloods treated blightborns who dared to step out of line. This was just like what had happened to me, what had happened to Florence.

Vaughn hadn't fallen. He'd been attacked. It was written all over his face. It was in the way he was refusing to meet our eyes.

I tried to keep my voice low and steady, but my anger was barely restrained. "This wasn't an accident, was it, Vaughn? Who did this to you?"

Vaughn winced, his face tightening as if in shame. He opened his mouth, then shut it again.

But his silence was answer enough.

"Who was it?" I pressed. I caught Florence giving me a dissuading look but I didn't care. "Was it highbloods? Which one?"

"Highbloods?" Florence gasped. She looked back and forth between us, her shock seeming to deepen. "Vaughn, if they–if they did this, you have to tell someone. You should go to the headmaster. We're supposed to be safe here."

I ignored her. Anything I'd said at this point would have offended her. *No one* was going to do anything about this. No one cared. No one but us.

My stomach twisted. There was only one person I could think of who would have had the influence and the cruelty to attack the boy who liked Theo Drakharrow.

"Was it Blake?" I asked, my voice cold. "Did Blake Drakharrow do this to you? Because of Theo?"

Vaughn's face crumpled, and though he didn't say the words, the guilt in his expression was all the confirmation I needed.

Before I could say anything else, the door at the front of the room swung open and Professor Hassan strode in, her cane tapping sharply against the stones.

Her severe expression immediately ended all conversations.

I clenched my fists beneath the desk, my mind still racing.

Blake still had the fluffin.

That was the only thing that made me pause and consider for one moment the sanity of my next actions.

But ultimately, even the little pup wasn't enough to stop me. Florence and I could sneak into the Drakharrow Tower and get it afterwards, I rationalized. We'd figure something out.

I stormed into Advanced Weaponry and paused in the doorway, scanning the room.

There. In the corner.

Fucking *shirtless* again. Of course he was. Cocky, egotistical asshole.

His back was to me. The sight of all that exposed skin and muscle made my chest tighten, but not with fear.

His narrow shoulders flexed as he worked the training bag, muscles rippling beneath the black tattoos that covered his pale skin like dark, forbidden scriptures.

Sure, he was gorgeous. He was also oblivious to Vaughn's suffering and guilty as sin for causing it.

Fury was boiling in my veins. But beneath the rage was something else. Something far more infuriating and far more shameful.

There was a pull when I looked at Blake Drakharrow. He was beautiful in the way that fire was beautiful. Raw and scorching. I hated it. Hated that my breath caught in my throat when I saw him like this. Hated that my heart raced. Not just with anger, but with something I'd sworn I wouldn't let myself name.

I thought of Vaughn. His black eye, his broken arm. I thought of the hopeful, sweet expression in his eyes when I'd run into him that night on the beach and he'd been on his way to see Theo.

Blake had done this to him because he was a blightborn. Because he thought Vaughn wasn't good enough for Theo.

Just like he thought I wasn't good enough for him.

Now was the time to end this.

I glanced around. I was early. The room was still empty, except for a few highblood students here and there, talking to one another or practicing warm-up drills. Professor Sankara hadn't arrived yet. This was my chance.

I squared my shoulders and started across the room, my pulse a drumbeat in my ears. As I neared him, I called his name.

"Blake."

He froze mid-punch, his back still to me, then slowly lowered his fist. Then he turned, casual but alert, the hint of a cool smile already tugging at his lips.

His gray eyes narrowed, taking me in with that lazy arrogance I'd come to loathe.

"What do you want, Pen–" he started to drawl.

I didn't give him time to finish. Before the words were fully formed, my fist was flying.

My knuckles connected with the sharp line of his jaw. The impact reverberated up my arm. It hurt. It also felt really good.

Blake staggered back, a flash of shock crossing his handsome face as he brought a hand up to his face, rubbing his jaw where I'd struck him.

"What the fuck was that for?" Blake roared.

His mocking arrogance and customary smugness was gone, replaced by something far more dangerous.

But before I could answer, a tall figure rushed towards me. I turned to see Coregon. The tall, dark-skinned young man eyed me warily. "You can't take on Blake, Medra," he warned, his voice surprisingly gentle. "Just walk away. He's stronger than you are. You don't want this."

But Coregon's words simply goaded me onwards. My fury was burning too hot to put out.

I stepped around Coregon and he let me, taking a few steps back.

"You know what this is about," I spat at Blake. My fists rose as I moved towards him, body moving into a fighting stance. "Let's go. You and me. Right now. No one's going to stop us. You know you want this as much as I do."

Blake raised an eyebrow. "Fight you?" he echoed, mockery thick in his voice. "I'm not going to fight you, little drag–"

My fist shot out before he could finish the sentence, but this time he was ready for me. He was fast. Inhumanly fast. He easily sidestepped my blow.

Before I could recover my balance, his hand shot out, catching me by the wrist and twisting my arm. Not hard enough to hurt but enough to keep me off balance.

I could feel his strength. His grip was like iron and no matter how I struggled, I couldn't shake him off.

But I was wild now. A frenzy of anger was giving me strength beyond reason. My dragon rider instincts finally triggering again? Maybe. Maybe there was something else to it, too, but I didn't have the time to stop and question what it was.

I swung again, using my free hand, and while Blake dodged, it was clear he wasn't used to fighting anyone in quite this state of reckless abandon.

My body collided against his and suddenly we were closer than we'd ever been before. His chest pressed up against mine. Even through the thin fabric of my training tunic, the contact was electric.

I hated how my heart stuttered at the sensation. Like I'd been doused in cold water.

Blake grunted. He was struggling to control me.

I didn't *want* him to control me. I wanted him to fight back.

I twisted in his grip, trying to throw him off, but he was too strong.

He managed to push me down, pinning me to the ground, his body hovering mine. The breath was sucked out of me as my back hit the dirt.

It was like with Visha all over again... but different.

Our faces were inches apart. My breath was coming in ragged gasps. Blake's lips were parted as he searched my face with a strange intensity.

I felt the weight of him pressing down on me, felt his heat against my skin. My pulse was thrumming in my ears. Not just from the fight, but from the proximity. My body was trying to betray my mind.

I twisted beneath him, lifting my hips to try to throw him off, and I saw him flinch. "You fucking coward. You're a monster, Blake Drakharrow. You thought you could hurt him and just get away with it? Hell no. Not while I'm around. "

He glared down at me. "What the hell are you talking about?"

"I'm talking about Vaughn Sabino," I snarled. "I'm talking about what you did to my friend. You don't know a fucking thing about friendship, do you? About loyalty? If you want to hurt someone I care about, you'll have to go through me first. You're going to pay for what you did to him."

Blake's eyes flashed with something I couldn't pinpoint. Anger, guilt, maybe even regret. He wiped at his lips where a small line of blood trickled, his eyes never leaving mine.

I wasn't bleeding, I realized. Not yet. He'd made sure of that.

But I wanted to. I wanted to hurt. I wanted him to make me bleed. Just like he'd done to Vaughn. I wanted Blake to reveal himself once and for all. To show me the monster I knew lay underneath.

The room felt too small, the air between us charged with tension. His face hovered over mine, his breath hot against my skin.

Gods, I could feel every inch of him.

Blake's gaze was dark, confused even. For a second, neither of us moved. His eyes flicked down to my lips, then back up, as if he wasn't sure what he wanted to do next, kiss me or kill me.

The moment stretched. The world around us had faded into silence long ago.

I felt dizzy, my body tingling with rage and a maddening sense of need.

I wrenched my body to the side, breaking free of his hold and jumping to my feet. I swung my fist again just as he rose up beside me.

He dodged, catching my wrist mid-swing.

"You really want me to hurt you?" His voice was sharper now, frustration seeping through the cracks of his control.

"Yes," I shouted. "Fight me, you fucking coward. Instead of always picking on someone weaker than you are."

I yanked my hand free and lunged again, this time landing a punch to his ribs. But before I could hit him again, he grabbed both my arms and twisted them behind my back, holding me tight against him.

I struggled, thrashing in his hold.

"But you're weaker than me, Pendragon," he breathed in my ear. "You know you are. Look at you. You're pathetic."

"Shut the hell up and fight me. Why won't you fight me?" I demanded, my voice trembling with rage. My body was burning, every muscle straining from the effort of trying to reach him. He was wearing me out and he knew it.

"Maybe you're not worth it," he murmured. "Did you ever think of that?"

I roared, thrashing in his arms. He held me tight, his jaw clenched, but I could feel the frustration in him mounting. If he was wearing me out, I was wearing him out, too.

I didn't want to admit the truth. Blake was different from Visha. I'd been training for months. If this was Visha, I'd have been more than a match for her this time. Blake *was* stronger than me. By a lot. But I still wasn't giving up.

I might lose today. But I'd work to become just as strong. No matter what I had to do. I wouldn't stop fighting him. I'd never stop.

I managed to break his grip on one of my arms and half-turned, trying to swing behind me, but he caught my wrist.

"You and all your friends," I panted. "You're all bullies. And you have the nerve to call me pathetic. Look in the fucking mirror."

"Stop!"

The word rang out across the training yard.

Instantly, Blake let go of me and stepped away.

I blinked, suddenly disoriented.

Professor Sankara stood at the entrance to the yard, his eyes blazing with anger as he strode towards us.

It was only then that I realized we were surrounded by a crowd.

Highblood students, blightborn students–there must have been a hundred or more gathered around. They'd come in from the corridors, and now stood there, whispering, their eyes wide with shock and fascination as they watched Blake and I.

I spotted a familiar face at the edge of the crowd. Vaughn.

I'd expected him to look relieved. But instead, he looked horrified. Was he afraid of retaliation? I'd have to reassure him later.

Still, a wave of guilt went through me. Had I done the right thing? Had this really been for Vaughn at all?

"Everyone to the arena," Professor Sankara barked. "The House Leader ceremony is about to begin and you are all expected to be in attendance."

The crowd started to disperse, the students raising their voices once more into an even louder murmur as they filed out of the yard.

Professor Sankara walked towards us.

"You are both in violation of Sangrathan law," he declared, his voice hard as stone. I stared at him. What was he talking about? "But you're needed in the arena, Drakharrow. Whatever this was will have to be dealt with later."

Blake went to move past me, then paused and glanced my way. Our eyes met.

He held my gaze for a moment, his eyes cold. Then he turned and walked away.

I was left in the yard alone, my fists still clenched by my side, trying to make sense of what had just happened.

A soft snuffling sound pulled me out of my fog. A faint whimper followed, then a tiny yap.

My eyes darted around until they landed on a large bag over in the corner where Blake had been practicing before I'd interrupted him. It was half-concealed by a stack of practice weapons, so I hadn't even noticed it before.

I walked over, my pulse finally beginning to slow to a normal pace after the fight. The bag was made of worn black canvas, the kind of duffel that just blended into the shadows. It was big enough to carry bulky training gear, the kind most highblood students would use to store their personal equipment.

But this one had mesh sides, open to let gear or sweaty training clothes ventilate.

I knelt down and unbuckled the top of the bag and there, nestled between some folded clothes and towels, was the fluffin. His wide, owl-like eyes blinked up at me. Then he yapped again, louder this time, and jumping up a little, licked my hand.

My stomach twisted in confusion. Blake had brought the fluffin to Advanced Weaponry. Why?

I looked the little creature over. He seemed to be fully healed.

Blake had brought the fluffin to give it back to me. He'd done what I'd asked and he'd been planning to return it. Then I'd attacked him and he'd been called away to the arena and forgotten all about it.

"Medra!"

I turned at the sound of my name.

Vaughn stood by the entrance.

Picking up the black bag and gently pushing the fluffin's head back down, I walked towards him.

"Vaughn. What are you doing here?"

"Why did you attack Blake Drakharrow?" He was chewing his lip nervously.

"You already know why," I said slowly. "He attacked you."

He shook his head slowly. "I didn't say that."

My heart sped up. "You didn't have to. It was written all over your face. Someone from Theo's house did this to you. Who else but Blake?"

Vaughn looked miserably. "It wasn't him."

His words hit me like a slap in the face.

"What? What do you mean it wasn't him?"

"We have to go, Medra. Attendance at the House Leadership ceremony is compulsory. *Very* compulsory." He grabbed my arm and I realized how frightened he was. "Let's go."

I followed him into the hall as he half-dragged, half-pulled me.

The corridor was empty. Bloodwing had never seemed so quiet.

I pulled away. "I'm not going anywhere until you tell me who did that to you."

Vaughn covered his hands with his face. "I didn't want any of this."

"I know," I said. "I'm sorry."

He lowered his hands and looked at me. "It was Coregon Phiri."

"What?" My head started to spin. "Are you telling me the truth, Vaughn?"

"It wasn't Blake," he said firmly. "It was Coregon. In fact..." He hesitated.

"What?"

"We have to go, Medra. At least walk and talk."

He started down the hallway again, half-running, and I chased after him.

"It could have been even worse," he said, tossing the words over his shoulder as he moved quickly down the next corridor. We were entering an area of the school I'd never been in before. "Someone found me on the beach. I was bleeding. I guess I'd passed out. They carried me back to the school. Left me outside the First Year infirmary. The healer found me right away. She said someone had been banging on the door."

"Theo?" I guessed.

But Vaughn shook his head. "I don't know."

My head was swirling. Just because Blake hadn't personally attacked Vaughn didn't mean he hadn't been responsible somehow. He could have commanded Coregon to do it.

But Vaughn's words had cast doubt on everything I thought I knew.

The halls were unsettlingly silent now that everyone had made their way to the arena. Our footsteps echoed as we hurried along, Vaughn leading me deeper into the school than I had ever ventured before. The stones along the walls began to darken.

As we rounded a corner, my breath caught in my throat. A wide trio of open arches led into the arena. The space was vast and open to the sky. Carved from huge stone blocks of deepest red, the arena had tiered seats that encircled the floor below.

Most of the seats were already full.

As we stepped through the arches, someone stepped towards me and grabbed my arm.

"Where the hell have you been?" Professor Rodriguez snapped angrily. He shook his head. "On second thought, never mind that now. You're late. Vaughn, go find a seat. Miss Pendragon, come with me. Everyone has been waiting for you."

CHAPTER 24

BLAKE

I watched Rodriguez usher Pendragon down the tiers of stone to her seat as I stood down below in the middle of the arena floor.

The floor featured moving stone platforms that could rise into the air during combat, adding another layer of complexity to a fight as they rotated and shifted unpredictably. But today the platforms were still and silent. I wouldn't have to worry about keeping my balance.

The most prestigious students from my house sat together in the first row, and there at the end were the two spots saved for my consorts: Regan Pansera and Medra Pendragon.

It was supposed to be a place of honor. Pendragon sure didn't look honored.

Regan had taken her seat a long time ago. She sat there now, the epitome of poise and control, her back perfectly straight, her silver-blonde hair arranged meticulously. She stiffened slightly as Pendragon sat down beside her and leaned away, as if touching the blightborn girl might sully her.

Regan was the perfect highblood girl. Popular and beautiful. Bred for power.

She stared ahead, indifferent, bored, waiting for this ritual to end. I knew she had no doubt I'd become House Leader today. But the confidence she had in me was meaningless.

Then there was Pendragon. Looking as if she'd love nothing better than to kill us all with her eyes. She was slumped slightly in her seat, obviously wishing she were anywhere but here. Her mass of fiery curls had grown only wilder thanks to our spat. Wisps and tendrils had escaped the leather tie she used to hold her hair back.

The freckles along her cheeks stood out even more when she was angry. And she was angry now. Angry and uncomfortable, glaring across the arena at me with a stubborn, reckless glint in her eyes.

My chest tightened. She'd attacked me with murder in her heart. And yet, idiot that I was, it was *her* I couldn't take my eyes off.

She was everything Regan wasn't. Unrefined, unpredictable. Burning with a fire I couldn't help but admire. Even though she clearly despised me.

Regan wanted me for what I represented, not who I was.

Power. Prestige. Status. Control. Everything that came with being a Drakharrow. Those were the things Regan lived for.

Oh, there was no denying she was beautiful. In the same way that ice was beautiful.

Regan would be an obedient consort. A perfect mother. Always loyal. She had been bred for this role and she played it well. From childhood, we'd been told we would someday be partners.

Yet I hated her. Hated her for everything she'd let herself become. Even though she'd done nothing less than exactly what she was told.

Whereas Pendragon didn't want me at all. She was willful, obstinate, and probably going to get herself killed one of these days.

Yet when I lay in my bed at night, after having rejected one of Regan's pathetic advances for the hundredth time, Pendragon's face was the one I couldn't get out of my mind.

It was a sick irony. The more she fought against me, the more this fucked up attraction to her grew.

Fighting her in the training yard just now had been almost as good as sex. It was probably the closest we'd ever get, if she had her way.

I knew I'd be replaying the way her body had moved as we fought in my head that night, over and over again. When I'd pinned her down, my body pressing against hers, her breath hot on my skin–I'd known in that moment it would be the closest I'd ever get to having her. The way she'd writhed beneath me, the soft curves of her body straining against my weight, her lips slightly parted as she gasped for breath... Fuck. It had almost undone me.

I'd stayed there like that as long as I'd dared, hovering over her, unable to take my eyes off the soft, tempting curve of her lips. The impulse had been so strong to just lean down and kiss her, right there in front of everyone.

She would have slapped me. Probably would have hated me even more.

But I couldn't help wondering if it would have been worth the humiliation.

Did she know how careful I'd been not to make her bleed? Not to break her perfect, soft, white skin no matter how much she goaded me?

I'd already been so fucking aroused that I knew if I'd scented even a drop of blood on her while we'd fought, I wouldn't have been able to restrain myself.

I groaned a little, remembering the sweetness of her body, the swell of her breasts. It had taken all I had not to reach a hand down and cup one of them through her tunic.

I knew that night I'd be jerking off as I imagined unfastening her trousers and sliding into the warm, wet place between her thighs.

Except, in my fantasies, Pendragon was always a *willing* participant. She'd moan her need for me, arching her hips impatiently. She'd tug my pants off, and cradle my cock, running her fingers down the hard length of it.

In my dreams, she wanted me just as much as I wanted her.

Fat chance of that ever happening in real life.

Belatedly, I realized Headmaster Kim had stood up and was speaking.

I knew I'd be expected to pay him a visit later. Probably with Pendragon. Did she even realize the serious crime she'd committed by fighting me like that?

Consorts had been banished or even beheaded for less.

One did not attack one's archon. Ever.

It was an unspoken rule, perhaps even an unwritten one. If it was unwritten, if it wasn't actually on the books, then perhaps we could use that to Pendragon's advantage. I could talk to Rodriguez after this was all over, see if he could point that out to Kim.

I felt an uncomfortable sensation, like an itch on my conscience.

What the fuck was wrong with me that I was thinking of ways to keep Pendragon from being kicked out of Bloodwing or worse? Instead of just letting it happen.

Because, a secret nagging voice in my head said, I knew exactly what would happen to her if she was expelled.

She wouldn't be free. My uncle would never let her go.

No, Pendragon was chained for life. If not to me, then...

Kim's chill voice broke through my thoughts. "For millennia, the leadership of our Houses has been determined by strength, cunning, and the will to dominate. Only the powerful may rule. Only the worthy may survive. 'Sanguis et Flamma Floreant' is our motto. Only blood and flame may flourish in these halls. From blood comes unity. From blood comes strength. From blood, legacy. From blood, power."

I sighed and crossed my arms over my chest, trying not to look too bored. It was basically the same tedious speech he'd given at every House Leadership ceremony.

Except this year would be even more tedious for the crowd watching. Today I'd be winning the House Leader position by default.

Headmaster Kim sure didn't seem pleased about that. "In an almost unprecedented historical moment at Bloodwing, we stand here today without a second challenger. Without a single soul brave enough to test their strength against House Drakharrow's favored son."

My claim to the house leadership was practically a birthright. No one had the guts to face me. I hadn't really expected them to.

Still, I had to admit it was too easy this way.

Catherine Mortis had to put down three other contenders to win her place. Even though we'd all known she'd come out the victor. One had even been her own cousin. Catherine was brutal and would do anything to win. She'd been merciless with her kills. Even more pitiless towards her cousin.

Lysander Orphos had two challengers to subdue before he took up the mantle of House Leader for Orphos. I hadn't really thought he'd had it in him, to be honest. He and his sister both looked so, well, fragile, sensitive. But he'd proved me and all his other detractors wrong that day. He'd killed with grace.

As for Kage Tanaka, only one highblood in House Avari had been stupid enough to challenge him. That fool was eliminated quickly and in the most stylistic way I'd ever seen. Kage was an incredible fighter and a strong leader. He was more cunning than either Catherine, with her brute force, or Lysander, with his daydreamy attitude. Tanaka would be a powerful ally some day. But in the meantime, we had an almost friendly rivalry. Things were less boring at Bloodwing with Tanaka around. He knew how to keep me on my toes. Like with his hilarious play at the bonfire that night. He'd evidently lost patience with Kiernan. Killing the lackey had practically been doing Tanaka a favor.

"Is this what we have become?" Headmaster Kim's voice had turned sharper, almost mocking. "Are we so weak, so cowardly, that none of you dare to rise to this challenge? What has happened to our legacy? To the blood that demands we fight for our place?"

My lips curled in a half-smirk, but my stomach twisted slightly at Kim's words. They were a dig. My very lack of challengers was casting a shadow over my ascension today. It made the victory feel hollow.

Never mind the fact that taking anyone on at this point would have been... bothersome. What Pendragon lacked in strength and speed, she made up for in raw chaotic force. Our fight had taken more out of me than I wanted to admit, even though I had to stand here now and pretend like I hadn't been impacted in the slightest. She'd pushed me hard. I wasn't fully spent but I wasn't where I'd have wanted to be to take on a challenger. Fortunately I wouldn't have to.

The problem was, I hadn't been feeding enough. I had to do so. Soon. I pushed the thought away and tried to concentrate on what Kim was saying.

"Blake Drakharrow stands here today, unchallenged," the headmaster continued. The man was getting on my nerves. Just wrap things up already. "Not because he is unworthy of a fight, but because none among his house has the courage to face him."

I glared at the back of the headmaster's head. Kim was taking it a little too far. I wouldn't stand to have my house shamed and it felt like that was exactly what he was trying to do. Make us out to be a bunch of cowards. When the reality was no one dared to challenge me because they knew it was pointless. They'd die. I'd put them down like the dogs they were.

It was better to defer to me than to waste their life needlessly. Just like with a wolf pack, my house of highbloods knew I was their alpha. I'd made that clear from the start. I'd done my duty when I'd served my brother Marcus as his second. I'd been loyal. Even though it'd killed me sometimes.

Then, when Marcus graduated, I'd made it clear that they all were to submit to me. And they had. I had to admit, Regan had been useful then. But of course, she'd wanted me in charge because that meant she gained status, too.

I'd had to kick a few asses to get everyone in line, but then it had been relatively peaceful. There was absolute loyalty among our house now. I'd have accepted nothing less.

Of course, the one outlier was Pendragon. But she was a First Year. When she came to Drakharrow Tower next year, she'd have to shape up. She'd risk embarrassing me even worse than she already had otherwise.

I smothered a yawn, as my mind continued to drift, tuning out the speech. I'd already won, hadn't I? I was moments away from receiving the gold pin. This was all just a formality. A reward for a position I'd never had any doubt I'd take.

Let's get this over with. My gaze wandered back to Pendragon.

Then I heard it. A growl. So soft I didn't think anyone else had even noticed.

My body tensed immediately. I recognized the sound.

My eyes darted to Pendragon's legs where my black canvas bag rested on the ground by her feet.

Neville—a stupid name but it was what I'd taken to calling the fluffin—had poked his head out. He was looking at me and growling, his tiny pointed teeth bared.

For a moment, I was shocked. Then I realized he wasn't growling at me.

Neville was looking behind me.

My reflexes kicked in just in time. I twisted to the side.

A blur of motion. A rush of air. A flash of silver.

Pain exploded along my side as I was thrown forward, sprawling face first onto the stone floor. For a few moments, I was disoriented. Ears ringing. Mind struggling to catch up with the sudden attack.

Who the fuck would dare...

The knife was yanked out of my side unceremoniously.

I groaned but pushed down the pain, using the same moment to flip onto my back, adrenaline surging as I locked eyes with my opponent.

For a moment, time froze.

Coregon.

The disbelief must have shown on my face because Coregon smirked. It was such an unusual expression for someone I'd thought of as a loyal follower. No, a friend.

Something in my heart sank. This was real. This was happening.

Whatever friendship I'd thought Coregon and I shared, it had just been an act. I'd been a fool not to know better.

My shock was quickly buried in a wave of anger. Anger at myself, anger at him. I tried to push myself onto my feet but Coregon was on me in an instant, the dagger still clutched in his hand.

Weapons were technically banned from the challenge. But students had snuck them in before. Generally, if you won, you got away with whatever you'd done to win. No one cared about cheating when everyone else was already dead. It just made you look more cunning.

Still, I'd always thought it was a coward's move and I'd said that to my group of friends more than once. The thought must have shown on my face.

"Don't look at me like that," Coregon hissed. "Don't you fucking dare. I had to do this, Blake. Someone has to put you down."

I had only one word for him. "Why?"

"Because you're weak."

The sound of the word stung more than the wound in my side. "Weak? How the fuck am I weak?"

"Because of her," Coregon spat, his voice laced with disgust. "The blightborn bitch. Pendragon defies you. She stands up to you. Hell, she attacked you today. And you, what do you do? You let her. You don't even punish her. You're supposed to be the leader of this House. And yet you can't even control a mere mortal."

My stomach twisted as the venom in Coregon's words hit me. How dare he. How fucking dare he.

I shouldn't have done it, but I did. I glanced across the arena to where Pendragon sat. She was leaning forward, her green eyes wide, all signs of boredom gone. Neville had leaped into her arms and she was cradling him.

Was she hoping Coregon would kill me? Probably.

But what would Coregon do to her if I died here today?

That was all the impetus I needed. I would decide what happened to Pendragon. Our fates were bound whether she liked it or not.

The dagger flashed as it arced towards my chest. But I was faster. I caught Coregon's wrist in a death grip, my muscles straining.

As I fought to push the dagger away from my body, Coregon fought back. We fell to the ground, grappling, neither of us giving an inch.

Around us the arena was coming to life, triggered by Coregon's appearance. The stone platforms that had been suspended in place were now shifting, rotating ominously around us.

I could hear the rasping sound of scraping stones as they moved into position and then out again, turning the arena around us into a deadly maze.

Scanning the arena and getting my bearings quickly, I jumped up onto a platform that had just risen behind me.

Coregon followed, leaping up onto it behind me just as the one he had been standing on descended.

I ducked as he swiped, then grabbed his arm, twisting it with brutal force.

The dagger clattered to the stone. I saw the panic in Coregon's eyes as my foot shot out and I kicked it away, down into the open pit far below.

I could have grabbed it. Used it against him.

But that wasn't my way. It wouldn't have been as satisfying.

I was tired. Muscles weary. Heart pounding.

Despite that, I knew I was going to win. There was no way I was letting Coregon Phiri take over House Drakharrow, even if it was only at Bloodwing. And there was no fucking way I was leaving Pendragon to him.

"You call me a coward," I panted. "Yet you brought a knife to a fist fight, Phiri, because you were so afraid to come at me. Who's the real fucking coward?"

Another platform hovered over us, larger than the one we were standing on, its shadow stretching across the arena floor below.

Coregon lunged again, throwing a wild punch that I just managed to dodge. The pain in my side was a fire now, but I ignored it. It would heal and I'd survive.

The same couldn't be said for Coregon. He'd fucked up today. It was just a matter of how long it would take him to realize it.

"You could have been my second. You could have been right by my side through whatever happened next. You unbelievable idiot. How could you have been so shortsighted? Here I always thought you were smarter than me." I gave a mocking laugh.

"Theo would always have been your second," Coregon growled. But I heard the doubt in his voice.

"Theo is a hopeless romantic with a flair for drama. He doesn't *want* to be anyone's second. But you're right. Now he'll have to be. He'll have to step up when you're dead," I shot back.

My eyes darted upwards as the platforms moved in closer, the gnashing of stone upon stone echoing through the massive chamber.

I saw an opportunity.

I ducked just as Coregon swung again, dodging the blow and using the momentum to shove him backwards–right into the path of the descending platform.

Coregon stumbled, his eyes widening as the shadow of the platform loomed over him. He twisted, trying to escape. But I was faster. I grabbed him by the throat, forcing him backwards.

"We sparred with each other almost every day," I snarled at him. "Yet never once did you realize I was always holding something back."

It was a strategy I'd been taught early on by my father. Never show your opponent what you're really capable of. Even if your opponent is one of your best friends. Even so, it hadn't been enough to save him.

Coregon's hands were like claws, nails raking down my arms with the desperation of a drowning animal. The stone platform above us continued its slow, inevitable descent.

"You think I'm weak?" My voice was filled with cold fury. "You have no idea what I'm capable of, Coregon. Now you're never going to find out. You won't be around for any of it."

I leaned in closer to him. "You're right about one thing though. I was weak. But not when it came to Pendragon."

Coregon's eyes were wobbling with panic as the platform lowered, now just feet above our heads. I held him firm, using all my strength to pin him against the stone.

"I was weak when it came to you," I continued. "You went behind my back when you attacked Vaughn Sabino. That's when I should have put you down."

"Theo is a fucking menace. A coward. He's an embarrassment to our house," Coregon managed to choke out. "Marcus came to me. I did what had to be done."

Marcus had come to Coregon? That was another betrayal that would have to be dealt with. But it could wait for another time.

I leaned in closer. "Theo is *my* cousin. He's my friend. That's all that matters. It's called loyalty, Coregon. Maybe if you'd shown some, you wouldn't be in this position."

"I know what you really are. If it isn't me," Coregon gasped, my hands tight around his throat. "It's going to be someone else. Someone else will take you down."

"Let them come." I glanced up as the platform lowered. "As for you, you won't have long to wait."

Coregon's eyes widened with fear, as the sound of grinding stone filled our ears.

"Blake—wait!" he gasped, his voice strangled. "I'm sorry. Please. Don't—"

But it was too late. The platform lowered, its descent slow and deliberate. I held Coregon's gaze. He knew there was no escape.

It was over in seconds.

The platform dropped with a sickening crunch.

I stepped back, breathing heavily as I watched the stone platforms all begin to grind to a halt.

The arena was silent.

I was trembling. I curled my hands into fists, trying to stop the shaking. The reality of what I'd just done was still sinking in.

Then the silence shattered. The crowd erupted. A wave of frenzied cheering and applause rolled through the stands.

I wiped a smear of blood from my face and straightened up, trying to look happy with my victory, my eyes scanning the crowd.

Everyone was on their feet, cheering for me. Highbloods loved bloodshed. They loved a brutal triumph. I'd added excitement to what they'd been expecting to be a dull school assembly. Even the blightborn students had been carried along in the frenzy.

Only one person in the arena wasn't cheering or clapping.

Pendragon.

She stood out like a flame. She clutched Neville to her chest, her eyes locked on me.

Our gazes met.

What was she thinking? Was she disgusted? I knew she couldn't possibly be proud. Did she even care about what I'd just done? Did she know how much Coregon had really hated her?

My mind raced, trying to untangle the look in her eyes. But she gave me nothing. Just stared back at me steadily as the noise of the arena crashed around us like a wave.

CHAPTER 25

BLAKE

I felt my lip split open as my head smashed against the wall.

Whatever pleasure I might have felt from surviving the House Leadership and Coregon's betrayal hadn't lasted long–if it was ever there in the first place.

I'd gone from a solo visit with the headmaster to being summoned by my uncle.

I licked the blood off my lips, resisting the instinct that screamed at me to fight back, to resist. Instead, I held still, jaw clenched with tension. The wound on my side from Coregon's knife was still throbbing. It would take a few days to completely heal. I'd bound it as best I could before coming here.

Viktor was a good few inches shorter than me, but even so, he seemed to hulk over me as I leaned against the wall, trying to fake the proper humility.

He was older than me by centuries. With that age came a power I could never hope to match.

Viktor might look like a typical blightborn man in his sixties. But the very fact that he showed any sign of aging at all spoke volumes.

He was one of the oldest vampires alive and possibly the strongest.

I spit out a mouthful of blood on the stone floor and considered, just for a moment, lashing out.

But I knew better. I stood no chance against Viktor.

Another blow came. This one a swift strike to my gut.

I doubled over, gasping for breath.

"You've embarrassed me," Viktor snarled, stepping closer. "You've embarrassed this House."

"Seems to be the theme of my day," I quipped, then instantly regretted it as Viktor's fist collided with my jaw again.

I struggled to stand straight, trying to push the nausea and dizziness away. But Viktor's words dug in deep.

"You've made a spectacle of yourself," Viktor snarled, his voice cold and biting. "Fighting with your betrothed in front of the entire academy."

I'd told Headmaster Kim that I'd started the fight.

Coregon Phiri was probably the only one who'd been close enough to witness what had really happened.

Fortunately he was now dead.

For a moment, I'd been tempted to tell Kim the truth. That I'd been defending myself. That I'd even held back. Pendragon had probably walked out of that training yard with a few bruises but otherwise not a scratch on her.

But the idea of Pendragon being summoned here to face my uncle's wrath instead of me made my chest tighten. I wouldn't subject her to it, no matter how much she might deserve it. I knew what Viktor was capable of. I wouldn't let her face that.

So instead, I'd lied.

I'd known Viktor would summon me. Though I hadn't expected it to be quite so soon.

"I was putting her in her place," I said. "She disrespected me and I dealt with it."

Viktor's expression twisted with anger. "You dealt with it? You made it worse. Knocking her around in private would have been one thing." Of course it would have. That was the norm in our family. At least, ever since Viktor had become its head. "Now *that* I could have condoned. But you fought her in public. The entire school thinks you can't control your own betrothed. A blightborn woman no less." He spat the word as if it were toxic. I knew he valued Pendragon's blood. That didn't mean he didn't simultaneously despise her.

My fists tightened at my sides. I knew what Viktor wanted to hear me say–that I'd failed. That I was sorry.

I couldn't bring myself to do it.

"She could have been expelled for that fight," Viktor continued, his fury plainly growing. "The Drakharrows have given buckets of gold to that fucking school. But Kim still runs it the way he sees fit. He could have had her executed. And I wouldn't have been able to prevent it. I wouldn't have learned of it in time."

"But she wasn't," I snapped. "He would have had to consult the board for something like that. Besides, I told Kim it was my fault. She's fine." I couldn't help adding sullenly, "I didn't ask for this, you know. I didn't ask for *her*."

Viktor backhanded me without a word.

He patiently waited while I wiped the blood off my face before he spoke again.

"I've held back today. You must be wondering why," he said. "The only reason I'm not beating you into the ground right now is because of what I heard about a certain blight-born boy walking around with some severe injuries." There was a gleam of satisfaction in Viktor's eyes. "I told you to put your cousin in his place. You did the next best thing. I hear you did quite a number on the boy."

I froze, my stomach twisting. I hadn't touched Vaughn Sabino. Coregon had been the one responsible. But Coregon was dead now. If he'd had been telling the truth, Marcus was the one who'd actually instructed Coregon to attack Vaughn. But evidently Marcus had gone behind my uncle's back when he'd talked to Coregon. Anything to make me look weak.

"Yeah," I muttered. "I told you I'd take care of it."

Viktor nodded, pleased. "Good. I won't have your cousin shaming this family. You did Theo a favor. The only thing I don't understand is why you didn't include him in your punishment. Or why you let the mortal boy live."

I shrugged. "Sabino's disfigured now. He might even lose the use of his arm. I thought he could be a warning to anyone else Theo might try to...entice," I lied, feeling sick inside.

Viktor nodded. "Fine. We'll try it your way. But another wrong move and Theo will find himself before me. You're welcome to tell him so."

I balled my hands into fists so tightly the nails bit into my palms. I hated how casually Viktor spoke about Theo and Vaughn, as if they were disposable. But I couldn't let my real emotions show. Not now. Theo was my responsibility and I had to protect him.

"Of course, then there's the matter of Kiernan O'Rourke," my uncle said. His face darkened once more and I knew I was in for it.

"Kiernan? What the fuck was wrong with what I did to Kiernan?" I asked in disbelief. "I thought you'd be happy about that."

"Happy?" Viktor roared. "His father was a valuable ally. Now you've destroyed that relationship with your hotheadedness."

I stared at him. "But the O'Rourkes are with House Avari..."

"Allegiances can change," Viktor snapped. In other words, Lord O'Rourke was a spy for Viktor. Or had been. "You have no idea the relationships I've been cultivating. The bonds I've been forging. All to strengthen this house, all to protect this family."

To strengthen *himself*. To gain more power for *himself*. Viktor Drakharrow only cared about one man and one man only. He was nothing like my father. And yet his power rested on my father's legacy.

He probably had spies in each of the other three houses. I wondered how many he had in Bloodwing, all scurrying back to tell tales about me to him.

"Kiernan was threatening to drink Pendragon. He disrespected me. I had to act," I said, meeting Viktor's gaze and refusing to back down.

The truth was, I'd lost control that night. When he'd touched Pendragon's blood, I'd seen red. Kiernan was doomed from that moment forward.

Kage Tanaka had understood that. Which was why he hadn't intervened. Kiernan had been an embarrassment to House Avari.

Or, the thought occurred to me, perhaps the Avaris had learned about the O'Rourkes' disloyalty. Had I punished Kiernan so Kage didn't have to? That would put a twist on things. I scowled.

"Did you?" Viktor sneered. "Or did you just want to throw your weight around like a fool? Now I have to clean up your mess. You don't think, Blake. You act without considering the consequences. You should be thankful I gave you the dragon rider bitch in the first place. Anyone else would have been grateful. Do you know the strength that lies in that blood of hers?"

Something in Viktor's voice made me pause. Something was off here but I couldn't put my finger on it.

Then I recognized it for what it was. *Hunger.*

My uncle was hungry for Pendragon. He was jealous. Jealous of me. That...was not a good thing.

I kept my voice steady. "I didn't ask for her. Give her to someone else if she's so valuable," I bluffed.

Now that I'd caught a glimpse of Viktor's own lust for Pendragon, I knew what would happen if I seemed too eager to keep the prize I'd been given.

"No," Viktor said, his lip curling. "She's yours now. But you will keep her in line using more subtlety in the future, or I'll be forced to handle her myself."

Just the idea of my uncle *handling* Pendragon made me want to vomit.

I clenched my jaw, anger simmering just below the surface, threatening to boil over.

Viktor abruptly shifted topics, saving me from myself. "There's unrest in the cities. The masses have been stirring. There are whispers of rebellion. Faint, but at times, I worry our control over them is weakening slightly."

I stayed silent, but my stomach twisted. I knew what Viktor meant by 'control.' A subtle, insidious magic, a lower form of thrallweave, kept the mortals compliant and worshipful.

Most blightborn lived their entire lives never knowing they were being manipulated. Never realizing we highbloods were gently pulling their strings.

At Bloodwing, this magic was less powerful. Different wards were set up over the school to protect the students within. These wards conflicted with the magic used over the city of Veilmar, among others. But the houses justified this by telling themselves that the blightborn students who attended Bloodwing didn't need to be manipulated–or not by much. They wanted to be here. They already adored us.

For the most part, I'd found that was correct.

Viktor's eyes flickered over me, sharp and calculating. "We can't afford weakness. Not now, Blake. Not with the city on edge. If word gets out in Veilmar that we have a dragon rider. Well... I've been preparing for that eventuality but I want her under our full control when it does happen."

My heart sped up. I wondered if my uncle was talking about speeding up our bonding. There was no real way to do that though. Not without Pendragon's cooperation.

Viktor started pacing back and forth across the room. "You don't understand the danger she poses. Keeping her alive... We had no choice that day in the Keep. But if word gets out that a dragon rider has returned, she could become a dangerous symbol. A spark for rebellion." He stopped in front of me, glaring down. "Which is why you need to keep her under control. Keep her at the school. Safe and under our power. Her entire life, she'll be watched and guided." His lips twisted into a cruel smile. "She'll never be anything more than what we allow her to be."

I stared up at him, trying to hide the shock I was feeling.

Viktor didn't know. He didn't have a fucking clue.

Rodriguez had told me he was teaching Pendragon thrallguard. Hell, it had been approved by Headmaster Kim himself.

And yet Viktor didn't know. He obviously didn't know.

I wasn't going to tell him.

My mind raced. How far had Pendragon come with her training? Probably not far enough to resist Viktor if he did have to use thrallweave on her.

"Is that all we want with her?" I risked asking. "To keep her as a pawn? She's a pretty useless pawn if you ask me. What kind of a symbol would she be for the blightborn when there are no dragons? Her blood carries power, nothing more."

"She's already a symbol," Viktor said. "A symbol of *Drakharrow* power. A symbol of our power over all the other houses. Do you not see that? Every man and woman in the Keep that day was hungering after her blood. We might have drained her in the Sanctum and shared her. A communal feast. But I gave her to one man. You."

A chill went up my spine.

"A very generous gift," I said slowly. "You truly honored me, Uncle. I see that now."

"I could have given her to Marcus," he said, studying me closely. "But Marcus has proven too reckless with his toys. She is too valuable for that. Not to mention..." He hesitated. I waited, all ears now. "Not to mention we still have no idea where she came from."

"You think she could be some sort of a spy?"

"The girl's ignorance seemed genuine in many ways," Viktor said consideringly. "Even if she were a spy, where would she have possibly come from? Who could have been keeping a girl with an appearance like that concealed? It seems impossible. But that doesn't mean she doesn't know more than she's letting on. She has no reason to trust us. And every reason to try to escape." His eyes met mine. "She cannot be permitted to leave, Blake. Ever."

I nodded. "I understand. I'll watch her. I'll keep her safe." I hesitated, then asked, "You say there's been unrest in Veilmar. I understand the killings have increased."

Viktor waved a hand. "Blightborns deaths. Easily dealt with."

Easily ignored, he meant.

"Blightborns clearly killed by highbloods," I said, trying to keep my patience. "If we want to maintain control..."

"It's a balance," Viktor said testily. "We must continue to preach restraint. We have your father to thank for that. A new way, he said. Well, your generation has grown up with this 'new way.' They are the weaker for it."

None of this was what my father had had in mind. But I said nothing.

"But the reality is," Viktor continued. "That vampires will be vampires. We can only show restraint for so long before suppressed desire boils over."

I nodded and started moving towards the door, hoping the interview was at an end.

"Blake."

I stopped in my tracks.

"As for Aenia..."

I took a deep breath, preparing for the worst. The moment dragged on.

"I've paid a visit to the Sanctum. Tell her your mother sends her love."

I nodded and pulled the door open.

BOOK 3

CHAPTER 26

MEDRA

A few days after the House Leader ceremony, I strolled towards my thrallguard lesson. I was hoping for another shot at the spellbook.

I hadn't seen Blake since that day in the arena. He'd been missing our Advanced Weaponry classes. Not that he really seemed to need them.

He'd killed Coregon in front of the entire school. It was the second time I'd seen him kill.

He was...very good at it.

Part of me still couldn't wrap my head around it. Coregon Phiri was dead. And he'd been the one to hurt Vaughn. Not Blake. I'd run hastily towards what I thought was the most obvious answer. Like a stupid, reckless fool.

Sometimes I tried to justify what I'd done. Just because Coregon had delivered the blows didn't mean Blake wasn't the one who was ultimately responsible. He'd probably told Coregon to go after Vaughn. There was no way it had happened without his full knowledge. I'd learned enough about the way the highblood chain of command worked, even here in the school, to get that.

After the House Leader ceremony that day in the arena, Rodriguez had told me to expect to be summoned to Headmaster Kim's office to talk about what had happened in Professor Sankara's class.

Apparently Sankara had already told him all about it. Rodriguez had looked almost frightened when he told me.

But the summons never came.

I was still here. Still going to my classes, eating in the refectory, sleeping in my room in the First Year dorm. Nothing had changed.

I'd supposedly broken some law by attacking Blake–and yet they hadn't punished me for it. I hadn't even been given detention.

Maybe the headmaster was just biding his time.

I made my way down the now-familiar corridor towards Professor Rodriguez's office. Oddly enough, thrallguard lessons had become the part of the day I most looked forward to. Rodriguez was tough but fair, never pushing me beyond what I could handle. I'd been learning, slowly but surely–how to compartmentalize, how to build mental walls that could withstand coercive power.

And Rodriguez... Well, he was just plain impressive. He knew so much. More than he ever let on. He had secrets to keep and the more I hung around him, the more curious I was to know just what they were.

I knocked once as I reached the door, then pushed it open and stepped inside.

My breath hitched.

Blake was sitting behind Rodriguez's desk, his long legs propped up on the wooden surface as if he owned the place. He was tossing Rodriguez's letter-opener up in the air, a small dagger with a dragon head pommel.

His white-blond hair fell lazily over his forehead. His white button-up shirt was unbuttoned just enough to reveal the top of the black tattoos that curled over his chest.

A smug smile tugged at his lips as I stepped inside the room.

"What the hell are you doing here?" I demanded.

"Rodriguez had to step out today. He asked me to fill in for him." He tilted his head, obviously enjoying himself to no end, his eyes gleaming with mockery.

All of a sudden I understood. Blake was one of Rodriguez's other pupils. One of the highbloods he tutored in thrallguard.

"For fuck's sake," I muttered, already turning around. "No thanks. Tell Rodriguez I'll see him at our next session."

Before I could reach the door, Blake was there, moving with lightning speed to block it with his body.

He shoved the door shut with a bang, then leaned against the wood. "Just where do you think you're going?"

My pulse quickened. But I refused to let him see how much I was rattled. "Get out of my way. You're not a professor. I don't have to listen to you."

"Actually..." Blake folded his arms behind his head. "You do. I may not be a professor, but I'm the next best thing. Your archon. I'm also your future House Leader now. Officially."

I glared at him. I wasn't about to offer my congratulations.

He leaned towards me slightly, his breath warm and minty against my ear. "Besides, we both know there's no way you'll get past me unless I let you."

His voice dropped, sending a shiver down my spine. "And I'm not in a generous mood today, Pendragon. You could even say I'm a little pissed off."

Belatedly, I realized there were fading bruises all along his jaw. I hadn't seen Coregon strike him there. I wondered how he'd gotten them.

Did it matter? Who cared if Blake Drakharrow was hurt? He deserved anything that came to him. Anything bad, that was.

My eyes narrowed. "Move."

He chuckled softly. "Feisty as always. But sorry, no can do, little dragon. We've got a lesson to get through and I mean to teach it." He reached a hand out, so fast I didn't see it coming, and brushed a strand of my hair off my face. "I'm looking forward to showing you how a real highblood uses thrallweave."

I slapped his hand away, my temper flaring. But I hadn't missed the subtle jibe at Regan. "Don't you dare fucking touch me."

Blake's eyes gleamed. He was having fun, the asshole. "I don't need to touch you to get what I want. And I want us to get to know one another better."

Without warning, he was in my mind.

The pressure hit me like a sledgehammer.

Blake didn't hold back. He wasn't Rodriguez. He battered at my mind with a savage strength, pushing at my defenses with a brute force I wasn't used to–or fully prepared for.

I gritted my teeth and forced myself to focus. This was what I had been training for. What was the point of the lessons if I couldn't go up against a real highblood?

I'd built my walls. I'd blocked off my thoughts. I could handle this.

But Blake was strong.

Each mental blow sent cracks shuddering through my defenses. The walls I'd spent weeks building began to fracture. I fought to keep him out, but it was like trying to hold back a storm with a piece of paper.

Blake was everywhere. Overwhelming me with his attacks.

I curled my fingers into fists, sweat beading on my brow as I pushed back with everything I had.

"Get out," I gasped, hoping the strain in my voice wouldn't betray how close I was to breaking.

The air between us felt charged. His proximity was suffocating.

My breath was coming in ragged little gasps. My entire body trembled from the effort it was taking to hold him off.

I hated the look in his eyes. He knew he was going to win.

Another strike. My walls buckled completely.

CHAPTER 27

BLAKE

On some level, I knew what I was doing was wrong.

Sure, I knew that.

I felt a little guilty. But it wasn't enough to stop me.

Pendragon had attacked *me*. Not the other way around.

And even though I'd won our fight, she'd still managed to humiliate me just by daring to challenge me in the first place.

If she hadn't made me lose face like that, would Coregon have fought me in the arena that day? Would my uncle have summoned me and beaten me to a fucking pulp?

Well, the last part, probably. It was a regular little Drakharrow tradition for the two of us.

There was something about me Viktor hated. Something that reminded him of my father. I knew he didn't treat Marcus the same way, no matter how out of control my older brother got.

I'd lied to save Pendragon. I'd covered for her to Kim. And she didn't even know it because Kim hadn't bothered to summon her along with me.

She had no idea what I'd done for her. That blissful ignorance really pissed me off.

Maybe I was truly beginning to lose it.

Rage simmered beneath my skin. The memory of Viktor's fist slamming into my face. The memory of holding Coregon down while he was crushed.

My whole body ached with the weight of rage. Everything was spiraling out of control.

Now here I was, taking it out on Pendragon.

So yeah, I was an asshole. But the truth was, I felt guilty when I slipped inside Pendragon's mind...but I also felt good. There was a thrill to it. A dark power.

I felt *her*. The real her. She was sweet. Intense. It was almost as good as tasting her blood might have been.

But I hadn't expected her to fight back so fiercely. It was clear Rodriguez had been doing a damned good job of teaching her. And yet, she still wasn't ready. Not nearly ready enough to face someone like my uncle.

Viktor wouldn't go easy on her. He'd tear through her mind like a tempest, leaving nothing but ruin in his wake.

Part of me wondered uneasily why he hadn't done it already. If he thought she might be a spy, why not search her?

Then a worse thought came to me. Maybe he already had. Maybe he'd already seen everything I was about to see and was just keeping what he'd learned from all of us. From me.

Earlier that day, I'd rationalized to myself that I was going to do this for Pendragon. I would push her to her limits to make sure she was strong enough to survive.

She didn't know that. She wouldn't believe me even if I told her.

But now, as I stood in Rodriguez's office, I knew I was also doing it for myself.

A high washed over me as I began to push past her defenses. She struggled against me and it was exhilarating.

Beneath that rush, the guilt and regret tugged at me again.

She wasn't like the others. She didn't deserve this. Not really.

I ignored the guilt and pushed harder.

I was in.

The first memories I grabbed onto were strange and disjointed. Nothing looked familiar.

I saw flashes of places that didn't resemble anything I'd ever seen in Sangratha at all.

I pushed past scenes of a strange beautiful city with a river running through it and a forest on fire. I caught hold of a memory that felt important to her. Recent, too.

My pulse quickened as I scanned through it. From Pendragon's viewpoint, I watched a woman with silver hair locked in a duel. She was facing a man—no, not just a man. He was almost like a highblood, but different. He radiated power. His entire being was charged with an energy I couldn't quite comprehend.

The woman with silver hair fought him with a passionate energy of her own. She was wild. Raw. Untamed. A chill went down my spine. She reminded me of someone. Of

Pendragon herself. And yet the way this woman was fighting was like nothing I'd ever seen before.

As I watched the fight, another figure caught my attention.

A dark-haired man stood by, his face covered with blood, watching the battle.

Then he turned and seemed to see Pendragon for the first time. His expression took on an intensity that made my stomach churn. The way he was looking at her–like she was *everything* to him. I saw the love in his eyes.

My hands clenched as hot jealousy flared inside me, sharp and painful.

Who the hell was he?

I had to find out. I had to dig deeper. I had to know who this man was, why he looked at Pendragon that way.

But then, out of nowhere, a voice echoed in my mind.

A woman's voice. Older and imperious. She sounded amused, but I caught the hint of a sharp edge. "Tsk, tsk," she purred. "You're not supposed to be here, little vampire."

I froze. It wasn't Pendragon's voice. It was someone else. Someone inside her *mind*.

Before I could even react, I felt a violent shove. As if an invisible force had taken hold of me and hurled me backwards.

I staggered and blinked, my back hitting the door.

But before I could regain my composure, I realized something else–something terrifying.

Pendragon hadn't moved. Her eyes were closed, her brows furrowed with concentration.

And then I felt it.

She was inside my mind.

My heart slammed against my ribs as I felt a presence, creeping along the edges of my consciousness.

It shouldn't have even been possible. Pendragon didn't know thrallweave. Mortals weren't supposed to be able to wield it.

But there she was, slipping into places she had no business being.

CHAPTER 28

MEDRA

What are you doing? I hissed at my mother.

Giving him a taste of his own medicine. Come on, don't tell me you don't want to. He deserves it.

How are you even doing this? I didn't know you were capable of anything like this.

Neither did I, she replied, sounding amused. *At least, not here. Not with them. And not from my... strange position.*

She was using me. Wielding me as an instrument as she went after Blake. I should have been horrified, terrified, shocked.

I was all three. But I was also letting her do it.

If you were capable of this, why didn't you help me when I was trying to keep him out? I complained.

But she ignored me.

Interesting, she mused, a moment later. *Very interesting.*

What? What's interesting? I demanded.

Here. Take a look.

She shoved him at me. Yanked me into his head alongside her.

The world tilted.

I felt my mother tearing through Blake's mind like a careless hand rummaging through old chests in an attic. She wasn't being subtle. She wasn't being careful. She was just yanking up lids and diving in.

Images, thoughts, and emotions swirled around me.

Gleefully, Orcades shoved a wave of them at me.

Emotions. A torrent of rage. So hot and fierce it nearly knocked me off my feet.

But it wasn't just anger. It went deeper than that. I felt Blake's grief, his pain at being forced to kill Coregon. I felt the sickening mix of fury and betrayal.

Underneath all of that, something else lurked.

Blake's anger at *me*. It was strong. So intense.

Emotions slid away, slipping like sand through my fingers.

A new memory emerged.

The world softened. Blake's mind settled into calm like the sea after a storm. I blinked and suddenly I was there, standing alongside him on a beach.

He was younger. Maybe eighteen. His face was more open, more boyish. He lacked all of the hard edges I'd come to associate with him. His nose wasn't as crooked. It hadn't been broken yet.

He was smiling, actually smiling, as he chased a small girl through the shallow waves.

His sister. Aenia. She couldn't have been more than three or four. Her giggles rang through the air as Blake splashed water at her.

She darted away from him, only for Blake to scoop her up and twirl her around as she screamed in delight, her pale ringlets bouncing around her face.

I could feel it. His joy. His protectiveness.

Love poured off him for this little girl.

It hit me like a punch to the gut. I hadn't thought him capable of love. Not in any real way. But it was there, undeniable. Coursing through him like a current.

Before I could even begin to process what I'd seen, Orcades' voice cut through the warmth of the memory.

Found something better, darling. Come and look at this.

The beach scene dissolved. I was thrust into a new memory.

Blake was in the headmaster's office. He was standing in front of Kim's desk.

He'd just come from the arena. He must have been summoned right after. He was bleeding from his side where Coregon had stabbed him, but he was trying to ignore the pain.

He was speaking calmly but there was tension in his voice. He was telling the headmaster that he had started our fight. That he had provoked me, goaded me into attacking him.

He was *lying*.

"If you have to punish anyone," he said, his voice steady but tired. "Punish me, Headmaster Kim. It was my fault, not Pendragon's."

"You don't get along with your consort," Kim said, his eyes watchful.

"No, sir, I do not. She's not a highblood. Nor does she show the proper deference. That doesn't mean I think you should do what you've proposed."

"A consort who attacks an archon is a serious matter, young man," Kim said. "Consorts have been executed for much less."

My heart hammered. Kim had wanted to execute me?

"She didn't attack me. It was the other way around," Blake insisted. "It was an inappropriate loss of control on my part. I assure you, it won't happen again."

The headmaster waved a hand dismissively. "You may punish your consorts for their lack of respect however you see fit. Such is your right. However, we discourage doing so in such a public way. It upsets the blightborn students. I'm sure you understand."

"I understand, sir," Blake said.

"Very well, Drakharrow. If you are certain..."

But I didn't get a chance to hear the rest of what Kim was saying. My mother was already moving on, pushing me into yet another memory.

We were back in the arena. Blake stood down in the center of the floor, looking up at the crowd. I saw myself there, sitting beside Regan.

Blake's eyes lingered on me.

My pulse quickened. I could feel what he felt as he looked at me.

I felt his hunger. One that went beyond a craving for blood, though I felt his thirst for that, too. This was mingled with something deeper, more primal. He wanted me. Not just my blood, but *me*.

The need... It was tangled with something else. Something sorrowful, something hollow.

And then, before I could start to understand it all, the connection snapped.

I opened my eyes. Professor Rodriguez's office swam back into focus.

Blake stood across from me, his chest heaving. His eyes were wide with fury and shock.

For a moment, we just stared at each other, neither of us speaking.

"Aenia," he spat finally. "What did you see?"

I stared at him. That wasn't what I'd expected him to ask about.

"I saw you on the beach," I said slowly, not even completely sure why I was answering him. I didn't owe him this. I didn't owe him anything. Not after what he'd just done. "You were playing together. She was laughing."

He studied my face, as if searching for any sign I might be lying.

Then, he was gone.

The door slammed shut behind him.

I was in Rodriguez's office. And I was alone.

CHAPTER 29

MEDRA

I lay back against the pillows on my bed, *The Dark Art of Eternal Bonds* cradled in my hands, and scanned the page with the spell for the hundredth time.

Florence was in the library studying. She'd left me behind with clear instructions to go into her room at seven o'clock and feed the fluffin. The little animal had been safely ensconced in her chamber ever since that day in the arena. Blake had come to fetch his bag, but Florence had brought it to him herself. I hadn't even had to talk to him. Thankfully.

At least, the fluffin had been *mostly* safely ensconced. The pup had developed a bad habit of darting out the door anytime it was left open. He would disappear for hours, even overnight, then reappear outside of Florence's room with a happy yap.

At least the pup felt comfortable navigating the school and finding his way back.

In the meantime, Florence was desperately fighting her conscience. We weren't supposed to keep pets so she was breaking the school rules. But since she was a warden she was also getting away with it–for now. Some of the other students had glimpsed the fluffin. They'd kindly offered their silence...in exchange for the occasional chance to cuddle with the adorable creature.

Florence was basically offering bribes in the form of fluffin snuggles.

But I wasn't about to point that out to her.

While Florence had gone off to the library, Naveen had gone to practice in one of the training yards.

But just in case one of them decided to walk in, I'd pushed a heavy chest in front of my door.

The ritual had to be performed at night, under the open sky, and in a place of ancient power.

I already had a place in mind. I'd use the Dragon Court. There was no doubt it was a place of power. The sculptures seemed to have been standing there for centuries. Not to mention there was a grove of trees there and part of the ritual involved using the earth.

The Dragon Court was usually empty during the day time. I was sure it would be completely quiet at night. No chance of interruption.

Then came the ingredients.

One was easy. I needed to use some of my own blood. Blood was the essence of the living soul. It served as the basic conduit for breaking the bond within me.

The next was a little more tricky. I needed the blood of someone I either loved or hated. It had to be a strong emotion. I only needed a few drops, but apparently the connection was key.

"Love and hate are the only emotions potent enough to fuel such a dangerous spell," the ritual text read. "They are the emotions that bind souls, making them the only ones strong enough to undo such bonds."

I already knew who I had to use. There was only one obvious solution. Blake Drakharrow. I hated him.

I might have tried to use Florence but our friendship was still fairly new. I wasn't sure if what I felt for her as a friend would count as a strong enough emotion.

I also didn't want to involve her in this in any way. So Florence was out.

Getting Blake's blood might have been a problem, but I'd thought of a possible way to do it.

Lastly, there were two ways the ritual could be cast.

One involved an anchor. The soul would enter an inanimate object and be bound to it until such time as the anchor was destroyed. Orcades could live for hundreds, even thousands of years, if she entered an anchor.

The downside to casting the ritual this way was that the caster could inadvertently become consumed by the emotion from the second conduit's blood, potentially transferring not just the soul they wished to expel, but part of their own essence into the anchor.

The other way did not involve an anchor. It was also safer for the caster.

I'd thought my mother would prefer the option with the anchor but to my surprise she chose the latter.

Now there was just the matter of getting my hands on some of Blake's blood.

Oh, and the tiny little issue of my technically not being able to do magic at all.

I'd basically failed all of Professor Wispwood's tests. That would have been enough to discourage most people from attempting what was probably one of the most difficult spells in existence.

The ingredients might have been basic, but the power required to make everything work was not.

And if I messed this up, the results could be disastrous. According to the book, a number of things could happen in the event of failure to cast the spell properly:

I could die. That was simple enough.

Or, my soul could be snuffed out. That was a different kind of death. My body would live on, but my mother would be in control. She'd basically get a second chance at life. I guess it was an outcome many highbloods would have loved.

Yet here I was, feeling fairly confident I'd be able to cast this thing successfully. Maybe it was arrogant of me to put so much trust in the very soul that had invaded me, but I didn't really see how I had any other choice.

I might not have had magic but Orcades did. She'd been incredibly powerful once. Now she'd promised me she'd put everything she had into helping me cast the spell successfully.

A few hours later, I slipped out of the First Year dormitory and made my way towards the arena.

At night, the school was quiet and bathed in torchlight.

When I reached the arena, there were no torches to light the rest of the way. Instead, moonlight cast an eerie glow over the huge colosseum, lending it a silent, foreboding air.

I walked slowly down the tiers of stone, my eyes scanning the ground in the center for any glint of light.

When I reached the bottom, I crouched low, moving from platform to platform, searching in between the wide cracks in the stones for the prize I hoped to find.

An hour later, I was sweaty and annoyed but I'd finally found it.

Coregon's dagger. The one he'd used to stab Blake. It was wedged between two stone platforms, much farther from the center where the fight had been than I'd expected. I'd been able to remember Blake kicking it off the platform and seeing it flying through the air that day, but not where it had landed.

I still couldn't believe Blake had given up the dagger in the first place. He'd taken a risk, choosing to fight Coregon without the weapon.

I picked up the blade carefully. The hilt was coated in dried blood. Blake's blood.

For a moment I wondered why Coregon had chosen the dagger. It was clearly not the finest weapon. Tarnish covered most of the blade in an ashen sheen. Faint writing snaked along the length of the blade but I couldn't make out more than a few letters under all the discoloration.

I looked around the arena. For a fleeting moment, I considered doing the ritual right there. It was certainly a place of power. I could feel the abiding presence of violence all around me.

But something about the arena felt wrong for this kind of magic.

I tucked the dagger beneath my cloak and left the arena behind, making my way to the Dragon Court.

The towering stone dragons took shape in the distance, their silhouettes stark against the moonlit sky.

When I arrived at the courtyard, it was as empty as I'd hoped.

I felt more at ease here. The grove that lay behind the red dragon seemed the perfect place, powerful and primeval.

I stepped into the space between the trees, my breath steady but my nerves already on edge.

Kneeling down, I pulled out the dagger, then two books. One I'd stolen from Rodriguez. The other I'd taken out of the Bloodwing library. It contained a simple spell to turn solid matter into liquid.

I flipped it open, then whispered the short incantation. I could feel Orcades presence swell inside me, lending me her aid.

So close, my darling. You're doing well, she whispered, her voice skimming across my mind like the gentle touch of fingertips.

I was hit with a sudden wave of loss.

Was this really what I wanted? I had never met Orcades in life. Never seen her face to face. Now my mother was present, within me, every day. She was full of power, not to mention a surprising amount of wisdom.

I'm not sure we're doing the right thing, I whispered back, a lump stuck in my throat. *Maybe we should put this off for a while. We have the book now. What's the hurry?*

No. Her voice was surprisingly firm. *We're doing what we must.* A pause. *Please don't misunderstand, my love. I have no wish to leave you. But this union of souls... It's wrong. I see that now. It's endangering you. And I would never want that, Medra. You deserve to live a long and happy life. As for me, I could never be happy living with the fear I might be threatening you somehow, child.*

I didn't respond.

The longer I'm here within you, she insisted, *the more danger you're in. I have no wish to live forever. That desire vanished the moment you were born. I would do anything to protect you. Now let me go.*

Tears slid down my cheeks. I ignored them and looked down at the knife. The dried blood had liquefied. The spell had worked.

Blake's blood shimmered darkly in the moonlight.

I tilted the knife and the blood dripped down the blade, pooling at the tip.

I had to do this now or I would never find the courage. I pressed the dagger across my palm, wincing as it cut me. Drops of blood welled on my hand. I rubbed them over the blade, letting them mingle with Blake's. A sharp sting shot through my hand, but it barely registered. My mind was fixed on the next part of the spell.

I held the dagger over the earth, letting the blood drip down onto the ground, and began to speak the ritual words:

By blood and breath, by night and sky,
The binding of souls I sever,
Let what was trapped be freed to fly,
No longer bound forever.
From heart to soul, from blood to bone,
Let life return where stone has grown.
What's chained away, shall now take flight,
Awakened be the soul tonight.

The final words hung in the cool night air as I finished.

I waited for something to happen.

Did it work?

My heart sank. We'd failed.

I can still hear you, I said sardonically. *So, no, it didn't work. Fuck. What do we do now?*

We don't use curse words, for one, my mother chided.

Really? You're going to lecture me about that now, of all times? I exclaimed. *I would have thought you'd be more worried about the fact that, oh, I don't know, that you're still* here.

It is strange, Orcades said thoughtfully. *I feel different. And yet as you say, we're still intertwined.*

I stopped breathing for a moment. Realization hit me in the head like a brick.

I stared down at the dagger in my hand.

"Oh, shit," I whispered aloud.

Well, that was only our first attempt, my mother continued, still oblivious to what had happened. *We'll try again tomorrow night. If that doesn't work, there are always other books. We'll figure this out, Medra, one way or another. I suppose I was too greedy to think I might simply go free. Perhaps the option with the anchor would have been simpler somehow.*

I think you're right, I said slowly. *It would have.*

A pause. *You sound rather certain about that, darling.*

I am certain, I said, gritting my teeth. *Because it's already happened. You aren't in my head anymore, Mother. You're in this dagger.*

A longer pause this time.

By the gods, I think you might be right. Oh, for fuck's sake. Of all the slip-ups. I should have foreseen this. You were holding the object as the blood fell.

I bit my tongue to keep from laughing hysterically.

But we used the right words, I reminded her. *We used the spell that would free you. Not the incantation for the anchor. So why didn't it work?*

She sighed. *That's magic for you, darling. Magic is a fucking mess.*

Oh, we're allowed to curse now... I meant to tease her, but the words caught in my throat as the ground beneath my feet suddenly trembled.

A shudder ran through the Dragon Court as all around us the castle walls began to shake.

I fell backwards, hitting the rough bark of a tree, my hand still clutching the dagger.

The trees swayed slightly, leaves rustling in the unnatural wind.

Then the wind fell silent. The ground stopped shaking.

I breathed a sigh of relief. *What the hell was that?*

Some sort of minor earthquake, I suspect, Orcades said thoughtfully. *Perhaps this place is built over some sort of a plate in the earth. Like the ones in the arena. They shift from time to time, you know.*

I frowned. I was about to say that sounded as preposterous as a theory I had once read in a book that claimed the entire world of Aercanum was being carried on the backs of four prancing unicorns when suddenly, I saw movement across the courtyard. I slunk down closer to the ground, my head leaning against the tree trunk.

Blake Drakharrow strode into the Dragon Court. He scanned the area, clearly checking to make sure no one had followed him.

I knew he had heightened senses as a vampire. I wondered if those extended to being able to see in the dark.

Nervously, I crouched even lower into the shadows.

Blake walked swiftly towards the grove and my heart sped up. If he came much closer, he'd see me.

But to my relief he stepped behind the sculpture of the red dragon. Bending down, he touched something on the ground. One of the flagstones.

I heard the rasping sound of stone on stone and risked raising my head a little.

There. On the ground amongst the flagstones, I could see a small area of pitch black. An opening of some kind had appeared.

Blake glanced around one more time. Then, he stepped down into the opening. A hidden staircase.

Follow him, my mother suggested. *You know you want to. We'll deal with this situation later.*

I nodded, quickly wiping the dagger off on the grass, then sliding it into my boot.

Slipping out of my hiding place, I moved towards the secret stairs.

CHAPTER 30

MEDRA

The opening was pitch black. I could see the first two steps, then nothing but darkness.

My heart was hammering. What was I doing? I had no idea where Blake had gone. What I did know was that he wouldn't take kindly to being followed. Especially if he caught me.

He was obviously up to something. Something he didn't want to be caught doing.

My pride was still burning from our encounter in Professor Rodriguez's office. He'd used me. Pried inside my mind as if he had a right to.

It didn't matter that I'd, eventually, managed to do the same thing to him. He'd started it!

I needed leverage over him and something told me now was the time to get it.

I heard a grating sound. There was no time to lose. The opening was starting to close.

Stepping down onto the first stair, I silently prayed the stone slab wouldn't decapitate me as I was halfway down.

The narrow staircase descended steeply. A few seconds after my head had cleared the opening, the stone slab shifted shut.

Inside the stairwell, the air changed immediately, thick with the scent of damp earth and mildewed stone.

The darkness was absolute.

I stumbled a few steps along the way down and caught my hand on the cold wall to steady myself. How the hell had Blake even found his way?

He was used to the dark, I realized. He had done this many times before. The steps were familiar to him. He didn't even need a light.

The steps seemed to go on forever. Each footstep echoed faintly in the deep silence. Just when I thought the darkness might swallow me whole, my foot hit solid ground. Cautiously, I took a few steps forward. Then a few more.

I stumbled, cursing, and nearly pitching headfirst down a second set of steps. Fumbling along the wall, I went down the next flight.

My pulse quickened as I finally glimpsed a glint of light there at the very bottom of the stairs. A torch, mounted to the wall.

The light was my beacon. I moved carefully towards it.

When I finally reached the torch, I could make out the faint outlines of a long, narrow corridor stretching out ahead.

A second torch was barely visible in the distance. I hoped there were more along the way.

The unsettling quiet magnified every sound. The shuffle of my boots on the stone. The faint swish of my cloak.

The silence pressed in on me. I wondered if there were rats down here.

What had Blake been doing down here, so far below the academy? How did he even know about this place?

Abruptly, the corridor opened up. I'd entered a vast chamber, the ceiling vaulting upwards overhead.

A torch flickered on the far wall. I took a few steps forward, then another...

And came face to face with a massive skull hulking out of the darkness.

Hollow eye sockets stared straight through me.

A dragon's skull.

It was enormous.

I don't think I had realized until that moment how large the dragons had been. The sculptures in the Dragon Court were huge, yes, but I'd assumed that was due to artistic license.

Now I was starting to understand the sheer scale of the beasts that had once flown over Sangratha.

No wonder the vampires had adored them. They were fucking terrifying to look at, even in death. I could only imagine how much more daunting one would be in flesh and blood.

The dragon's bone structure was jagged and angular, with ridges along its white skull rising up to form a crown of horns. Sharp, serrated teeth pierced from its gaping mouth, some cracked and crumbling with age, but most still jagged and fierce. They looked as if they could still tear through my flesh.

I reached out a hand cautiously and touched one. Sharp. I drew my hand back as if I'd broken an unwritten rule by touching the bones of the dead.

Are you seeing all of this? I asked curiously. *Can you see? Can you still hear me?*

I can. It's strange. I'm close enough to your flesh that I'm getting the visuals, but they're slightly blurred and a little faded. An echo of what you're seeing. She was quiet for a moment. *These creatures... They were really something, weren't they?*

I'm glad there are none around now, I replied. *Can you imagine me actually trying to ride one of these things? If this is its head, I can't imagine how big its body must have been. And those horns... Did they have them all over or just on their heads?*

Maybe riders used saddles? Orcades mused. *It would certainly have been safer that way.*

I don't think there was anything *safe about dragon riding,* I replied.

As my eyes adjusted, I noticed more corridors branching off from the chamber in which I stood. Over each archway a name was etched in stone. Orphos, Mortis, Avari, and... Drakharrow.

Blake's house.

It was obvious I'd have to choose one of the four. It might as well be the devil I knew.

Taking a deep breath, I stepped into the Drakharrow corridor.

My eyes darted from side to side. Along the walls were massive alcoves. Each one housed a dragon skull. They varied slightly in shape and size.

All of these dragons must have been Inferni. The red dragons that flew for House Drakharrow. I remembered what Blake had claimed. That the Inferni breed was volatile and unreliable.

If there were still dragons, I'd be stuck riding a red. Flying an Inferni for House Drakharrow.

I thought of the dragon statue I'd climbed. Nyxaris was his name. A Duskdrake. They were the dragons of House Avari.

I wondered if they'd been better-tempered than the Inferni. For the sake of their riders, I hoped so.

I walked slowly along the corridor.

Even in death, these creatures were indomitable. It felt as if they were watching me, their hollow eye sockets fixed on me as I moved through the catacomb, intruding on their graves.

Where were the rest of their bones buried? Or had they been burned? What would it take to burn a dragon? Was it even possible?

A rustling sound startled me. I looked down just in time to see a rat scurrying along the floor. I pressed my lips together to stifle a scream, my heart hammering in my ribs.

It's only a rat, my mother said mildly.

Oh, and you had a lot of contact with rats in your life, did you? I shuddered. *Rats. I hate rats.*

The corridor was beginning to widen as I walked.

Soon, I could see moonlight spilling in from outside. I ran towards it.

The passageway had opened to a view of the sea.

As I walked along the open corridor, I began to notice caves and openings dotting the cliffside ahead.

These must have once been dragon lairs. Or nests.

The knowledge hit me like a wave. Dragons had lived once. Truly lived. Mated and had their children here in this place.

Bloodwing Academy had not just been dominated by highbloods back then. It had been a place for riders to come and to learn and study. And they had brought their dragons with them.

I felt a strange pang of sorrow. A sense of loneliness I hadn't anticipated. A few hundred years ago and I could have been attending Bloodwing with fellow riders. People like me.

Now here I was, alone.

I had friends, I reminded myself. Florence and Naveen. Even Vaughn, if I could still call him that.

But there was a difference between them and I. Almost as much of one as there was between blightborn and highbloods.

I shook my head, trying to clear my mind. Blake had a head start and I had no idea if he had even come this way. But I kept walking, following the trail until I reached another staircase, this one leading back underground.

I hesitated for a moment, then descended the steps. This stairwell was even more narrow than the others had been. The air was colder here, the walls slick with moisture.

As I walked, the passage grew more cramped, the ceiling lowered, and the darkness felt more oppressive. My hands were coated with damp slime from trailing them along the walls. I wiped them on my cloak.

The stairs bottomed out and I walked along a crooked tunnel.

We were beneath the sea.

The restrictiveness of the small stifling space nagged at me, but I pressed on.

After what felt like hours, I finally reached another set of steps. Fortunately, these ones led upwards.

I mounted them gratefully, my legs burning from the effort as I ascended. The stale air of the tunnel gave way to something fresher.

At the top of the steps, I stood on a landing. A wooden ladder led to a hatch over my head, like one that might be found in a cellar.

I climbed the ladder and pressed my ear against the wood of the hatch, straining to hear. The faint murmur of voices drifted down and the sound of music, light and lively.

I pressed the hatch open and was greeted with a wave of rich scents. Ale and herbs. Garlic and rosemary.

It was a storeroom. Kegs of ale and crates of bottles of liquor were stacked in corners, while bundles of herbs hung from the rafters. Root vegetables were piled in sacks and stacked in wooden crates on high shelves.

The voices and laughter grew louder as I slipped into the room and closed the hatch softly behind me.

Slowly, I opened the door leading out of the storeroom just a crack and peeked out.

I blinked as a warm light spilled inwards.

A tavern. Much larger than I'd expected. Bustling and bright. Cozy in its disorderliness.

I caught the scent of spilled ale, roasting chicken, and freshly baked bread mixed with the faintest hint of pipe smoke. The sound of laughter and conversation floated toward me. Someone was playing a harp over in the corner. A lighthearted song that made my feet twitch.

My eyes roamed over the room. Besides a bar lined with stools, the room was filled with round tables and chairs, most of them full of patrons. The walls were lined with bookshelves, every inch crammed full of books. Some patrons stood by the shelves, holding volumes in their hands or searching the shelves.

I watched as a man wearing a pointed red hat went up to the bar and requested a room. The place doubled as an inn then, as well as a bookstore. Tripled?

I scanned the crowd of people but there was no sign of Blake, though I did see a few people who looked like they might be highbloods. He could have slipped into any of the adjoining rooms or disappeared up the flight of stairs leading to the guest rooms.

I gnawed on my lip. Maybe I should have felt frustrated. But instead I felt surprisingly free. I was here now. Why not explore?

Presumably this was Veilmar. I had never even seen the city. We had skirted around its edges on that first day Blake had found me.

There was just one problem. My hair.

I quickly shut the storage room door, then pulled my hair into a tight knot and wound a strip of black ribbon around it, making sure no strands of telltale red were left dangling over my face. When that was done, I pulled up the hood of my cloak.

I waited until no one was around, then slipped out of the storeroom, pulling the door shut behind me.

The wooden floor beneath my feet creaked softly but the sound was lost in the buzz of noise from the tavern.

I moved across the room, then paused. A group of students, all highbloods, sat around a table, laughing and jesting among themselves. It was past midnight on a school night. Perhaps they were Third or Fourth Years who had been granted special privileges from Headmaster Kim.

Or perhaps they'd just snuck out, like I had.

I grinned to myself as I headed for the door. I was eager to see the city. Eager to see the real Sangratha. A place that wasn't full of highbloods.

I should have known nothing would be as I'd hoped.

As I stepped out of the inn, the first thing that caught my eye were the children.

They were huddled against the walls of the buildings across the street. They were dirty and their clothes were tattered and threadbare.

My stomach twisted as I saw the signs they held.

"Need Blood?"

"Feed on me please."

"Blood for Sale. Cheap."

The signs were misspelled, scrawled in messy and sometimes illegible lettering.

My breath caught in my throat as I saw how young some of the children were. The smallest couldn't have been more than five. Her face was streaked with dirt and tears as she huddled next to an older girl.

There was a movement to my right. I watched in stunned silence as a highblood emerged from the shadows of an alley. He moved silently towards the oldest boy in the group of children, who must have been about twelve. The boy shot to his feet without hesitation, his sign dropping to the ground as he wiped his nose with the back of his sleeve.

Eagerly, he took the highblood's outstretched hand. Together, they disappeared down the street.

Disgust roiled in my gut. This world was so broken.

"Sad, ain't it?"

I turned sharply. A woman had come out of the inn behind me. She leaned against one of the wooden poles along the inn's porch, a half-empty mug of ale dangling loosely from her hand.

She hiccuped and covered her mouth.

I glanced back at the children, unable to keep the horror from my voice. "Why are they out here? Shouldn't they be home?"

"Poor mites haven't got no homes, do they? Parents are dead, most like." She glanced around furtively. "Killed, you know. There's been more killings of late."

My heart sped up. "What do you mean? What sort of killings?"

The woman was too much in her cups to wonder about my ignorance.

"*Murders*," she said, drawing the word out with relish. "The blood drained from each and every one."

"So highbloods killed them?" Of course. Why wasn't I surprised?

"Highbloods?" The woman's eyes widened. "Who said anything about highbloods? Of course not! What a strange thing to say."

I gaped. "But you said their blood was drained. Who else but a highblood would have done that?"

The woman laughed nervously. "Why, a mad man. Or woman, for that matter. A murderer. Who knows why they do the sick things they do? Killing for fun. Horrible, ain't it?"

"You're telling me," I said slowly. "That there have been a number of murders in which the victims have been exsanguinated–"

The woman looked at me blankly.

I rolled my eyes. "It means drained of one's blood," I explained. "The victims have been exsanguinated but no one will consider that a highblood most likely did it?"

The woman's face took on a skittish expression. "The highbloods wouldn't do such a horrid thing. They're our protectors." She pointed. "I pray at the Temple of the Blessed Bloodmaid every day, you know. And you should, too." She looked down her nose at me.

"Saying such things could get you into a heap of trouble. We don't speak that way about highbloods. No siree." She shook her head and belched again.

"Do all blightborn feel the way you do about the highbloods?" I asked, as I stared at her. In other words, were they all this stupid or was this poor woman the exception?

Her eyes widened as if she couldn't believe I was bothering to ask. "Why, of course they do." She closed her eyes and took a deep breath, then recited, "We serve the blood, we serve the line. The highbloods lead, by right divine. In blood we trust, in grace we stand. The highbloods guide us, hand in hand."

My jaw must have dropped a little because when she opened her eyes she gave me a disapproving frown. "All little children learn the verses. Have you forgotten your Creeds of Faith?"

I licked my lips. "My parents weren't particularly religious."

"Not religious?" She looked horrified. "I don't know what that even means. Are you saying you didn't go to the temple? Didn't make a blood offering every name day?" She started to back away. "What a strange girl," she said, sounding uneasy.

"Yes, well, goodnight to you, too," I called sarcastically, as she darted back inside the inn.

I looked up and saw the sign that creaked in the night breeze above the door.

The Wandering Page.

Was this one of Blake's hangouts? Had he even come this way? For all I knew there were multiple ways off the island. Maybe each house had a secret passageway of their own. Would I run into Catherine Mortis or Kage Tanaka next?

My stomach plummeted as I thought of something awful. Had Blake come here to *feed*? Had he stepped out of The Wandering Page and grabbed a child, just like that other highblood man had done?

No. Blake Drakharrow might have been many other horrible things but he wouldn't harm a child. I had to believe that. Didn't I?

But he does need to feed, my mother's voice said from my boot.

Oh, you're still here, are you?

You get sarcastic when you're worrying about something, you know.

I had no idea, I said. *Thanks for telling me.*

Of course, my dear. You know, I might come in handy tonight. There's something to be said for having something sharp with you as you walk down dark streets alone.

She was right. That didn't mean I'd be taking her with me everywhere from now on.

Consider this a special occasion, I said. I felt a twinge of guilt. *We'll figure out a way to free you fully soon. I swear it.*

Of course, we will, she said with false cheer. *I have no doubt of that.*

I looked around. It was growing late and I had no idea where to go next. My eagerness to explore Veilmar had dissipated.

I glanced at the children again. I longed to do something to help them. But what? I couldn't exactly smuggle them back to my rooms.

Did Florence know about their existence? Had she grown up seeing beggar children like these and simply become jaded to the idea of children selling their blood?

Something brushed against my leg and I jumped. I looked down, half-expecting to see another rat.

"You!"

It was the fluffin.

"Did you follow me?" I demanded. My eyes narrowed. "You're a sneaky little thing, aren't you?"

The fluffin gave a happy little yap, then wagged his fluffy tail and ran a little ways ahead of me. He barked again.

"You want me to follow you?" I put my hands on my hips. "Is this where you've been sneaking off to? Florence is going to have a conniption when she finds out."

Are we really about to follow this dog? My mother inquired, sounding half-amused, half-curious.

Unless you have a better idea, we are, indeed, about to follow the dog, I said with a sigh, starting to follow the fluffin down the street. *And it's called a fluffin. You already know that.*

I do, but I'm not about to use such a ridiculous name, Orcades said with a sniff. *It resembles a dog and so a dog is what I will call it.*

I sighed. *I believe it's more like a fox mixed with an owl. Let us simply resign ourselves to the absurdity of this situation and make the best of it.*

I ran to catch up with the fluffin.

The cobbled streets of the city shone as the moon rose higher overhead, the stones slick with moisture from the nearby sea. I followed the little creature, weaving through winding alleys and side streets, the noise from The Wandering Page fading behind us.

After a while, we began to enter a new part of the city.

A seedier part. The street lamps were more scarce here, and what light they cast was dim.

The further we went, the more the city seemed to decay. The buildings were older here, their stone facades crumbling or their wooden slats covered with peeling paint. Figures slumped in shadowy doorways, eyes following me with suspicion or indifference.

The fluffin trotted on without hesitation, a tiny spark of color in an otherwise dark place.

My senses prickled with unease. I could have picked up the fluffin and gone back the way we'd come, returning to Bloodwing.

Or could I? I wasn't completely sure I could find the way.

Finally, the fluffin stopped, sitting on his haunches across from a building that stood out amongst the others.

The windows were aglow with dancing red candles. A wooden sign hung above the door, its red paint faded but still legible: The Drained Rose. There was a picture of a flower, a rose presumably, painted below the words.

The red candles, the name...

Outside, several blightborn were lounging casually, cups and goblets held loosely in their hands. Most were leaning against highbloods—each one beautiful and seeming utterly indifferent to their tawdry surroundings. One of the blightborn, a young man of my age, was laughing drunkenly, his hand caressing the arm of a highblood woman who was whispering something in his ear.

Another blightborn girl, perhaps twenty or so, stood silently near the door, her gaze vacant as a highblood man trailed his fingers down her neck, looking at her hungrily.

I felt a wave of revulsion. This was a blood brothel.

I stared at the blightborn with morbid curiosity. Was this really a choice? Or was it desperation like with the children I'd seen?

The fluffin had sat down patiently by my feet. Now he jumped up and made a yapping sound.

"Hush," I whispered. But my eyes followed the direction the fluffin was looking.

Blake Drakharrow was coming along the street towards the brothel from the opposite way. And he wasn't alone. Professor Rodriguez was walking beside him.

The two men were deep in conversation. They seemed to be arguing. I slunk back into the shadow of the building so they wouldn't see me.

I couldn't hear them from this distance, but the tension in Rodriguez's face was unmistakable. He gestured sharply at Blake, his voice low but intense.

My mind whirled. What could they possibly be arguing about? Rodriguez was obviously tutoring Blake in thrallguard. He'd trusted him enough to have the older student fill in for him as my tutor.

But this wasn't the place for a thrallguard lesson. Why were they really here?

I inched forward slightly and was considering stepping out and confronting them when Rodriguez suddenly peeled away and stormed off down the street.

Blake remained where he was. He watched Rodriguez leave but didn't seem perturbed.

After a moment, he rolled his shoulders, adjusted the cuffs of his black jacket, and headed for the entrance of The Drained Rose.

I looked down at the fluffin. My mind screamed at me to turn back but something stronger was pulling me forward.

I'd come all this way. I wasn't about to turn back now.

"Wait for me here," I whispered to the fluffin. "Can you do that?"

The fluffin looked up at me from his large owl-like eyes and gave a soft yip.

"Is that a yes? I won't be able to find my way back without you, you know," I whispered.

Do you expect the animal to actually answer you? my mother asked incredulously.

I ignored her. Pulse drumming in my ears, I headed for the door of The Drained Rose.

CHAPTER 31

MEDRA

The heavy oak door creaked as I entered. Immediately I was struck by the garishness of the brothel. The place was decorated in shades of crimson and gold, with thick velvet drapes and brocade-covered chairs lining the walls. Ornate brass chandeliers hung from the ceilings. There was a sense of opulence without a sense of elegance.

Something brushed past my feet and I looked down to see the fluffin.

I cursed under my breath and darted forward, trying to catch him, but it was too late. The fluffin darted into the foyer.

Pulling my cloak tighter around my head to hide my hair, I followed the pup deeper into the room.

The hour was late, but from the sounds of it, The Drained Rose was still going strong. Voices and laughter filled the air, mingled with the scent of perfume, wine, and sweat. Something subtle lay beneath it all. The faint aroma of blood.

A little ways inside the foyer stood a wooden counter. There was a sign on it: "Madame Illustra will return shortly. Wait here."

Behind the counter, a grand double staircase curved upward on either side, meeting at a landing before continuing to the second floor, which was encircled by a balcony that overlooked the room below.

I took a few steps forward and glimpsed Blake. He was nearing the top of the stairs. As I watched, he disappeared along the corridor.

Before I could even react, the fluffin scampered up the steps ahead of me.

"Dammit," I muttered, tugging at my cloak again.

I ran up the stairs behind the fluffin, trying not to lose track of it.

At the top, I paused. Blake had disappeared.

Then I spotted the little fluffin. He was trotting confidently down the hallway, his little paws pattering against the worn red carpet.

I followed, trying to keep my head down, and avoiding the gazes of the patrons who were wandering down the hall.

But one of them, a leering highblood man with greasy white hair and a half-buttoned shirt stained with blood, reached for me as I passed him.

"What you got under that cloak, sweetheart?" he sneered, pulling at the garment.

I jerked away and quickened my pace, praying he wouldn't follow.

Laughter followed me, but I didn't hear footsteps. I glanced back a few moments later, and the hallway was clear. I let out the breath I'd been holding.

The fluffin had stopped in front of a door at the end of the hall. He stood there, pawing the door, waiting for me.

I thought about knocking, then thought better of it. I pushed the door open and stepped inside.

The room was empty. A large, four-poster bed sat in the center, draped with scarlet satin sheets. A cloying perfume hung in the air.

Blake was nowhere in sight.

Then I heard it.

His voice. It sounded so clear.

I looked around. The fluffin gave an excited yap and darted over to a tall wardrobe in the corner.

I frowned and followed. Pulling the wardrobe door open, I peered inside.

"You brilliant, sneaky little creature," I murmured, looking down at the fluffin who bounced up and down happily.

A peephole had been drilled inside the wardrobe, going right through the wall that connected this room to the next.

Hesitating only for a second, I stepped inside. The smell of mothballs filled my nostrils.

I peered through the hole.

There was Blake.

He must have just entered the room. I watched as he shrugged off his jacket and tossed it casually over a chair. He wore a black linen shirt underneath, open at the collar. His sleeves were rolled up, exposing the black tattoos that coiled up his muscular forearms.

Every line of his body seemed cut with precision. I found myself holding my breath as I watched him. Why did the bad ones have to look so good?

Blake raised a hand to his face and pushed back a lock of pale blond hair, then glanced across the room.

My heart caught in my throat.

On the bed, a blightborn girl lounged against the headboard. Her dark hair tumbled around her shoulders. Scantily clad in a short little dress of red lace, her golden-brown skin caught the candlelight perfectly.

She was beautiful. She was also watching Blake with unconcealed admiration, her gaze roaming over him as if he were a prize.

Her lips curled into a seductive smile as he strolled towards the bed.

A shiver went down my spine. Was I really going to watch this?

Yes. Yes, I fucking was.

My heart pounded in my chest as Blake darted forward in a sudden movement and lowered his head towards the blightborn girl's neck.

The girl's head jerked back, her breath coming out in a gasp, as Blake's fangs sank into her skin.

It should have been a grisly scene. This puncture of flesh, the slow trickle of blood.

And yet, it was anything but.

The blightborn girl wasn't writhing in pain. Instead, her eyes fluttered shut, as she tilted her head back a little more to grant Blake better access. Her body arched towards him, her hands reaching out to clutch the sleeves of his shirt, as if she craved more of the sensation he was giving her.

My stomach twisted, torn between disgust and the embarrassing heat rising between my thighs.

Watching Blake feed was unsettlingly intimate. His hands gripped the girl's waist, firm but not possessive, holding her steady as he drank.

Yet there was a coldness to his actions, as though his mind was detached from the ritual. He didn't caress her, didn't embrace her. He simply took what he needed.

At least, that was what I told myself as the girl's soft erotic moans filled the room.

Blake seemed unbothered by her reactions. He must have been used to them. His only interest seemed to be in the blood he was taking.

I tracked the motion of his throat as he swallowed mouthful after mouthful from the girl's limp body.

I could have looked away at any time. Yet I didn't.

Finally, after what seemed like an eternity, Blake stepped back.

His chest was heaving. His mouth was smeared with a trace of the girl's blood.

I felt a strange anger fill up inside me as I looked at the red wetness on his lips. As if the girl had marked him in some way she had no right to.

Blake's fangs shone briefly in the light, before retracting. He wiped at his mouth with the back of his hand, clearing away the drops of blood.

The girl sat up on the bed, her eyes half-lidded, her skin flushed. She pouted. "Is that really all you want from me?"

Blake didn't answer. His face was impassive as he reached into his trouser pocket and pulled out a leather pouch. He placed it on the bedside table and the girl grabbed for it, spilling the contents onto the coverlet.

She huffed softly, her fingers brushing over the gold coins. "It's too much," she muttered, sounding sulky. "You always overpay."

She slid off the bed and moved towards him, her fingers reaching for the collar of his shirt.

I felt a knot in my stomach. She wanted him. She wanted more from him. Had he used thrallweave on her? Enchanted her somehow? I didn't think he'd needed to. She'd clearly wanted this.

But then, she'd been raised from birth to idolize people like Blake, I reminded myself. To see them as purer than she was, better than she was. Of course, she wanted him.

Still, I hoped he'd reject her.

I needn't have worried. With a frown, he brushed her hands away.

"Maybe the next time you come to call, I won't be here," she said petulantly. "Or maybe I'll be with someone else. Some other highblood man. It would serve you right. What would you do then?"

"I'd pay the next girl," Blake said coolly, picking up his jacket from the chair and shrugging it back on.

I choked back a laugh. He was one cold bastard. I should have pitied the girl. But I didn't. There was something about the possessiveness she was showing towards Blake that I didn't like.

I watched the jacket slide over his shoulders. He was leaving. I felt a flicker of smugness rise inside me.

Smug, that is, until a cold hand clapped firmly over my mouth.

I was yanked out of the wardrobe. A man's hand wrapped around my waist.

"Well, well," a low voice growled in my ear. "What have we here? Does someone like to watch?"

My heart raced, breath ragged against the highblood's palm.

"A new girl," the man muttered. "I've drunk my fill tonight, but I always like a new girl."

I felt my hood being pulled down. The ribbon was wrenched from my hair. My curls cascaded down around my shoulders.

There was a sudden silence as the man took in my appearance.

Then I felt fingers move through my hair. I tried to yank my head away but he held tight.

"What have we here?" the man murmured. "Such pretty hair." He sniffed at it. "You even smell different. Unique. I've never tasted one like you before."

Panic flared inside me at the thought of this man putting his teeth into me. I twisted, jerking free of his grip, and leaned down, pulling Coregon's dagger from my boot.

I spun around, my hand moving fast, and drove the blade deep into the closest part of him I could get to—his thigh.

The man howled in pain and staggered backward, knocking over a wooden chair.

I looked him over quickly. I'd half-expected to see the man I'd run into back in the corridor. But this was a different highblood. He wore a black domino mask over his eyes and a crimson cloak. There was blood all around his lips—blood he hadn't bothered wiping away, as if he liked looking like that.

I glanced at his hands. They were covered in blood, too. My heart sped up. This man had done more than simply *feed* tonight.

And he wasn't done with me yet. Rallying with more speed than any mortal, his face contorted in fury and in a flash, he was on me again, seizing my wrist and pulling my arm back with a painful twist.

I cried out in agony, but didn't drop the dagger. My eyes darted around the room in desperation.

There. On the floor. The fluffin was lying motionless. The highblood must have kicked him earlier. The sight filled me with a sudden, blinding rage.

Stab him again, my mother demanded. *Use the knife. Hurry. He's not going to let you out of this room, no matter what he might claim.*

But I couldn't fight him off, no matter how I twisted. He was too strong.

I remembered something I had learned in my History of Sangratha class. That high-bloods grew stronger with age. Before now, I'd only fought against highbloods my age–Visha, Blake. I might have been close to a match for them...but I wasn't one for this man.

"I should bring you to the Sanctum," he muttered as he fought me. "Turn you in. You've been hiding from them, haven't you? Naughty, naughty. You're special. That hair. But you smell so good. I think I'll keep you for myself. Will you scream like my other girls? I don't like my girls damaged. Not until I'm ready to do it myself. Drop the knife, little girl. Don't make me break your fucking wrist now, girly."

He was close to it. I could feel my bones coming close to the snapping point. My eyes were burning with pain.

The door to the room slammed open with a splintering crash.

CHAPTER 32

BLAKE

I'd been coming to The Drained Rose long enough to know that most of the time you just had to look away. Madame Illustra *wanted* you to look away. Sometimes her girls– and boys–had rough customers, and it usually wasn't anything they couldn't handle. Hell, some of them liked it that way.

Most of Madame's workers enjoyed what they did. The low level coercion that we highbloods had spun over the blightborn in Veilmar and the rest of Sangratha made mortals more pliable to suggestion. But they still had a measure of free will. If one wanted to feed, one needed the blightborn to be willing–or one had to overpower them or use thrallweave. Something which most highbloods had no qualms about.

In any case, I was used to hearing the sounds of rough feeding and even rougher sex.

But this was different. The sounds were different.

And then I'd heard Pendragon scream.

Now I took in the scene, my heart pounding.

Pendragon, her cloak ripped off, her hair wild, cascading down her back.

Her dress was torn. It was fucking *torn*. I saw red.

The highblood brute had hardly noticed me. He still had his hands all over her. Clawing, pawing at her, his intentions sickeningly clear.

"Get your own girl, my friend," the highblood called back over his shoulder. "I've found myself a new girl and she's mine."

Mine.

Mine.

Mine.

The word echoed in my head and fire erupted in my veins.

"I'm not your fucking friend."

I launched myself at him, moving faster than I ever had in my life.

One moment, the highblood was latched onto Pendragon like a leech. The next I had ripped him away, my hand twisting into the man's collar as I hurled him against the wall with all my strength.

He was older than me. Probably stronger.

But not now. Not tonight.

The sickening sound of bones cracking echoed through the room. But it wasn't enough. Not nearly enough.

The blood pounded in my ears as the man crumpled to the floor, dazed but still alive.

That simply wouldn't do.

Mine, he had said. Mine.

I didn't know why I knew it with such certainty then but I did. The word pounded through my blood. It spread through my bones. *Mine.*

Medra Pendragon was mine. And I was prepared to die before I let any harm come to her.

It didn't matter if she believed it. If she accepted it. It didn't matter if she hated me. I'd believe it enough for both of us. She was mine and she always would be.

My heart might have been black, my deeds as dark as night, but she was mine to protect, mine to keep safe, with everything I had to give.

She thought she was trapped? I was the one trapped. Trapped with this feeling I couldn't get away from. The need to possess her. To dominate her until she accepted me.

I grabbed the man by his throat, yanking him up with ease. The highblood gasped, clawing at my arm in desperation. But my grip was like iron.

"She's not yours," I hissed. "I want to hear you say it."

There was no mercy in my eyes as I looked at him, holding him up off the ground.

I slammed his head against the wall, hard enough to crack the plaster. A trail of blood was left behind.

"She's..." The man choked. "She's yours."

"Mine," I growled, my voice thick with jealous rage. "You don't get to touch her–*ever.*"

The man's voice came out as a rasp. I could hear the blood bubbling in his throat. "For–forgive me..."

But there would be no forgiveness. Not tonight. Not ever.

I tightened my grip, twisting the highblood's neck with a sickening crack that reverberated through the room. The man went limp in my grasp.

I flung him to the floor, his body crumpling in a heap.

Breathing hard, I turned towards Pendragon.

She stood there, frozen, clutching her cloak to her chest as if trying to hide her torn dress. Her eyes were wide with shock.

Our gazes locked.

I reached for her arm, expecting her to slap my hand away. But to my surprise, she let me.

I led her towards the door.

"Wait," she said, her voice hoarse. She pointed down at the carpet.

Neville. The fluffin lay on the gaudy red carpet. His little chest was rising and falling slowly.

"Fuck," I growled. "He did that?"

She nodded tightly.

I suddenly longed to kill the man all over again.

I let go of her arm and scooped the little pup up into my arms.

"Come on," I said, hoping she'd comply for once in her stubborn life. "I'm taking you and Neville back."

CHAPTER 33

MEDRA

I was following a vampire.

Because I had no other choice, I told myself. The fluffin–whose name, apparently, was Neville, of all the ridiculous names–had been my way back home. At least Blake knew where we were going.

Still, I waited until he'd led us into the tunnel beneath The Wandering Page before I spoke up.

"What the fuck was that back there?"

He'd grabbed a lamp from off the shelf in the storeroom. Now he carried it in one hand and the limp fluffin in his other.

"What do you mean?" he asked, not even pausing to look back at me.

"I mean..."

"You mean you followed me," he interrupted. "You followed me into a place you had no business being and where you had no chance in hell of being able to take care of yourself."

There was no point denying it. Still, "You're saying *you* had a right to be there? You snuck out of school. You wouldn't have snuck out if you'd been allowed to leave."

"No one would have stopped me."

"Then you snuck out because you didn't want anyone to see where you were going. Why?" I thought of the girl. "Why use a sellblood? I thought House Drakharrow had its own thralls."

A pause. "We do."

"Then why not feed from them?" I asked. "Or does it just get you off to go to brothels?"

"Why not mind your own fucking business?" He shot back. "Oh, wait. You can't. You're clearly obsessed with me."

"I beg your pardon?" I sputtered. "I don't think so."

"Really? Then why follow me? No, not just follow me. Why follow me all the way into The Drained Rose? You could have gone anywhere in Veilmar, but instead, you were in the next room over. Did you watch me feed, Pendragon?"

He stopped and turned around, holding the lamp up higher so he could see my face. I felt my face flushing. Godsdammit.

He sneered. "You did. You *watched* me. And you fucking liked it."

He took a step towards me and I backed up.

"Stop it," I said automatically. "Don't do that."

"Don't do what? Come near you? Why not? When it's obvious you want me to. Why can't you admit it, even to yourself?"

My blush deepened. I felt furious with myself. "In your wildest dreams, Drakharrow. Not every woman on earth wants you."

"Not every woman, no. But you do." He smirked. "Did you watch the entire time I was feeding? Or did you look away? Was it too much for you?"

I didn't answer.

He lowered his voice, looking at my neck. "I can give you the same pleasure I gave her. Anytime you want. All you have to do is say the word. Just one little word. 'Please.'"

I snapped. "No fucking way. Keep your hands and fangs off me. Besides, you're not allowed to take blood from me. You said so yourself."

His smirk deepened. "You don't even know how it works."

"Then tell me," I demanded.

He shook his head. "No way. It's more fun like this. Maybe someday you'll figure it out."

I refused to beg him for information. "Fuck you, Blake."

"Now who's dreaming, Pendragon?" He laughed.

"Let's get one thing straight," I said, stabbing my finger into his chest. "I'm not yours. I don't know how to get it through that thick highblood skull of yours..."

"Oh, so you admit I'm thick?" He smirked again.

I threw up my hands. "I'm not yours. Stop saying that word around me. It gives me the creeps. You and that word. *Mine.* I'm not yours. I never will be."

He gave an exaggerated yawn. "Whatever you say, Pendragon. I noticed there wasn't a single 'thank you, Blake' in there. Even though you know I saved your life tonight. Yet again. For someone who doesn't want to belong to someone else, you sure do a shitty job of taking care of yourself."

I gritted my teeth. "Maybe if all of you highbloods weren't so feral, I wouldn't have to worry about protecting myself."

"Not all of us are feral," he said, his eyes roaming down my body. "Some of us are all about control."

"Keep telling yourself that," I retorted. "You're just as bad as that highblood who attacked me."

To my shock, fury filled his eyes. I'd gotten to him.

"We're not all like that," he spat.

"That man had clearly been murdering blightborn girls. I saw children out on the streets, begging for someone to pay for their blood. Their parents had been killed, drained of their blood. Who else would do that besides a highblood? Tell me, Blake, why do you all pretend to be so civilized? So restrained? When really you're all just monsters inside?"

He moved so quickly that I could barely register the blur of his body before he was in front of me, his face an inch away, his breath hot against my skin.

"You think I'm like him?" he growled. "You think I want this? You think I want to be tied to some mortal? To a blightborn who despises me?"

I glared at him, my chest tightening.

"But you're right about one thing, Pendragon. Why should I fight so hard to leash the monster inside when you're so determined to bring him out?"

Before I could even respond, his lips crashed against mine.

Blake's hand cupped the back of my head, his fingers tangling in my hair as he deepened the kiss, his tongue sliding possessively into my mouth.

For a moment, I was too stunned to react, caught up in the sudden heat that was shooting through my body.

Then, to my shame, I found myself kissing him back. The taste of him overwhelmed my senses. I hated it. Hated him. Hated this. Hated how good it felt. My heart was racing. My skin tingled.

I clenched my fists by my side, desperately trying to control the storm of emotions that were sweeping through me.

And then it was over as quickly as it had begun.

Blake pulled away, breathing hard, his gray eyes dark with a mixture of triumph...and confusion.

He turned away from me and stalked down the tunnel.

I stood there, frozen for a moment, my hands trembling.

Then I followed.

"Well, at least now we know where Neville has been going," I finished, sinking down onto Florence's bed.

"Neville?" Florence's eyes were wide. I'd woken her up when I'd brought the fluffin back.

Blake hadn't said another word to me until we reached the Dragon Court. Then all he'd done was shove the fluffin at me and tell me to bring it to him if the pup didn't recover by the next day.

I'd wanted to ask him why he didn't just take the fluffin, but I hadn't.

Hadn't dared.

Florence was looking at me curiously. I colored.

"Um, Blake Drakharrow seems to have named the fluffin Neville," I confessed to her.

We looked at each other, then burst out laughing.

"Neville?" Florence sputtered. "*Neville*? Why Neville?" She gawked at me. "Are you really saying the fluffin–I mean, Neville–has been sneaking away to visit your..." She stopped herself just in time. "To visit Blake Drakharrow?"

She fell backwards onto her bed, giggling again. "That might just be the most ridiculous thing I've ever heard."

"Hey, you're the one who loves highbloods. Can't a highblood love a fluffin?" The question sounded so silly, we burst out laughing again.

"A highblood can do whatever they want, I suppose," Florence said at last. "But Blake? I mean... I would never have taken him for a fluffin-lover."

"Florence, please. If we don't stop putting Blake in the same sentence as a fluffin, I'm never going to be able to stop laughing," I groaned.

"What I don't understand is why Neville keeps coming back here," Florence said, leaning over to pat the fluffin's fluffy head. Neville perked up a little, then fell back asleep. He seemed to be recovering after his nasty ordeal with the highblood.

"Maybe they're not allowed to have pets in Drakharrow Tower either?" I suggested.

She shook her head. "I'm pretty sure the highbloods are allowed to do whatever they want over there. That goes double if you're a House Leader."

"Maybe Neville–" I suppressed a giggle. "Maybe he keeps trying to get back to Blake, but Blake keeps sending him back to us?"

"That would make sense. But it's also a little sad. Why doesn't Blake just keep him?"

"I mean, I guess it might be a little embarrassing for the big, bad House Leader to keep a fluffin?" I said, snorting with laughter. "Poor Neville. He deserves better than Blake."

Florence looked at me consideringly. "So do you, I guess."

I blushed. "I mean, he did save me from that highblood. Do you think I should have thanked him?"

"Do you? You said yourself the highblood would probably have killed you."

I looked away. "I don't know. Blake's different from anyone I've ever met. He's not... fully evil, I guess. But he's certainly not good either. He's selfish and controlling. He acts like he owns me. But he doesn't want me to get hurt. It's confusing."

I hadn't told her Blake had kissed me. It was too humiliating. I'd only told her that he'd killed for me. Which was somehow slightly better. I wasn't sure why.

"What do you think of him feeding from a sellblood?" Florence asked, eying me curiously.

"I was going to ask you that same question," I said.

She tilted her head, her dark eyes thoughtful. "I think it says something about him. Something neither of you might want to admit."

"Something bad?"

"No, the opposite. He'd rather feed from someone who's willing. He didn't hurt her, did he? The sellblood girl?"

I shook my head. I hated thinking about her. "No, she seemed to enjoy herself quite a bit, in fact."

"I can't believe you watched," Florence said, a little admiringly. "That was rather daring."

"Blake Drakharrow doesn't have a right to privacy, as far as I'm concerned," I countered. "I wasn't trying to be daring. I just wanted to figure out what he was up to."

I thought of Professor Rodriguez. How he and Blake had met outside The Drained Rose. It was clear it wasn't for the first time either.

"But speaking of daring," I said slowly. "I have a dare for you..."

Back in my own room a little while later, I lay beneath the blankets, unable to sleep even though I knew there were only a few hours left before I'd have to wake up for class.

My head was spinning and it wouldn't stop.

Mine.

It wasn't the first time he'd said it. But it felt like the first time I'd actually been truly listening. And at that moment, my heart had quickened. My useless, traitorous heart.

I forced myself to think of something else.

Professor Rodriguez's book still lay on my bedside table. I couldn't risk keeping it much longer. Florence had promised to help me get it back into his office the next day. She'd distract him while I slipped inside and shoved it back on the shelf.

I'd placed Coregon's dagger high on a shelf. I'd managed to shove it back into my boot before Blake had noticed me carrying it. I'd have to find a sheath for it. Then perhaps I could carry it around, without having Orcades exposed to everything I saw or did.

Part of me was glad she was still here. But I knew this wasn't what she'd hoped for.

Tomorrow was the start of Wintermark term. In a few weeks there would be festivities, a school break, even a ball. I knew Florence and Naveen were excited about the first real school holidays. It turned out Naveen played the flute and planned to audition to join the school band.

The last autumn leaves had fallen days ago. The air had turned crisp and cold.

I fell asleep and dreamed of snow and dragons.

BOOK 4

CHAPTER 34

MEDRA

*W*intermark

The once vibrant colors of autumn had faded away in the last few weeks. Leaves had fallen, swirling in gusts of color around our feet as we walked through open courtyards to class, and then vanished like embers extinguished in the night, swept up by the omnipresent but always subtle school staff. The trees were all bare now, their branches skeletal.

Mornings at Bloodwing were met with a thin veil of frost, painting the windows and cobblestones in the courtyards and open halls silver for a few brief hours. I dressed in a cloak or heavy sweater and scarf every morning before leaving my room.

As if to make up for the absence of the leaves, house colors were more evident with the changing of the seasons. We First Years wore wool cloaks of midnight blue or silvery gray, embroidered as ever with the school crest, our pointed hoods pulled up to block out the biting winds that had begun to swirl through the corridors. Classrooms were heated. Hallways were not and many had windows open to overlook the sea, the shutters of which were only closed at night.

House Drakharrow students marched through Bloodwing's halls in clothing of rich black and deep crimson, wool scarves shot through with red, knotted around their necks. House Avari students strutted by wearing black cloaks with silver-trimmed hoods, polished leather boots with silver laces snaking up their calves.

House Mortis students moved through the halls in white wool scarves and red cloaks. While students from House Orphos stood out like peacocks in their dark gold scarves and purple cloaks lined with silk.

The air had sharpened, turning our breath into clouds of mist each morning. By mid-day, the frost would melt and we'd sling our cloaks over our arms or race back to our dormitory to stow them back in our rooms. But soon, Florence said, the sunlight would wane earlier and earlier, the wind would become a howl, and snow would blanket the school.

It wasn't all bad though. We were only a few weeks away from our first real break from classes. For fourteen blissful days we'd be free from the bondage of books and parchment. There was even a special midwinter festival, Frostfire, which would be celebrated over the break.

Some students went home over the Wintermark break. But most tended to stay. The festivities for Frostfire were supposed to be worth it. Some years, visiting delegations from other schools in Sangratha would even attend–and Bloodwing would send their own delegations in exchange. But this year it would just be Bloodwing students. I wasn't sure exactly why.

Frost was still stubbornly clinging to the stone pathways as I made my way to the refectory one evening.

The vast hall was warmed by the glow of torches and the fires burning along the walls in two huge hearths. Supper was in an hour and students were slowly beginning to trickle in. I smelled hot cider and apples and cinnamon buns.

The normally austere space was gradually being transformed in preparation for the approaching Frostfire Festival. Dark green garlands of evergreen hung along the walls, dotted with bright red berries. Arrangements of pine and ivy had been artfully set as centerpieces on each long table. Scattered amongst all the greenery were little carved wooden ornaments of red birds, orange foxes, and other winter animals, their vivid colors standing out as bright splashes among the darker shades.

The effect was cozy, festive, and inviting.

On the far side of the refectory, a normally empty space had been set up with a stage. The Bloodwing Ensemble, the school orchestra and choir, were in the middle of a rehearsal for the upcoming festival.

I slid onto a bench at an empty table as music curled through the hall. In the first row of the orchestra, Naveen stood holding a flute. As I watched he lifted the instrument to his lips and began playing a delicate solo that made me think of a bird flying on a winter wind. Despite his modest size, Naveen had a quiet confidence. His posture was straight and his fingers nimble as they danced across the flute's keys. His melody faded just as the rest of the orchestra swept in, harmonizing with him to carry the song forward.

I pulled off my cloak and folded it up beside me, glancing around the hall. One of the House Drakharrow tables was nearly full. I saw Blake, Regan, Quinn, Theo, and Visha. They were laughing and talking. Well, all of them except Blake. He was staring down at the table moodily, his hands steepled in front of him. If he'd noticed me come in he gave no indication of it. Visha looked up, narrowed her eyes at me, then turned and said something to Regan.

I quickly looked away. Blake and I had been ignoring each other since that night we'd returned from Veilmar. And that was how I preferred it.

As for Regan, I knew I'd have to talk to her one of these days. But for weeks, I'd been putting it off.

I spotted Catherine Mortis on the far side of the room. The House Leader looked as if she was enjoying herself thoroughly. Her two thralls were seated on either side of her. If you could call it seated. The three women's bodies intertwined as they kissed and embraced, oblivious to the room around them.

For a second, I was unable to look away. They reminded me of a coil of snakes, writhing and slithering, their intimacy on full display without a care in the world for anyone watching.

Only someone with as much privilege as Catherine would feel so comfortable necking in the school refectory. I'd seen professors chide other students for much less. I seriously doubted any of them would approach Catherine, however.

Besides, I doubted Catherine was doing it for anyone's benefit but her own. This wasn't exhibitionist. It was simply entitled.

Catherine reminded me of Regan a little. But honestly, Catherine scared me a little more. Whenever I happened to pass her in the halls, she acted as if we were all beneath her notice. This was just one more example.

My gaze wandered away from Catherine to one of the tables reserved for students from House Orphos.

A young man was sitting alone, his eyes on the orchestra. Lysander Orphos. Naveen had pointed him out to me once briefly in the halls, but I'd never officially met him.

There was an ethereal quality to the House Orphos leader. In profile, his features were finely chiseled, even delicate. His long, silver-white hair was swept back, half up in a loose bun, while the rest fell in waves around his shoulders.

Lysander's focus was entirely on a girl in the orchestra who was playing the violin. The girl's eyes were closed as her bow glided over the strings. She, too, wore House Orphos colors. She resembled Lysander a great deal, though her features were softer, more delicate. I decided this must be Lunaya Orphos, Lysander's younger sister.

As I watched them, Lysander's gaze shifted and our eyes met. His own were a pale blue. He stared at me, completely uninhibited. But there was nothing threatening in his expression. After a moment, he inclined his head. I returned the nod.

It was a gesture of respect. Nothing more. But at that moment, I reconsidered the reputation of House Orphos. There was something about Lysander. He may have been quiet, even dreamy, but I didn't see either of those things as signs of weakness.

As the music reached its climax, the practice seemed to wrap up. Naveen packed up his flute, said good-bye to some of his band mates, then jumped off the stage and came towards me wearing a broad grin.

"Well?" he asked, plopping down across from me. "What did you think? Pretty dull, right?"

"I think you've made all of us other First Years look bad," I teased. "That was incredible, Naveen. Why didn't you tell us you'd been given a solo?"

He shrugged modestly, but I could tell he was happy I'd noticed. "Just lucky, I guess. The ensemble leader said I had a good ear for the piece. I guess I didn't mess it up too badly."

"It was beautiful," I said seriously. "Does Florence know?"

He shook his head, blushing slightly. "Not yet. I was thinking of surprising her. You know she's always in the library or staying after class when I have practice."

Unable to decide on a single course of study yet, Florence had done the unthinkable and committed herself to both. At least for now. Instead of choosing a strategist or healer path for the Wintermark and Springrise terms, she'd balked and refused to drop any classes. Instead she'd actually gotten permission to add more courses to her timetable.

As a result she now seemed to have a paper due almost every day and had taken to staying late after many of her classes to get extra tutoring from her professors. All of whom seemed to adore her, of course. Why wouldn't they? Florence was serious, studious, hard-working, and brilliant.

Whereas Naveen and I were, well, coasting through. Neither of us had failed any classes yet. We had midwinter exams coming up soon, but neither of us seemed too worried about them. Apparently the ones to panic over were the ones at the end of the Springrise term, just before the summer break. That was when the real culling would happen. At least a third of the First Years wouldn't be back next year, Florence had told me conspiratorially. If she herself was worried, she never let on.

As for me, if fighting Blake hadn't gotten me killed or kicked out, I somehow doubted flunking an exam would do so. Still, I wanted to do as well as I could. I might not have been as perfect a student as Florence, but to my surprise I found myself putting my head down and working harder than I ever had for any of my tutors back in Camelot. Any of them but Odessa, that is.

As I studied Naveen's glowing face, an idea was growing in my mind.

I wasn't sure I should risk putting it into words though.

I raised an eyebrow. "That's a nice idea." I paused, then added, "She's going to be so proud of you when she finds out. You're going to sweep her off her feet with that solo."

A flush creeped up Naveen's neck and I grinned.

"Florence already told me you're the only First Year to make it into the band, let alone get a solo."

Naveen put his face in his hands and groaned theatrically. "And now the real pressure's on. The Frostfire Festival is coming up fast. Soon there will be a lot more people listening to us."

"And one special person in particular," I prodded, my eyes twinkling.

He looked up at me with a guilty expression. "You've figured it out, huh?"

"It took me long enough, but yeah, I think so." I looked at him thoughtfully. "How long has this been going on, anyhow? You said you had a girlfriend before you came to Bloodwing."

"How long? I met Florence when I was eight."

I choked. "You've liked her since you were *eight*?"

He shrugged, the blush returning. "More or less."

"Did you ever think of, oh, I don't know... *Telling* her that you like her?"

He shook his head resolutely. "Nope. Not happening."

I stared at him. "Let me get this straight. You'd rather go out with other girls instead of taking a chance and telling the one you actually like how you really feel?"

He nodded seriously. "Safer that way."

I rolled my eyes. "I take it your last girlfriend didn't exactly break your heart."

He grinned. "Nope. I might have broken hers though. She was hoping I'd turn down my invitation to Bloodwing and stay with her. So were my parents. They always hoped I'd stay home and wind up with a nice dwarven girl."

"But you wanted to go where Florence went?" I said softly.

He nodded. "I couldn't let her go alone." He paused. "And I won't risk our friendship for something so stupid."

"I wouldn't exactly call it stupid, Naveen. Not if you really love her." By the gods, listen to me, giving relationship advice as if I had any idea what I was talking about.

"Have you ever been in a similar position?" Naveen asked curiously.

I shook my head. "Definitely not. I mean there have been... people. Men. Sure. But they were basically just flings. I've never been in love."

Naveen's blush deepened. "I'm not even sure that's what this is."

"And you'll never find out," I teased. "Not if you never take a chance and tell her."

He looked away. "I've thought of telling her at the Frostfire Festival. There's a ball, you know. I'll be there as part of the ensemble. I know Florence will have permission to go. Her grades are certainly good enough. I was thinking of asking her."

"Yes, ask her," I said immediately. "I'm sure she'll say yes." At least, I hoped she'd say yes. What if Florence liked someone else? I decided I'd try to ask her.

"You can't tell her about any of this, Medra," Naveen said, as if reading my mind. "Promise me."

I nodded slowly. "Fine. I promise. I won't, I swear it, Naveen. But life's too short not to take chances. You've been waiting since you were eight. Why not just tell her and see what she says? What's the worst that could happen?"

"The worst that could happen is I'd be destroying the best and longest friendship I've ever had," he answered.

I laughed. But I could see he really was afraid. "I don't think Florence would end a friendship over something like that. Do you?"

"If I knew how she'd react, I'd have done it a long time ago," Naveen said morosely. "But I don't. It's a big risk." He looked around the refectory and sighed. "At least this year we're together as First Years. But next year..."

"Next year we'll all be in different houses," I said softly. "I get it." We wouldn't be seeing each other as often then. Unless we were lucky enough to all wind up together. "But then, isn't that the reason why now is the perfect time to tell her?"

"She has a lot on her mind. She's taking so many classes." He ran his hands through his hair, leaving half of it standing on end.

I hid a grin.

A shadow fell across our table. I looked up to see Regan standing there. Two highblood girls were with her. I remembered their faces from that night at the bonfire. Larissa and Gretchen. Neither had seemed like the brightest candles in the room.

"What's so funny?" Regan said with false sweetness. "Care to share?"

I stiffened, my good mood instantly draining.

Naveen glanced down at his hands, clearly not wanting to engage with the highblood girls.

But Regan and her friends weren't about to let it go.

"You know, Larissa," Regan drawled. "I think the little dwarf thinks his flute solo might actually impress someone. I mean, maybe if it was a show for children."

She and the other two girls laughed as if what she'd said was hilarious.

Larissa leaned down, icy blonde curls framing her pretty but cruel face. "Oh, Naveen," she cooed. "You're not seriously planning on embarrassing yourself in front of the entire school at the Frostfire Festival with that terrible solo, are you? I mean, I've heard dying cats sound better." She laughed loudly.

I suddenly remembered seeing Larissa in the ensemble. She'd been standing in the second row and also holding a flute.

"Naveen is more than ready for Frostfire," I said firmly, narrowing my eyes at her. "Unlike some people, he actually earned his place in the orchestra with skill."

I had the satisfaction of seeing my jibe hit home as Larissa's face flushed with anger.

Gretchen looked down at me, her lips curling. "So protective of the dwarf. Why? Are you two screwing? Blake won't like sharing with a dwarf, will he, Regan?" She laughed, but Regan, I noticed, did not. "But then, you must be used to having to look out for your little misfit friends. Especially since none of you will ever fit in here yourselves."

Gretchen's gaze passed over me with disdain, as if to say nothing about me was good enough to be in the same room as them. Then she looked at Naveen. "Better hope you don't wind up in House Drakharrow next year, dwarf boy. We don't tolerate losers like you."

I ignored her and looked up at Regan. "I liked you better that first day of class when you were pretending to be kind. Jealousy doesn't suit you, Regan. Maybe you and your friends should focus more on your own lives rather than trying to tear everyone around you down. We all have to work together here, you know."

Larissa and Gretchen gaped at me, while Regan's face flitted between anger at the "jealousy" comment to confusion.

"Well, isn't she a naive little thing?" Gretchen said finally. "Let's go, Regan. I don't want to be seen hanging around the loser table for too long."

"See you around, little blightborn bitch," Larissa said, in a sing-song voice.

The two girls started walking away. Regan began to follow. I was surprised she wasn't leading their little pack.

Maybe that was why I decided now was my chance.

Sliding off the bench, I stood up quickly. "Regan, can I talk to you alone for a minute?" I looked down at Naveen. "I'll be right back," I mouthed. He nodded.

Regan hadn't acknowledged my request. But she hadn't walked away either.

She waited for me as I walked into the aisle, then started walking alongside her.

"What do you want?" she snapped. "Make it quick."

I rolled my eyes. "Fine. I know the Consort Games are coming up."

She glanced at me. "Oh, you know that, do you? What else do you know about them?"

"I know we're supposed to work together," I said as calmly as I could. "To survive. That sounds pretty important, doesn't it? Survival."

She tossed her head. "I'll survive with or without you."

"Yes, but it doesn't have to be without me. We could help each other. Work as a team."

She narrowed her eyes. "I thought you didn't want any of this."

"If you mean Blake and being part of this little triad, then I still don't. But I do want to live. Don't you? Wouldn't we be stronger if we helped one another?"

She didn't respond. I watched her face. Was she considering what I'd said?

"I don't know all of the details of these Games, but we're clearly supposed to be proving ourselves. Won't it make you, you know, *look* better if we work as a team? Isn't that what Blake would want?"

Instantly, I knew I'd said the wrong thing.

Regan narrowed her eyes at me. "Why are you even still here, *bitch*? You play at being one of us. Always trying to get Blake's attention. It's pathetic. Things were better between us when you weren't here."

I took a deep breath and tried to keep my temper in check. "Fine. I take it that's a 'no.' But there's still time for you to change your mind. Think about it. We don't have to like each other to work together."

I turned and walked back to the table before she could say anything else.

I sank back down on the bench across from Naveen.

"You know, Naveen," I said slowly. "Sometimes I think this place might actually be growing on me."

He smiled sympathetically. "And then?"

"And then I have to talk to highbloods."

I looked around the refectory, at the blazing fires, the greenery on the walls, the chattering students. "I mean, if I'm being honest… I love Bloodwing more than I would have thought possible. But being around all of these vampires…" I shook my head, my mind going back to the terrifying encounter I'd had with the highblood man at the brothel. To the moment Visha had shoved dirt in my face and shown me her knife. "I don't know. Doesn't it just make you feel *weak* sometimes? Powerless? Gretchen was right. We'll never fit in. We're not meant to."

I half-expected Naveen to wave the highblood flag of loyalty like Florence usually did.

But instead he nodded. "All the time. Sometimes I think I made a mistake in coming here. Even if it was for a good reason."

"Was it just because of Florence?" I asked, curious. "Or do you really want to be a scout?"

"It was mostly for Florence," he admitted. "I could have stayed at home and been a scout for my own people. Dwarfs are blightborn, yes. But highbloods mostly leave us alone."

"You could still leave," I said. "No one would judge you. Well, I wouldn't. I'm sure Florence wouldn't either."

He shook his head. "You can't leave once you've been accepted. I mean, it's not like I really had a choice once I got the letter, even if my girlfriend thought I did. They would probably have come for me, even if I'd tried to refuse."

"They must have thought you had a lot of potential then," I said, trying to be optimistic. "If they wanted you that bad."

He shrugged. "Maybe. But they make mistakes, too. That's why so many First Years wind up getting kicked out. It's a make us or break us thing, the first year here. And sometimes I don't know if I'm going to make it."

I looked at him in surprise, suddenly wishing I hadn't brought up this subject. "Of course you are, Naveen. Look at you, you're doing great. You have a solo in the ensemble. A highblood is *jealous* of you. Jealous of a blightborn!"

"Maybe that should make me feel great. But honestly, I kind of wish they'd given the solo to Larissa," he said darkly.

"You don't really mean that," I said, shocked. "What would Florence say?"

"Florence is going to make it through the academy and be a brilliant highblood prize. She will always fight for them, Medra. No matter what she sometimes says. She looks up to them and always will." Naveen dropped his voice and leaned closer. "If she'd been in your position, she'd have been thrilled."

"What do you mean?" I shifted on the bench, suddenly uncomfortable.

"I mean she'd love to be a consort," he said sadly. "I'm sure of it. She wouldn't want someone like me. She has too much ambition for that."

"You could become a brilliant scout," I said loyally. "Like Professor Stonefist. For all I know I'm sitting across from the next Grimblade."

He gave me a wry smile. "Sure. But I doubt it."

"Don't be so sure, Naveen. You probably didn't think you were going to get into the Bloodwing Ensemble. Or get that flute solo," I said, suddenly losing my temper with him a bit. "But you did. Have some confidence in yourself. If you want to win Florence's heart, I promise you, that'll help more than anything else."

He studied me. "Maybe you're right."

"I am," I said resolutely.

I knew I was right. I was pathetically, pitifully right. I knew that from personal experience. Confidence was attractive. And arrogance? Well, it turned out sometimes that was even better.

Hating someone didn't mean you could take your eyes off them. Which was why I couldn't take my eyes off Blake Drakharrow even though I knew what an asshole he was. He was the walking, talking embodiment of highblood haughtiness. And I was the pathetic girl who'd been secretly sneaking glances at him this entire time.

He hadn't looked at me once.

Unable to help myself, I turned my head and glanced over at the Drakharrow table. It was mostly empty now. Only Blake and Visha remained. They were talking. Did it matter about what?

I sighed. "So, tell me more about the Frostfire Festival."

"What do you want to know?"

I shrugged. "I don't really know anything about it. Other than that you'll be playing a solo."

"That'll be the highlight of the entire festival," he joked.

"I'm sure it will be," I said, giving him an encouraging grin. "What else will happen?"

"You'd be better off asking Florence..." He started to say.

I cut him off with a groan. "That's what you always say."

He smiled sheepishly. "Fine. But I've never actually *been* to it."

"I thought Frostfire was celebrated all over Sangratha."

"It is. But I'm sure Bloodwing's traditions will be different." He looked thoughtful. "I know there's a feast. The Feast of the First Flame. Everyone sits down in the refectory for that on the first night of the festival. If it's anything like the one back home, there'll be visiting guests and performances. I'll be performing with the ensemble that night."

"What else?" I asked. A feast didn't sound so bad.

"There are some little traditions that they seem to do everywhere. Like ice sculpting contests. Things that are just part of winter. But I'm sure Bloodwing will make an even bigger deal out of them." He thought for a moment. "And then there's the ball."

I frowned. "A ball?"

He nodded. "You'll be expected to go, whether you want to or not. I'm pretty sure it'll be mandatory since you're a consort. For the rest of us, well, we don't have to go but we can be awarded the privilege. Though, for First Years, we can't attend unless we come with a partner to dance with."

"So you have to ask Florence," I said quickly. "Perfect."

He grimaced. "We'll see."

"Is there a theme to this ball?"

He nodded. "It's called the Dance of the Longest Night. It's held on the Winter Solstice."

"A ball, a feast, ice carving." I ticked them off on my fingers. "None of this sounds especially vampire-ish to me."

Naveen laughed. "That's why you should ask Florence about the rest." His face turned serious. "There is one part of it I just remembered that you probably won't like. But we'll all be expected to take part. Even back home, we'd do it."

My heart sank. "Oh? And what's that?"

When I got back to my room that night, I found a note that had been slipped under the door.

I unfolded it and read: "Dear blightborn bitch, go fuck yourself. I work alone. I hope you die a slow and painful death in the Games. I can't wait to watch. Love, Regan."

CHAPTER 35

BLAKE

Thank the Bloodmaiden for vampire reflexes. I'd been gawking at Pendragon like a fool, but every time her head seemed to be about to move in my direction, I'd glance away so she'd have no idea.

I'd noticed Regan looking at me strangely once or twice but I didn't think she'd seen anything. I still glared at her to put her in her place. I was her fucking archon and she knew it.

Things between us were rocky. I mean, they had been all last year, if not before that. But now, with Pendragon thrown into the mix, they were worse. Regan had always been insecure. I think she actually thought her feelings for me were real.

She knew I didn't reciprocate. Honestly, I found it hard to take her "feelings" for me seriously. I didn't think they were based on anything more than her hunger for power and status. Being paired with me gave her both. She seemed to think "love" should be part of the bargain. But that wasn't how it worked. I wasn't obligated to love her.

We'd been paired together to be mates out of political convenience. Because my uncle needed to shore up power and Lord Pansera had shoved his daughter in front of him at the perfect time. I had no idea if my father would have ultimately approved of our match, especially considering how Regan had turned out. Even though our families had grown up together and Regan had always been pushed my way, I'd always hoped he'd let me do my own choosing. After all, he'd wound up with my mother–and with only her. That had been their choice. They'd opted not to form a triad, even though they might have been stronger with a third mate.

Sometimes I wondered if my father would still be alive if he'd formed a triad. Who could say.

I wasn't the only one with my head in the clouds as we sat in the refectory.

Theo wasn't even pretending to listen as Regan and Quinn went on and on about what they were going to wear to the Dance of the Longest Night and what they were going to eat and who they were going to talk to–and not talk to, of course.

He was too busy staring across the refectory at Vaughn Sabino, not even caring who saw.

I looked over at the blightborn boy. Sabino's arm was no longer in a sling. He had it perched on the table and was holding a quill as he scribbled something on parchment. That was a good sign. I knew that Sabino had wanted to be a scout. Coregon had bragged that the blightborn wouldn't be able to become one now, thanks to the damage to his arm. Maybe Coregon hadn't done as much harm to the boy as he'd liked to think.

I winced, thinking about Coregon. Sometimes I still couldn't believe he was really gone. Deep down, he'd been even more of a cold-blooded asshole than I was. But he'd hidden it well.

There were times it would have been nice to have him back. Or at least, useful. He'd been good at helping me to shut Regan up, to put her in her place. He'd helped me keep everyone in line.

He really would have been a good choice for my second.

But now I knew what he'd really been thinking. That I hadn't been capable of managing my house on my own.

I gave Theo a playful punch on the arm. "Hey. Stop staring." I said it low enough that only he'd be able to hear.

He jerked his head up, then glared at me.

"What are you looking at me like that for?" I said, frowning. I lowered my voice again. "I'm not the one who did that to him."

He shook his head. "Right. And you expect me to believe that."

I felt my face flush. "I do expect you to believe that. Because it's the truth."

He looked at me. "Next thing you'll tell me Uncle Viktor didn't tell you that you had to keep me in line. Keep me from humiliating our family with my little 'indiscretions.'"

I leaned towards him. "You know I don't give a fuck about your indiscretions."

But there was no way I was going to tell him the truth about just how little Viktor cared about him. Or Marcus.

I slung my arm around his shoulder. "You're my second now, Theo. We have to trust each other."

He shrugged my arm off and stood up. "Maybe you should pick someone else."

He slunk out of the refectory before I could think of the right thing to say.

"Shit," I muttered under my breath.

The girls were still gossiping about some bullshit.

It was only when Quinn brought up the Consort Games that I tuned back in.

"You must be looking forward to putting that little Pendragon bitch in her place, Regan," Quinn gushed. She was such a suck-up. She'd managed to crawl so far up Regan's ass I didn't think she'd ever come out again. But then, Regan loved that sort of thing. She only wanted girls around her who would worship her.

"Oh, I am, believe me," Regan started to say.

I slammed my palms down on the table. "What was that?"

Regan fell silent.

I slid down the bench and positioned myself across from the three girls. Regan, Quinn, and Visha.

Visha was the only one who met my eyes.

"Regan, you know my position on the Consort Games," I said firmly. "And you're going to toe the fucking line. Aren't you?"

Regan twirled a strand of hair around her finger and sighed.

"Regan, look at me, dammit."

She sulkily met my eyes. "Yes. Fine. I am. You know that. A girl can still dream, can't she?"

I rolled my eyes. Only Regan would dream of murdering her fellow consort. Well, maybe not only Regan. It happened once in a while. But it wasn't supposed to.

"You don't want to piss off old Uncle Viktor, now do you, Regan?" I reminded her.

I hated myself for doing it, but I reached a hand forward and lightly cupped her cheek. "Or me, baby. Right?"

Her gaze softened as she looked at me. "Of course not. You know I'm a good girl."

"The very best," I said, letting my voice take on the hint of a drawl. "Such a good girl for me."

She bit her lip. "Blake..."

I knew exactly what she was going to ask later. She'd want to come to my room that night. She wanted to come to my room every fucking night.

But I'd shut her out months ago. It had driven her crazy. I hadn't even let her go down on me. No matter how sex crazed I'd felt sometimes. And it had been pretty bad at some points.

I wasn't sure exactly what was wrong with me. But Regan had lost all appeal. Even in bed. And she had a good body, there was no denying that. She was exceptionally... bendy.

It was all Pendragon's fault. Ever since that day I'd found her. Even covered with that prick, Barnabas's blood, she'd been a breathtaking sight.

I thought of that day constantly.

Medra Pendragon might have been the most infuriating girl I'd ever known. She certainly ignited my worst emotions. And yet I'd never get that vision of her out of my head. Naked and yet still looking down her nose at me. Breasts splattered with blood and yet standing as tall and straight as a queen.

She was a blightborn. She shouldn't have been capable of doing what she did to me.

But it was like she didn't even understand what she was.

She wasn't like other girls who fawned over me and bent to my will. I'd sampled plenty of those in my first year at Bloodwing. Even Regan had fallen into that category eventually, though at first she'd pretended to have an actual backbone and mind of her own. It had all been an act. She'd been trying to hold my interest. And it worked–for a little while.

But no, Pendragon met me with brutal words and cold glares. She made it clear she had no intention of falling at my feet. Yet despite that–no, fuck, because of it–I couldn't stop thinking about her.

There was something about being challenged that made her irresistible. That glimmer of rebellion in her eyes, like a light that promised to never go out. The way she resisted what most girls would normally crave.

I couldn't shake her from my thoughts. If I'd at least been able to just *taste* her, then maybe I'd have been able to get her out of my head. But even that was impossible. To do so would undo exactly what my uncle claimed he wanted us to get out of this.

Hell, part of me suspected he never wanted me to taste Pendragon–because he planned to take her for himself.

And that thought made me see blood red. It would *never* happen, not while I lived.

I didn't want to stand up to Viktor. I fucking hated the man, but I wasn't an idiot. I knew he was stronger than me.

Still, I'd do it, even if I knew it was suicidal, if I thought there was a chance it would keep Pendragon out of his slimy old hands.

In a world where everyone else bowed to us, she stood tall. Defiant and unbroken. It made Regan hate her. But to me, it only made her more alluring.

I closed my eyes for a moment. Remembering her perfect breasts. That thatch of red curls between her pale thighs.

Every night I jerked off to the same thing. Just different variations.

My favorite fantasy this week involved going down on her. She'd push me away, tell me to get out of her room, then she'd change her mind and grab me by the hair and pull me back, shoving my head down between her legs.

I'd lick long and deep, tasting her sweet saltiness, while she moaned. She didn't want this. And yet she did. That was what made it so fucking good. Knowing we couldn't stand each other. Yet knowing we couldn't keep our hands off one another.

I'd reach a hand up to cup one perfect breast, rubbing my finger over her nipple until it was taut, while my tongue circled her clit and she arched her hips against me.

I'd bring her to her climax, swift and intense, and then I'd climb over her, letting her get a good look at me. I'd tell her this was what she'd done to me. She'd bite her lip and tell me she needed me inside her, couldn't wait another minute.

I'd bend down and kiss her sweet lips while I wrapped my hands in that gorgeous mane of red curls, all spread out around her head like a halo of flame, and then I'd slide inside of her. I'd try to be slow and gentle, but soon I'd be out of control. She'd be clawing at my back, begging me to take her harder, faster...

Visha cleared her throat and I jerked out of my reverie, suddenly remembering where I was.

I sighed and ran my hands over my face, shifting on the bench to get more comfortable. It was fucking humiliating. It was also ironic. Pendragon had been given to me as a prize and yet I couldn't even claim her. She was untouchable. I couldn't even feed from her without our bond getting stronger first. Of course, she didn't know that. If she did, she'd never let me get close to her ever again.

Regan and Quinn were standing up to go. They pecked each other on the cheek as if they actually cared about each other. It was sweet in a nauseating kind of way.

"You're not coming, Visha?" Regan said, looking down at the dark-haired girl.

Visha shook her head. "I'll just hang here until supper time. See you back in the tower."

Regan looked at me with a question in her eyes. "Blake..."

I shook my head. "I'll see you back at the tower later on, too." Then I looked away.

Regan stood there a moment longer then walked off. I heard her start chattering like a magpie again as she ran into Larissa and Gretchen. The third and fourth meanest girls at Bloodwing, after Regan and Quinn.

I watched as the girls approached Pendragon's table. Her friend, Sharma, started looking uncomfortable. They were putting him through the ringer, no doubt. Pendragon's face grew more and more angry. Then she snapped at them. I watched Larissa's face redden with embarrassment and had to stop myself from bursting out laughing.

Then their conversation seemed to wind up. To my surprise, Regan lingered. Pendragon stood up and followed her. She talked to the other girl for a minute. Whatever they were discussing didn't seem to make her happy.

I thought I knew what it was about.

I turned back to Visha. She pushed a hand through her short-cropped white hair. She liked to change up her style. Last week she'd shaved it down almost to the scalp. She looked pretty badass. Unlike Regan's other friends, Visha had a mind of her own.

It had taken me a while to realize that. I still didn't think Regan had.

"You still pissed at me for what happened with Pendragon?" She said, with typical Vaidya bluntness.

I met her violet gaze. "I was for a while. I told you to test her. Not fucking beat her to a pulp and try to knife her."

She shrugged. "It was too tempting to resist."

I nodded. "Fine. Let's move on. You got a taste. But I won't tolerate it if you take another. Do you understand?"

Slowly, she nodded. Unlike Coregon, Visha knew what I was really capable of. I knew she'd fall in line.

"The Consort Games are coming up," I said to her. "Have you decided?"

She blew out a breath. "Fuck, Blake. That's a big decision."

"I know," I said carefully. "The biggest one of your life. Don't wind up like me."

She rolled her eyes. "I'm more worried I'll wind up like Regan, if I'm being honest."

"I don't think you'll ever have to worry about that happening," I said quietly.

She studied me. "You really don't think she'll listen?"

I shook my head. "I doubt it. She's not usually a risk-taker, but I think I know her well enough to know this is one risk she'll think is worth taking."

Visha nodded. "I think so, too."

"Good thing I've got you on my side," I joked.

She smiled wryly. "Just don't let Regan get the wrong idea."

"We'll talk fast," I agreed. "I think you already know what needs to be done."

CHAPTER 36

MEDRA

It was the same dream I'd had for the last seven nights in a row. Wasn't seven some sort of a lucky number?

I lay tangled in my sheets, my body tense.

I was back in the training yard, fighting with Blake. Heart pounding. Adrenaline coursing through my veins.

I sat astride him, the weight of my body pressing against his.

But this time there was a dagger in my hand.

I pressed it to his throat.

My breathing was ragged. So was his. I could feel the pulse of his life beneath my trembling fingers.

For the first time since we'd been forced into this twisted bond, I felt truly powerful.

I was in control. I could end everything in an instant. Stop all the hatred, all the confusion.

I was filled with a strong emotion. Joy.

Or was it? Why was I hesitating?

Blake stared up at me. His gray eyes were dark with fury and hatred. But beneath it, I glimpsed a hint of fear.

I relished the weight of the blade, focused on the pale skin of his throat. He was at my mercy. All I had to do was push down.

A rush of power was building up in my chest. I'd be free of him.

I faltered. His gaze caught mine and for a split second, I saw something more there.

Raw desire.

It was like looking into a mirror. The realization struck me like a blow, the breath fleeing my lungs.

His lips twisted into a half-smile.

Slowly, he reached up and grasped my wrist. I let him.

"Do it then," he whispered, his voice rough and taunting. "You want this, don't you? Finish it now."

His grip grew tighter. "But that won't be enough, Pendragon. Haven't you ever killed a highblood?"

He moved my hand lower, until the dagger was right over his heart.

"If you really want to end things, you'll have to stab me in the heart."

I gritted my teeth, every fiber of my being screaming at me to do it.

But I didn't move.

That pause was all he needed. In a heartbeat, Blake flew into action.

Surprising me with his strength, he flipped us over, and suddenly, I was the one pinned beneath him.

He had the dagger now, his hand still around my wrist, as he pressed the blade against my throat.

His face hovered over mine. His eyes were wild. So full of hate.

I knew he'd use the knife.

I closed my eyes, the pressure of the blade against my skin intensifying. This was how it was going to end. All because I'd been too weak and too stupid to kill him when I'd had the chance.

I braced myself for the cut. Would he feed from me as my life's blood spilled out?

Then his lips brushed my ear. "I could kill you right here, right now, little dragon."

The words sent a jolt down my spine.

Then the pressure at my throat was gone. I heard a clattering sound as he tossed the dagger away.

"You had your chance to end this," he growled, his breath hot against my skin. "You failed. And now...you're mine."

Then his lips were on mine.

The kiss was rough. Urgent. Possessive. Everything I'd been denying I wanted.

For a heartbeat, I froze.

My first instinct was to push him away. But in the next moment, I felt my hands betray me. I clutched his shirt, pulling him closer instead.

I was furious with myself. In my head, I knew he was no good for me. But my body knew what it wanted and was refusing to deny it for another second.

Heat coiled low in my stomach and the need I'd been fighting for so long surged to the surface.

I was lost in the kiss, lost in him. The way he kissed me was commanding–a storm of anger and desire. Every nerve in my body screamed with need, my mind spinning from the intensity of it.

I couldn't think, couldn't breathe. Couldn't resist him.

Blake's hands slid down my body, his fingers brushing the exposed skin of my waist, leaving a trail of heat in their wake.

My hands tangled in his hair, pulling him closer against me, as my mind screamed at me to stop.

His tongue slid against mine, sending a bolt of lightning through my body, and I moaned.

His fingers roamed over me, finding their way beneath my clothes. His hands cupped my breasts and I shivered, arching upwards, silently begging for more.

"You're mine," he growled against my lips.

I hated myself for how much I wanted it to be true.

"I hate you," I whispered, even as my body melted with his touch.

His teeth grazed my lower lips and I felt his fangs, reminding me just how dangerous he truly was.

His dark voice filled with cruel satisfaction. "You could never hate me as much as you want me."

And then his hands were tugging my trousers down and his fingers were between my legs, slipping into the wet space between my thighs. I trembled against him as he slid in and out of me, bringing me closer and closer to the edge.

The dream shifted violently.

The training yard quaked.

I looked around in terror as the stone walls surrounding us began to crack and crumble, pieces of rock breaking off and tumbling to the ground.

"What is this? What's happening?" I demanded.

Blake looked down at me, his gray eyes strong and steady. "The dragons are coming."

My heart slammed against my chest as the walls collapsed, revealing a dark gaping space beyond.

A shape moved, massive and terrifying.

A dragon–huge and ancient and filled with unspeakable power–rose from the wreckage of the wall, its wings spreading wide, its glowing yellow eyes locked on me.

The beast let out a deafening roar.

I opened my mouth to scream and the sound of my own voice tore me from the dream with a jolt.

My eyes flew open.

I tossed my legs around, trying to untangle them from the wreckage of my blankets, my heart still racing from the nightmare.

Something was wrong.

The room was shaking. The First Year tower trembled as if it would crumble apart, just like in my dream.

I shot out of bed, my feet hitting the cold floor as I stumbled towards the door and ran down the hall towards Florence's room.

Naveen was already there. He had a hand against the wall, bracing himself.

"What the fuck is happening?" I shouted.

The shaking stopped.

Florence's door flew open. She stood there in a white nightdress, her black hair loose around her shoulders. Her eyes were wide and frightened.

Other students had come out into the hallway. The corridor filled with the sound of panicked voices.

I saw Vaughn Sabino come to stand near Naveen. His arm had been out of the sling for a week now.

"Quiet everyone," Florence called, raising her voice to be heard over the din. "Quiet please."

Slowly all the First Years turned towards her.

"I'm not sure where the other First Year Warden is," Florence said. Her voice was calm. I glanced at Naveen, knowing only he and I could probably tell how nervous she still was. "But I need you all to be quiet and to listen to me."

"Probably drunk or being sucked," I heard Naveen mutter to Vaughn. The other warden, Thomas, didn't take his duties as seriously as Florence. I wasn't sure why he'd even been selected. Then I'd found out he was a thrall to one of the students in House Avari. That was probably why. Maybe he was busy with his highblood right now.

The First Years had all turned towards Florence.

"Thank you. Now, please listen. The tower is not going to fall," Florence reassured them, her voice firm. "This castle was built centuries ago and was enchanted to withstand almost anything. Even dragon attacks." Her lips twitched a little. "And I think we all know there's no need to worry about one of those."

There was a titter of nervous laughter.

"I've already spoken to Professor Wispwood about the last quake we experienced a few weeks ago," she continued. This was news to me, but I knew Florence was spending a lot of time with Professor Wispwood after class. "She told me that it was nothing to worry about. Islands like the one Bloodwing is situated on often experience ocean tremors. Sometimes there will be nothing for decades, then there will be a span where you get a bunch all in a row over a few weeks or even days. It's very common."

Her words began to settle around the hall and I could almost feel the relief coming off my fellow First Years.

"Even if we did get hit by something like a tidal wave caused by one of the tremors," Florence continued. "Bloodwing was built high enough above sea level that we would remain safe. Nothing can reach us here."

Some of the students began talking again, but their voices were lower, less panicked. They seemed reassured.

Florence clapped her hands together briskly. "Now, I need you all to go back to your rooms. The tremors are over. Go to sleep. Everything will be fine. I'll check in with Professor Wispwood and the headmaster in the morning, and I promise you, if there is any cause for concern, we will let you know."

The crowd began to move, thinning out of the corridor as the students moved back to their rooms.

I turned to Florence. "That was impressive."

She shrugged modestly but looked pleased. "Just doing my job."

"And Thomas isn't," Vaughn pointed out.

She sighed. "He's probably snuck out again. Can you call it sneaking out if you're going to feed a highblood student? I've never been sure about that."

"I didn't know First Years could be used as thralls," I said.

"Yes, well, apparently Thomas 'belonged' to this highblood before he arrived at Bloodwing. They came here together from the student's family estate. It's rare but it's acceptable. What's more unusual is Thomas being made a warden." Florence looked frustrated. "I don't see the point of it. He hardly helps the First Years at all."

"Highblood nepotism knows no bounds." I peered past her into her room. "Where's Neville?"

"Gone again," Florence said, pushing a lock of black hair off her face. "Probably to Blake. I hope he's all right."

I shook my head dutifully, but a part of me wondered if Neville slept on Blake's bed. The memory of the dream was still fresh in my mind. Suddenly my own bed seemed very cold and empty.

"Sleep in my room tonight?" Florence suggested.

"Sure, great idea," Naveen quipped. "Sleepover party, Vaughn?"

Vaughn smiled. It was the first time I'd seen him really smile in a long time.

Florence punched Naveen's arm playfully. "I meant Medra."

"Oh, right. That makes sense," Naveen agreed. "I'm still hurt though."

"I'd have invited you if I didn't happen to know you snore like a bear," Florence said, giggling. "We used to have sleepovers when we were little," she explained to Vaughn and I.

We said goodnight to Naveen and Vaughn, and then I followed Florence into her room.

Once we were snuggled up under her blankets, I started to relax. Florence slept with a huge, heavy comforter on top of the other blankets. Its heaviness was nice. Like a warm hug.

Like Blake's body pressing against you, said an evil voice in my head. I told it to go to hell.

"I got invited to the Dance of the Longest Night," said Florence, her voice starting to drift. "Did I tell you?"

I sat up in bed. "No, you most certainly did not. By who?"

Please say Naveen, I prayed.

She hesitated. "I actually received two invitations."

"Oh, really? I'm not surprised. You'll probably get a dozen more before the ball," I teased. "After all, you are the most brilliant girl at Bloodwing. Not to mention one of the most beautiful."

"Ha. I don't know about either of those things," Florence said, scrunching up her nose. "I work hard. That's all." She hadn't dimmed the lamp by her bed yet and I could see her black eyes were bright with excitement.

"You work very, very, very hard. Now tell me who asked you," I prodded. "You know you want to."

She blushed slightly. "One was a student from House Orphos."

"A highblood?" I asked in alarm.

She shook her head. "No, a strategist. Ebbot. He's a Third Year. We've studied together a few times. You know I've been taking some advanced classes."

"Is he nice?" I ventured. "Handsome?"

"He's nice," Florence said, after a pause to consider. "I'm not sure about handsome. I have to admit, I was surprised when he asked me. I hadn't thought about him that way. He's brilliant though. We'd have a lot to talk about."

"It might be nice to have someone in your field to go with," I said cautiously. I was hoping the other invitation wasn't from a highblood. "And the other?"

Florence waved a hand. "It was just Naveen."

"Oh." I wasn't sure what to say. Not without revealing anything. "Well, Naveen is a good friend. He'd be fun to go with. He'd make you feel comfortable, right?"

"That's what I was thinking, too." Florence sighed. "I should probably give Ebbot an answer one way or the other tomorrow."

I hoped she'd pick Naveen. But I wasn't sure I should say that out loud. It might sway her the other way.

"Well, no one's asked me yet," I said, throwing my head back down on the pillow. "And they probably won't." I grinned ferociously at her. "Because I'm the weirdo redhead blightborn dragonless dragon rider girl."

Blightborn students seemed scared of me half the time. And highbloods were just plain nasty.

I thought of something horrible. "Wait. Please don't tell me I'm locked into going to this thing with Blake and Regan."

Florence shook her head and relief flooded through me. "You don't have to attend with them. Not if Blake hasn't specifically asked you."

"He hasn't. Thank goodness." But the irrational part of me felt offended that he hadn't. Which was ridiculous. Despite all that Theo had claimed at the bonfire that night, I knew Blake would go with Regan.

"But you will probably have to dance together at least once," Florence went on. "It's tradition."

"I guess I can manage a single dance." I tried to imagine slow dancing with Blake Drakharrow and couldn't quite manage it. "I tried to ask Naveen about the Frostfire

Festival but he told me to ask you. He thinks a lot of you, Florence. What's it like having a friend who adores you so?" I decided to risk teasing her a little.

She laughed. "Naveen is silly. He probably could have given you just as good an answer. What did you want to know?"

I thought for a moment. "So far Frostfire seems so... I don't know. Sweet? Cozy? Not like a highblood tradition at all. Although Naveen did mention we'd have to visit the Temple of the Bloodmaiden."

"Yes, that's true." Florence bit her lip. "We're expected to make a blood offering."

I frowned. "Like on your name day? Why didn't you ever tell me about that tradition?"

"I guess I never even thought to. Sometimes I forget that you don't know anything about Sangratha, Medra. Even the most minor things like how we celebrate our name days are new to you."

"Giving the highbloods some blood on your name day doesn't seem like much of a celebration to me," I said with a shudder.

"Well, we're not giving it to one highblood specifically. We're offering it to the Bloodmaiden," Florence replied.

"I still don't understand what the Bloodmaiden really is. A goddess of some kind?"

Florence nodded. "The story goes that when our world was new, a demigoddess—half mortal, half divine—sacrificed herself and let her blood be spilled to save the world. But her family were determined to avoid her fate. Her mother and father and siblings dipped their head into her blood and drank. She saved them and they were granted immortality."

"They stole her blood, cheated death because they were too selfish to help her save the world, and were turned into vampires," I translated.

Florence grimaced. "That's one way of looking at it. Not an interpretation I'd ever bring up in Professor Hassan's class."

I laughed. "I'll remember not to."

"Anyhow, some of the demigoddess's brothers and sisters refused to drink her blood."

"I don't blame them," I chimed in unhelpfully. "Gross."

"Gross but powerful," Florence countered. I thought of what Naveen had said. About how Florence harbored great ambitions and might have been happy to be selected as a highblood's consort. I wondered if it was true. "The brothers and sisters who did not drink remained mortal. A lower life form."

"Blightborn," I supplied.

"Right. They were looked down on at first. Then came the histories you've already heard in Professor Hassan's class."

"The highbloods were the blightborns' salvation." I snorted. "I remember."

"Regardless of what you believe," Florence went on. "Highbloods and blightborn revere the Bloodmaiden. There are temples devoted to her across Sangratha. Some women even enter into her service and live their entire lives there." She shot me a curious glance. "Did you know Blake Drakharrow's mother is in the Sanctum?"

"At a temple?" I said in surprise. "No. How would I have known that? Why?" I was surprised a woman from such a powerful family and house would choose to enter into a life of seclusion.

"When her husband died, she left her family. As far as everyone knows, that's where she went. To the Bloodmaid's Sanctum. The most sacred temple in Sangratha. No one has seen her since. I assume Blake and his family are in touch with her somehow though."

"I don't like the sound of having to give blood at this place," I said with a groan.

"It's not so bad. You'll see. Naveen and I can go first. You can watch... us..." Florence yawned.

"We should go to sleep," I said guiltily, remembering how hard she'd been studying. "You need your rest."

"Sounds good," Florence said dreamily.

The room was quiet for a while. Then she spoke again. "Who do you think I should go with, Medra?"

"Naveen," I said promptly. "You'll have fun with Naveen."

"I'm sure you're right." She yawned again. "Even though he probably only asked me because he thought no one else had. He had a girlfriend back home, you know."

"I know," I said. "But they broke up, right?"

But there was no answer. Florence had fallen asleep.

In another few minutes, so did I.

There were no more dragons in my dreams that night.

CHAPTER 37

MEDRA

A few weeks passed by.

Wintermark term exams came and went.

I'd passed all of my classes. I'd even surprised myself with some of my marks. I'd received a C (Commendable) in Restoration with Professor Rodriguez. Part of me thought he was as surprised as I was. I couldn't do healing magic, but the theory was fascinating and I was excited to get into more alchemy work in the next part of the course. I'd gotten the highest mark possible in Basic Combat for Blightborns–an E for Excellent, and another Commendable in Advanced Weaponry with Professor Sankara, which I thought was more than fair considering the incident with Blake.

The only class I'd received the second-to-last lowest mark possible, a W for Weak, was History of Sangratha. The class itself was engrossing. Professor Hassan's lectures were usually full of interesting historical tidbits. But she'd hated me since that first day I'd arrived late and no matter how I tried to keep out of her way and no matter how hard I worked on my essays, nothing improved. She'd actually failed me on one paper and accused me of plagiarism. So I was thrilled to have passed with a W. It was better than flunking out completely.

Florence's marks were all stellar which was no surprise. Es across the board. And Naveen seemed happy with his marks, too, though he wouldn't show them to us.

Ever since Florence had accepted his invitation to the ball, he'd been looking a little high strung. But I put that down to his nervousness over the Dance of the Longest Night. Not only was he worried about his solo but now Florence would be there on his arm.

Since the night of the second quake, my dreams had changed.

Blake had been banished. He'd been replaced by the dragon.

The dreams were all pretty much the same. Bloodwing was crumbling around me. Sometimes I was running through the halls and trying to save Florence or Naveen or Vaughn or other random blightborn students.

All while a huge dragon with massive flapping wings rose up out of the rubble, roaring all the while.

There had been a few more tremors, but they'd happened during the daytime and Florence had been right–none of the professors seemed very concerned.

Now we'd reached the last day of term. It was lunchtime. I walked down the corridor with Florence towards the refectory, my breath fogging in the chilly air.

The weather had turned bitingly sharp and a heavy snow covered the campus. But despite the cold, Bloodwing was buzzing with anticipation for the upcoming school break and the Frostfire Festival. Most of the First Year students seemed to be staying at school for the break rather than returning home.

While Naveen and Florence were going to the Dance of the Longest Night together, I had no date for the ball. No one had even asked me. But I was determined not to get in their way by being a third wheel.

I'd told Florence I'd found out I had to go with Blake and Regan. It was a lie, but she'd bought it. Now I could stay out of the way and let her and Naveen get in some alone time. I'd be fine on my own. I'd play the wallflower, staying on the sidelines and watching the dancing, participating only if I absolutely had to. Then I'd leave as early as was acceptable.

As we rounded a corner, my thoughts still wandering, I stopped dead in my tracks as a tall figure stepped out of the shadows, blocking our path.

Another instant and I'd recognized who it was.

Kage Tanaka.

The highblood house leader had an oversized presence. He was nearly as tall as Blake. He stood with his back straight, legs spread in a rigid posture that spoke of someone used to maintaining authority. His white-blond hair, gathered in a bun at the back of his head, with the sides shaved close, gave him a fierce, edgy look. His crescent moon tattoo peeked up over the high collar of his black, silver trimmed jacket.

"Miss Pendragon." His voice was rich and smooth. But there was a sharp edge underneath that told me not to underestimate him. "I wondered if I might have a moment of your time?" He glanced at Florence. "Alone."

Florence looked at me questioningly. When I nodded, she slipped down the hall ahead of us. I knew she'd grab a table in the refectory and wait for me.

"Kage," I said, my voice wary. "What do you want?"

"Medra, isn't it? Such a beautiful name. May I have your permission to use it?"

I hesitated. "I suppose so."

It would be a refreshing change from Blake constantly snapping "Pendragon."

He smiled. "Thank you, Medra. I've been watching you for quite some time now."

My head spun at this revelation. "Have you? Why?" I thought of that night at the bonfire. Kiernan had claimed Kage wanted us to join him. It had seemed to be true, but I hadn't thought anything of it since then.

The leader of House Avari gave me a small, knowing smile. "Let's just say I admire your spirit. It's rare to see someone so...unyielding."

"Unyielding towards highbloods, you mean?"

He nodded. "If you want to put it that way. You stand apart here. Others in your position might have broken."

"I don't break easily," I snapped. Though it had been a close call at times.

"I respect that." Kage's dark eyes lingered on my face, appraising me with a slow, deliberate gaze that made my stomach flip. "Maybe it's the hair. Like the fire of a dragon, you're impossible to tame."

What exactly was happening here? Was Kage Tanaka really paying me compliments?

"Well, thank you," I said slowly. "But that doesn't answer my question. What do you want?"

Kage leaned against the wall, his black eyes watching me carefully. "I want you to come with me to the Dance of the Longest Night."

I blinked, unsure I'd heard him correctly. "I beg your pardon?"

"I want you to be my date for the ball." His tone was matter-of-fact, as if it were the most natural request in the world. "That is, unless you already have one."

I didn't. He knew I didn't. Somehow.

"Why me?" I asked, my voice coming out sharper than I'd intended. "You could ask anyone. You're a House Leader."

"Because you don't belong at Drakharrow's side. He doesn't deserve you. And you know it." His voice dipped, becoming more intense. "You're not a girl who belongs at the feet of someone like Blake. I know you wish you had never been shackled to him by his uncle. Why not show him you'll never belong to him?"

"You think I'm going to go with you just to spite Blake?"

"Let me show you that you don't have to be just a pawn in the Drakharrows' game." He gave me a slow grin. "If you accept, I can promise you one thing, Medra. I'll make sure to give you the night you really deserve."

I swallowed, unsure of how to respond to that. It was an invitation, in more ways than one.

Was I really considering going to the ball with a highblood? What would Naveen and Florence say?

I knew there was more to this. Kage wasn't just being nice. He wanted to use me as leverage against Blake. But did it really matter? When that was exactly what I'd be using him for, too?

"Can consorts even attend with someone other than their archon?" I asked carefully.

Kage shrugged. "It's not specifically forbidden, but it's rare. I have no problem with us being the exception. I'm not one to play by the rules." He took a step towards me. "You're impossible to ignore, Medra. There's something unique about you and it's not just your rider blood. You deserve to be treated with respect. Not as some obligation."

The way he said my name, the way he held my eyes with his... Kage's charm was undeniable, yes, but I wasn't naive enough to fall for it completely. He probably didn't mean a single word he said.

But if I could use him right back... Salvage something of the ball. I imagined what Blake would think when he saw me standing beside the school House Leader. His rival.

Kage was right about one thing. I didn't belong to Blake. Maybe this would be a way to prove that once and for all.

"By the way, there's something Drakharrow probably never thought it worthwhile to tell you about a triad union," Kage said, his dark eyes gleaming with a challenge. "If you refuse to accept the bond, they may not be able to hold you to it."

My heart started to pound. "What do you mean? Are you saying there's a way out of this?"

"Not yet. But if things go on the way they have been between you two then Blake may never be able to feed from your blood. Not properly, anyhow. He won't be able to draw power from your blood if you don't give your consent. Consorts are supposed to strengthen their archon but you'd be a hindrance. You'd be free of him in the one way that really mattered."

Excitement sped through me, but I tried to tamp it down, still suspicious of Kage's motives. "But if we did bond fully?"

I wasn't sure I wanted to know the answer.

But Kage just smirked. "Consorts take lovers all the time. It's accepted. Highbloods are rarely satisfied with just one or even two partners. Blake won't be able to stop you from enjoying the pleasures of life."

I wasn't so sure about that. How much freedom would I really have when I finally left Bloodwing Academy? I suspected the Drakharrows planned to keep me somewhere on their own terms and that I wouldn't be given much fresh air. That is, if I didn't get away from them somehow first.

Making Kage my ally might not be such a terrible idea.

"Fine. I'll think about it."

Kage's dark eyes sparkled with amusement. He straightened and stepped away from the wall. "Don't take too long."

He gave me one last lingering look before disappearing down the hall.

CHAPTER 38

MEDRA

The Frostfire Festival had officially begun.

As night fell on the first day of the festival, a grand procession of students, professors, and house leaders set off from Bloodwing Castle. First and Second Years were bundled into carriages with Bloodwing's faculty, six or eight at a time, while some of the older students and the house leaders led the way on horseback.

This was the Night of Silent Offerings, in which we would make our way to the Bloodmaid's Sanctum and be expected to give up some of our blood in a fucked up highblood tradition.

My nerves were on edge as I found myself seated between Florence and Naveen in one of the carriages. They were talking about the festival, but even though I tried to keep up, my mind was elsewhere.

Last night I'd sent an acceptance note to Kage Tanaka. I had no idea if I'd made the right choice but I was committed now.

The carriage rocked slightly from the strong winter wind coming off the sea as we crossed the long, iron bridge leading towards Veilmar. Once we reached the mainland, we turned east and passed over another bridge, this one leading to the island that housed the Sanctum.

As our procession neared, the temple came into view.

Perched like a white nest on a dark cliff, the Sanctum was striking in the winter's twilight. Built from luminous white stones, it gleamed like a pearl against the stormy sea, soaring into the sky, its center dominated by narrow spires that rose in jagged symmetry. The closer we came, the more the building's sheer size became evident.

I exchanged a glance with Florence, who gave me a small, reassuring smile. I'd told her about Kage's invitation. She'd been shocked but supportive.

Naveen was staring out the carriage window, wide-eyed. I knew he had been to temples before, but this was his first time visiting the Sanctum. Normally it was reserved solely for highbloods. There were other temples in Veilmar where blightborn were welcome to worship.

When the carriages halted, we were escorted out, faculty and house leaders guiding us through the outer gates.

I looked over at the grand doors of the Sanctum. An image of the Bloodmaiden had been carved into the white stone lintel. Her expression was serene, her hands cupped, as though she held her own lifeblood in them. I shivered.

As we made our way closer, lanterns lit the path, illuminating the towering white walls ahead of us.

The House Leaders and the faculty moved among us, talking quietly amongst themselves. They had all done this before. Tonight was nothing new for any of them, even the blightborn Professor Rodriguez or the halfborn Professor Wispwood.

Blake walked among the rows of students. His black cloak caught the breeze and it billowed out around him, as he swaggered about as if he owned the place.

We had been instructed to remain silent once we reached the Sanctum and already a hush had fallen over the students.

Two doorways marked the entrance as we approached. One for blightborn, the other for highbloods. It was pretty clear which was which.

Around the blightborn archway were carved symbols of cupped hands dripping blood.

By contrast, the highblood door was more ornate, with shining brass inlays in which reliefs had been etched of vampires standing tall and proud, their hands raised as they reached up to cup the Bloodmaid's chalice.

We filed through the archways in two lines. Most of the blightborn students around me were silent and walked with their heads down, as if in reverence. I was not about to imitate them. I wasn't going to bow my head in this place.

The highblood students were less disciplined. They whispered in hushed tones, their voices carrying through the quiet.

A few professors made their way through the crowd, shushing them. I watched as Professor Rodriguez marched up to where Regan stood whispering and laughing with Quinn and Gretchen.

"Shut up." Rodriguez's cold voice cut through the night air.

Regan looked so shocked that I had to stop myself from laughing.

"Don't make me have to tell you girls to be quiet a second time or you'll all have detentions with me, winter break or not."

Regan scowled but fell silent as Rodriguez stomped away.

We had neared the archway. Florence and Naveen walked through the blightborn doorway first. I followed.

Inside, the interior of the temple atrium was vast and lit only with flickering candles. Beyond the atrium I could see the nave and part of the inner sanctuary, where the blood offering would take place. Rows of white stone benches were divided by two broad aisles. On the far end stood an altar, a solid white slab of marble over which towered a statue of the Bloodmaiden, her hands in the cupped position.

I watched as, one by one, blightborn students approached the altar. Each was handed a small ceremonial dagger by a temple votary. With a quick slice across the palm, they let a few drops of their blood fall into a silver basin at the altar's base.

Afterwards they knelt in prayer, as if paying homage to the Bloodmaiden's sacrifice. Ironic, as I didn't see how any of them had actually benefited from it.

The highblood students did not offer blood. Instead, they approached the altar from a different aisle, moving towards it with a practiced formality. They bowed their heads in silent prayer as they neared the altar, kneeling down and murmuring words of devotion before taking a small red tablet from a silver tray offered by one of the votaries, each of whom wore flowing white robes cinched at the waist with red braid. Florence had already told me the tablets were each stained with a single drop of blightborn blood and represented the Bloodmaiden's sacrifice.

I watched in revulsion as each highblood placed a tablet in their mouth, then swallowed it.

As I stood in line, waiting my turn, I felt like even more of an outsider than usual, here in this ancient place of vampire rites and mysteries. I pulled my cloak a little tighter around me. Did I really have to go through with this barbaric ceremony and offer up blood to a goddess I had absolutely no intention of ever worshiping?

After my experiences in Aercanum, I'd had enough of so-called gods and goddesses for one lifetime.

As I stepped forward in the line, my hood slipped from my head. I shook my curls out, letting my hair free now that we were out of the blustering wind. As I did, my gaze was pulled to Blake. He had approached one of the votaries. All of them were women. I wondered if male highbloods were permitted to serve in the Sanctum.

Blake was pointing to me. I felt a prickle of unease as the votary's expression changed instantly, her eyes widening as she took in my hair. She clutched her robes in her hands and then hurriedly crossed over to where Professor Sankara was standing on the other side of the foyer. The highblood teacher had been looking bored. Now he snapped to attention as the votary whispered something urgently into his ear. His silver brows knitted together as his dark eyes slid towards me.

Blake had moved to join Sankara and the votary. Now the three of them conferred in hushed voices, with unmistakable glances in my direction.

I scowled. What now? Would I have to give more than the usual amount of blood? I had a bad feeling it would be something like that.

My pulse quickened as Blake broke away from the group and came towards me.

"Pendragon," he barked, breaking the silence. Every student around me snapped their heads in our direction. "Get out of the line."

I blinked. "Why?"

"You don't need to make an offering," Blake said, his voice brusque. "You're exempt. Like the highbloods."

I frowned. Little did he know that was the worst possible thing he could have said to get me to do what he wanted. "But I thought..."

"Don't think," he snapped, gray eyes narrowing. "Get out of the line, Pendragon. Now. That's an order."

My heart raced as my natural defiance threatened to bubble up. Then I realized how stupid I was being. Of course, I didn't actually *want* to have to make an offering.

"Fine," I muttered, stepping out of the line, with a shrug in Florence and Naveen's direction. "What now?"

"Now you wait." Blake smiled smugly. "Unless you'd prefer to enter the nave and pray quietly."

"No, thank you," I said quickly, managing to bite my tongue and not share what I really thought about the whole revolting proceedings.

I walked away from him to stand in a quiet recess flanked by two tall white marble pillars. As I leaned against the wall, I thought about Blake's dismissive command. Kage was right. Blake didn't respect me. Best scenario, we were trapped with one another. Worst case, he wanted to use me. Either way, I was determined to break free. I might be stuck in this world, but that didn't mean I had to be tied to him.

I froze as two familiar voices drifted towards me.

Regan and Quinn. The two girls must have finished their prayers at the altar and now were walking around the outer perimeter of the foyer, out of the professors' earshot. If I stayed where I was, they wouldn't be able to see me.

I quickly found myself caught up in their whispered conversation.

"Another boring offering night," Quinn griped. "I can't believe we have to wait while all of these cattle are bled." I scowled, knowing she meant the blightborn. "My knees hurt from kneeling on that stone step. Do you think we prayed long enough?"

"We looked like perfectly pious highblood bitches," Regan answered.

They both snickered.

"Besides," Regan continued. "I'd have thought you'd be used to going down on your knees by now. I've heard it's all you do for Edward Ashveil."

"Don't you dare judge me, bitch. It fucking worked, didn't it?" Quinn said with a laugh. "He begged his father and I've been approved as one of his consorts. I'll be in the Games with you this year. Making it nice and official."

Oh, great. Quinn was going to be part of the Consort Games. I doubted that boded well for me.

"Are you going to the Adoration Rite this year?" Quinn asked Regan.

"I'm not invited. Not until I'm officially Blake's consort," Regan muttered. Interesting. So it wasn't completely official yet. What Kage had claimed might be the truth. "I can't believe it. It's not like I'm some random blightborn. They know I'm with Blake. We've been betrothed for years. I'm entitled to attend."

I suppressed a snort of laughter. She was entitled all right.

Quinn made a sympathetic noise.

"It's not fair," Regan went on. I could practically picture her pouting. "Blake can go if he wants to. He's Lord Drakharrow's nephew and a House Leader. He can basically do whatever he pleases. But he says he can't bring me with him."

I wondered if Blake actually could but just didn't want to.

"My father is going," Quinn said. "He's in Lord Drakharrow's inner circle. He says this year will be *very* exclusive. Lord Drakharrow has something special planned."

"Well, exclusive or not," Regan replied testily. "By next year I'll be a full consort if all goes well at the Games. They won't be able to keep me out."

"I wonder who they've found to play the Bloodmaiden for the Rite this year," Quinn mused. "She's always lowborn trash, but some years I've heard she can be quite pretty. I've heard girls fight for the part. It's a great honor for a blightborn girl."

Regan scoffed. "Of course it's an honor. She's pampered before the rite, treated like she's some sort of queen. No wonder they compete just to be chosen. It's the only time they hold any value in their entire pathetic lives."

"But the girl never gets to go home," Quinn pointed out, sounding almost doubtful.

"Please. She gets to stay in the Sanctum. With highbloods all around her. Living in luxury in the most holy place in Sangratha. A blightborn girl would never have it so good wherever she comes from. Most of them live in complete squalor, you know. Have you seen some of those hovels they call homes in Veilmar? Blightborn don't deserve the honor, if you ask me," Regan snapped.

My stomach twisted, but I stayed perfectly still, listening.

Regan and Quinn were talking about this rite as if it were some kind of fairy tale for the blightborn girl. But I didn't see it that way. Nothing good ever came of being chosen by a highblood.

"I wonder if Marcus Drakharrow will play the First Highblood this year," Quinn said, her tone gossipy. "He's so good-looking. Even more handsome than Blake."

"Are you joking? Blake is better-looking by far," Regan said, sounding annoyed. "And Blake doesn't have Marcus's disgusting reputation with women. Besides we won't be there to see it, so why hope? Maybe your Edward will be selected for the part next year. Now that would be something to see."

"He does have some fine...endowments," Quinn admitted.

Both girls broke into giggles, which they quickly stifled.

I remembered Marcus. I'd seen him that day on the dais in the Black Keep. He resembled Blake, but was broader, a few inches shorter. I wondered if he was stronger. Did that come even with just a few years' age difference?

"Maybe it'll be Lord Drakharrow playing the role," Regan said, lowering her voice. "Father says the council has encouraged him to take the part. Either way, it's sure to be someone powerful."

"Ew, gross," Quinn complained. "Lord Drakharrow? Can you imagine? Maybe Blake will do it next year. Wouldn't that be an honor?" I could tell she was trying to goad Regan.

"No, I don't think so," Regan said, her tone frosty. "I'd tell him not to do it. You know he always listens to me."

I managed to suppress a snort of skepticism. The two girls' voices faded away as they started walking again.

I stayed where I was, trying to piece together all that they'd said. The Adoration Rite. A blightborn girl to play the Bloodmaiden. A highblood man to play First Highblood. Something told me this rite wasn't like the Night of Silent Offerings. This was something darker. And Blake might be involved.

I clenched my hands into fists, mind already made up.

I'd attend this Adoration Rite myself and find out what was really going on.

There was only one problem: I'd have to find a way to get there.

CHAPTER 39

MEDRA

Two days before the Dance of the Longest Night, Kage sent me a dress.

It arrived in a sleek black box, tied with a ribbon embossed with tiny silver stars. When I opened it, the fabric spilled over my fingers, shimmering like liquid night.

The dress was in House Avari's colors, black with silver accents. The bodice was tightly fitted with a deep V neckline that plunged daringly, framed by thin satin straps that showed off my shoulders and left most of my back exposed. Flared layers of tulle made up the skirt, which had been embroidered with silver half-moons. A high slit ran up one side of the dress, reaching all the way up to mid-thigh.

A note had been tucked into the folds of fabric. "Medra, you don't have to wear this, but I would be honored if you did. House Avari's colors suit you."

I hesitated, holding the note in my hands. Then I set my jaw. I owed House Drakharrow no allegiance. Why shouldn't I accept the gift?

Now, I stood in my dorm room with Florence, cinching the laces of the bodice.

"You look amazing," Florence said admiringly.

I twirled in front of the full-length mirror, feeling the gown swish around my legs. "I've never worn anything like this before." I glanced down. The slit was certainly high enough.

"Well, I would never have guessed. You're going to fit right in. The ball is full of girls in extravagant gowns, all trying to outdo one another." Florence's eyes twinkled. "But in that dress Kage sent, you're going to outshine them all. I can't wait to see the look on Regan's face when she sees you."

I looked at Florence. She was wearing a modest gown of midnight-blue with capped sleeves. The dress hit her legs just above the knee, showing off shapely calves and ankles.

"Your dress might be more understated but you look gorgeous, too, Florence," I said loyally. "You can't hide that body under a cloak forever you know." I smiled as she blushed.

We set to work on one another's hair. Florence pinned up half of my red curls, leaving the rest loose around my shoulders, then threaded silver ribbon through my updo. It was a tousled, wilder look that paired well with Kage's daring gown.

When she was done, I pulled Florence's long, straight, dark hair into an elegant twist and pushed in some pins capped with seed pearls around it to hold it in place. She looked graceful and sophisticated, exactly the way she truly was.

"Are you nervous?" Florence asked as she readjusted one of the pins in my hair.

"A little," I admitted. "Are you?"

Florence tilted her head. "I would probably be more nervous if I wasn't going with Naveen."

I smiled. "He puts you at ease. That's a good thing. You know, he..." I was just about to say something along the lines of not underestimating Naveen's potential when there was a knock at the door.

One of the First Year girls stood there. She was dressed in a tunic and trousers, clearly not planning to go to the ball.

"Medra, you have a guest waiting in the Common Room."

I thanked her and glanced at Florence. "I guess I'll see you there."

I hurried down the winding staircase. As I reached the bottom, my breath caught. A tall figure was standing by the fireplace. For a moment, all I saw was the silver hair and slender tall frame. My heart sped up. Blake.

Then the figure turned. Kage.

He was dressed in a formal black jacket, trimmed with silver and perfectly tailored to his slim, muscular build. A silver brooch, shaped like a crescent moon, was pinned to his left lapel. He looked handsome and regal, with his high cheekbones catching the light and his dark eyes shining like black onyx.

His lips curved into an appreciative smile as his gaze swept over me.

"You look exquisite." His dark eyes traveled up to my hair. "The dress suits you. It sets off your hair. Like fire against the night sky."

I felt my cheeks warm at the lavish compliment. I fingered the silver embroidery of my gown, momentarily lost for words, which rarely happened. It certainly never did with Blake.

Before I could properly respond, Kage reached into his jacket pocket and pulled out a small black velvet bag. "I thought this might complete the look."

He emptied the pouch into the palm of his hand, revealing a delicate silver necklace with a pendant shaped like a half-moon.

"May I?"

He stepped behind me and gently fastened the pendant around my neck. For a moment, his fingers lingered against my throat and a shiver went down my spine.

I found myself wondering whether I could ever feel anything for Kage Tanaka. Would he even want me to? What was he getting out of all of this, besides a perfect opportunity to infuriate Blake?

And besides, who was to say Blake would even care? It might have been sheer arrogance on my part to think he'd be bothered by my showing up to the ball on the arm of another man.

"Perfect," Kage murmured, stepping back. "You're perfect."

He offered his arm. "Shall we?"

I hesitated for only a moment, then took it. Together, we left the Common Room to make our way to the ball.

The refectory had been completely transformed.

The long rows of tables and benches had been removed. Large circular tables draped with white linen tablecloths had been set up in their place, all decorated with dark evergreen garlands intertwined with pale blue roses, their petals dusted with glittering frost.

Long, thin, icicle-like chandeliers made of crystal hung from the ceiling. The walls had been enchanted with some sort of a charm. They shifted as they displayed images of snowflakes, swirling from one end to another.

Beneath our feet, the floor seemed to sparkle and gleam, enchanted with a pattern of frosted blue ice.

At the far end of the room, in the center of the stage, a great silver clock had been hung up. It counted down the hours to the end of the solstice night.

As I stepped into the room with Kage at my side, I spotted Regan and Blake. They were standing with a group of students from House Drakharrow.

Blake had his back to us, but Regan was facing the entrance.

She looked stunning as always, though her dress was a little predictable. A bold red satin, short and tight, that clung to every curve, leaving little to the imagination.

Regan's eyes widened and her jaw went slack as Kage led me inside. I watched, curious, as she grabbed Blake's arm and whispered something urgently to him. He turned slowly, then froze.

His gaze locked onto mine and the world seemed to pause.

I watched his jaw tighten and his eyes grow dark and stormy. A shiver went down my spine.

He was displeased. It was the reaction I'd anticipated, the reaction I'd wanted. I glanced at Kage. He was smiling slightly, his eyes also on Blake.

I lifted my chin, determined to ignore everyone from House Drakharrow and focus on the man standing by my side.

Kage led me to a table full of students in House Avari colors. None of them were familiar to me, but they smiled in a surprisingly friendly way. One boy stood up and offered me his seat.

I took it gratefully as the girl beside me leaned over. "I'm Evie. Is this your first Frostfire Festival at Bloodwing?"

I nodded. "Yes. Pleased to meet you."

Kage took the seat beside me, his gaze sweeping over the room before returning to me. "Forgive me for saying it again," he murmured against my ear, his voice low and husky. "But you look ravishing tonight. You're the most beautiful woman in the room."

I felt a flush creep up my neck, but tried to mask it with a polite nod. "That's very kind of you. Thank you."

Next to smooth-talking Kage, I felt slightly awkward and out of place but I was determined not to show it.

Evie leaned over again, a mischievous smile on her lips. "Just so you know, Kage has never brought a date to one of these things before."

I glanced at Kage, raising my eyebrow.

He shrugged casually.

I was about to respond when I caught a flash of red and white. Turning, I saw Catherine Mortis making her way towards us. The House Leader always had a bored, prideful air about her, but tonight, it seemed even more pronounced.

To my surprise, she was without her blightborn companions. Instead, she was flanked by two highbloods, one male and one female. They stood behind her, looking beautiful and similarly bored.

Catherine's gaze, I belatedly realized, was focused on me.

"I like your dress," she said, as she neared the table. Her tone was approving, but her eyes still held their customary superiority. "Black and silver." She glanced at Kage. "Good choice."

I wasn't sure if that last part was directed to me or to Kage.

"Thank you," I said, feeling slightly uneasy under the scrutiny.

Catherine Mortis lingered a moment longer, looking down at Evie. "Save me a dance later, won't you?" she said, waving a slender hand.

Evie flushed with pleasure and nodded.

Then, with a small nod to Kage, Catherine moved on, her two companions trailing behind her.

Once she was gone, I turned to Kage, my curiosity piqued. "Were those her consorts?"

He nodded. "They're not official yet. But her father has approved them. They'll be in the Games with you."

I remembered what I'd heard about Catherine. She preferred women. But she'd chosen one male consort. For breeding, I assumed. What a decision to have to make. But I supposed noble highbloods were used to those kinds of compromises.

"Where are *your* consorts?" I blurted out, before I could stop myself. "I'm sorry. Is that in poor taste?"

Kage smiled and shook his head. "I don't have any yet. In House Avari, archons make their own choices. We're at Bloodwing for years. I still have plenty of time to decide." His gaze slid over me, with the hint of a suggestion.

I felt a mixture of intrigue and discomfort at the implication but before I could reply, Kage stood up.

"The orchestra is playing."

I glanced over at the stage and saw that he was right. The Bloodwing Ensemble had begun to play and I'd been so distracted I hadn't even noticed. There was Naveen in the front row.

I scanned the crowd and found Florence. She sat at a table near the stage with some other First Years, talking and laughing. I wondered what would happen between her and Naveen tonight. Would Naveen work up the courage to tell her how he really felt?

Belatedly, I realized Kage was offering me his hand.

"Shall we dance?"

CHAPTER 40

BLAKE

Fuck me.

That was the first thought that went through my head as I saw her walk into the room in a dress that seemed to silently scream at me "please peel this off my stunningly beautiful body."

My reaction was visceral. Like a punch to the heart. An immediate tightening in my chest.

Then I saw the colors she was in. Black and silver. The shades of House Avari.

And next to her? Looking so smug I wanted to knock his perfect white teeth out? None other than fucking Kage Tanaka.

My eyes honed back in on Pendragon. What was she wearing around her neck?

A silver half-moon pendant. A mark. A claim. Kage may as well have branded her with his fangs.

I clenched my jaw so tight I thought it might break.

The dress, the necklace, the sight of Kage there by her side. It was a power play. Kage was flaunting her. We'd always been rivals. He was the only one at the school anywhere close to being at my level.

Now he was trying to deliberately provoke me.

Well, it'd worked. He'd triggered something so primal and possessive inside of me that I could barely keep it under control.

Kage turned to say something to Pendragon and I saw his eyes linger over her cleavage. I wanted to stab his fucking eyes out for even daring to look. How could he look at her like that when she so obviously belonged to me?

No matter how furious I felt, I couldn't deny one thing.

Pendragon was the most stunning woman in the room.

I could hardly tear my eyes away from her.

And yet I knew I had to. Because I could feel Regan's jealous eyes boring into me. In another minute, others would start to notice my obsessive attention and I'd look like even more of a laughingstock.

Regan's voice cut through my thoughts. "Blake, darling," she purred, tugging at my sleeve. "You're staring."

I ignored her, watching as Kage led Pendragon through the crowd and over to one of the tables reserved for House Avari.

Regan's hand slid over my chest, her touch unwelcome but persistent.

"Blake, you're not listening to me," she said, her voice sulky.

I forced myself to look away.

Regan smiled up at me. "That's better. The dancing is about to begin."

"I'm not interested," I said coldly.

Regan huffed in annoyance. "You're being such a bore tonight, Blake."

"And you're being a petulant bitch, as always," I snapped cruelly. "I didn't invite you here, so don't look so hurt. Go find someone else to bother."

I turned away, but not before I saw her face fall. My mood had soured. Suddenly, I didn't want to be near anyone. I stepped into the crowd and began to prowl the edges of the room.

I couldn't leave. I was obligated to be here as House Leader.

And as House Leaders, Tanaka and I were also not permitted to attack one another. No matter how much I might long to break that rule, I knew I'd be in a huge pile of shit if I did. Worse than what had nearly happened to Pendragon when she attacked me.

Everywhere I looked, I saw Pendragon and Kage.

As soon as the orchestra began to play, Tanaka led her up to dance.

I had to admit, Tanaka had good taste. It was clear he'd picked out the gown for Pendragon. The neckline was certainly low enough. My colors would have suited her better, but even in black and silver she was absolutely gorgeous. Her fiery red hair gleamed against the dark fabric of the gown. The dress was striking, revealing, clinging to every curve of her body in a way that made my throat go dry.

It killed me to watch Kage lead her around the room.

I'd stalked in a circle and now I'd reached the Drakharrow group again.

Regan was talking too much, laughing too loudly. She touched my arm and tried to pull me back into the group but I yanked away. I knew I was being an asshole, but I hadn't asked her to the ball tonight and it pissed me off that she was acting as if I had.

I hadn't asked anyone. I knew Pendragon would have turned me down flat. The idea of that rejection was just too much to stomach.

A slow song started and I watched as Kage put his hands on Pendragon's waist, guiding her into the steps of the melody.

Every instinct in my body was telling me to march across the floor and rip her away from him.

The idea that Kage might actually believe that this night might end with him in Pendragon's bed made my blood boil. There was no way I was going to let that happen.

I reminded myself that I was the only man in the room who knew what she looked like beneath all of that silk and silver. I could remember every detail. The perfection of her breasts, the curve of her hips, those long luscious legs.

I stole a glance at the dance floor, stealing a glance at the swell of her breasts as they lifted against the satin edge of the black dress.

I imagined pulling the edge of the gown down and exposing the tip of one straining nipple to the cool night air as my hot mouth landed on it.

Fuck. I had to stop torturing myself or I'd be hard all night.

Kage might think this was all just some game. A move to rile me up by flaunting Pendragon. But I knew her better than that. Didn't I? She was stubborn, defiant, and there was no way she'd let Kage put her in his little box.

I hoped I was right.

And yet, as Kage spun her around and I watched her face light up in a smile that seemed genuine, my fists clenched at my side. She'd never smiled at me like that. She seemed happy. Like she was really having fun.

I'd known she would laugh in my face if I'd extended an invitation tonight. But now, as I watched her with Kage, I felt a sting of regret for not even trying.

I needed a drink. Something to take the edge off.

I reached the bar and ordered a glass of bloodwine. I needed something strong enough to drown out the image of Kage and Pendragon swaying in each other's arms on the dance floor.

Just as the bartender handed me the goblet, I heard a familiar voice beside me. I turned to see Kage, ordering two drinks—one for himself and one for Pendragon.

"Bloodwine for myself and spiced wine for the lady," Kage said smoothly.

I drained my glass and then slammed it down, feeling the stem snap. The bartender took one look at me and quickly swept it away.

I turned to face Kage. "Spiced wine? Really? How do you know what she likes to drink?"

Kage turned slowly to look at me. "It's the little things, Drakharrow. When you spend enough time with someone, you pick up on them."

I clenched my jaw, as he smirked. "You think spending a few hours at a dance means you know her? You don't know a damn thing about her."

Kage wasn't even in any of our classes. House Avari had their own Advanced Weaponry sessions. When had he spent time with her? Had they been seeing each other without my realizing it?

Kage leaned casually against the bar. "I'm getting to know her. Medra's full of surprises, isn't she? There's so much more to her than meets the eye."

I took a step towards him. "If you know her so well, then you must know she's not the type to fall for a few fancy words and some cheap wine."

Kage raised an eyebrow. "Maybe not. But she seems to be enjoying my company tonight, doesn't she? After all, you've been watching us closely enough to notice."

"Enjoy the moment while it lasts," I snarled. "You'll never know her the way I do."

Kage smiled, but his tone turned icy. "The way you do? That's funny. From where I'm standing, it doesn't look like you know her at all. Or that she wants you to. Are you just afraid to have her realize that someone else might treat her better than you ever would?"

A rush of rage rose in my chest. My hands itched to wrap around Tanaka's throat and wipe off his smug expression.

I held back. Barely. I wouldn't give Kage the satisfaction of drawing me into a scene here, in front of everyone.

"She's not a game, Kage," I said, my voice tinged with warning.

Kage's eyes gleamed with amusement. "If she's not a game, then why are you playing it so badly? No need to be so jealous, Drakharrow. At least try and keep your shit together."

The urge to hit him was almost unbearable.

"Jealous?" I spat. "I'm not jealous. I just don't like opportunistic snakes."

Kage's smile didn't waver. "Whatever you say. Just remember–you've done nothing to make her yours. She's a gift you've never appreciated. So maybe the problem isn't me, Drakharrow. Maybe it's you."

The blood rushed to my ears.

Kage leaned towards me. "And now look at you. You're just standing on the sidelines," he murmured. "Watching her slip through your fingers. How does it feel? You had your chance, Drakharrow. And now? She's with me."

I wanted to splatter Kage's blood all over the ballroom floor. But I couldn't. Not here. Not with everyone watching. Especially as I knew Pendragon would see it as a sign of weakness.

I gestured to the bartender for another bloodwine, trying to swallow down my fury. "You're treading on dangerous ground, Tanaka. Enjoy the night while it lasts."

I took a deep breath as Kage walked away.

I just had to get through the rest of the night. There was too much at stake for me to fuck this up now.

Somehow I made it to midnight without strangling Kage or throwing him across the room. It was a Frostfire miracle, really.

I watched as the clock ticked towards twelve. When midnight chimed, with it would come the Longest Night Waltz.

I stood near the edge of the dance floor, watching as the orchestra prepared. Archons were supposed to dance with one of their consorts. This dance was reserved exclusively for highbloods. Even though I hadn't officially asked Pendragon to the ball, there was no way in hell Kage was claiming her for this one.

Spotting her over near the punch bowl, talking to her friend, the quiet dark-haired girl, Florence, I straightened my jacket and marched over.

When I reached her, I didn't waste time on pleasantries.

"Dance with me," I said, holding my hand out.

I saw her hesitation. Her brows furrowed. I'd caught her off guard. For a brief moment, I saw the desire to refuse flash across her face.

"This dance is for archons and consorts," I said stiffly.

I was basically commanding her. But I didn't care. There was no way I was dancing with Regan.

I could tell she didn't want to cause a scene. Especially as the entire ballroom was watching us.

"Fine," she said, placing her hand in mine. Her voice was distinctly lacking in enthusiasm.

Still, I felt triumphant as I led her onto the dance floor just as the lights dimmed for the waltz.

The dance was a time-honored tradition. A way of closing out the longest night of the year and celebrating the forging of bonds for the new one to come.

I gripped Pendragon's waist firmly, pulling her a little closer than was strictly necessary. I was relieved when she didn't resist.

I wanted her to feel my presence. To know I was here with her, for her—more than Kage or anyone else ever would be.

"You know," I began, as we glided across the floor. "They say that whoever you dance with during the Longest Waltz will share a deep bond with you in the coming year. It was a mortal tradition, originally. A tad sentimental but rather romantic, don't you think?"

Was this really me talking? Part of me wanted to slap myself. I was taking a chance. A chance of looking like a huge idiot.

Pendragon didn't respond right away. Her gaze was fixed over my shoulder, as if she was trying not to meet my eyes.

I felt a sting of frustration coil around me as the silence stretched. It had been a subtle gesture that meant more than it seemed. And yet, she didn't seem to care.

When she finally spoke, her voice was chilly. "Blake, you've treated me like shit for the first half of the year. I doubt that's going to suddenly change in the new one just because we're dancing."

Her words hit me like a punch in the gut. I hadn't expected her to speak so plainly and her bluntness caught me off guard.

A sharp retort rose to my lips. But I hesitated, as memories flashed through my mind.

The insults, the humiliations, the way I'd pushed her over and over again. She didn't even know the half of it.

She was right. I didn't want to admit it. But she was. I clenched my jaw, replaying every interaction we'd had.

I thought back to that first day I'd seen her. Naked and covered with blood. I'd been captivated from that first moment no matter how much I tried to convince myself otherwise.

It would have been so much easier to want someone like Regan. Someone who threw herself at me.

But no. It was Pendragon. Always Pendragon.

The more she tried to push me away, the more I wanted her.

She'd gotten under my skin in a way no one else ever had. This feeling wasn't just hate anymore. There was something else here. Something deeper.

Something that terrified me.

Maybe it was the bloodwine, but suddenly it seemed to me that love and hate might not be that different. Ultimately, weren't they just two sides of the same coin? I wasn't sure which one I was feeling right now, but one thing was certain. I *wanted* her. More than I'd ever wanted anything.

And I wanted her to want me back. Even if she hated herself for it.

"Whatever I've done, it was only to make you stronger. You're mine, Pendragon, and that won't ever change." The words slipped out before I could stop them.

I could feel her tense beneath my touch, her body stiffening against me.

It was true. She was mine. No one else's. Not Kage's. Not anyone's.

But she was tensing up in my arms. Her back straightened. Her head jerked up.

She looked at me, eyes narrowing, her face a mask of anger.

"I will *never* be yours, Blake Drakharrow. When will you get that through your thick highblood head?"

Before I could respond, before I could try to fix the mess I'd just made, she was gone. She tore herself out of my arms and stalked off the dance floor, leaving me standing there, stunned.

The room felt like it was closing in. I felt the gazes of the other students searing into my skin.

In the distance, I caught a glimpse of Kage Tanaka smirking, clearly enjoying my humiliation. But I noticed Pendragon hadn't gone running to him.

I hadn't meant to say those exact words, to push her away like that. But now, standing there alone, the weight of my failure came crashing down on me and I thought of my uncle's threat.

He could take her away. Give her to someone else. Or keep her for himself.

But this wasn't over. Not by a long shot.

My eyes followed Pendragon as she disappeared into the crowd, clearly heading towards the doors. My heart thudded painfully.

I wanted her. Needed her in a way that was starting to be a problem.

If she wasn't going to come willingly, I'd take a different approach.

I walked off the dance floor and back over to the bar where I tossed back another glass of bloodwine. The liquor mixed with blood went straight to my head. Just like I wanted it to.

I felt calmer as the warm haze filled me up. Everything would be fine. There was still time. I'd gain the upper hand, get back in control. I'd make her see that she belonged with me, one way or another.

The night was far from over.

CHAPTER 41

MEDRA

I was shaking as I left the room, quivering with rage.

Blake Drakharrow could go straight to hell.

I swiped at my face, feeling the wetness on my hand. I wiped it away savagely. My emotions were a tangled mess. A knot of anger, hurt, and something else I didn't want to even try to name.

I found a bench along the corridor outside the refectory and sank down onto it, leaning back against the cold stone wall.

I could still feel the press of Blake's hands, lingering on my waist, and I hated it.

Students were beginning to trickle out of the ballroom, their laughter and chatter spilling into the hall.

I saw some couples sink into the shadows, their arms wrapped around one another. Some ran past me, giggling, hand in hand. Apparently the Dance of the Longest Night was also a great night for getting someone into your bed.

I hadn't even said goodnight to Kage. Part of me didn't want to. Who knew what he was expecting, what he might feel he was entitled to. But I had to give him credit. He'd been a perfect gentleman all evening, which was more than I could say for Blake.

I pressed myself further back on the bench, part of me just wanting to disappear. But then I saw Florence emerge from the ballroom.

"Medra, are you all right?" Florence asked, as she came over. "You rushed out so fast..."

I tried to smile. "I'm fine. Just needed some air."

"Blake was being an asshole again?" she asked sympathetically.

I nodded. It was easier than telling her exactly what had happened. "How did your night go? Where's Naveen?"

Florence glanced back. "He's still inside, helping the ensemble pack up."

With a pang of guilt, I realized I hadn't even paid attention to Naveen's solo. I'd been too absorbed in my own problems, first distracted by Kage, then by Blake. Naveen must have performed it while I was dancing with Blake.

I hadn't heard a single note.

"I didn't even really hear his solo," I admitted. "I feel terrible."

"He'll understand," Florence reassured me. "He probably won't even ask you about it. It went really well though. He played beautifully. Not a single wrong note. He looked so happy. Don't worry, Medra. He had a good evening. This was everything he wanted."

I studied her face. "Really? Everything? Did he...say anything to you?"

Her nose scrunched. "Like what?"

I sighed. That was a "no" then. "Never mind. I'll tell you later."

"Come on, walk back to the First Year tower with me. We can sit in the Common Room and listen to everyone gossip about their night," Florence suggested. She winked. "And you can tell me all about Kage Tanaka and Blake Drakharrow fighting over you."

I groaned. "Not sure if that's something I really want to relive."

My eyes caught movement from behind her. Blake had just exited the refectory. There was a bottle of red liquor in his hand. I watched as he tipped it to his lips. His movements seemed slower than usual, languid, as if he'd already had too much to drink.

My pulse quickened. This was my chance.

Florence was still standing there waiting for me.

"Go on without me," I said quickly. "I'm going to go for a walk. Clear my head. I'll meet you back in the Common Room later."

Florence hesitated. "Are you sure?"

"I'm fine, really," I said. "I'll see you back there."

Florence nodded and left me sitting in the shadows.

Blake was heading in the opposite direction, away from me, and I thought I had a pretty good idea of where he was going.

I waited until Florence disappeared down the opposite end of the hallway before I stood up and began to follow Blake.

He was halfway down the corridor now, his gait slightly unsteady. Clearly he was intent on drowning his sorrows in that bottle he was drinking from.

I'd have to be careful. He was probably furious with me. I'd humiliated him, and not just once tonight, but repeatedly.

I trailed him through the winding corridors of the academy, moving steadily but cautiously. One wrong move and he might sense me. I had no idea how much the liquor he was drinking would actually dull his vampire senses.

When we reached the Dragon Court I smiled in satisfaction. My guess had been correct.

It was cold in the courtyard. I was still only dressed in the gown from Kage and the winter chill was biting. Even so, I hung back, watching as Blake moved toward the opening to the secret stairwell. I waited until the last possible moment before darting down after him, the passage closing over my head as I ducked inside.

The air was warmer the further down I went. This time I knew the way. But only to a point.

I knew Blake wasn't going to take the same path tonight.

But I also couldn't risk running right into him in the dark. I held back, listening for his footsteps, then matching my pace to his.

Eventually we reached the vaulted chamber where the massive dragon skull loomed in silence.

I hung back, watching as he strode right to the arched doorway labeled House Orphos.

I followed at a distance as he moved through the Orphos catacombs where the skulls of the house's long-dead dragons lay asleep in their alcoves, hollow eyes looking out into darkness.

The catacombs finally ended and Blake moved into a deeper tunnel. We descended, step after step, down endless narrow passages. The temperature dropped and the scent of mildew and brine filled the air. I knew we must be heading beneath sea level again, just like before. But this time I was betting we wouldn't end up in Veilmar.

Eventually, I lost the sound of Blake's footsteps. I hung back, waiting to see if I could pick them up again. Either he'd gone on too far ahead of me to hear them or he'd paused because he'd heard me behind him.

Finally, I had to risk it. I moved on.

There was no one ahead of me. The passage was empty.

The tunnel I was in continued to stretch ahead. I must have walked for at least an hour in the darkness, pressed in on all sides, knowing that above me was only a layer of rock protecting me from the entire weight of the sea.

Just when I felt like I couldn't take the confinement any longer, I found myself ascending. Steep, curving stairs took me higher and higher. My legs burned from the climb. As

I rose, the walls gradually began to change. The rough, damp stone gave way to polished white marble. Torches appeared at intervals in iron sconces along the walls.

The stairs ended. I was on a landing but there were no doors. No hatches that I could see. Blank white marble walls surrounded me.

But I knew I was in the right place when I spotted the bottle of liquor Blake had been holding, tucked away in one of the corners.

Before I could change my mind, I reached for the bottle and took a long swig. I choked. It was strong stuff. I felt it go straight to my head. I took another swallow. I needed courage tonight and if this was what was doing it for Blake, I'd have to hope it would do the same for me.

I noticed a slight indentation in one of the marble walls, barely discernible. I pressed my hand against it.

There was a soft click and a panel slid open, just a crack. I wedged my hand in and pulled it towards me, then looked out. No one was around.

I stepped out, pulling the panel almost all the way shut behind me.

Just as I'd expected, I'd emerged in the Sanctum of the Bloodmaiden. But this time, I was in a completely different part of the temple. One of the upper levels.

A balcony wrapped around the mezzanine on which I stood, overlooking a vast, open courtyard below.

Soaring marble columns ringed the space. Tall white candles lined the edges of the balcony, casting a warm glow across the pale marble. Vines covered with lush white flowers draped along the railings.

I took a step forward, holding my breath. Blake was nowhere in sight. But no one else seemed to be up on this level either.

I crept towards the balcony rail, my heart pounding in my chest. Reaching it, I crouched down low, and peered through the balusters.

At least two stories below the level on which I crouched, a group of highbloods had gathered. They wore long black robes and silver masks that covered their eyes and the upper part of their faces, leaving only their mouths exposed.

In the very center of the courtyard stood a large silver bowl, sitting atop a pedestal. Silver chains hung down over it from the ceiling above, swaying ever so slightly.

On the far side of the courtyard, a black throne-like chair stood empty, waiting for an occupant.

The faceless figures stood around the bowl, as though waiting for something.

They didn't have long to wait.

The low, resonant sound of a gong echoed through the chamber and I jumped.

The crowd of masked highbloods stilled, turning towards the far end of the courtyard.

I tensed as a figure in a black robe and black half-mask stepped into the space. He moved slowly, deliberately. The masked highbloods parted for him, bowing their heads as he passed.

He reached the black throne, turning gracefully before lowering himself into the seat. A second gong sounded.

A young woman in a long, gauzy white robe stepped forward from the shadows.

Unlike the others, her face was unmasked. She was smiling and seemed unafraid. Her hair was loose and dark and wavy. She walked slowly across the courtyard, her bare feet padding silently upon the stone floor.

The masked highbloods made way for her, bowing low to the ground as she passed, as if she were their queen.

Or their goddess.

My pulse quickened, unease tightening my chest.

The woman in white came to a stop before the black throne.

I watched from my hidden perch as the masked man rose slowly to his feet. His black robe billowed slightly with the movement.

"Bloodmaiden, will you accept my offering to you?" he intoned. The words were filled with ritualistic solemnity.

The young woman in the white robe lifted her gaze to meet his.

Her voice was clear and calm as she replied, "Yes. Will you accept mine?"

A strange ripple of anticipation coursed through the masked crowd.

The man on the throne nodded. "I will."

He turned to the crowd of assembled highbloods, sweeping his hand toward the woman. "Let the union of the Blessed Blood begin."

"Let it begin," the crowd murmured in unison.

The man surveyed them. "Will you worship her?"

The highbloods' voices rose in a chilling chorus. "We will."

My breath caught as I watched the young woman climb the steps to the throne. The closer she got to the man, the heavier the air seemed to become. Thick with mystery and dark tension.

My mind was swirling with confusion. What the hell was happening?

The woman reached the top of the steps and then, to my shock, climbed onto the man's lap, straddling him without hesitation.

The scene felt wrong. Perverse. Yet the act was full of sensuality.

My thoughts were racing wildly, just as a hand clamped down over my mouth.

"Caught you," Blake's voice murmured into my ear.

CHAPTER 42

BLAKE

I had her right where I wanted her.

"You didn't actually think I didn't know you were following me, did you?" I whispered against her ear.

I yanked her to her feet. I could feel her trembling.

"They'll see us," she whispered.

So, she was afraid. She was right to be. She had no business being here and if anyone else but me had found her, the votaries would have slaughtered her without a second thought, red hair of a rider or not. Of course, Viktor would have been furious. But it would have been too late. She had violated the Sanctum by coming here uninvited.

"No one is up on this level and no one down there is going to bother looking up." But just in case, I blew out the nearby candles, throwing us both into shadow.

Once she felt slightly safer, she tried to pull away from me. "You bastard," she hissed. "Let go of me."

"Hey, you're the one who followed me, Pendragon. No one made you come here. Did you really think vampire senses were so useless that I couldn't hear you stomping along behind me?"

"You didn't the last time," she shot back.

The last time I'd been so desperate to get to a blood brothel and feed that I hadn't taken my usual precautions. I'd dismissed my qualms about any noises I'd heard as my imagination. But now that I knew she knew where the passage out of Bloodwing was, I'd never make that mistake again.

But I decided to fuck with her.

"Maybe I wanted you to follow me. Maybe I didn't care. Ever think of that? Maybe I liked it when you watched."

She stiffened in my arms.

"Just like you seem to like watching right now." I nuzzled my face against her cheek. "Can't take your eyes off them, can you?"

"What are they doing?" she whispered back.

"Watch and see."

Down below, the girl playing the Bloodmaiden sat upon the masked highblood's lap, her white robe a stark contrast to his dark garments. Innocence waiting to be marred.

The silence in the courtyard seemed to thicken as the highblood raised his hands to the girl's shoulders. Slowly, he began unfastening the clasps that held her robe in place.

The girl remained still, her eyes half-closed, her chest rising and falling in slow, deep breaths.

The man's hands moved lower, tracing the length of the girl's arm before moving down to the curve of her waist. There would be no rush tonight, only the gradual reveal of the woman beneath the white robe.

The masked observers stood in silent reverence for the rite. But despite their air of sacred solemnity, the atmosphere was undeniably carnal.

I felt Pendragon's breath catch in her throat as the clasps finally unlocked and the white robe slipped off the girl's shoulders, revealing an expanse of lush white skin.

The girl's breasts were on the smaller side, but firm and high. Her dark red nipples puckered in the cool air. The Sanctum always made sure to pick a lovely blightborn specimen.

But it wasn't the girl down below who had my attention. It was the one I held in my arms.

My hands gripped Pendragon's waist, holding her steady. Her hands had slipped over the balcony rail, and she peered forward. She seemed to have almost forgotten my hands were there, a single layer of fabric keeping my skin separated from hers.

The rite had her captivated. Unable to look away.

I leaned forward slightly, burying my face in her hair. She smelled incredible. Like fresh fallen leaves with a hint of jasmine. And underlying it all, the iron tang of blood.

"What are you doing?" she asked suddenly, her voice uneasy.

But still she didn't pull away.

"I call truce," I murmured lazily. "A one night truce. You don't want me to make you leave, do you? Should I call for the votaries? Have you thrown out? Because that can be arranged."

She hesitated a moment before shaking her head.

"Good. Stay then. Here, with me. I'll keep you safe. If anyone finds us, I'll say it was my fault. That I brought you. I broke the rules."

"You'd do that? For me?" She sounded shocked.

As if I hadn't already protected her, time and again.

I said nothing, just slid my hands slightly lower down her hips.

She gasped slightly as her eyes moved back to the spectacle unfolding below.

The highblood man was skimming his hands over the girl's smooth, white breasts. His fingers played with her nipples, stroking and squeezing.

The girl leaned back, her head tilted upwards, throat bare and exposed.

The highblood man leaned forward. Not to the girl's neck, but to suck one pert nipple. Together we watched as he drew the luscious bud into his mouth and licked and teased it with uninhibited abandon.

The girl moaned, her hands moving up to clutch his shoulders, her fingers grasping at his black robe.

Hundreds of eyes watched as the man pushed the girl's robe down around her waist, exposing the curve of her spine, the delicate swell of her flared hips.

He cupped her body, drawing her closer towards him, her breasts flattening against his chest as he moved his mouth to hers.

They kissed deeply.

"She's enjoying it." Pendragon's voice was shrill with disbelief. Her body hadn't stopped trembling since I'd grabbed her. "I don't understand."

I couldn't stand it another moment. I had to get closer to her. I let go of her waist with one hand and raised it to brush away the hair from her neck on one side, then lowered my mouth until it was inches away from her skin. As close as I dared get. For now.

"So are you," I pointed out. "Enjoying it, I mean. It's a beautiful scene. The girl is lovely and willing. Why shouldn't she accept pleasure? But she's nowhere near as stunning as you." I brushed my other hand down her body, skimming the flat plane of her stomach and then inching lower.

She reached down and grabbed my hand, stopping it in its tracks. "Stunning? Since when do you give me compliments like that, Blake Drakharrow."

I grinned to myself. The words were strong but her voice was weak. I could sense her hesitation, her confusion. She was vulnerable. Defenseless.

"Surely you know how much I want you, Pendragon," I murmured. "How much I've wanted you since that first day I saw your unbelievably beautiful naked body."

Her hand had frozen over mine. She hadn't pulled it away, only stopped me from going any lower.

"I haven't been able to get you out of my head since then," I confessed. "I want to feel your body against mine. I want to bury myself inside you. Don't you understand how much I crave you?"

Maybe it was the bloodwine talking, but I had no shame left. I risked it all. I lowered my mouth to her neck, not to feed, but to suckle her sweet skin. I kept my fangs in check, simply moving my mouth over that sweet, sensitive flesh.

She gasped. "What are you doing to me?"

"Nothing you don't secretly want me to do, little dragon. I won't feed from you, if that's what you're worried about. I swear it on my life."

I teased my tongue over the curve of her neck, wishing I dared turn her around and taste her lips. But I knew the spectacle unfolding below was what was driving her desire. She wanted to watch. And I wanted to watch her watching.

"On some level, you need this," I murmured against her neck. "No matter how hard you've tried to deny it."

"Oh, gods," she moaned, tilting her head back slightly to give me greater access.

I pushed gently against her hand, silently begging her to release me. She let it fall away.

I moved my hands down her body, skimming her hips, grazing her thighs, then trailed them back up, letting them linger against the sides of her gown, the sides of her breasts.

She gasped at the contact. Even through the fabric, it was electric.

I moved my mouth to one of the black straps of her gown and worked it slowly off her shoulder with my teeth.

Down in the courtyard, the man had gotten the blightborn girl completely out of her robe. She sat astride him, fully naked, as he fondled her breasts with one hand, caressing her hips with his other, his mouth still moving over hers.

The scene was incredibly erotic.

But not as erotic as the feel of Pendragon's gown slipping down off her shoulders.

I pushed her other strap down then moved my fingers to the top of her bodice, and before she could stop me, slipped my hands into her gown and cupped her breasts.

She gasped and arched against me slightly, making no move to stop me.

My mouth went to her neck, kissing and licking hungrily, as I took her nipples between my fingers and worked them until they were rigid and stiff. The gown kept getting in my way, pushing against my hands. I shoved it roughly down to her waist, baring her fucking perfect breasts.

She raised her hands then, as if to cover her breasts modestly.

"Shy, little dragon?" I nudged my mouth against her skin, breathing a kiss onto her shoulder. "You've got nothing to be shy about. Everything about you is sheer perfection. Surely you know that."

I felt her shake her head slightly. I smiled against her neck. I had her just where I wanted her. Fuck but she was beautiful. Beautiful and all mine.

I couldn't get enough of her. I stroked her breasts, reveling in the heat of her skin.

Her hair brushed against my face, the curls soft and light, as I bent my head further down, kissing and licking her shoulders and nuzzling my mouth against the nape of her neck.

I was hard, so fucking hard for her. I pushed myself forward against the back of her gown, letting her feel what she'd done to me, and she moaned.

"This is the power you have over me. This is what you do to me every day, Pendragon. You drive me wild. I can't look at you without longing to fuck you."

She clutched my hand abruptly. "Look."

Down below, the highblood man had moved his mouth to the girl's neck. He drew her closer, smoothing her hair off her neck, then yanked her head back. I watched as his fangs shot out, glinting under the dim light before sinking into the girl's skin.

Pendragon stiffened, as if unsure if she should run or stay.

"No," I murmured. "Keep watching. Look."

The girl's body arched, her breath catching in what seemed like a mix of pleasure and release.

Her fingers tightened on the man's shoulders, gripping him hard as he fed.

Blood trickled down her throat, running in rivulets over her bare breasts. Every few moments, she trembled, her head falling back in a perfect display of surrender and ecstasy. The man's grip on her waist tightened as he fed, drawing long pulls of blood.

Finally he withdrew, his mouth rimmed with blood. He ran a finger delicately down the girl's throat to her collarbone, then along the curve of her breast, tracing the trickle of blood before lowering his mouth to suck the droplets off.

In my arms, Pendragon let out a soft moan, as if in frustration.

I knew what was coming. So did the girl playing the Bloodmaiden.

The question was, did Pendragon?

The man's hands were down around his robes. Slowly, he parted the fabric, exposing his long, hard cock.

The blightborn girl writhed impatiently as she felt him press it against her clit.

She rose up, pressing her hands against his shoulders as if too eager to wait. Then, bold with lust, she lowered herself onto him.

Her moan of pleasure broke through the silence, the sound thick with hunger and desire. Slowly, she began to ride.

"I know what you want," I whispered in Pendragon's ear. "I know what you need. The only question is, will you let me take care of you?"

I slid my hands down her bare stomach, feeling the smooth firm planes of her flesh.

"Just watch," I murmured. "Just watch them. Let me do this for you. Let me give you what you need. What you've always needed from me but have never dared to ask for."

I moved, as if to push her dress from her hips, but her hands shot out. They were shaking as they closed over mine.

"Fine," I said, my voice husky with want. "I get it. The dress stays on."

At least half of it.

I raised a hand to her hair and ran my fingers through it, then grabbed a handful and pushed her head down, not roughly, but not exactly gently either. When I had her half-bent over the balustrade, I raised the back of her skirt.

She was naked underneath. Even in the shadows I could see the pale swell of her perfect ass. I ran my hand gently over it, then slid my hand between her legs.

I suppressed a groan. She was soaked. Wetness dripped over my fingers.

"Fuck, Pendragon. You sure know how to make a man feel wanted."

She squirmed with embarrassment under my hand and I grinned.

"What's the matter? No witty comebacks now that I've got your pussy in my hand?" I slid a finger inside of her while another began to work the sweet soft rise of her clit.

She trembled against me and a moan escaped her lips. Louder than before.

Without hesitation, I let go of her hair, my free hand flying to clamp down over her mouth. It wouldn't do for us to be discovered up here. Not at this perfect moment.

She squirmed, trying to fight against me, but I held her tighter.

"Hush now, little dragon," I scolded. "You don't want everyone to know what a bad girl you've been, do you?"

I started playing with her. Flicking and stroking her soft folds, slipping a second finger into her wetness.

It wasn't enough. I wanted to be inside her. Wanted to sink my cock into her pussy so fucking badly, to feel her quiver and tighten around me, to spread her thighs as far apart as they could go as she rocked back and forth against me.

But I wouldn't risk taking things that far. Not now. Not tonight.

Tonight would be for her and her alone.

I nudged her legs a little further apart, enjoying her resistance.

Of course, if she'd really wanted me to stop all she'd have had to do was bite my hand or hit me. I'd have backed right off. Reluctantly, but I'd have done it.

I wanted her willing or not at all.

But she didn't do any of those things. She wanted this. No matter how much she wanted to deny it. So I'd take the silent treatment. As long as it meant I could also take her.

Below us, the blightborn girl was moaning as she rhythmically rode up and down on the highblood man's cock, her breasts bobbing with each rise and fall of her hips.

The masked man had returned his mouth to the girl's neck and was feeding again. Trickles of red slid down the girl's body and were smeared against her skin by his greedy hands as he grasped her breasts, her hips, her buttocks, urging her on and on.

Meanwhile, my fingers were sliding in and out of Pendragon, working her clit in small circles, as I matched the girl's feverish rhythm below. My fingers thrust in and out of her tight, willing body as her breathing grew more and more ragged, her muscles clenching and tightening around my hand.

She was close now. So fucking close I could feel it.

"That's it," I murmured. "Come for me, little dragon. You come when she comes. You can feel it can't you? The power of it all. The sheer lust."

I longed to lower my face between her thighs and taste her slickness. Would she taste the same way she smelled? Like brine mixed with jasmine? Like iron and salt?

I settled for driving her mindless with my fingers. I'd pleasure her until she broke, sobbed, cried out my name, muffling the word against my hand.

Her hips were rocking against me now, shamelessly riding the waves of pleasure I was giving her, lost in sensation.

The girl playing the Bloodmaiden was nearing her climax, too. Her cries of pleasure were filling the courtyard.

The masked highbloods had given up their semblance of stiff disregard. They were disrobing one another, forming pairs and trios and piles of naked flesh. Coupling one with the other, men with women, women with women, men and men, like writhing masses of tangled snakes. I lost count of the breasts and cocks and tongues spread out over the white marble floor, atop their discarded black cloaks. Only their masks remained, tightly fitted to conceal their faces.

"I could slide my cock into you right now, little dragon," I whispered, unable to help taunting her. "I could fill you up, spread you wide. Would you like that?" I stroked my fingers in and out. "Would you want me to part your hips, slide my cock into your wet pussy? Would you ride me like you'd ride a dragon? Like that girl is doing down below?"

She gasped, her body jerking at the sound of the words. Just the idea of my cock inside her was doing this. I felt myself grow harder at the knowledge that I'd turned her on that much.

I circled my thumb over her clit as I rocked my hand against her, fucking her with my fingers as hard as I dared.

I felt her groan against my palm as her frame shook. She was close.

Down below the blightborn girl was, too. I watched as she arched backwards, her breasts damp with her own blood as she rode the highblood man harder and harder.

"That's it," I whispered in my little dragon's ear. "Come for me. That's what you've always wanted, isn't it? To come hard for me?"

I felt her clench around my fingers. The cliff was beckoning.

CHAPTER 43

MEDRA

My head was swimming. Below us, the courtyard had become a blur of black masks and flowing naked flesh.

My breath came in shallow pulls. The bloodwine. It had made a haze of every thought, knotting my mind into a cloud of confusion and heightening my worst desires.

Letting Blake touch me had been a very, very bad idea.

I should have run when I'd had the chance.

Would he have let me? Or would he have held me here and forced me to watch?

It didn't matter. He *hadn't* forced me. I'd stayed.

I hadn't elbowed him in the stomach or shoved him away. I'd let him slowly undress me, baring my body to the air as he ran those strong hands of his wantonly over it.

Now he was inside me. Fucking me. His fingers thrusting in perfect rhythm. And all I could think about was how good it felt, how sweet the release would be when he finally let me come.

I was close now. My body was responding to him as if it had been waiting for this all its life.

I hated myself for my reactions. But even more, I hated how I didn't want him to stop.

Each touch of his fingers sent a torrent of flame dancing across my skin.

My eyes flicked back to the courtyard where the girl rode up and down on the high-blood's lap as he fed on her, lapping at her blood with a predatory yet seductive hunger.

His feeding was somehow heightening her sensations. Is this what it would be like with Blake? I tried to imagine his fangs sinking into my flesh.

I couldn't tear my eyes away from the blightborn girl even though I knew every bit of this was wrong. Watching her was like watching my own transgressive desires unfolding. Raw and unfiltered for everyone to see.

Blake's hand rocked into me, his fingers thrusting again and again. I arched backwards, a moan stifled against his hand. It was humiliating to have him quiet me. But there was something incredibly erotic about him holding me captive, too.

I whimpered as his thumb skimmed over my clit.

His name was on the tip of my lips. I'd come so close to saying it already. Somehow, I'd managed to hold back.

Down below the girl had reached the peak of her frenzy. She slammed her body down onto the highblood's cock again and again, her cries of pleasure filling the courtyard as she rode him.

The sight of her there, the sound of her, the knowledge of her ecstasy–all of it was driving me straight towards the edge. The pressure built up inside me, hotter and hotter.

I was almost there.

"Come for me, little dragon. Fly over that cliff and fucking soar," Blake murmured in my ear.

And then there it was. I was coming. I was lost in the feeling of heat rushing through me. Rich warmth flooding my body. I was a dragon, exploding in fire like a shooting star in the night sky.

I muffled a scream against Blake's hand, my body throbbing in the overwhelming rush of release.

Below us, the girl's cries rocked the marble chamber as she climaxed, her pleasure unleashed, completely wild with abandon.

Emotions flowed through me as I came back down to earth, my heart beginning to settle into something like a normal tempo.

Relief. Shock. Awe.

I had never come like that before. So fast, so hard. Not for anyone. Not for any of the awkward stable boys who'd put their lips between my thighs, hardly knowing what to do. Not for any of the young courtiers I'd let slip into my bed.

It had never been like this before. So intense. So fucking good.

Of course, it had to have been Blake.

He slipped his hand out from me, as if with the utmost reluctance, then slowly drew the bodice of my dress up over my breasts and helped me slip my arms through the straps.

I could smell myself on him. The raw scent of sweat and salt and desire. It turned me on even now to know I was all over him, coating his hand with my slickness.

It was primal and crude. He'd marked me, entered me, filled me up with himself. But I'd left my mark on him, too.

If this was how good his fucking fingers felt, I could only imagine how... No, I was *not* going to let myself think that. I wouldn't, couldn't go there.

Blake's mouth was hot against my ear, his hands tight and possessive on my waist. "You're mine, Pendragon. Let another man touch you like I just did and you'll find out just how much of an asshole I can really be."

I jerked away from him, the aftermath of pleasure suddenly shifting to disgust. "You just had to ruin it, didn't you?"

He shot me a look of confusion, as if I'd wounded him somehow. "Wasn't it good for you?" He shook his head. "You were perfect. Incredible. Everything I'd ever imagined."

Part of me wanted to admit he'd been pretty good himself. But instead, I looked down at the courtyard.

Something had happened while we'd been standing there talking.

The girl. What was happening to the girl?

"What the fuck is this?" I hissed, my voice brittle. "What the hell is going on?"

He moved back towards me, standing at my shoulder as we looked down at the scene below. His hand hovered at my waist, still possessive, but this time I made no move to push him away.

Suddenly, I was too afraid for that.

CHAPTER 44

BLAKE

I t was a good fucking question.

What were they doing?

I'd never actually attended an Adoration Rite. But I hadn't wanted to let Pendragon know that, lest she feel even more uncertain about staying where she was.

I knew the rite involved a blightborn girl who would freely give an offering of her body and her blood in front of the congregation–now predominantly made up of my uncle's most loyal followers and the top ranking nobles from each of the four houses.

Afterwards, the girl was promised riches and glory. Her family was well-compensated but she could never return to them. She would spend the rest of her days in the Sanctum, cared for by the votaries of the Bloodmaiden.

At least, that was what I had always thought happened.

Like most of the younger highbloods, we'd only learned about the rite through whispers and rumors. Through overheard bits of information pillaged from our parents and elders.

Now, as I looked down at the blightborn girl slumped over the throne, I knew with certainty that she was dead.

Around the throne, the masked highbloods were rising and pulling their robes back on.

The highblood man stood up, lifting the Bloodmaiden into his arms. Blood still trickled from the fang marks at her throat.

He'd done that. He'd killed her. He'd murdered her for the rite. Was it always this way? Or had something gone horribly wrong?

I was a highblood. I should have known better than to even ask that question.

Limp in his arms, the blightborn girl looked almost peaceful, her pale face framed by the gleam of blood trickling slowly from the puncture marks on her neck.

The crowd of masked highbloods parted as the man walked between them, towards the silver bowl in the center of the courtyard.

Without a word, he reached up with one hand and pulled down the long silver chains that dangled from the ceiling. The links clinked softly as he began to wrap them around the girl's ankles. Other masked onlookers stepped forward. Together they helped him pull the chains taut, then hoist her body up into the air.

The blightborn girl's body swung gently above the silver bowl.

A soft pattering sound broke the silence as blood from her throat began to drip into the bowl below.

I stood perfectly still beside Pendragon, my hand still frozen at her waist, staring down at the silver bowl as the blood pooled.

Slowly, the basin began to glow with light.

The energy radiating from it was palpable. Humming through the courtyard like a low and steady pulse.

I realized what must be happening. The blood was powering some sort of enchantment. A powerful one.

Then it clicked into place.

The girl was fuel.

The glow around the bowl grew stronger, illuminating the faces of the masked highbloods standing around it.

My jaw tightened as I understood. The coercive magic that kept the blightborn compliant, relatively docile. This was how it was achieved.

There was a sickening twist in my gut as I glanced down at Pendragon. She was frozen, her face pale, her expression a mix of shock and horror.

My hand tightened instinctively on her waist and she jerked her head up.

I saw it then. The look of complete betrayal.

She thought I *knew*. She thought I'd purposely made her stay to watch...this. A girl's life force being drained away to fuel a magic that controlled thousands of innocent lives.

I nearly laughed. Then I caught myself. There was nothing funny about the look in her eyes.

She yanked out of my grasp and sprinted away from me.

I glanced down at the courtyard below before following, praying no one would spot us. If I'd thought letting her stay was risky before, now I knew things would turn deadly in a heartbeat if we were caught.

She was moving fast, heading back to the panel that led to the secret staircase, but my vampire speed made it easy to catch up.

I closed the gap between us, stepping in front of her.

Without thinking, I reached out and grabbed her by the shoulders, shaking her a little.

"Pendragon, stop," I hissed, my grip tightening as she tried to pull away.

Her eyes were wild with anger.

"Just calm down." The words came out rougher than I'd intended.

"Calm down? After what I just saw?" She yanked herself free again, stepping back as if my touch burned her. "How dare you tell me to calm down after you stood there and let me watch that... that horror."

"I didn't know," I blurted out. "I didn't know she was going to die. You have to believe me."

"Oh, you knew." Her voice was trembling with rage. "You knew exactly what was going to happen. I may have been an intruder but you were an invited guest. You were supposed to be down there, with them, weren't you?"

I struggled to keep my composure. "Both things can be true. I'm telling you the truth."

She gave a bitter laugh. But I saw there were tears in her eyes. "You knew she'd be sacrificed. You had to have known. You know who I believe didn't know?" She paused. "Regan."

I stared at her. "You think Regan would have actually cared? You think she would have stopped them?"

She shook her head slowly. "No. I think you highbloods all keep secrets from one another. But you–a Drakharrow–you're in on the worst secrets of all. You're sick, Blake. You're a monster."

"I didn't know," I tried to say again.

"Stop lying," she shouted.

Her voice was too loud.

I jerked into action before I could stop myself, darting forward to grab her. In an instant I had her tossed over my shoulder.

In another second, the panel had opened and shut. We were in the stairwell. I flew down the stairs with her struggling in my arms, beating at my back with her fists.

Only when we were far enough inside the passage did I finally put her down. Then I reached into a recess in the wall and pulled out the lamp I had hidden there.

As I lit it, she slapped me full across the face.

I grimaced but made no move to retaliate.

I watched as the tears fell from her eyes.

"You knew," she said quietly. "The bowl. The chains. What else would they have been for?"

My heart thundered in my chest. "It wasn't supposed to happen like that. The bowl is always there. Not the chains. I knew they'd take some of her blood. But she was supposed to be willing."

"Oh, she was willing all right." Pendragon's voice dripped with irony. "So willing she fell for your highblood bullshit, hook, line and sinker. That's the only part of it that…" She trailed off, shaking her head.

I felt a drop of water hit my face. One of her tears.

"She didn't suffer," I said softly. "If that's what you meant. I don't think she even knew it was happening."

She sniffled. "It doesn't make it any better."

"I know."

"What was it for? What the hell was it for? Why did they kill her?" She stepped closer, her face twisted with disdain. "Tell me the truth for once in your life."

My throat tightened as I struggled with what to share. The weight of the lie I was about to tell pressing down on me. But how could I possibly tell her the truth?

I hesitated, my voice caught in my throat.

"Tell me!" Pendragon's voice cracked, her fury showing through. She shoved me hard in the chest, pushing me backwards. "What was all that blood for?"

My jaw clenched. "Magic. Some sort of a spell."

"For what? What were they doing?" she persisted.

I ran my hands through my hair in frustration. "I don't know. They didn't tell me. They didn't even tell me she was going to die. I guess tonight was supposed to be my… initiation. If I'd shown up."

Pendragon covered her mouth. "Kage."

Even now, I felt rage rising at the sound of his name on her lips. "What about him?"

"He's a house leader, too. Was he there?" she demanded. "Wearing one of those masks?"

I shook my head wearily. "I have no idea. He might have been. But it wasn't mandatory to attend. It's supposed to be a privilege. They knew we had the ball tonight. Maybe Kage stayed at Bloodwing." I wondered if Catherine Mortis or Lysander Oprhos had been in the Sanctum.

"A privilege," she said with sarcasm. "Right. What a wonderful fucking privilege. As if you aren't all privileged enough. So what *privilege* was the spell for this time? What sick tradition? You already think you own us. You sacrifice blightborns as if we're worthless. You already control this entire cursed kingdom..."

Her eyes widened, horror dawning in them.

I stayed silent.

"Oh, my gods," she breathed, taking a step back as if I'd struck her. "That's what this is all about, isn't it? The spell. It's like thrallweave. It's to control the blightborn in the city. To keep them compliant."

My stomach dropped, the truth hanging in the air between us, thick and oppressive.

Her voice broke. "How could you? How can you be a part of this? Why do you hate us so much?"

My throat tightened as I saw her pain. I stepped towards her, desperate to comfort her somehow.

"Stay back," she whispered. "Stay away from me. Don't you dare fucking touch me."

I swallowed. "I didn't choose this. None of this is what I wanted. I was born a highblood." I took a deep breath. "Some highbloods murder blightborn to feed, yes. You probably figured that out already. But it's never supposed to happen at Bloodwing. And I...do not. I swear that to you, Pendragon."

"Why?" she challenged me. "Why not kill us for your food? Why limit yourself? Why hold back?"

"Because the idea sickens me," I burst out. "To take a life like that. For that reason. Not to protect myself or to protect..." I'd almost said "to protect you." "Or to protect another. Not in self-defense but simply out of willful indulgence. I hate the idea of it. And so did my father. He tried to change things."

"And then he died," she said simply.

I nodded tightly. 'Yes."

"So why don't you do something about it?" she said, her voice deceptively soft. "You stand by and let these people die. You let them murder that girl. You could stop it, but you don't."

My heart twisted. "You think I could have stopped that, even if I'd known? Gone up against that many older highbloods? They would have killed me just like they did her."

"No way. You're a Drakharrow," she spat. "A fucking prince of the Blessed Blood. Your uncle is the most powerful vampire lord in Sangratha."

"None of that would have mattered to them," I said, trying to control my frustration. "You think my uncle would try to save me? He was down there with them. Wearing one of those masks. Fuck, he might have been the man on the throne for all I know."

For a second she froze. Then a look of complete revulsion came over her face.

"I think I'm going to be sick," she muttered, turning away.

I grabbed her arm, then quickly released it as I saw the look on her face. "Look, I know all you want to do is run away but you need to listen to me."

"I don't have to listen to a single damn thing you say," she snapped.

"Yes," I snarled. "You do. If you want to live, you do. And if you try to run, I will stop you. So you will stay and you will listen. Don't make me touch you again."

I could practically see her gnashing her teeth. If she'd had fangs of her own, she'd have ripped my throat out.

"Fine," she finally spat. "Speak."

I took a deep breath. "You can't tell anyone about this. None of it. Not what you saw, not what you've learned. If you say anything, you *will* be killed. Do you understand? They'll kill you. And not only you."

Her face was pale but her eyes were full of fire. "Really, Blake? You're trying to scare me into silence?"

"I'm trying to make you understand how serious this is," I growled, hoping the desperation would be evident in my voice. "You think I want to threaten you? You think I enjoy all of this? What I'm telling you is true. You can't say anything. Not a word. Not to your friend Florence. Not to that dwarf you hang around with. No one. If you do, they'll be killed–right along with you."

Her lips parted slightly. "Florence..."

I nodded, my voice softening slightly. "Yes, Florence. If you care about her. About any of your friends, you'll keep quiet."

I felt like a complete and utter asshole. But what else could I do?

For a long moment, neither of us spoke.

I watched her mind race as she clenched and unclenched her fists at her side. I understood. Her world had just unraveled at the seams. And now there I was, trying to sew things back together with lies and guilt.

"Fine," she finally whispered. "I won't say anything."

I exhaled. "Thank you." I could feel the tension in my shoulders loosen a little.

I gestured ahead of us in the direction of Bloodwing. "Let me go first. My night vision is better."

I stepped carefully around her and started walking.

A few moments later, I could hear her begin to follow. She kept her distance. I held the lantern high enough that she'd be able to see the path.

The night hadn't turned out quite the way I'd hoped it would.

Now Pendragon hated me even more than she had before.

But not as much as I hated myself.

CHAPTER 45

MEDRA

The night's horrors weren't over. Not even close.

I followed Blake through the darkened tunnels, my mind racing. I kept my eyes on his back, unable to shake the memory of the girl's lifeless body hanging over the silver bowl.

I had so many more questions I wanted answers to. But before I could confront him again, we'd somehow reached the First Year tower and a new kind of chaos descended upon us.

The ball had ended hours ago and so I had expected the Common Room to be deserted. Instead it was filled with people, most of them looking frightened and panicked.

"Medra!" Florence's voice sliced through the noise as she ran towards me. "Where have you been?" She grabbed me by the shoulders and pulled me into a hug. "I was so worried about you."

She barely glanced at Blake, her attention locked on me. Before I could answer, she continued, "It's one of the housekeeper's children! A little girl. Poppy. She's gone missing. Professor Rodriguez is organizing search parties."

Sure enough, I caught sight of the dark-haired faculty member in the center of the crowd, his face haggard as he pointed at students and barked orders.

I blinked, suddenly feeling exhausted and disoriented. "What do you mean she's gone? She's a child. Maybe she just wandered off."

I thought of all the times I had gone sneaking around the castle in Camelot, without a word to my poor nurse.

"No, you don't understand." Florence's gentle voice shook. "There was blood. On her pillow."

Blood. My stomach churned, the memories of the rite surging through me like a flood wave.

The servants at Bloodwing were all blightborn, of course. They mostly worked at night, while we students were asleep. They lived in the lower reaches of the castle. We hardly ever saw them. Their children mostly lived away from them, attending blightborn schools in Veilmar. But I knew many had come home for the Frostfire Festival, to celebrate with their families.

These were humble people, just doing their jobs while we–the privileged students, and yes, I included myself in that category for once–attended our classes at the academy.

Their children should have been safe. They were innocent.

I thought of the soft patter of blood filling the silver bowl and shivered.

It was happening again. Now. Here. Tonight. This time to an innocent child.

Panic swelled in my throat.

I turned slowly to Blake.

His face had gone even paler than usual. His expression was grim. "I have to go."

"Where?" I demanded, stepping in front of him. I glimpsed the look of surprise on Florence's face. "You can't just leave. Not now."

His jaw clenched, his eyes darting towards the entrance. "I have to find out what's going on."

"You know something, don't you?" I said accusingly, lowering my voice. "You're not leaving me behind. If you know something, tell me. I'm coming with you."

"This isn't a fucking game," he growled. I sensed his frustration. And beneath it, fear. "Stay here. Where it's safe."

I tilted my face up towards him stubbornly. "You want me to stay quiet about tonight? Then I'm coming with you. If you know where that girl is, I'm coming."

Florence was watching us, her brown eyes wide. I tried to give her a reassuring smile.

Blake glanced at her. I knew he was wondering if she'd overheard.

"Pendragon is coming with me," Blake said, his voice gentler than usual as he looked at my friend. "I'll bring her back to you soon."

Florence pushed her spectacles up the bridge of her nose, then nodded slowly.

I touched her arm briefly, before I followed Blake out of the tower and back into the hall.

There was no doubt in my mind that he knew exactly where he was going.

He led us to the Dragon Court again, his pace much quicker than before. As we slipped down into the passageway, he strode ahead with purpose.

When we reached the vast chamber with the massive dragon skull at its center, the imposing stone doorways marked with the four house names loomed ahead.

Blake paused, nostrils flaring, as if he were tracking something elusive in the air. He tilted his head slightly, sniffing like an animal.

Then with a low grunt of recognition, he strode into the passage marked Avari.

My heart raced. Did this have something to do with Kage?

Blake's speed left no room for my questions. He moved through the Avari dragon catacombs without a word and I followed as quickly as I could, trying not to lose sight of him. I knew he was already holding himself back so I could keep up.

This time, when we reached the end of the dragon tombs, the passageway led straight down. We descended steep staircase after staircase, delving down into the earth itself.

At first, the stairways were plain stone. Then their style began to change, shifting into a different kind of architecture, nothing like anything I'd seen at Bloodwing. These stairways seemed even older than the academy itself.

The stairs ended and we entered a new passage. Some of it had collapsed almost entirely, stone crumbling into dust and rubble.

Blake climbed over large fallen stones, then reached back for my hand without a word, guiding me through the narrow gaps.

Each time his hand grazed my skin, I trembled. Whether from fear or revulsion or something else, who could say?

The tunnels opened onto a vast space. The remnants of once-grand architecture surrounded us, cracked and crumbling but still awe-inspiring in their craftsmanship. Panels of gold and glittering green stones shone from buildings stretching upwards twenty or thirty feet or more.

My breath hitched. Dwarven ruins. Magnificent and lost to time.

I felt like an intruder in a forgotten world. Did anyone else even know these were here?

As we walked through the ruins, a sound broke the stillness.

A girl's high-pitched giggle, eerie and out of place.

A sharp, terrified scream followed. It sounded as if it had come from a much younger-sounding child.

My blood ran cold.

Blake's reaction was swift. He ran forward toward the sounds.

I chased after him and we ran through crumbling streets until we reached another open area, surrounded by half-collapsed buildings.

A small girl, no more than four or five, lay crumpled on the ground. Over her crouched Blake's sister, Aenia. Her mouth was slick with blood as she leaned over the younger child, sucking greedily.

My stomach twisted, Aenia's cruel laughter still echoing in my ears.

But Blake didn't hesitate. He lunged forward. In a heartbeat, he had grabbed Aenia and yanked her off the little girl.

The small highblood screamed and snarled in response, her eyes wild as she bared her fangs at her brother. She thrashed about in his arms, scratching at his face with viciousness like a savage animal.

"Aenia!" Blake barked. His voice was sharp with authority but it didn't seem to even reach her. She writhed in his grasp, trying to sink her teeth into him as if she'd lost all sense of who and where she was.

"Grab the child," Blake snarled in my direction, his voice full of urgency. "Quickly."

Aenia's nails left trails of blood on his skin as she hissed and scratched but Blake didn't falter. He held her firm as I darted forward.

For a moment, I stood, frozen, looking down at the little girl's body. Poppy. That was her name. She looked like a lifeless doll. Blood was flowing freely from the wounds at her throat.

Then I saw it. She was breathing. Only just.

"Give me something," I cried, desperately, turning back to Blake. "Anything. To stop the blood."

Shifting Aenia under one arm, he somehow managed to peel off the jacket he was wearing and tossed it to me. Quickly, I ripped one of the sleeves off and tied it around Poppy's neck as tightly as I dared, then wrapped the rest around the little girl and lifted her up into my arms.

She was so light, so fragile. I could feel the warmth of her blood soaking through Blake's jacket, sticking to my skin.

Before I could move towards the way out, Aenia let out a feral scream of rage and broke free from Blake's grasp.

She fell to the ground in a heap then leaped to her feet and dashed towards me.

But Blake was faster.

In a blur of motion, he came between us.

"Aenia, stop!" Power flowed through the words. His voice carried the unmistakable command of thrallweave.

Aenia froze mid-lunge, her body trembling violently as she tried to shake off his hold. Her tiny fists shook at her side, her face twisted with fury. But she couldn't move.

I'd had no idea he could do anything like that. That he could use thrallguard on another highblood. Then I wondered if anyone really knew what Blake Drakharrow was truly capable of, least of all me.

Blake scooped up Aenia again, holding her more tightly, her arms pinned at her sides.

"Can you get the girl back to the tower alone?" His voice was strained but controlled.

I nodded tightly. "I think so. What are you going to do with her?"

Blake didn't answer.

"You can't keep letting her hurt people." The image of the little fluffin I'd found injured on the beach flashed through my mind. "First it was the fluffin. And now look at her! I know she's your sister, but she nearly killed this child. How many others has she already killed that you don't know about?"

"It's none of your concern. You think I don't already know all of this?" Blake snarled.

"I have no idea what you know and don't know," I said slowly. "Or if you really care."

"I'm here, aren't I?" he spat.

"Then what are you going to do about it?" I demanded. "Because if you don't stop her, she'll keep hurting people. She would have killed this girl and you know it. What happens next time?"

Blake's gaze darkened. "This isn't the time or the place for this conversation. I'll handle Aenia. You just take care of the girl."

"How?" I started to say.

He turned towards me, his face dark with fury. "Maybe you didn't hear me the first time, Pendragon. Take the girl and get out of here. *Now.*"

He didn't use thrallguard, I'd give him that much. But there was power in his voice nonetheless.

I took a step back. "Fine. So you'll just keep covering for her, protecting her, while she tears apart blightborn children as if they're nothing." I shook my head. "I guess I'm an idiot for thinking any highblood would actually care about something like that."

Blake's face hardened, but he didn't reply.

I turned and began to walk back through the dark tunnels, cradling Poppy in my arms.

The little girl's breaths were weak and shallow, but reassuring in their steadiness.

As I passed the room with the large dragon skull the ground beneath my feet suddenly shifted. A low rumble began, growing louder and louder, causing the very stones underfoot to vibrate.

I picked up my pace, half-running, half-walking through the dim passageways.

Chunks of stone began raining down from the ceiling. I stumbled, my knees hitting the cold, hard ground. As debris fell around us, I curled my body over the little girl's, shielding her as best I could.

The tremor finally passed leaving silence in its wake.

When I was sure it was over, I struggled back to my feet, legs wobbling as I held the child close.

Fifteen minutes later, I finally reached the First Year Common Room. I burst through the door, sweat pouring down my face.

Florence rushed towards me.

"Medra!" she cried, as she took in the sight of the wounded girl. "Poppy! You found her. Thank the Bloodmaiden." Her shoulders sagged in relief.

I cringed at her choice of words, but knew this was not the time.

Professor Rodriguez was crouched by the hearth, stoking the fire. When he saw me, he rose quickly. Crossing the room, he took the girl from my arms and placed her gently upon a couch. He knelt down beside her, unfastening my makeshift tourniquet, and pressing his fingers gently against the wounds at her neck.

"Fetch her mother," he ordered one of the speechless students standing nearby. The boy ran off immediately. "You." He pointed to another student, a cowering girl. "Go fetch a healer. Tell them to bring a litter she can be carried in."

Minutes later, we could hear the poor mother's panicked sobs from the hallway before she even appeared. The housekeeper was a pretty blightborn woman with long black braided hair. She fell to her knees beside her daughter, cradling Poppy's face. Tears streamed down her cheeks as Rodriguez continued his ministrations.

"Medra, what happened? Where did you find her? Where's Blake?" Florence asked softly.

Her eyes scanned my face. I couldn't find the words to answer her. Nor did I want to. Not truly. I couldn't tell her what I'd seen.

If the little girl remembered her ordeal in the morning, she could share it with her mother. But I prayed she would forget.

Exhaustion was weighing down upon me. The events of the night were finally crushing me with horror and guilt.

I shook my head. "Tomorrow," I said, putting her off.

I climbed the stairs to my room, every step heavier than the last. My mind spun, replaying every last painful detail from the moment I'd left the First Year Common Room earlier that night with Kage.

The rite. The things Blake had done. The things I'd let him do.

I'd let him in. Let my guard down. For a moment, I had wanted him.

It had been a mistake.

He had saved the little girl. But he'd also saved her monster.

Aenia's feral eyes, filled with hunger and madness, flashed before me. And there was Blake. Holding her back.

Protecting Poppy and I. But also protecting the highblood who threatened us both.

I fell onto my bed, too exhausted to even turn down the covers.

The last thing I remembered as I fell asleep was the feeling of his hands on my skin...and the shame that had come from wanting him.

BOOK 5

CHAPTER 46

BLAKE

Springrise

I lay in my bed, staring up at the dark crimson canopy, one hand absentmindedly stroking the soft fur of the fluffin curled up beside me.

I'd given up trying to send Neville back to Pendragon and her friend, Florence. He went where he wanted, when he wanted. Secretly, I found it kind of flattering that more and more he seemed to want to be with me.

There was something comforting about having him around. Not to mention the fact that the little ball of fluff had basically saved my life that day in the arena when he'd warned me about Coregon's approach.

Neville made a small sound of contentment in his sleep, nestling closer against me.

Usually the animal's proximity would help to calm my restless mind. But tonight, not even Neville could settle my unease.

I'd returned from feeding in Veilmar earlier to find Pendragon standing smack dab in the middle of the Dragon Court.

For a moment, I'd been frozen in my tracks. Had she been following me again?

For the last few weeks, she'd completely ignored me. Refusing to even look at me when we passed one another in the halls.

Then I realized she wasn't looking at me. In fact, her back was to me.

She was talking. But there was no one around.

I walked over to her and stopped with a jolt. She was in a night dress. The loose white gown clung to her tall slender frame. Her hair was down, red curls flowing down her back.

I'd stepped up to her cautiously. Her voice echoed through the air, but the words were strange and foreign.

Then it hit me.

She was speaking Classical Sangrathan.

I hadn't heard anyone ever speak the dead language outside of my father's lessons. He'd insisted his children learn the Old Tongue. I knew enough to recognize it, to hear it when it was spoken. No one really used it anymore though, except in rituals or in texts so old they required translation by a linguist before they could be read.

Yet here was Pendragon, speaking it fluently.

I moved closer to her. She paid me no mind. Her eyes were glassy and unfocused.

Because she wasn't truly *there* at all. She was sleepwalking.

I tried to wake her, calling her name, but there was no response.

I glanced around, half-expecting to see someone else, whoever she'd been talking to, my senses on edge. But whoever it was must have been a figment of her imagination—someone in a dream. There was no one around us except the four stone dragons, lifeless and silent as always.

I stared up at them, shivering slightly.

The Dragon Court held power. Perhaps not even we highbloods understood the nature of that power fully.

I felt the urge to get Pendragon out of there. There was no way I was going to leave her alone in the courtyard in her nightgown in the dead of night.

I gripped her shoulders and shook her gently.

Nothing. Her lips kept moving, her eyes remained unfocused.

Knowing I wasn't going to get anywhere that way, I gave up. Scooping her up in my arms, I marched out of the Dragon Court.She didn't struggle. She didn't fight back. She just leaned her head against my chest.

I'd held my breath for a moment, expecting her to wake up and punch me in the face for touching her.

Then I started to relax.

I half-expected her to keep talking to herself, but instead she stayed silent. Her eyes remained open, watching me as I walked.

Now that I was back in my room alone, I had to admit it had been fucking creepy.

But also weirdly nice.

She'd been so relaxed as I held her. It'd felt so natural to have her in my arms like that. I'd sniffed her hair, still damp as if freshly washed. She'd smelled of jasmine and vanilla. Her body was warm and soft against mine.

Part of me had longed to bring her back to my room, put her on my bed, and just... sleep beside her.

But I knew what would happen if I did.

So I took her back to the First Year Tower. Woke up her friend, Florence. The dark-haired girl's face had been shocked when she'd seen Pendragon in my arms. Then her expression had shifted into one of mistrust. Whatever Pendragon had told her about me, Florence certainly didn't like me now. I wondered if she knew about Aenia.

When I left, Pendragon was still dazed, only just beginning to come out of her stupor.

I figured Florence could tell her what happened. Maybe she'd even leave out the part where I brought her back. That might have been for the best.

Neville rolled over in his sleep and I rubbed his stomach. He let out a little grunt of happiness, then started snoring.

I grinned down at him. If only Pendragon was as simple as a flufifn.

But she wasn't. She was a puzzle wrapped in a mystery with extra secrets sprinkled on top.

She was the most complicated person I'd ever met. And the most infuriating. Just when I thought I might have come close to cracking her code, she'd slap me in the face and shut me out again.

The Consort Games were coming up and, if I was right, she was in for a world of trouble. In some ways, I'd laid the groundwork for her as best I could.

But there was still more I could do to help her. The problem was, I knew she wouldn't fucking let me.

She didn't trust me. She wouldn't let me near her.

And if I wanted to protect her in the best way I knew how, she'd have to let me get closer to her. A lot closer.

I frowned down at the fluffin as I stroked his fur.

She'd never accept my help willingly. She was too damn stubborn. But there was one way I might be able to get her to come to me.

It would mean taking a risk. A big one.

But if it worked, if she'd accept my protection, we'd both come out of the Games the stronger for it.

Not to mention I'd be a hell of a lot closer to getting what I really wanted.

CHAPTER 47

MEDRA

I walked into Professor Rodriguez's office, ready for our thrallguard lesson.

As soon as I entered, I knew something was off.

Rodriguez sat behind his desk, his dark brows drawn into a deep frown, his lips set in a thin, unforgiving line.

I froze in the doorway as I spotted the book that lay in front of him. *The Dark Art of Eternal Bonds*. The one I had "borrowed" weeks ago.

"Sit down, Miss Pendragon," Rodriguez said, his voice terse. There was no trace of the warmth I'd grown used to in our recent lessons.

I did as he said, my palms growing clammy.

My mind was racing with excuses and possible explanations, but none of them seemed good enough.

The problem with Professor Rodriguez, I decided crankily, was that he was decidedly *not* an idiot. He was the kind of teacher who always knew when a student had been bullshitting him. If anything, it was a miracle it had taken him this long to catch me out.

"So," he said, fixing me with a piercing gaze. "How did you enjoy the book?"

I swallowed and tried to keep my voice even. There was no point in denying anything. "How did you know I took it? Why didn't you ask me before?"

His eyes narrowed. "Are those really the questions you want to be asking me right now, Miss Pendragon?"

I squirmed in the hard wooden chair. There must have been some sort of an enchantment placed upon the book. Something that told him who had last read it. Why hadn't I thought of that before? It was too late now to do anything about it, in any case.

"Why did you need the book?" Rodriguez's voice was deceptively soft.

"I... I had a problem and I thought it might help me solve it."

"Did it?" he asked sharply.

I shook my head. "Not in the way that I'd hoped." That was basically the truth.

Rodriguez's mouth twitched in a faint grimace. "Interesting."

I glanced down at his desk and for the first time noticed something else was there laying beside the book. My essay on dragons. I had finally turned it in last week.

"Tell me," Rodriguez continued, his voice frosty. "What did the book teach you about dragons?"

My heart sped up. "Dragons? It... It didn't. I mean, there wasn't anything about dragons in there." I thought for a moment. "Or if there was, I didn't notice."

For a second I could have sworn he looked disappointed. Then his eyes narrowed, his expression darkening. He flicked my paper towards me across the desk. "This paper is an embarrassment, Miss Pendragon. A child could have written it."

My face flushed hot. "I've had so much going on in my other classes..."

"I gave you extension after extension, Miss Pendragon," he shot back. "More fool I. When a student usually asks for an extension I am always inclined to deny it. Yet I had high hopes you might actually make good use of yours."

Knowing I had disappointed him, that he thought the paper unworthy of his time–that actually meant something to me. I felt hot with humiliation.

"Look, I'm sorry, all right? I'll do better. I can rewrite it. I'll read everything you told me to read. I can stay at lunch to work on it. Or after class," I said desperately.

I was praying he wouldn't do the one thing I was most afraid of and cancel our thrallguard sessions. I didn't know when exactly but I knew the Consort Games were coming up soon and I felt as if I was finally getting somewhere. Once or twice in the halls, I'd felt the prickling of a highblood student, trying to pry into my mind. I'd successfully managed to shut them out each time. But these were just students. As Blake had said, older highbloods would be much more of a challenge. I still had a long way to go if I wanted to be able to protect myself.

Rodriguez scowled and leaned forward. "It's too late for that, Pendragon. I would have thought that you of all people would have been most eager to learn everything you could about dragons. But instead you act as if you actually care about your other classes. As if you're taking all of this bullshit seriously. I thought you didn't even want to be here."

"I didn't... I mean, I don't," I said lamely.

But he was right and we both knew it. Something had changed. *I'd* changed.

Had I bought into the highblood propaganda without even realizing it or just fallen into an easy routine? Either way, I'd grown complacent.

Part of me had started wanting to be here. Bloodwing, for all of its horrors and cruelties, had begun to feel like home.

"And now," Rodriguez continued, ignoring me. "You give me this half-assed excuse for an essay. Do you even care? You have no idea what's at stake here, do you?"

My temper rose. "How the hell would I when you haven't told me anything? You keep things from me and yet you expect me to somehow learn? To care. Why should I care? All the dragons are dead and gone." I leaned forward. "Speaking of half-assed bullshit, what about you, Professor? Why were you meeting Blake Drakharrow in the middle of the night in Veilmar?"

His eyes flashed. "Don't. Don't even go there, Pendragon. I'm warning you." He leaned back and took a deep breath, as if trying to calm down. "I thought you wanted to survive. That you'd use the knowledge you found to help you get through the Consort Games, to help you... prepare."

I blinked at him, utterly confused. "I don't understand. What knowledge? What do dragons have to do with anything?"

"It doesn't matter now, does it?" he snapped. "You're obviously not as clever as I'd hoped. And now we have a bigger problem."

I bristled at the insult, but knew his frustration was at least somewhat understandable. I hadn't held up my end of the bargain. But at the same time, it felt like he was talking in riddles.

He leaned forward, his dark eyes holding me in place. "Do you know what a legacy is, Pendragon?"

I narrowed my eyes and swallowed a witty retort about the breadth of my vocabulary. "Yes, I believe so."

"There's a legacy I've held onto," he said, his voice lowering slightly. "It's been passed down through my family for generations. A legacy of dragons and their riders."

My heart skipped a beat. "What kind of a legacy exactly?"

"The subject we're talking about," he said slowly. "Is the most dangerous one in existence."

I swallowed, taking in the gravity of his words.

"Some say there was a time when dragons and their riders ruled these lands. Not highbloods."

My mind raced at the possibilities. "How do you know this? Are you saying this is real history or just a legend?"

Rodriguez smiled thinly. "The only way you're ever going to have a chance in hell of finding that out now is if you survive the Consort Games."

I could feel my frustration rising. "So that's it? I'm supposed to risk my life in these Games and you're going to just sit there judging me?"

Rodriguez raised an eyebrow.

My temper flared. "It sounds to me as if you need me to survive more than you're willing to admit. Why don't you help me instead of just dancing around everything?"

Rodriguez tilted his head. "There's already someone out there who's willing to help you. The question is, will you let them?"

I knew immediately who he must mean. I scowled. "Blake Drakharrow?"

Rodriguez nodded. "I didn't say it would be easy."

He pushed back his chair. "This meeting is at an end. We'll reschedule our thrallguard session. Be here tomorrow at the same time." He smiled at me coldly, then pointed to the door.

Shaking my head, I marched out of the room, unsure if I should be feeling apologetic, ashamed, or furious. Maybe all three.

When I got back to my room the next evening after dinner in the refectory, a note had been slipped under my door. My heart sped up.

I picked it up, unfolded it, and read.

The handwriting was neat and slanted, written in black ink, and decidedly masculine.

"Midnight. The Dragon Court. Come alone if you want a weapon to wield against me."

I stared at the words. There was no doubt in my mind the note was from Blake.

What the hell was this? Some kind of a trap?

Blake was dangerous. He was a killer. He was a highblood. I had no idea what kind of evil shit he was really involved in. The Adoration Rite had just been a taste of the corruption that ran through the veins of this dark and twisted kingdom—and through his own.

But Florence had told me how he'd brought me back the other night when I'd been sleepwalking.

I'd had restless nights of late and when I woke, I couldn't even remember what I'd been dreaming about. I never used to sleepwalk. I supposed I should have been grateful it had been Blake who'd found me and not someone else.

Regan would probably have just shoved me over a cliff.

The promise of learning something about Blake that could tilt the balance of power between us in my favor was too tempting to ignore. And then there was the advice Professor Rodriguez had given me.

When midnight came around, I slipped out of the Common Room and navigated the winding corridors until I reached the open expanse of the Dragon Court.

The night was cool and crisp. A light snow was falling, coating the statues with white.

Blake stood in the middle of the court, his back to me. His tall frame was draped in his customary black coat, the fabric hugging his lean, muscular shoulders. He turned his head slightly and my heart caught in my throat, taking in his knifelike cheekbones, his angular nose. He was imperial, imposing, perfect in his imperfections.

He might have been mine. If I'd really wanted to claim him.

My heart skipped a beat as he noticed me and turned fully around, his gray eyes glimmering with a hint of latent danger.

In his own terrifying way, I knew Blake wanted me. In his own terrifying way, he might even believe he cared about me.

But I knew the truth. He wanted to own me, possess me, use me up.

What he felt was the same thing I did–desire merged with loathing.

If I let those dark impulses consume me, I knew it would be my undoing.

"So," he said, his voice low. "You came."

I crossed my arms over my chest as if I could protect myself from his presence. "I'm here. What do you want?"

He looked amused. "No, 'thank you?'" He shrugged. "I suppose I should stop expecting to ever get one."

"You're right," I snapped. "You should. Stop getting your hopes up."

His lips curled. Then he gestured to a stone bench that lay over in the grove of trees behind the dragons. "You might want to sit down for this."

"I prefer to stand," I said coldly.

He shrugged. "Suit yourself."

He walked over to the grove of trees. Reluctantly, I followed.

He sat down on the bench, stretching his long legs out in front of him. "I want you to do something for me."

I tensed up. "Of course you do. Of course there are strings attached. I should have known." I turned to leave.

"I'm a highblood, Pendragon," he called. "There are always strings attached."

When I kept moving, he shot in front of me. "It's about Aenia."

There was a strange undercurrent to his voice.

"What about her?" I asked cautiously.

"If you want to know something that could hurt me, then you have to promise me something in return first," Blake said.

I narrowed my eyes. "What exactly am I agreeing to?"

"I've learned the Consort Games will begin in less than two days," he said, watching my stunned reaction. "Let me protect you so that you survive the Games."

"Protect me?" I said scornfully. "You won't even be there. I'll be going in alone." I pulled my cloak more tightly around me. "Besides, most of the consorts survive."

After my alarming meeting with Rodriguez, I'd begged Florence to come to the library with me and together we'd read up on the murky history of the Consort Games. There wasn't a lot to go on but ultimately, it was clear that the Games weren't supposed to eliminate all of the consorts. They were supposed to be a test. Yes, consorts died sometimes but that wasn't the point of the Games. These were noble highblood youths, after all. The kingdom needed to preserve them.

"Yes, but those are consorts who work together," Blake pointed out, to my annoyance. "They aren't alone."

"Regan will be alone, too," I said, tossing my head.

"No," he said. "She won't be. You'll see. You really think you have a chance as a blightborn? If you think you can go in with no preparation and no advantages, you're stupider than I thought, Pendragon."

This was much too close to what Rodriguez had said for my liking.

"Fuck you, Blake," I said. "I took on Visha Vaidya on my very first day, remember?"

"Yeah, I remember her winning and shoving your face into the dirt. And she'll be there, you know. She's a potential consort, too."

That wasn't the best news.

"She won because she cheated," I snapped. "I won the first round, fair and square."

"And what? You don't think they'll cheat in the Games?" He ran his hands over his face, as if he was actually worried about me.

"Are you making a similar offer to Regan?" I demanded.

He laughed but I sensed tension there. "Regan doesn't need it."

"I have rider blood," I pointed out. "I might not be a highblood, but I'm not exactly a regular blightborn either."

I also had one secret weapon I wasn't about to tell him about.

"Yes, but what if it's not enough?"

I shook my head. "This is just... bizarre. Stop pretending you care, Blake."

CHAPTER 48

BLAKE

"I care because I want you and Regan to both make it out of this," I lied. "Now do you want to know how I can help you or not?"

When she hesitated, I shrugged. "Fine. It's been nice knowing you, Pendragon."

I moved to go but she stepped in front of me.

I grinned.

"Get that self-satisfied look off your face," she spat.

I held my hands up in mock surrender.

She wasn't going to like this next part. I was bracing for her reaction.

"Fine," she said, tapping her foot impatiently. "What's the big tip? What do I have to do? Paint the refectory with blood? Sacrifice another blightborn virgin in the Sanctum?"

I flinched, and so did she as the cruel words left her mouth. She wasn't hardened enough to make jokes about that yet. I wasn't even sure if I was.

"If it involves you drinking me," she hissed. "Then the answer is absolutely fucking not."

I smirked. "It doesn't. All you have to do is drink some of *my* blood. Think you can handle that?"

She took a step back. "You can't be serious," she said, wrinkling her nose in disgust. "No. Hell no."

I sighed, resisting the urge to point out that any other girl at Bloodwing would have been flattered. I'd never even made the offer before. But Pendragon didn't care about any of that. She didn't care about our ways or traditions. She didn't care about the power the blood of the four houses held.

After what we'd both witnessed in the Sanctum, I supposed I didn't blame her.

"You agree to drink my blood," I said. "And I'll tell you a secret no one else knows. One that will give you power over me. One that could even get me killed. You'd like that, wouldn't you? Admit it."

Something dark flickered in her eyes and I hoped I wasn't making the biggest mistake of my life.

"Well?" I said, trying to look impatient. The truth was, I didn't really want to tell her. Part of me might have even been hoping she'd say no. But if she did, she'd be screwed.

"What will it do for me?" she demanded. "Your blood."

I searched for the right words. "It'll give you an edge. Make you stronger. Faster. Give you a little taste of my vampire abilities. Temporarily, of course."

I pulled a small vial from my pocket and held it up so she could see the red liquid glistening inside. "You won't even have to touch me. Just drink this. It'll help you survive."

She stared at the vial in my hand as if I were trying to poison her. "Drinking your blood is just as bad as touching you."

I tried to laugh it off. "You might be right."

For a long moment, she glared at me. But then her hand reached out slowly for the vial.

I watched her uncork it, then tilt the small glass bottle to her lips. My eyes fixed on her slender pale throat as she swallowed.

There was something erotic about watching her take part of me inside of her.

She downed the blood, her expression twisting in discomfort. But she didn't gag or spit it out.

"Good girl," I said with a smirk.

She gave me a dirty look, then wiped her mouth with the back of her hand and handed the empty vial back. "There. I did it. Now let's get the bullshit over with. What's your deep, dark secret, Blake?"

I slipped the vial back inside the pocket of my coat. "Aenia. She's not my sister. Not really."

Her eyes widened slightly. "What?"

I walked past her, moving to stand at the edge of the grove, looking down at the churning sea below.

"My brother Marcus... You saw him that first day, up on the dais with my uncle." I turned to look back at her and she nodded. "Right. Well, he's the kind of highblood you'd hate. If he ever comes near you, you should run in the opposite direction. He loves the hunt."

I wasn't sure if she would understand what I meant.

I took a deep breath, steeling myself for her reaction to this next part. "What I mean by that is, he loves to kill. He doesn't use thralls. He prefers to hunt and then to feed. He slaughtered Aenia's real family. He left her to die. She was barely two years old. I found her, bleeding out." I paused, swallowing hard. "I turned her."

Pendragon had walked up beside me. I could feel her by my shoulder. Now she stiffened. "You turned her? What does that mean?"

"I mean I made her," I said bluntly. "Made her like us. She was a blightborn. I made her a highblood." I shoved my hands in my pockets. "Though not everyone would see it that way."

"What do you mean?"

"I mean there's another name for those like Aenia. Foulbloods they're called. Blightborn who have been turned." I turned to look down at her. "Most of the time, they're hunted down and killed."

"But she was only a child," Pendragon whispered. "Would they have really done that?"

I shrugged. "Who knows. What matters is I botched it. I was too young to know what I was really doing. Too young to have even attempted it. My mother found me with Aenia. I begged her for help." I cleared my throat, finding it suddenly thick with emotion. "She helped me hide what I'd done. She took Aenia and went away for a while. When she returned, she claimed Aenia as her own child to protect me."

Pendragon was staring up at me. I couldn't tell if it was disgust in her eyes or something else. "You let everyone believe she was your sister, this entire time?"

"Marcus probably suspects. He's an idiot but he's not quite that dense. And I'm fairly sure my uncle knows." Viktor used it as something to hold over me. It gave him more power to control me. "But if anyone else knew the truth, they could kill Aenia and be well within their rights. Or me."

"Why you?"

"Because I broke the law, Pendragon. I'd be called before a tribunal. My uncle would probably get involved but he wouldn't be able to shield me, not entirely." Even if he actually wanted to and I had my doubts. "Representatives from all of the four houses would each select a judge. They could decide to execute me."

I stepped away from her and sat back down on the stone bench, clasping my hands together. "I was too young to know how stupid what I'd done was. I thought I was saving her."

To my surprise, she came over and sat down on the bench. Though not right next to me. In fact, she sat as far away as was possible without falling off the bench.

"But you did," she said slowly. "Save her, I mean."

"It would probably have been kinder to leave her to die." I sighed. "She's alive now, yes. But look at how she's living. She's losing her mind. You saw how she is. She's becoming feral. Wild. It's always a risk when you turn someone. She's a danger to herself and to others."

Pendragon looked at me, her eyes narrowing. "I'm glad you see it that way. Where is she now? What did you do with her?"

I scowled. I'd known this was coming but I wasn't about to be interrogated. "She's somewhere safe. Where she's not a danger to anyone."

She stared at me. "And what about Marcus?"

"Marcus?"

"You said that he killed Aenia's family. What would a tribunal have to say about that?"

I didn't reply.

She threw her head back and gave a bitter laugh. "I thought so. It's so fucked up. At Bloodwing, blightborn are treated almost like equals. I think you really fool us into thinking you see us that way half the time. But we're not. We'll never be, will we? Nothing would happen to your brother for killing Aenia's family, would it? What he did probably isn't even against the law. Tell me, Blake. Tell me I'm wrong."

"You're not," I said, frowning. "But such unrestrained violence is looked down upon these days. Most highbloods exercise far more control than Marcus. There's a system. Most of us follow it. My uncle encourages restraint." I said the words as if by rote. But I knew the system could crumble apart at any moment. That the balance we had right now was precarious. Maybe Viktor even wanted it to fall.

"We need blightborns," I said, trying to hide my real thoughts. "Most highbloods know that. You fulfill roles that we need."

She shook her head. "We're *useful* in other words. But you don't really value our lives or see us as individuals to care about."

"That's not true," I retorted. "Some highbloods value their thralls greatly. Blightborn can be brilliant healers, strategists, scouts."

"As fodder for your armies when you go to war with one another, you mean," Pendragon cut in.

I ran my hands through my hair in frustration. "Whatever. I've told you what I came here to say. I've given you an advantage. Use it how you will."

I stood up.

"So that's it?"

I looked down at her.

"You're just going to trust me with a secret that could get you and your sister—no, your *child*—killed?"

I kicked at a rock on the ground. "I'm completely at your mercy. Is that what you want me to say?"

"No, what I want you to say is 'thank you, Pendragon, for letting me get that weight off my chest.'"

"What the hell are you on about?" I asked angrily.

She stood up. "You only told me that because you wanted to. You wanted me to know so that I would feel guilty about Aenia just like you do. That's manipulative and fucked up, Blake, even for you."

I snapped. I stepped up into her space, bumping my chest against hers.

She gasped and took a step back.

"Everything I have done has been to protect you. We're bound, you and I, whether you like it or not. Marcus is a monster. He's also my family. Which makes him *your* family. Aenia is... She's a child."

"Is that how you see it?" she scoffed. "You think you owe them your loyalty? You know, the truth is that Marcus probably deserves to be put down even more than Aenia."

I hissed. "Don't ever say that. Don't ever speak about my family that way."

But in my heart, I already knew she was right. I'd known for a long time.

"We're done here," I said, turning away from her. "Good luck in the Games."

CHAPTER 49

MEDRA

The next day, I walked through the halls of the academy after my classes were finished. The air seemed lighter, humming with the promise of spring. But my heart was heavy and even the glimpse of green buds on the ivy climbing the stone walls or the soft breeze that carried the scent of fresh earth weren't enough to lighten my mood.

My conversation with Blake still rang in my ears.

Aenia wasn't his sister; she was his creation. His mistake.

The revelation had shaken me more than I cared to admit.

In some warped sense, Aenia was more than a sister to Blake. She was his *child*.

Beneath his cold surface, a weight of guilt lay on Blake's shoulders. He had tried to save an innocent girl from one monster and instead had condemned her to a life just as monstrous.

Now he was living with the consequences.

I passed beneath a stone carved archway and shivered. The air in the halls was still cool, but the bite of winter was disappearing. Outside, the snow was melting and soft green shoots of grass were pushing up in the courtyards. Signs of change, signs of spring.

I moved down a corridor leading to the First Year Common Room.

Blake Drakharrow was reckless. He was arrogant. He was a bully capable of cruelty and brutality.

Yet he had also tried to be a hero.

He'd done something that was decidedly not in his own best interest. He'd broken highblood law to save a blightborn he didn't even know. He'd risked his own life and his future.

Now he was tangled in a dangerous web of deceit. Because the older Aenia grew, the stronger she would get–and the more out of control. From what Blake had suggested, her mind was decaying and it sounded as if there was no way to reverse the process.

My mind turned to Blake's mother. Lady Drakharrow. I didn't even know her first name.

She must love Blake a great deal to risk so much to protect his secret, to shield a blightborn child–one who other highbloods would have left to die–and claim her as her own. The decision could have come with dire consequences for both of them. Yet Blake's mother had taken that risk for him.

And Blake? He clearly felt love for the girl, or some semblance of it. I wasn't sure if highbloods were even capable of love. The emotion seemed beyond them in some ways.

But whatever it was, I couldn't shake the feeling that the loyalty he felt towards Aenia could lead to even more destruction.

After all, if he had felt nothing for her, he would have put her down already. That was something I hadn't been able to say aloud the night before. Instead, the words had floated there in the air between us–unspoken, unacknowledged.

I sighed and lifted my satchel of books and parchments a little higher on my shoulder. The worst part of all of this was having to admit that while Blake wasn't a good person–he had proven that time and again–he *might* not be entirely evil either. He was capable of guilt, of admitting mistakes–well, not when they came to me–and of carrying a weight of responsibility.

But sooner or later, he would be forced to choose between his guilt and his love and a chance to end the terrible thing that Aenia was becoming.

I paused with my hand on the doorframe of the Common Room, realizing that for the past night and day my thoughts had been consumed with Blake Drakharrow even more than usual. My feelings towards him felt sharper, more intense. Not to mention there was an unsettling awareness that was following around like a nagging shadow. All day I had felt more conscious of his presence somewhere in the school, even when we weren't sharing a class.

My body felt differently, too. There was a restlessness in my limbs, like my muscles were constantly tense and primed for action. I'd had to actually hold myself back in Basic Combat earlier that afternoon, afraid I might accidentally hurt someone. I wondered how the feelings might have manifested if I'd had Advanced Weaponry. Part of me itched to try myself against a highblood.

And lastly, there was an annoying ache in my neck. Almost as if it were bruised. I'd found myself rubbing it throughout the day, as if I'd received an injury there I'd forgotten about. But this was more than pain. There was this... *pull*. As if I wanted something, needed something that I couldn't quite put my finger on. A pull in my throat tugging me towards *him*.

I frowned. It was maddening. But I was sure all of these things were symptoms of drinking Blake's blood. Ones he had conveniently failed to mention. Or maybe he had no idea they even existed. Were these side effects because I was blightborn? Either way, they were sure to be temporary. I just had to deal with them for now and get through the Consort Games. Blake had made it sound as if the effects of his blood would wear off soon after that.

I pushed the door open and stepped into the Common Room.

Several First Years were scattered about, talking quietly in armchairs by the large windows or reading quietly in one of the nooks by the bookcases.

My eyes fell upon Naveen. He was slumped on a couch near the fire, staring morosely into the flames.

Naveen'd been distant towards Florence and I ever since the Frostfire Festival. I'd assumed it had to do with disappointment. After all, he hadn't worked up the courage to tell Florence how he felt that night at the dance. I'd put it down to his regret, but had expected him to get over it. There would be other chances.

But now, looking at him, I wondered if that was all there was to it.

I walked over to the couch. "Hey, you."

He grunted slightly but otherwise didn't respond.

I grimaced. He clearly didn't want company but sometimes it wasn't about what you wanted but what you needed. I decided the time was past for leaving him alone with his dark thoughts, whatever they were.

I sank down on the couch beside him, dropping my bag onto the floor.

"You all right?" I asked softly. "You've seemed kind of... off lately. You want to talk about it?"

Naveen ran his fingers through his short, dark hair. As usual, he wound up looking like a cranky hedgehog. I hid a smile.

He shrugged, still staring into the fire instead of looking at me.

"Is this about Florence?" I ventured. "Look, I know you didn't talk to her like you wanted at the ball. There will be other chances though, Naveen. You see each other all the time. Do you want to practice on me... maybe?" It might have been a terrible idea, but I wasn't sure what to suggest exactly.

He shook his head. "It's not about Florence. Well," he corrected. "Not just about Florence." He glanced at me. "It's just everything," he admitted. "I don't know what I'm going to do."

Now I was really alarmed. "What do you mean? What else is going on?"

He slunk lower on the couch. "I failed one of my classes."

I tried to hide my shock. Our last exams had been at the end of the Wintermark term. Naveen hadn't confessed this then. He'd let months go by without telling someone. And he'd still been permitted to attend the ball.

"Well," I said carefully. "Just one class isn't too bad. Maybe you can make it up? Retake the class? Have you talked to the professor about it?"

Naveen scowled. "I failed a class... and I got a 'W' in two others."

I blinked. I knew "W" stood for Weak. So that was three classes he wasn't doing well in. I wondered which ones they were. I knew for a fact that he'd passed Basic Combat. He and Professor Stonefist got on well and she'd even commended him in front of the class a few times.

"A 'Weak' is basically the same as a fail," Naveen said miserably. "That's three classes I'm flunking."

"We have Springrise exams coming up at the end of term," I said slowly. "Maybe you'll do well on those. Now that we know, Florence and I can help you study. We can quiz you, make sure you're more prepared."

"Maybe." He didn't look convinced. "But more likely, by the end of the year, I'll be out of here."

There was something in his expression I didn't understand.

"Well, even if that does happen, there's more to life than Bloodwing, right?" I reminded him, trying to cheer him up. "There must have been other things you wanted to be, besides a scout for the highblood houses. Your family lives in a dwarven city. There must be other paths you could take. What do your parents do? You have siblings, right?"

"You don't understand," Naveen said, almost angrily, cutting me off. "I knew you wouldn't. When you attend Bloodwing, you're committed, Medra. It doesn't just end if you fail."

I furrowed my brow. "I get that." But I wasn't sure I did. Florence had never fully explained.

"Best case scenario," Naveen continued. "Is that they make my family pay for everything. All the tuition fees are waived for successful students. They assume we'll pass so your family isn't responsible for anything up front. But this is the most expensive school in Sangratha. If you fail and you're actually sent home, your family has to pay for your failure. It's a massive amount, Medra. My family could probably manage it. We're not poor. But the shame, the humiliation. My father would be furious."

"If that's the best case scenario?" I asked tentatively. "What's the worst?"

Naveen hesitated, glancing around the room nervously. "Most students who fail never go home again. They're sent elsewhere. I think it's mostly assumed they're sent to a highblood house to work as indentured servants." He put his head in his hands. "I guess after Springrise, I'll be continuing my friendship with you and Florence by letter."

"What?" I exclaimed. That sounded little better than slavery. I lowered my voice. "How can they do that? You really can't go home? Ever"

Naveen shrugged. "I don't know. I guess it's the same thing as making your family pay off your debt. But that's just a guess. And I'm not even sure that is the worst case scenario. Other students I've talked to think they might..."

Before he could say more, the Common Room door opened and Florence walked in beside Vaughn Sabino. They were both talking and laughing. When they spotted us, they headed straight for the couch.

Naveen's eyes widened in panic. "Promise me you won't tell them," he whispered urgently.

I nodded quickly. "Of course not," I said, just as Florence and Vaughn reached us.

The dark-skinned, lanky boy plopped down beside me with a grin and stretched out his long legs comfortably with a sigh of relief. Florence sat down more primly in an armchair by Naveen, tucking her skirt around her legs.

"So, how about that Basic Combat class?" Sabino asked, still smiling. "It was a rough one, right?"

I couldn't help grinning back at him. Over the last few weeks, Vaughn had seemed to be returning to his usual self. The bruises had faded. His arm had healed amazingly well. So well that he'd been permitted to stay in Professor Stonefist's class. She'd made sure we'd all taken it easy on him for the first while. But lately she seemed to have no qualms about pushing him just as hard as the rest of us.

I had never spotted Theo with Vaughn again since the night of the bonfire. I wondered if Vaughn blamed Theo for what had happened to him. If so, I didn't really blame him.

Each time I saw Theo Drakharrow around the hall, he did little more than nod to me. He hadn't been beaten like Vaughn had– or if he had, he'd hidden it well–and yet his former air of carelessness and theatricality seemed to have diminished. Secretly, I thought it was a little sad.

But still, I reminded myself, Theo was a Drakharrow. He was a part of a dark and twisted family. And as a highblood, he needed blood to survive and keep his powers up. Just because I didn't see him drinking from his house thralls in public like Catherine Mortis didn't mean it wasn't part of his regular routine.

I tried to focus on what Vaughn was saying.

"I think Stonefist is going to finally start throwing some stealth lessons our way."

I nodded, thinking back to the class. "She said we're finally getting closer to where she wants us to be in terms of hand-to-hand. It would be nice to have a change of pace."

Florence had been listening. "I still can't imagine what it is you do in those classes," she said, wrinkling up her nose slightly in distaste.

I laughed. "We pummel each other for hours," I said jokingly. "But I promise, it's fun. Really, we've been practicing disarming and grappling for weeks now. But Stonefist says none of that would be enough for those who wind up as scouts if they don't also have skill in stealth."

"And she's not wrong," Vaughn said, leaning back against the couch. "Of course, it's not as if we don't have time to acquire the skills. It's only our first year, after all. I've heard some First Year cohorts don't even get into stealth training at all by the end of Springrise. Professor Stonefist can be kind of a stickler if she thinks you're not ready."

"Better that than letting us get too far ahead of ourselves, I guess," Naveen chimed in.

I was happy to see him taking part in the conversation. We continued to chat about the class, talking about who seemed to be struggling the most with the newest grappling technique we'd been taught, and speculating on when Stonefist might let us finally switch to something more interesting.

When the conversation finally lulled, Florence jumped up. "Come on, let's head down to the refectory. I'm starving."

The great hall was buzzing with the usual crowd of students unwinding after the day's classes. The scent of freshly cooked food hit my nostrils and made me realize just how hungry I was.

My eyes drifted over to the House Drakharrow table. Blake sat there, beside Theo and Regan. But he had his back to me.

My hand absently reached up to my neck, brushing against one of the sensitive places Blake's mouth had been that night in the Sanctum. With a little huff of annoyance, I yanked it back down as I realized what I was doing.

I sat down at a table with my friends, filling my plate, and forcing myself not to look at Blake's back.

Had he lied to me? Today had been just another ordinary day. Yet he'd promised that the Consort Games would be held soon. Maybe I'd been wrong to trust him, to drink that vial—even with all he'd confessed about Aenia.

After finishing up dinner in the refectory, I said goodnight to Florence and the others and then made my way to my room, suddenly exhausted. Clearly that vial of Blake's blood I'd drunk wasn't about to give me insomnia, even if it did heighten my strength and senses.

The conversation I'd had with Naveen lingered in my mind.

Part of me felt guilty knowing I now had to keep what he'd told me from Florence. I suspected she'd have had a much better idea of what to do to help him.

I decided I'd have to talk to Naveen again alone and try to persuade him to talk to Florence—about his grades, even if nothing else. Maybe Florence's mother, Jia, would know of some options for Naveen. Surely there was a way he'd be able to repeat the class he'd failed, do some make-up assignments, or retake his exams.

If worse came to worse, maybe I could approach Blake and demand he help out somehow.

Which made me remember why he'd told me about Aenia in the first place. He'd claimed he was giving me leverage. Something to use against him.

I yanked off my clothes and tossed them into the hamper, then pulled on a robe and lay down on my bed.

Leverage. What did Blake really expect me to do with knowledge that might get him killed?

I thought of how I might use it. I could go to someone like Headmaster Kim, I supposed, and reveal what Blake had done. If Blake was telling the truth, then he'd be pulled up before some sort of highblood tribunal and would face the full wrath of Sangratha's highblood laws. He could be executed. I assumed Aenia would fare no better.

Not so long ago, the idea of Blake being horribly tortured and killed would have brought a smile of joy to my face. I hated him then. Hated him for how he'd treated me, for his cold superiority, for the betrothal I'd never asked for.

But now things were different. Without meaning to, I'd come to know him better. I couldn't ignore the fact that he'd done what he'd done to try to save Aenia.

When I looked at him, I didn't see the same person he'd been at the start of the year.

I wondered what he saw when he looked at me.

I lay back on my pillow, staring up at the star-covered ceiling.

I could get rid of him once and for all. The question was could I really live with that on my conscience? And would I be better off without him?

There was no way Lord Drakharrow was going to let me go. If Blake was out of the picture, who would they give me to next? Marcus Drakharrow? I shuddered.

Pushing myself up on my elbows, I looked over at the item on my nightstand. Coregon's dagger with Orcades' soul trapped inside. If Aenia was a symbol of Blake's failure, the dagger was equally one of mine.

Most days, I brought the blade with me. Even tucked into my boot, Orcades could take in most of the things around me.

Each night before sleep claimed me, I'd gotten into the routine of reaching for it and speaking with her.

I sat up and pulled it into my hands.

Mother?

At first there was only silence.

Then, *Medra?* Orcades' voice had changed over the last few weeks and this worried me. Her tone was softer. Each time she sounded a little more distant. As if she were speaking from a place further and further away. There was a dreamy quality to her words. A detachment that hadn't been there before.

Were you asleep? I asked cautiously. *Did I...wake you?*

You know I don't sleep anymore, she said with a sigh. *But I... I was dreaming.*

How could one dream without sleeping? But I didn't point out the contradiction.

I was dreaming of the sky. I was flying over the sea.

You're not in the sea or the sky, I reminded her, a little sternly. *You're here, with me. Remember?*

She gave an almost wistful sigh. *The blade. My prison. How could I forget?*

I felt a stab of guilt. *I'll take you with me tomorrow,* I promised. *I shouldn't have left you here all day without me.*

My heart sped up as I suddenly wondered something. Was my mother on the same track as Aenia? A path leading to madness? Was she losing herself the longer she stayed in the dagger, confined and chained? I couldn't imagine how horrible it must be.

Is being in the dagger worse than being stuck inside of me? I asked.

Worse, came the answer almost immediately. *But it's not so bad.* I felt a warmth from the blade, as if it were pulsing slightly. I squeezed the hilt in my palm, wishing I was actually clasping the hand of a flesh and blood woman and not a piece of metal. *You didn't mean to, Medra. It's not so bad,* she said again.

Having her try to excuse my accident was almost worse somehow. It didn't ease the guilt I felt.

I wondered if Professor Rodriguez would help me if I told him the truth. I looked over at the books about dragons he'd given me. I'd been going through them. I still wasn't sure exactly what I was supposed to be looking for.

I slid the dagger under my pillow, my hand still wrapped around the hilt. It was the only comfort I had to offer.

Goodnight, Mother, I whispered.

I closed my eyes, sleep beginning to pull me under.

But my slumber didn't last long.

A rough hand clamped over my mouth, yanking me awake. Filled with panic, my eyes shot open. But before I could scream or take anything in, a soft cloth was pressed against my face. A sweet, sickly smell filled my nostrils. I thrashed about but my limbs were suddenly heavy and sluggish.

Everything went black before I could even begin to fight back.

CHAPTER 50

BLAKE

I sat in the stone bleachers of the arena, my body tense, eyes locked on the massive projection veil that hovered over the pit.

Beside me, Theo was fidgeting restlessly.

I resisted the urge to join him.

Here we were, safe in the stands. While somewhere out there, the woman tethered to me by blood and by fate would soon be walking headfirst into unknown dangers.

I hadn't been able to stop replaying our meeting from two nights ago in my head. The image of her standing in front of me, tossing back the vial of my blood. Maybe it was weak of me, but part of me was regretting not telling her the whole truth.

But there was no point in thinking about it now.

The Consort Games were about to begin. I'd done what I could for her. Now I just had to hope it would be enough.

The Games were not supposed to be impossible to win. For most highblood consorts, they were a test of strategy, of the consorts' ability to work together and to survive. Nothing more.

But Pendragon was going into them with a target painted on her back.

My jaw clenched, my gaze going back to the enormous semi-translucent veil projected overhead where the area's enchantment would soon begin to reveal the consorts' journeys.

Other teams would be working together, pooling their strengths. Pendragon would have to rely on her instincts—and on my blood coursing through her veins.

"Regan's been sharpening her knives for weeks now," Theo muttered beside me. "Think she has a chance?"

I knew he didn't mean Regan. He hated the woman. We both knew she was about to openly defy me. Despite the humiliation that would bring, on the one hand, Regan's defiance would play into exactly what I wanted.

On the other hand, Pendragon had a lot to lose.

I clenched my hands into fists on my knees.

The consorts would have been taken from their beds in the dead of night, drugged, and brought to a special dormitory reserved for the sole purpose of the games, located on a small island not far from Bloodwing.

Right about now, they'd be waking up. Professor Wispwood would be casting an enchantment over each one. The spell would allow everyone in the arena to see what the consorts experienced, permitting us to become spectators.

The island wasn't designed to kill. But accidents always happened. Every year, a few consorts died. Either from sheer stupidity or bad luck.

I hadn't answered Theo's question. I didn't want to admit just how worried I was. But I suspected he could sense it.

Around us, the usual crowd of highbloods and blightborn were taking their seats. I saw a number of faculty members sharing a row together. There was Rodriguez, the bastard, looking completely unconcerned as he sat down next to Professor Sankara. I knew he wanted Pendragon to get through this as badly as I did, and yet when I'd practically begged him to help me give her some kind of an advantage he'd claimed he'd already done what he could.

Some of the highbloods in the arena were consorts in their second or third year, or beyond. They'd already passed the Games. Now they were settling in to watch this one as entertainment. They had nothing to worry about. They could sit beside their co-consorts and their archons, knowing their places were secure.

Who would I be sitting beside when this was all over?

A figure striding down the rows of stone caught my attention. Vaughn Sabino. He looked as if he'd recovered well from the injuries Coregon had dealt him. I'd made some inquiries. I knew he still had a chance of making it as a scout.

Out of the corner of my eyes, I saw Theo notice Vaughn. His whole body stiffened. He shifted away from the aisle uncomfortably as Vaughn passed.

Something in my gut twisted. I knew Theo had liked Vaughn. Before everything had gone to hell.

"Have you seen Sabino lately?" I risked asking.

Theo's eyes shot towards mine, giving me a black look that could have melted stone. "Why? You going to report me to dear Uncle Viktor?"

I frowned. "Theo, I didn't... Is that really what you think?"

"Don't bother," he snapped. "I doubt Vaughn ever wants to talk to me again after what he went through. Wasn't that the entire fucking point?"

"I didn't tell Coregon to do what he did," I said, lowering my voice.

"The Prince of the Blessed Blood doth protest too much. But, sure. Whatever you say, old boy," Theo said tightly. I wasn't sure he believed me but I was also getting sick of denying his accusations. "I was supposed to learn my lesson, right? Like a good little boy. Stay away from the bad blightborn boy forever. Or was it all males in general?" His lips twisted cruelly, distorting his normally easygoing features in a way I hated to see. "Don't worry. You and Coregon made sure of that."

Guilt hit me square in the chest. I hadn't known what Coregon was going to do. But I sure hadn't warned Theo about any of it when I'd had the chance. Viktor had made it clear that Theo's dalliances with other males were not going to be tolerated within our house.

"I suppose I should just be grateful Coregon didn't punish me, too. Is that it?" Theo said, half-snarling, half-hissing the words. "Should I be grateful, Blake?"

"He wouldn't have fucking dared," I said automatically.

"So you'd protect me, is that it? But not someone like Vaughn?"

"I had no idea what was going to happen to Sabino. I swear," I growled. "Coregon stepped out of line. He's gone now, isn't he? But if you expect me to protect every man you get a crush on..."

I was being cruel. Cruel and unfair. And I knew it.

I saw Theo flinch.

"Don't worry," he said coolly. "Do you really think I'd risk stealing some happiness for myself if it could result in another person's disfigurement, dismemberment, or decapitation? I'm not that shallow. No, I'll just follow your example and be fucking miserable doing whatever Uncle Viktor tells us to do. Isn't that your great plan?"

"I didn't ask for any of this," I said, my voice low. "I fucking hate this." But I didn't dare to say more. Afraid I might give away some truths with my lies.

Theo looked away, his jaw tight. "Just leave it, Blake. It's done." His voice sounded tired. He slouched back on the bench.

I tried to settle back into my seat, but my mind was churning with thoughts of Pendragon and now Theo. A light touch on my shoulder pulled me from my thoughts.

"House Leader?"

I looked up to see Lucian Aleron standing over me. Visha Vaidya's archon wore a sleek black tunic embroidered with red thread, its billowing sleeves cuffed just below his wrists. His long, pale blond hair was tied in a tail at the nape of his neck with a black ribbon. Silver rings glittered on his slender fingers.

Lucian was polished, I'd give him that. But there was something pompous about him that had always grated on my nerves. He liked to play the role of archon to perfection. Lucian wasn't a fool, but he lacked Visha's steel.

Lucian's other consort, Evander Sylvain, was out there on the island with Visha right now. Lithe and tall, he had delicate features that gave him an androgynous look. Lacking Visha's fierceness and Lucian's ingratiating ambition, Evander was softer, more introspective, lacking the typical highblood ruthlessness. The best quality he brought to his triad was loyalty–to Lucian, to Visha, and to House Drakharrow–and thus, by extension, to me.

The irony of it all wasn't lost on me. Lucian and Evander were generally believed to be a love match. Lucian's father had approved the union, with the condition that Visha be added in to strengthen the pair.

In contrast, there was no way in hell Theo would be permitted to select male consorts.

But our uncle's prejudices remained mostly hidden from other highbloods for now, even within House Drakharrow. The key words being "for now." I had no doubt he'd try to extend his reach as soon as he dared.

I thought of Visha and the task I'd assigned her. I trusted her to be ruthless, to do what was needed. Lucian and Evander lacked her fire. Eventually, Visha would control both of them easily, whether she was their official archon or not.

I looked back at Lucian, wondering what had brought him here.

He smiled at me, but there was a hint of unease in his eyes. "I thought you'd want to know. Before the consorts were taken, Regan Pansera formally requested that the Crown of Bone be used on Medra Pendragon before the Games began."

My blood began to boil. I started to spring up from my seat. Theo's hand held me down.

"Steady, cuz," he warned. "Don't make a scene."

He knew what this meant. So did Lucian.

But Lucian didn't need to see how much the idea of Pendragon being under threat bothered me. Let him think I was simply furious at Regan's defiance.

Still, I couldn't hold back a growl. "How did this happen?" I demanded.

Lucian took a cautious step back. "She's of dragon rider blood and a blightborn no less. Regan's argument was compelling–and valid as far as I could tell." He dropped his voice. "I happened to be near the Headmaster's office."

He'd eavesdropped in other words. But I didn't care how he'd found out.

"Thank you for informing me," I said stiffly. "Good luck to you and your consorts in the games."

He nodded. "The same to you, Drakharrow. Just thought you'd want to know."

My jaw clenched but I forced myself to sit on the bench and feign calm.

I glanced at Theo. I knew he liked Pendragon. We both knew what the Crown of Bone meant for her.

Crafted from ancient dragon bones, the crown was rarely used and usually had to be requested by a consort's archon. It was an artifact reserved for testing the loyalty of consorts who were chosen from blightborn bloodlines.

The crown could peer into a blightborn's mind, forcing them to confront their deepest loyalties and fears. It would make them select someone from their lives–someone they cared about. Only a blightborn would be chosen, of course. The consort wouldn't even realize what they'd done. The decision would be unconscious and by the time they figured out what had happened, it would be too late.

I ran a hand over my face, as if trying to wipe away the worry I felt. No one could see, no one could know how much this was all getting to me.

The crown might destroy Pendragon. And Regan, that venomous bitch, had known exactly what she was doing when she'd requested it be used.

But there was absolutely no way I could stop it now.

Approximately six hours from now and this would all be over. I was betting on Pendragon being a survivor. What didn't kill her would make her stronger. Right?

CHAPTER 51

MEDRA

My eyes fluttered open, my head pounding with a dull ache. I lay on a hard cot in a shadowy stone cavern. Slowly, I propped myself up on my elbows. Around me were rows of other cots. All of them were empty.

My heart sped up. Had they started the Games already? Had I missed them?

Before I could move, I felt something being lifted from my head. I looked up and saw Professor Wispwood standing over me. The blonde, halfborn professor looked down at me with sympathy in her eyes, then murmured, "Good luck."

She walked across the room carrying something in her hands and placed it in a wooden box. A white circlet. Why had it been on my head?

The last thing I remembered was falling asleep in my own bed.

No, the last thing I remembered was *dreaming*. I'd been dreaming of Florence and Naveen. We'd been talking and laughing together in the Common Room. It'd felt so real.

I sat up groggily, then groaned. The cloth. I remembered the sickeningly sweet scent of it pressed to my mouth and nose. I'd been drugged. Had I been affected worse than the other consorts? Was that why everyone else was gone?

I glanced down at myself. I was in my underthings. There was a small table beside the cot. On it sat a neatly folded pile of clothes. A plain tunic and trousers of a dark, sturdy material sat beneath a leather vest, lined with pockets. On the floor next to the cot was a pair of familiar leather boots.

I pulled on the clothes, unable to shake the sense of panic. Everyone else was gone. They had a head start.

It was stupid but I supposed some part of me had held out the faint hope that Regan might have changed her mind.

But no, here I was—all alone.

I started to pull on my boots. My fingers brushed against something cold. Coregon's dagger.

Stay calm, Orcades voice rang in my head. *Don't draw attention.* Professor Wispwood was still organizing instruments on the far side of the room. *Get up. You need to get moving.*

I pulled on the boots the rest of the way, carefully keeping the knife tucked alongside my right calf. I'd been hoping to bring the dagger in with me. That had been my plan all along. But I hadn't exactly been given a chance to pack.

Had the other consorts been given weapons? Or only me?

The soul-imbued dagger gave me a slight advantage. But considering I'd been left here alone and was the last one out, it might not be enough of one.

I walked out of the cavern and into the light. It looked to be about mid-morning. I raised a hand to my eyes, squinting. The daylight was almost blinding after the darkness of the underground dorm. My legs felt wobbly, as if they belonged to someone else. What the fuck had they given me? Whatever it was, I hoped Regan had gotten it, too.

My boots sank slightly into the damp earth as I scanned my surroundings. The air was thick with a humid heat. A stark contrast to the cool spring we were experiencing back at Bloodwing. This was another world altogether. I stood on the edge of an island—lush, almost jungle-like, with towering trees draped in vines that created a dense canopy over-head.

The foliage around me was rich with the smell of wet bark, damp moss, and flowers.

I walked forward through the trees and reached a dead end. A gorge lay in front of me, separating the underground dormitory from the main part of the island. Below, a thin mist rose up from the depths of the gorge.

My stomach dropped as I spotted the only way across. A stone platform, barely wide enough for two people, jutted up out of the mist, perched on top of a high stone pillar.

But there was only one. It was close to me. I could jump onto it if I tried. But leaping onto it would only get me part way across the gorge.

I moved towards the cliff's edge and caught sight of two figures standing on the other side.

Visha Vaidya looked back at me, her hands on her hips. The last time we'd crossed paths the girl had tried to beat me to a pulp.

Behind her stood a tall, slender boy with silver hair. He looked less than pleased. They'd clearly been arguing. Visha seemed to have won the debate.

Evander, I thought, remembering the male consort's name. Florence had been telling me about some of the recently formed triads. Visha had been paired with an arrogant, sulky-looking highblood named Lucian and another consort named Evander.

"Pendragon!" Visha called across the gap. "Wait. You'll never make it across alone."

I ignored her and stepped to the edge of the cliff, gauging the space between the cliff and the platform.

I jumped.

I wobbled as I landed, flinging my arms out to steady myself. Damn that drug they'd given me. There was no way the other consorts were suffering these after effects, considering I was the last one here.

I stood on the platform, waiting for something to happen, but nothing did. I'd expected the next platform to rise, providing me with a way across. Shit.

"You need a partner to get across," Visha called, sounding annoyingly smug. "It won't work otherwise."

She stepped towards the edge of the cliff, her violet eyes gleaming. "Did Professor Wispwood mention you're being timed? The platforms will all disappear in a few minutes. Including the one you're standing on. You're the last one to emerge."

"Thanks for the helpful information," I called back, sarcastically. "And you're both doing what? Just waiting on the other side to watch me fail?"

To my surprise, she shook her head. "I'm going to help you across. I need you to promise not to attack me when I come towards you."

My heart pounded. "Why the hell would you do that?" I shook my head stubbornly. "I'm not an idiot. There's no way I'm trusting you."

Visha moved a little closer to the edge. "You have no choice. The clock's ticking. You're the last one. And maybe you've failed to notice this but Regan is long gone."

"Why would you help me?" I demanded. "You hate me. You tried to kill me."

"Kill you?" Visha rolled her eyes. "So melodramatic, you blightborns. If I'd wanted to kill you, you'd be dead. I was testing you." She shrugged. "So I got a little carried away."

"Regan sent you after me," I accused. "Why the hell would I trust you now?"

Visha smirked. "Regan wasn't the one who sent me to fight you that day. Though, of course, she was thrilled that I did."

I stared at her. "Then who did?"

"I'm sure you can figure it out on your own."

I felt a lump in my throat, but savagely pushed it down. "Blake."

She nodded. "Turned out you weren't as weak as we thought. Way to prove me wrong. Now are you going to just stand there or are you going to let me help you across?"

"I don't understand," I said. "Blake sent you after me then. But now he's what? Told you to help me survive this?"

"That basically sums it up." Visha nudged her fellow consort. "Right, Evander?"

Evander frowned but said nothing.

"Evander isn't thrilled with any of this, so if you could decide what the hell you're doing soon, that would be great," Visha explained. "We need to get going."

"Why would Blake want you to help me now?" I demanded.

Visha threw up her hands. "Look, you and Blake can figure all of this out and talk about it once you've survived the Games. Sound good? It's none of my business. He's the House Leader. I'm just doing what I'm told."

She leaned forward slightly and to my surprise, a pillar began to rise up out of the mist, just a few feet in front of her.

"There," she said with satisfaction. "Thought so."

She jumped onto the first pillar, then leaned forward again and the next one rose.

"If you've already crossed once with your consort," she explained, slightly out of breath as she leaped to the next platform, drawing nearer and nearer to me. "Then the platforms will let you go backwards. But you can't go forward the first time alone."

She jumped to a pillar as it rose across from the one I was standing on. One more to go.

I spread my legs a little more, willing myself to keep my balance. I still felt woozy. I tried not to look down at the rolling sea of mist below us.

Visha glanced over at me. "So, what's your decision? You going to fuck this up and get us both killed or you going to catch me?"

She didn't wait for me to respond. She jumped.

I clutched her shoulders to brace her as she landed and she gasped.

I shook my head. Despite our history, I had to admire her tenacity. Visha was tough as nails. Behind her, the platform she had just been standing on was descending once more.

Visha was shaking her head. "You don't look so great, Pendragon. What the hell did you do to yourself?"

I pushed my hair off my face. "I must have been drugged. We all were, weren't we?"

"Some of us more than others from the look of it." She eyed me up and down, then shook her head. "That fucking bitch Regan. She must have paid someone off. No wonder it took you so long to come out. Evander wanted us to move on and in another minute we would have."

I glanced across at where the tall pale young man stood. I didn't really blame him. He just wanted to survive.

"What you're doing right now–helping me. Isn't that cheating? Won't you both get into trouble?"

"Funny, now that's what Evander said," Visha replied. "You worried about us, Pendragon? How sweet. So you'd rather I didn't cheat to save your life?" She shrugged. "I mean, it's a little late now. Shall we get moving?"

I gripped her hand and together we leaned forward. The next platform rose up.

We jumped for it.

"Steady," Visha shouted as I lurched forward abruptly, dizziness clouding my vision. "Get it together, Pendragon." She swore under her breath, but didn't let go of me.

"I'm sorry," I gasped as I staggered upright.

She swore again, muttering something about Regan, then glanced across the gorge at where Evander was watching us. He'd started pacing, his hands shoved into the pockets of his trousers.

"You'd better get ready to catch her," she shouted across the gap. "You hear me, Evander?"

The pale blond-haired boy nodded tersely and stepped a little closer to the edge of the cliff.

"We're running out of time," Visha said tightly. "Let's go."

She yanked me forward and I took the next jump with her, stumbling only slightly.

We slammed onto the next platform. I fell to my knees.

"Are you going to let her get away with this?" Visha asked, looking down at me and shaking her head.

"Who? Regan?" I said breathlessly. "What choice do I have?"

"Blake must be so pissed," she muttered. She grabbed my hand. "Get ready. Last one."

We leaned forward together and the next platform rose up in front of us.

I focused hard, trying to clear the fog from my head.

We jumped onto the final platform. Evander leaned forward, his hands extended.

"Come on," he said gruffly, nodding to me. "Take my hand."

I grabbed onto him gratefully and Visha and I stepped across the crevice onto solid ground.

Behind us the pillars remained in their ascended position for a few moments longer. Then they began to shake and rumble. Within a few seconds, they had crumbled into the gorge below.

I sank down onto the damp earth, taking deep breaths.

"Well, that's that," Visha said, looking down at the gorge.

"So cheating is allowed? Or tolerated?" I glanced at her and Evander. They both seemed fine. Not shaky on their feet. I knew the effects of whatever drug I'd been given would eventually wear off. But if Visha hadn't been there, I would have been screwed. What had Professor Wispwood thought? Had she tried to wake me to no avail? Then I had an awful thought. What if she'd been the one who'd administered it? Could faculty *do* that? "You won't be punished for helping me?"

Visha and Evander exchanged a look.

Visha shrugged. "Probably not. I doubt it. If Regan can get away with all of her bullshit, I doubt they can punish us for ours."

"What would have happened to me if you hadn't helped me? If I hadn't been able to make it across on my own?"

"You probably don't want to know," Visha said smoothly. "Blake would have been furious though."

In other words, I'd have died. Would Professor Wispwood have done it? Or someone else? For all I knew, Bloodwing had a special executioner on staff.

And if I'd died, Blake would have been unhappy. Because he actually cared about me? Or because it would have been a blow to his precious reputation?

"Not to mention his uncle," Evander muttered. I wondered if that was how Visha had gotten him to comply. If he was more worried about Viktor Drakharrow than about Blake.

"All right," I said, taking a breath. "I guess I'm on my own from here." I thought of something else. "That white circlet that Professor Wispwood took off my head when I woke up. What was it?"

Visha's eyes widened slightly and she exchanged another look with Evander.

She cleared her throat. "I wouldn't worry about that right now."

I narrowed my eyes. "What was it, Visha?"

She sighed. "I didn't see it. But if it's what I think it is, then it's called the Crown of Bone."

"Bone? What kind of bone?"

"Dragon bone. It's part of an old tradition. They probably used it because you're a blightborn. Don't worry about it right now." She must have seen the stubborn look in my eyes. "Look, all you need to know is that you can still get out of this place if you try."

"Fine. So what's next?" I demanded. "You two obviously know a lot more about what to expect than I do."

Visha shrugged. "We'll split up for now. You'll wander around. Just hang out. Try not to fall into any traps. Don't get eaten by any wild animals. If you're still feeling groggy then stay out of Regan's way if you see her."

"And then?" I asked cautiously. "That's it? That's all there is to it?"

"Of course not. That would be too easy, wouldn't it?" Visha snickered. "Get across the island. Meet us on the other side. There's sure to be at least one or two more challenges. You'll need another consort's help for at least one of them. Evander and I will be there waiting. One of us will help you finish this."

"Not if I beat you there first," I said automatically.

Visha raised an angular eyebrow. "That's the spirit."

She stepped towards me and lowered her voice. "Just watch out for Regan. I know she sees this as her chance to get at you now that Blake's not around to stop her. You're in rough shape. This probably isn't the best time to take her on." She glanced at Evander who had turned his back to us and was staring into the trees, tapping his foot impatiently. "Look, I'd stay with you but Evander is scared we're going to get in trouble for all of this. I doubt we are. It's clear that we can push the boundaries. I think they *want* us to. Besides, Regan's the one who tore up the playbook first. She's breaking all of the rules. We're just helping to even the field. I've got your back, but I have to have Evander's, too."

Our eyes met. I stared into Visha's violet ones, still unable to quite believe I was going to trust her.

I nodded. "All right."

She started to walk away.

"Visha," I called. She turned back. "You really did all this just because Blake told you to?"

"For Blake, sure. But not just because of him. I fucking hate Regan," she said with a grin that showed her pointed fangs. "I've been waiting for this for years. I can't wait to see what happens to her after today." She shot me a thoughtful look. "You're not as weak as you look either, Pendragon. Get your shit together and you'll be fine. Go drink some water. Good luck out there."

"Good luck," I echoed as she walked away with Evander.

For the next hour or so, I moved through the dense jungle, the thick, humid air making the fabric of my tunic stick to me like a second skin. Before long, I'd removed my vest and tied it around my hips. Then I pulled off my tunic, ripped away the bottom half and used the extra fabric to tie back my hair so the heavy curls weren't sticking to my face and neck. My midriff was now exposed and I supposed I might get a few more insect bites, but at least I could breathe better this way.

The heavy fog from the drug was lifting. At times I felt a wave of dizziness but I could mostly push it away. And something else was starting to kick in. The effects of Blake's blood. I could feel them working my way through my system. I was under more stress and strain. I figured that was kicking the effects of the blood into high gear. I could feel the change in my body, the power coursing through me.

Ever since my fight with Visha that day in Advanced Weaponry, I'd been honing the advantages of my rider's build with Professor Sankara's help. But no matter how hard I'd worked, I knew there was no way I would ever be as strong or as fast as a highblood.

But today? I wasn't so sure. That feeling of powerlessness I'd had when I woke up was dissipating. Did I have Blake to thank for that?

I came to a small stream and knelt down beside it. The water was clear and cool as it trickled over the rocks. I cupped my hands and drank deeply. The cold water washed away some of the residual blurriness that still clung to me. I felt stronger now, more myself.

I stood back up, wiping my mouth, and leaned back against a tree, looking ahead. By my guess, I was about halfway around the island by now. If Visha was right, we'd meet up on the other side, just in time for the next test. I hoped she'd keep her word and wait for me.

Just as I began to move again, a blink of movement in the trees caught my eye. My instincts kicked in and I dropped and rolled, just as a small silver blade came flying through the air and landed in the trunk of the tree right where I'd been standing.

There was a rustling sound. Regan stepped out from the underbrush to my right, a sharp rapier in her hand.

There was another sound, this time from in front of me. Gretchen emerged, twirling a small throwing knife between her fingers, a cruel grin on her face. She wore a belt across her shoulders, loaded with at least three more of the small blades.

Someone whistled from directly above me. I glanced up to find Quinn perched in a tree, a bow in hand and an arrow already drawn, aimed squarely at my chest.

Regan stepped out in front. "Look, girls. The little blightborn lamb has lost her way. What? No dragon to protect you?"

I tried to keep my expression neutral, as my eyes flitted between the three girls. "What do you want, Regan?"

Regan sneered. "Oh, nothing much. Just to teach you a lesson about taking what's mine."

"I've got the best seat in the house," Quinn called, from where she perched high in the tree. "Let the show begin."

Gretchen danced up and down on her feet. "Oh, this is going to be fun."

I sighed. "This again? I've never wanted Blake. You know that."

"I know he's far too good for you, blightborn bitch," Regan spat. "As am I. You pollute us both with this unnatural alliance."

My temper started to rise. Not this Blood of the Blessed shit again. "Does Blake know you're here? Attacking me like this? What's he going to do when he finds out?"

"It doesn't matter," Regan hissed. "He's not here to protect you anymore. Blake and his misguided sense of duty. I don't understand it, but after today he'll finally be free. You've been a thorn in my side since the moment he dragged you in, covered in dirt. I could tell even then that you thought you were something special. Better than the rest of us. Well, you're about to learn a lesson in true superiority. Gretchen and Quinn and I are going to teach it to you."

I tried to keep my face impassive. "I don't think I'm superior but I sure as hell don't think I'm beneath you either. You know I've always wished we could be friends. I wanted us to work together."

Regan laughed. "Right. Keep telling yourself that. As if I'd ever stoop so low. I know exactly what you want, Pendragon. Blake Drakharrow's cock inside of you. You little slut. You want him in your bed, don't you? But just because he's abandoned mine doesn't mean I'm going to give him up to you so easily."

I was astonished. Not least of all at her admission.

I sighed. It was time to take a different approach and stoop to her level. "Well, I can see why he doesn't want you. Who would want a snide whiny bitch sucking them off?"

Regan screeched like a parrot. "How dare you!" Her eyes narrowed and a slow smile stretched across her face. "This has gone on long enough. Pull that blade from the tree behind you and stick it in your throat. I command it."

I turned towards the tree trunk, taking in the sight of Gretchen's throwing knife embedded in the bark.

Slowly, I pulled it out. I looked down at the blade.

Then I tucked it into my pocket.

"Sorry, but that's not going to work anymore, Regan," I said calmly, as the thrallweave she was using continued to wash over me, hit the wall I'd built and skim away.

I didn't feel the compulsion like the last time she'd attacked me. Then it had been unbearable, undeniable. This was a different kind of pressure. Strong and insistent, yes. Pulling at my mind, trying to find a purchase. But I had practiced for this very moment. I'd partitioned my thoughts, dividing them, hiding the core of myself in my mental shadows. So far inside that Regan couldn't reach, even if she'd had the ability to. And I doubted she did. She wasn't as skilled in thrallweave as I'd once given her credit for. Rodriguez and Blake were much more proficient.

With a smile, I slammed my wall up hard, shutting her out. The sudden snap of mental threads nearly sent her reeling. I laughed at the look of shock on her face.

Gretchen looked back and forth between us, uncertainty on her pretty face. "What's happening, Regan?"

"The bitch shut me out," Regan panted. "Someone taught her how to block us."

She narrowed her eyes at me. "Who was it? Who taught you? I'll fucking kill them."

I smiled slowly. "You could try. But I doubt you'd succeed. You see, Blake and I have enjoyed a lot of time together. He *loves* getting me alone. To practice." I wasn't sure what I was doing. Only that seeing the expression on her face made it worth it. "He really enjoys our private tutoring sessions. Why don't you ask him about them yourself? If you make it back, that is."

"Blake?" Regan spat. "You're lying!"

I shrugged, keeping my stance steady. The dagger was in my boot. I could reach for it if I needed to. But it didn't escape me that I was outnumbered three to one and that Quinn had a bow pointed at me. "Think what you want. I know denial is easier for you."

I took a step closer towards her, my eyes locked with Regan's. "But you know all you really have to do is ask Blake."

I lunged forward, reaching for her rapier.

Regan reacted, but she'd lost a few precious seconds. My hand gripped her wrist, twisting hard. My body crashed into hers as we fell to the ground.

The damp earth shifted as we rolled across it, locked in a struggle.

The blood was pulsing in my veins. I felt as if I were filled with power. All of a sudden three against one seemed less of a concern and more of a fun challenge. I could do this. I knew I could.

Regan twisted against me, trying to get the upper hand, but I slammed her arm into the ground, forcing her rapier hand down with all my strength.

Regan growled, fighting me with renewed fury as she tried to roll me off her. I could feel her weight shifting, feel the sheer effort of her desperation to win this fight. She was a highblood. She was stronger, faster. For a split second, doubt crept into my mind.

Then I saw something in Regan's eyes. The same doubt reflecting back at me.

I gave a ragged laugh, giddy at the sight of it, my grip tightening. "You expected this to be easy, didn't you? So sorry to disappoint. Any guesses as to why things aren't going your way?"

"You're nothing but a blightborn," she hissed, her beautiful lips curling in disdain as she tried again unsuccessfully to slam me back into the dirt. "I will crush you like the pathetic bug you are."

I leaned towards her. "I have to admit something, Regan. I have a secret that might make that more difficult than you're expecting."

Regan froze. "What?"

I smiled slowly. "Can't you tell just from looking at me? I can feel him inside me. I would have thought it was written all over my face." I put my lips to her ear and whispered, "Blake gave me a little taste of something special."

"You're lying." Her eyes widened with fury and disbelief. "You're fucking lying. He wouldn't."

I'd hit my mark. For a moment, I wondered if I'd done the right thing. Then my heart hardened.

My strength surged, fueled by the vampire blood coursing through my veins. Blake's power was amplifying everything–the thrill of the fight, the sight of Regan beneath me, suddenly vulnerable and exposed. The power was intoxicating.

Regan thrashed and let out a scream of rage.

"Believe what you want," I murmured. "But we both know it's true."

A flash of silver. Before I could react, the sharp bite of steel sliced into my shoulder. Pain flared. But the wound didn't paralyze me as it should have. My vision sharpened as I turned and saw Gretchen, her hand still outstretched.

The rage inside of me was rising, burning hotter by the second, the pull in my blood urging me onwards to kill, kill, kill the ones who were trying to hurt me.

Don't lose yourself, Medra. Focus. My mother's voice. *All you need is to get out of here.*

I shut it down, ignoring her.

Bloodlust coursed through me. Urging me to end this, to finish it once and for all. These girls wanted me dead. They were here to kill me.

Why shouldn't I return the favor?

I yanked the knife from my shoulder, my eyes narrowing with fury, and threw it back at Gretchen with all my strength. The blade hit the highblood girl square in the face, slicing her cheek open. She screamed, clutching at the flap of skin as she stumbled backwards, blood pouring from between her fingers.

"Bitch," Regan screamed. "You think you're better at us just because you've been sipping from Blake's cup? You lying little cheat."

"Cheat?" I glared down at her. "Oh, that's rich coming from you."

I grabbed Regan's wrist, twisting unmercifully and the rapier fell to the ground. I grabbed it and held it over her face. It would be so easy. So easy to let go and finish it. To never have to look at Regan again.

Unbidden, Florence's face came to my mind. Her calm steady gaze. The kindness of her smile.

I took a deep breath and tossed the rapier far into the trees.

Just as I began to relax, the arrow whistled through the air, striking me in the other shoulder.

I gasped, the force of it knocking me off Regan and onto the ground. My vision blurred for a moment from the pain. But through the haze, I could already feel the wound beginning to heal.

"Not... like... this..." I growled, the blood pounding in my ears.

I yanked the arrow out of my shoulder, ignoring the pain as I cast it aside. Regan was already coming towards me. I moved faster, catching her by the ankle and tossing her to the ground, then leaping atop her. I pulled the dagger from my boot, throwing the sheath onto the ground and held it poised over her face.

I saw the look of terror in her eyes, the raw fear.

You might need her. Think carefully, Orcades' voice warned.

For a moment, I didn't care. I wanted to let the bloodlust take me over completely. This rush felt good. I could bury Coregon's dagger in Regan's evil little heart and be done with it. After all, she deserved it after everything she'd done to me.

I pulled my arm back, then lifted my hand and struck Regan directly under the chin with the heel of my palm. For a moment, her head rocked back and forth. Then her body went limp.

Breathing heavily, I stood up and turned my gaze to Quinn, who still sat up in the tree, her bow drawn.

"I don't want to kill you," I called up to her. "But I will if I have to."

Quinn let the arrow fly.

CHAPTER 52

BLAKE

Theo turned towards me. "What did you do?" he hissed.

We could see everything the consorts were experiencing. We couldn't hear them though.

Still, it wasn't too hard to figure out what was going on between Pendragon and Regan. Or to see that something in Pendragon had changed.

She'd started off slow. I'd been terrified for her. Regan had clearly paid someone off because the drugs they gave the consorts weren't supposed to linger in their systems for that long. Pendragon had nearly missed the first challenge altogether.

When she'd made it across the gorge, I'd breathed a sigh of relief. Thank the fucking Bloodmaiden for Visha. She'd lingered far longer than I thought she would, ignoring Evander's clear pleas to get going. The girl had a backbone of steel and some serious potential.

I glanced at Theo. He didn't trust me and while I understood that, it also didn't make him great right hand material.

Theo was still looking at me expectantly.

I shrugged him off. "I did what I had to."

"You're insane," he whispered. "This could ruin everything. You put her at risk."

"At risk? I saved her. Regan was going to cheat anyway," I hissed. My gaze lingered on the images up on the veil, on Pendragon and the way she moved–stronger, faster than she'd ever been before.

Theo's jaw tightened. "Still, you know this isn't how it's supposed to go. They're supposed to work together. Not…" He gestured helplessly at the projection just as Pendragon pulled the knife out of her boot. Regan might have managed to arrange for a little extra drugging but I'd snuck a surprise in for Pendragon, too. Good thing I had since Regan and her friends had brought their own surprises with them. "Whatever the fuck this is. It's all falling apart. If Viktor catches wind of it..."

"I'll handle it, Theo," I interrupted, forcing myself to remain calm. "Don't worry about it."

Consorts weren't meant to destroy each other like this and the whole thing didn't exactly reflect well on House Drakharrow. But Regan had set the whole thing in motion as soon as she'd pulled Gretchen and Quinn into her scheming. She'd tried to stack the odds, to sabotage Pendragon from the start. I was just leveling the playing field. Or at least, that's what I was telling myself.

I risked a glance at where Headmaster Kim was sitting further down the tiers. His eyes were glued to the veil, his face impassive. As far as I could tell, he didn't look as if he were about to jump up from his seat and call the whole thing off. I doubted he'd interfere.

But as for what came after the Games were over? That was a toss up.

All I knew was, I'd protect Pendragon. No matter what.

Regan was on her own now. It was only a matter of how long it would take her to realize she was out in the cold.

I watched Pendragon deal with Quinn, then stand over Regan.

She wasn't going to kill her. I knew that. But it took her a moment to come to that realization. My blood was flowing through her, making the urge to violence stronger than it would normally be. It was actually incredible how well she was resisting its pull.

"How goes it, little brother?"

My head jerked up. My brother Marcus stood there, pale blue eyes looking down at me coldly. His mouth curved up in an arrogant smile.

Looking at my older brother was like looking in a mirror in some ways. Standing a few inches shorter than me—something that never failed to drive him crazy, Marcus was stockier and broader, with a physique built for raw strength rather than finesse. His pale, silvery-blond hair was cropped shorter than my own. His jawline had more of a square cut to it, too.

He was an intimidating bastard, I'd give him that. The scars that littered his arms and neck were reminders of his ruthless exploits. I wondered whether the consort he'd murdered had left any marks behind on my brother. I hoped so. She'd certainly earned it.

Viktor loved Marcus's brutality—as long as he was the one wielding it.

Knowing he had our uncle's favor just made Marcus more dangerous. His smile rarely reached his eyes and when it did, it was usually at someone else's expense.

Like mine, right now.

Beside me, I felt Theo tense, shrinking into himself. He hated Marcus. I didn't blame him.

Marcus swaggered down the step and slid into our row, forcing me over.

"Well, well," he drawled, his eyes moving to the screen. "Your little dragon rider's doing better than I would have expected, brother. Must be a lot of work keeping those two ladies in line outside of the Games though. You ever need any advice on how to manage them both, you know where to find me."

I kept my eyes forward.

But Marcus didn't do well with being ignored.

"What's up with Theo? He looks as if he's seen a ghost. What's got you so nervous, cuz?" Marcus leaned around me to ruffle Theo's hair like he was a child.

Theo flinched but didn't say a word.

"Leave him alone, Marcus," I growled.

Marcus smirked. "Relax. I'm just having fun. We're family for fuck's sake. Theo knows I'm only playing, don't you, cousin?" He lowered his voice and leaned closer. "It's funny though. I've always thought it's pathetic how soft you are with him. You think you're really doing him a favor by coddling him?"

My fists clenched, but Marcus wasn't through. His gaze shifted to the veil projection where Pendragon's figure was moving swiftly through the island terrain.

He whistled, long and low. "Pretty thing, isn't she? Those long legs. That tight ass. I can see why you've bailed on Regan. Really, I can."

My head snapped towards my brother. I glared at him.

Marcus grinned, clearly relishing my reaction. "Careful, little brother," he drawled. "She might not stay yours for very long. Uncle Viktor has his eyes on her. Hell, I might just take a liking to her myself. You know I've been looking for a replacement for Allessandra."

I tried to control my breathing. "You still have Amaris."

Marcus scowled. "She's no good by herself. She's gotten boring."

I didn't point out that this was probably because Marcus had killed her twin sister.

There was no way my brother was getting within an inch of Pendragon. I'd fucking die before I let that happen.

Marcus tilted his head towards mine. "I'm sure I could make her scream in a whole new way," he said, his voice dipping suggestively.

My restraint shattered. I shot to my feet, my muscles coiled. Theo looked up at me in a silent plea for me to stay calm, but I ignored him.

"You think you could handle her, Marcus?" I hissed, my voice low and deadly. "She's stronger than she looks. You're not taking anything from me. Especially not Pendragon. Our bond's nearly complete, and you know what that means."

My older brother's grin faltered, a hint of uncertainty betraying his bullshit bravado. "Is that so?" he asked, trying to sound nonchalant. "Uncle Viktor didn't think you'd gotten far."

"I was planning on surprising him with the news," I lied. "He told me to keep her controlled and soon she'll be mine. Fully bonded. And there won't be anything you or Viktor or anyone else can do about it."

Marcus's lips curled in annoyance. "We'll see about that," he said, rising to his feet, his playful tone gone.

I stabbed him in the chest with my finger. "Why don't you scurry back to Uncle Viktor like a good little fucking lap dog and tell him I have everything under control?"

Marcus's body went tense. If we weren't in the middle of a crowd of people, I knew he'd have decked me one.

"This isn't over, little brother," he muttered, as he moved into the aisle.

I sat back down, trying to calm the fire inside of me.

"You shouldn't have said that," Theo groaned. "Now he'll come after her for sure."

I knew Theo was right. Still, "Let them try," I muttered.

CHAPTER 53

MEDRA

Instinct kicked in. Highblood instinct. Blake's instinct.

Before I even had time to think my hand had shot out and with a sharp, audible snap, I caught the arrow mid-flight.

I stared down at it in disbelief, my palm wrapped around the shaft.

Above me, Quinn froze, her eyes wide.

For a long moment, we simply stared at each other.

Then something stirred inside me. A savage urge rising to the surface, too powerful to resist.

Blake's blood had flipped a switch in me, igniting something dark and wild.

My muscles tensed with inhuman power, Blake's blood and my rider's body meshing together in a ferocious combination.

I lunged towards the tree and before Quinn could even blink, I'd scaled the trunk, clambering from branch to branch with skill not fully my own.

I landed beside Quinn on the tree limb where she sat, my feet hardly making a sound.

She let out a strangled gasp and scrambled backwards.

But there was nowhere she could go.

I moved towards her and this time, I didn't stop. I didn't hold back.

I drove the arrow into her side, ignoring the sickening sound of flesh tearing. Quinn gasped, her eyes widening with shock as the force of the strike pushed her out of the tree.

Her body crashed through the branches as it plummeted down before hitting the ground with a thud.

I dropped down to the forest floor beside her, landing lightly on my feet.

For a moment, I stood there, looking at my fallen opponents.

Regan's unconscious body was still sprawled in the dirt. Now Quinn lay gasping in pain beside her.

I felt nothing. Certainly not guilt.

I turned and walked out of the clearing, Blake's blood still pulsing in my ears.

I stood at the top of a hill, looking down at the scene in front of me.

A domed stone building lay in the distance, silhouetted against the sea. A dock lay behind it with small boats tied up. I assumed this was how they were getting us home. Those of us who made it that far, anyhow.

Below, I could see Visha and Evander waiting near the entrance. They weren't alone. There was a line of other consorts ahead of them. All anxiously awaiting their turn.

As I came down the hill, Visha rushed up. "Have you seen Regan?"

I blinked. "You told me to avoid her."

Still, the guilt must have shown on my face.

Visha's eyes narrowed. "But you didn't, did you?"

"I had no choice," I admitted. "She ambushed me. Gretchen and Quinn were with her."

The hint of a smile crossed Visha's face. "Gretchen limped down here a while ago, looking a little worse for wear. Her consort is furious at her." She tilted her head. "But Regan? You didn't kill her, did you? I sure hope not, because you're going to need her."

My eyes widened. "What? Please tell me you're joking. I thought you said you or Evander would help me."

"Is she dead or not?"

"No, but I knocked her out. I left her back there." I gestured to the forest behind me. "Way back there."

Visha cast a quick glance at the line of consorts. "Well, you'd better go get her. You need your consort for the next test and a substitute won't cut it. Both of you need to spill a drop of blood into some bowl before you're allowed to enter the dome. And once you enter, you don't come out again. If you can't find Regan, you're both going to be screwed. Evander and I can't help you." She had the decency to look sympathetic but that wasn't much consolation.

"Fuck," I swore. "I can't believe this."

Visha chewed her lip. "I'd help you go and get her if I could. But Evander..."

The tall, silver-haired boy was standing at the end of the line, watching Visha and I.

I nodded. "I understand. It's not fair to him." Just like being paired with Regan had never been fair to me. I glanced over at the domed building. "What's waiting for us in there anyhow?"

Visha hesitated. For a moment, the fierce, unshakeable girl looked uncertain. "I don't know exactly." But something in her voice told me she did know. She just didn't want to tell me. "But I have a bad feeling about it."

I ran a hand over my hair, brushing loose tendrils off my forehead. "Great. Fantastic."

I turned away, my boots digging into the dirt as I started my trek back up the hill.

"What are you going to do?" Visha called.

"Get Regan," I shouted from over my shoulder. "I'll drag her back here if I have to."

But when I arrived at the clearing, it was empty.

Regan and Quinn were gone.

I cursed under my breath, eyes narrowing as I scanned the ground.

Broken twigs. Flattened earth. Quinn's blood on the grass.

I crouched down, touching the spot where I'd knocked Regan out. If only I'd made her bleed a little. Would dried blood count for the next challenge? Quinn had left plenty but it wasn't hers I needed.

I took a deep breath, inhaling, my senses prickling with clarity.

There it was. Regan's scent. Sweat mixed with dirt. The hint of lavender and musk. Apparently Regan had managed a spritz of perfume, even in the jungle.

Quinn's scent hung in the air, too. The tang of her blood mixed with fear and dirt and sweat.

I sniffed in one direction, then another.

They'd split up. Regan had gone one way and Quinn another. Why hadn't they stayed together?

How did I even know any of this?

There was more to it than Blake's blood. My mind flashed to Rodriguez's cryptic words about my rider's heritage. Was this what he'd meant? Could I activate some instinctive ancient training?

I had no dragon, but the instincts of a rider were in my bones. Blake's blood must have been intensifying them somehow, stirring up senses I had no idea I'd even possessed.

I was born to do this, I told myself, trying to channel tranquility. Sure, the effects wouldn't last. But they were useful for now.

I took another deep breath, letting my senses guide me, honing in on Regan's scent while ignoring the alluring aroma of Quinn's fresh blood. I wasn't a highblood. I didn't need blood. I needed Regan Pansera.

I could feel her pull now, faint but present.

I turned in the direction she'd gone.

Dodging low-hanging vines and branches, I moved as quickly as I dared. Each step felt purposeful. My body knew where it was going. My blood was guiding me.

All right, so a little of Blake's was in the mix, too.

Regan's scent grew stronger, sharper, as I ran through the dense foliage.

I leaped over fallen logs, my steps light, all trace of dizziness and grogginess gone. I'd never felt so attuned to my surroundings. So powerful.

Suddenly, the scent faded.

I slowed my pace, heart pounding with anticipation.

I felt like a predator. A hunter.

Was this how Blake felt all the time? With me?

Regan was close. I could almost taste her. When I found her, I knew I'd have to control myself. Control that part of me that was Blake, the part of him that wanted to kill, wanted to feed. I suddenly wondered how he managed to keep himself in check at Bloodwing. Was this how he felt when he was near me? Was this how all highbloods felt all of the time? It was an uncomfortable idea.

A new thought came to me. I slid Coregon's dagger down my palm, then began to turn in a slow circle, holding the knife outwards slightly.

It's your turn to shine, I muttered to Orcades. *Time to step up.*

Dear girl, I thought you'd never ask, came my mother's voice. *But do try not to kill Regan when you do catch her. From what Visha told you, it sounds as if you need her alive.*

I'll do my best to resist, I said grudgingly. *But she started it.*

Orcades laughed. *She's in the trees. Get ready.*

Taking a page from Quinn's playbook, is she? I grumbled. *Where?*

Jump to the left, Orcades snapped. *Now.*

I did as she said, tumbling to the side then springing back to my feet.

Regan hit the ground with a grunt of shock. She'd expected me to be her landing pad but I'd denied her that.

I walked up, sorely tempted to kick her in the ribs.

Instead, with a sigh, I offered her my hand.

"Fuck off, bitch," she groaned gracelessly. She had a hand to her head. I guess I'd hurt her more than I'd realized when I knocked her out. But she was still walking and talking, so it must not have been that bad. "And give you a chance to stab me with that dagger? I don't think so."

So she was unarmed. She hadn't found her rapier in the bushes. Good. I'd wondered about that.

I sheathed the dagger, tucked it back into my boot, and held up my hands. "I'm not going to stab you, Regan."

"Why'd you come back?" she asked sulkily.

"The real question is, why are you still here?" I said, shaking my head as I looked at her wobbling on her feet. "Why didn't you head to the other side of the island?"

"I got lost," she admitted. "Quinn left me. No thanks to you."

I snorted. "Right. I'm so sorry your two pals got hurt trying to kill me. They got what they deserved."

"And now you're here to finish me off while they're not around," she hissed.

I rolled my eyes. "Tempting though that idea is, it turns out I need you."

I took a step towards her. "Let me rephrase that. We need each other. If you want to get out of this place. Unless you'd rather live up in the trees for the rest of your days."

"Blake helped you," she spat. "He gave you his blood. He obviously doesn't care if I live or die here."

We had to hurry. There wasn't much time left. I thought of the line of consorts. We'd be the last ones to arrive if this kept up. I wondered how long it took each pair to get through whatever challenge they had to face in the dome.

"Can we speed this up or do you have a long self-pitying monologue planned?" I said, waving my hand. "You can hash things out with your boyfriend when we get back."

"He's not my fucking boyfriend and you know it. He hasn't let me into his room in months. Not since you got here."

I hadn't actually known that. Theo had suggested it, yes.

I must have been shallower than I thought though because a warm feeling of relief flowed through me.

"Not my problem," I lied. "Tell someone who cares. What matters is that we're both stuck with him for now. So let's just get out of here."

I took another step towards her. "You can hardly stand. Don't make this harder for yourself. If I have to, I'll tie you up and carry you."

Regan lifted her eyes upwards as if we were being watched.

Which, I suddenly realized, we were. We were a spectacle for the entire school. Just like Blake had been that day in the arena when he'd had to kill Coregon.

"Can they hear us, too?" I asked her, suddenly curious.

She shook her head. "No, thank the fucking Bloodmaid."

Good. So they hadn't heard what I'd told Regan about Blake helping me with his blood. I felt oddly relieved. I didn't want him to get into trouble, not when what he'd done for me had actually worked.

"What's the point?" Regan whined. "I'm probably going to get kicked out of the triad, kicked out of Bloodwing. I'll be a laughingstock." She kicked at a rock, her pretty face petulant.

I really doubted I'd be that lucky. But I bit my tongue.

"Get a grip, Regan. If you don't get out, what'll happen? We'll live on this island together forever? I can think of a long list of people I'd rather be stranded with."

"Live?" Regan laughed nastily. "Oh, no, we won't *live*. They'll kill us both. But knowing I took you down with me might make it worth it." She tilted her head as if considering the option.

I clenched my jaw. "Or you can live another day and plot your revenge."

She eyed me thoughtfully. "Appealing. Slightly more appealing."

"Good. Then let's get going," I snapped, losing patience with her. "Everyone was already there. Except you and Quinn. We're going to be the last."

I started striding back through the jungle, praying she'd follow and I wouldn't have to do what I'd threatened and actually carry her. I felt powerful enough to manage it, but she'd severely slow me down.

Within a minute, I heard the snap of twigs and rustle of grass as she trailed after me.

"What exactly do you need me for?" she asked after a few minutes had passed. "What's the next challenge?"

"All I know is they need some of each of our blood. We have to enter a domed building together. No one seems to know what's inside." Well, Visha might have had a pretty good idea. Though she hadn't wanted to tell me.

"Did Visha tell you that?" Regan guessed. "That traitorous bitch. How dare she take Blake's side."

"Yes, you seem to have a lot of traitors in your life," I quipped. "Once we're out of here, you might want to do some soul-searching about why that is."

"I think I'd rather drink a few thralls and fix my broken nails instead, thanks." She sighed and I didn't have to turn my head to know she was looking at her hands. "Fuck. They'll never be the same."

I held back the comments that were on the tip of my tongue and instead continued leading the way back to the dome.

CHAPTER 54

MEDRA

We were the last ones.

The outskirts of the dome were empty as we approached.

The pair of heavy stone doors leading the way inside sat slightly ajar.

In front of them was a stone pillar topped with a small offering bowl and a knife. Despite the many pairs of consorts who had come before us, the bowl was empty and the knife was clean.

Another highblood mystery. I wondered if Professor Wispwood had been here, working her magic.

"Well, this is it," I muttered, glancing at Regan. "You want to go first or should I do the honors?"

Regan lifted her chin. "I always go first, Pendragon." She stepped forward and lifted up the ritual knife. With a swift motion, she cut a small mark in her palm and let a few drops of blood dribble into the bowl.

The stone doors groaned, cracking open further, but not fully. We were only halfway there.

"Your turn," Regan said, holding the blade out to me.

Instinctively I reached for it.

The second my fingers brushed the handle, Regan yanked the blade forward, slicing it across my forearm instead of my palm. I gasped as blood poured from the wound into the offering bowl.

"What the hell?" I hissed, clutching my arm as crimson continued to drip onto the ground. Yet I could already feel Blake's blood working inside me, healing me. The tear in my flesh was starting to close.

Regan smiled darkly. "Whoops. Sorry. My hand must have slipped."

I glared at her as the doors opened with an ominous creak.

Regan laughed and strode into the building without a backwards glance.

Resisting the urge to pull her back by the hair, I took a deep breath and then quickly tore a piece of cloth from the edge of my shirt to wrap my arm, before following her.

Inside the dome, the atmosphere was cold.

Darkness swallowed us as soon as we entered. But as the doors slammed shut behind us, torches flared to life one by one around the walls.

I glanced at the wall to my left and then stepped up to it, grabbing the two swords that had been hanging there. Beside them hung two small shields, bucklers. I tossed one of each to Regan and she caught them.

"Try not to stab me in the back," I muttered.

She batted her eyelashes. "I make no promises."

We walked inside the interior of the dome. It was a lot like the arena. A central, circular chamber with a domed roof. There were no tiers of seats though. The building was empty except for us.

Almost empty.

Two creatures stepped out slowly from the shadows as more torches along the walls flared up to illuminate them.

I froze.

Beside me, Regan was shaking her head. "You've got to be kidding me," she said, sounding annoyed. She took up a fighting stance and brandished her sword as the two creatures slowly advanced. "Not these things again. They used these last year. Can't they come up with anything better for these pathetic losers when they flunk out?"

I couldn't even find the words to answer. All I could do was stare.

The creatures were grotesque amalgamations of what had once been students–blight-born students. Human flesh had been combined with arachnid traits. Legs split into eight limbs. Mouths split into mandibles that dripped and clicked as they moved.

From what Regan had just said, it sounded as if this was a common challenge in the Games. Turning former students into monstrosities.

I thought of all the consorts who had come before us. Of all the battles that had already been fought in the dome today.

Maybe, just maybe I could have steeled myself to face those...things. If one of the students hadn't been someone I knew.

Naveen scuttled slowly towards me, the twisted creature that held his soul a horrible mockery of the sweet, goofy boy he had once been.

His brown skin, once warm and full of life, had taken on a sickly, blotchy hue. Patches of thick, dark hair sprouted in uneven clusters along his arms and back. Where his legs should have been were now eight jointed limbs, thin and spindly, jutting from his sides. They bent and clicked unnaturally as he moved in stilted steps.

His back was hunched, the spider-like limbs supporting a stretched, elongated frame, hardly human at all, giving him a lopsided, horrifyingly insectoid appearance.

And his face. Oh, gods, his face. His boyish features were twisted into a nightmare, eyes bulging and black like a spider's, devoid of all human emotion. Predatory. Rapacious. Sharp mandibles extended from his mouth, twitching grotesquely and dripping with a viscous liquid.

Beside me, Regan was unphased. If anything, she seemed amused by my horror.

She gave a low, mocking chuckle. "Get a grip, Pendragon. Choking up already? Guess I don't need to worry about planning my revenge after all. Your little friend is going to finish you off before I can."

She darted across the room as my stomach turned. Part of me wanted to slap her sideways. But Naveen–if any part of him really was Naveen anymore–took another step closer and my focus shifted back.

From the corner of my eye, I saw Regan engage the second monster. A spider-like creature I could just barely recognize as a First Year girl. She'd shared a piece of parchment with me in History of Sangratha once.

I turned back to Naveen, trying to block out the pain I was feeling.

I forced myself to shove away the memories of Naveen's infectious laughter in class. His goofy smile. Tried to forget about how he'd never be able to tell Florence how he felt now. He'd never be able to tell us anything again.

My hands were trembling. I wanted to run but there was nowhere to go.

Naveen lunged.

I barely raised my buckler in time. The force of the blow sent me stumbling backwards, arm throbbing from the impact.

He was fast. One of his legs caught me in the side, slicing through my shirt. Pain bloomed instantly.

He was moving again, his spider limbs propelling him forward with terrifying speed.

I dodged, rolling to the side as Naveen's mandibles snapped down inches from my face.

The air was filled with the clicking and clattering of his legs as he turned to face me again.

"I can't do this. I fucking *can't*." I heard my voice crack.

You have to. You have to be strong, Orcades' voice insisted, piercing through the fog. *You have to let go of him. He's gone, Medra. This isn't him. Not anymore.*

I drew a deep sobbing breath. *It's too hard. Those motherfuckers. They planned it. All of it.*

There was a pause, as if she was hesitating. *The crown.*

No, I said. *No, no, no.* Then I thought of the dream I'd woken up from. Of Professor Wispwood lifting the circlet off my head.

The pain stung even worse. *They made me choose,* I said hollowly. *They got into my head and they made me choose this. I did this.*

You didn't choose this, Orcades insisted. *Not consciously.*

But I did. It could have been Florence.

Florence, the sweet, smart, bookish girl who I had come to love like a sister.

The crown had sat atop my head, piercing my thoughts with its bitter powers. And it had seen something I'd never have admitted out loud. That I loved Florence more than Naveen. It had taken my two dearest friends and made a mockery of friendship, of love, of loyalty.

The only thing you can do for Naveen now, my mother said, *is let him die with dignity.*

Dignity? I let out a choking hiccuping sob and rolled away as another spider-like limb pierced down where I'd just been. *How can there be any dignity when they've done this to him?*

It's a mercy killing, my mother said softly. *Think of the boy's parents.*

I knew she was right. That didn't make it feel any less like a betrayal.

The creature that was once Naveen let out an inhuman screech and darted towards me with unnatural speed. I dodged, but this time I wasn't fast enough. Maybe I didn't want to be.

One of his long, spindly legs caught my side, slashing me open with sharp, needle-like claws.

I knocked it aside with the buckler, then rolled away, clutching at my ribs, feeling the blood seep through my fingers.

For a moment, pain coursed through me and the thought crossed my mind: What if I just let it happen? Blake's blood couldn't heal me fast enough if I just let Naveen attack me over and over again. It would be painful but quick. This entire nightmare would finally be over. I'd have escaped.

Don't you dare, my mother's voice warned sternly. *You end him now before he ends you. Think beyond yourself. Beyond this moment. Take courage. Beyond the darkness lies the light.*

Light.

I tried to do as she said. I thought of Florence. Her kindness and her brilliance.

I thought of Blake, whose bullying had evolved into a strange protection. Blake who I couldn't quite bring myself to fully hate.

I even thought of the fluffin, ridiculous Neville with his soft fur and happy nature, scooting back and forth across the school, unable to decide if he belonged to Florence or to Blake. He saw something good in each of them, something maybe even I hadn't fully glimpsed yet.

They were waiting for me. Blake didn't want me to fail. He'd given me his blood to make sure I got out of here.

I thought of Naveen's parents. My heart ached. I owed them this much. Their son deserved a peaceful end. Better he find his rest at my hands than at Regan's.

Tears blurred my vision. I blinked them away, determination filling my chest.

The spider-creature charged again, its legs clattering against the floor in a horrifying rhythm.

I dodged to the side, ignoring the sting of my wound.

I was faster this time. I didn't hesitate.

I swiped at one of the spider's legs, severing it at the joint. Naveen screeched in agony, staggering back.

I thought of Florence, watching back at Bloodwing, and the tears poured down my face.

I knew what I had to do. But my sword felt heavy in my hand.

Naveen lunged again. I tried to block but one of his massive legs crashed into my sword arm, knocking the blade from my grip. It fell to the floor, skidding out of reach.

I ducked down, yanking Coregon's dagger free from my boot.

Let's finish this, my mother murmured softly. *Together.*

Naveen darted forward again but I was ready. I dove and drove the dagger into the spider's capacious chest, right where its heart should have been. I ripped the knife savagely back and forth, tearing a wide swathe in the creature's underside.

Guts and viscous black fluid rained down on me. I gagged. Overhead, the spider-creature convulsed violently and collapsed.

I stood over it, looking down into its black eyes. Was Naveen still in there? Looking back at me somehow?

I wiped at the tears on my cheeks, my heart heavy.

I could taste the blood magic, my mother said, her voice filled with disgust. *The dark sorcery that bound him. His soul was already gone. You just gave his body peace.*

I nodded, closing my eyes, trying to let the weight of her words sink in fully. Naveen had already been lost. The highbloods did this to him, not me.

But I couldn't escape the feeling of guilt. The Crown of Bone had been placed upon my head. I was the culpable one.

From across the room, I heard a scream. My eyes snapped open.

Regan was fighting her own monster. Blood ran down her arms as she raised her sword, trying to keep the creature at bay.

Her cocky arrogance had fled.

You don't owe her anything, my mother reminded me.

I glanced across the room. The doors on the opposite side had opened halfway. I could slip through them, leaving Regan behind.

Regan had tried to kill me. She might put things to rest after this. Or she might do it again.

Leaving her would be the justice she deserved.

I clenched my teeth. *I can't.*

Cursing under my breath, I sprinted across the room. The creature had cornered Regan, its long legs pinning her to the floor.

I didn't hesitate, I threw my buckler at the spider-like monster, hitting it square in the back.

The creature shrieked and turned towards me. I refused to look it in the eyes. A First Year girl. This was a First Year girl once.

"Hey!" I shouted, waving my arms like an idiot and backing away. "Come and get me!"

Behind the creature, Regan was rolling to her feet. She grabbed the sword she'd dropped as I continued to distract the spider, trying to give her the opening she needed.

It was enough.

Regan ran forward and plunged her sword into the creature's side, piercing its hide. She withdrew the sword and stabbed it again, then a third time. The monster screeched and writhed, collapsing to the floor.

Regan wiped the blood from the blade on her thigh and shot me a haughty look I knew only too well.

"What took you so long?"

I bit back a retort.

We didn't say another word to one another as we turned and headed towards the doors.

CHAPTER 55

MEDRA

Two days later, I sat on my bed in the First Year dorm, knees pulled up, arms wrapped around them. Beside me, Florence leaned against my side, her head on my shoulder. We'd both been crying.

The weather reflected both our moods. Storm clouds were gathering outside the diamond latticed windows.

The skin around my eyes felt as if it had been rubbed raw from all of the tears I'd shed since the Games had ended.

But the tears weren't the worst part. What I couldn't escape was the guilt that twisted inside me like a knife, sharp and relentless.

Florence shifted, wiping at her red eyes. "I can't believe he's really gone," she whispered, for what must have been the hundredth time that day.

I slipped my arm around her. This wasn't about me, I reminded myself. It was about Florence. It was about Naveen's parents.

I'd already started writing the Sharmas a letter. Florence said she'd write one, too, and we could send them together.

"A few days before the Games," Florence said suddenly. "Naveen said he had something to tell me."

I froze. "He did? What did he say?"

"I think you already know." Florence's voice was small. "He said you'd already guessed."

"Oh, Florence." I sighed. "He told you how he felt about you?"

I felt her nod. "He told me he loved me. I didn't know what to say. I told him... I told him I needed time to think."

Her voice cracked and I tightened my hold on her.

I felt her start to sob. "But I'll never be able to talk to him again now. I asked for time but he had no time left. I didn't know."

My throat constricted. I wanted to comfort my friend, wanted to say the right words.

But every moment we sat here together it was all I could do to keep the torrent of guilt from slipping out of my throat.

It was my fault, I silently chanted. I'm sorry. It was my fault. I did this. Forgive me.

I'd saved Florence. I'd doomed Naveen.

How could I ever tell Florence any of that? How could I tell her I'd somehow made a choice that had cost our friend his life?

I swallowed hard. Even so, my voice trembled when I spoke. "Florence..." I shouldn't ask. I didn't really want to know. "Were you in love with him, too?" The words tumbled out.

There was a long silence. I hated myself for asking.

"Never mind, you don't have to answer that," I said. "I'm so sorry for asking, Florence..."

"I... I don't even know," Florence whispered, interrupting. "I didn't have a chance to figure it out. I thought there would be time. I thought maybe we could try..."

She broke off, turning her head and burrowing it against my shoulder.

I bit my lip hard enough to taste blood.

Naveen was gone. Florence had lost her chance. What if this was it for them? True love. What if they'd been meant to be together and now they'd both lost their chance at happiness?

If it hadn't been for the crown, Naveen might still be alive. There were other kids like him, students who hadn't passed the year at Bloodwing, who were being kicked out in disgrace but hadn't been killed. I'd heard most were being sent to highblood households to work as servants. Indentured labor. It was horrible, but at last they were still alive. They hadn't all been sent to be slaughtered in that domed arena, as sick tests for us to pass or fail.

There was a soft knock at the door.

We both tensed. Florence quickly wiped at her eyes with one of the many handkerchiefs littering the bed. But it was no use. Her face was flushed and blotchy. I was sure mine was no better.

I stood up stiffly, my limbs heavy from sitting for so long.

I ran my hands through my hair. I hadn't brushed it in days. Taking care of myself had somehow seemed wrong. As if I didn't deserve it. Living should have been enough, shouldn't it?

I opened the door and there stood Blake.

For a second, I forgot to breathe. I'd forgotten how beautiful he could be.

Even now, looking disheveled and awkward and out of place.

He looked as if he hadn't slept in days. There were dark circles under his eyes. His usual cool, composed confidence was nowhere to be seen. He wore a white shirt. The top buttons were undone, revealing a pale triangle of skin with curling gold hairs and a glimpse of the black dragon. His sleeves were rolled up, baring his well-muscled forearms. His hands were shoved into his pockets.

His gray eyes moved from me to Florence, then back to me.

He cleared his throat. "I'm sorry to interrupt."

He looked like he wanted to be anywhere other than where he was. Yet when my eyes met his, I saw something soften there.

"What is it?" I said, keeping my voice low.

Blake hesitated, glancing at Florence. Then his jaw clenched. "You need to come with me. Headmaster Kim has summoned us. We're being called into a disciplinary hearing."

Florence slid off the bed. "A hearing?"

She pushed past me, going straight for Blake. I'd never seen her like this. "What for? What's going to happen to Medra? Is she in trouble?"

Blake looked down at her, his gray eyes surprisingly kind. "I'm not sure," he said patiently. "But if she is, I'll be right there with her. I won't leave her to face it alone. I promise you that, Miss Shen."

Florence said nothing, just stared back at him. "All right," she said finally. "Don't you dare leave her with *him*."

She meant Headmaster Kim. I knew she blamed him the most for Naveen.

Still, I was shocked at how she'd spoken to Blake. She seemed to be getting over her diffidence towards highbloods. Or maybe it was just him.

Blake's eyes were still soft as he watched Florence climb back up onto the bed. "We have to go. Try not to worry. I'll have her back soon. I promise."

I crossed over to Florence and put my arms around her. She gripped my wrist.

"Go," she whispered. "I'll be fine. I might go back to my room and sleep."

I nodded. I hoped she'd be able to rest. She needed it.

I didn't want to leave her, but it looked as if I had no choice.

I followed Blake out the door.

CHAPTER 56

BLAKE

Pendragon suddenly seemed so small as she walked alongside me.

Her red curls hung around her face, frizzy and tangled. She wore a long black dress over the same pair of lace-up leather boots she'd worn in the Games. The dress hung on her frame. Even in just two days she seemed as if she'd lost weight.

I hated seeing her like this. I knew she was grieving. Her pale freckled skin was red and blotchy. I could tell she'd been crying.

Any other girl would have looked like a wreck. But not her.

It unnerved me how beautiful she still was. I'd missed the sight of her face.

I jammed my hands deeper in my pockets, resisting the urge to say that very thing out loud.

She looked frail. But I knew she wasn't. No matter what she might believe about herself right now, I knew she was strong.

I wished I could figure out the right thing to say. I wanted to tell her how every second of watching the Games had torn me up inside. It'd been the worst feeling in the world.

And then, seeing her have to fight her friend. My heart had ached for her.

But the words wouldn't come. I wasn't sure she'd even want to hear them. Not from me.

Or maybe I was worried I'd sound weak. Expose too much of this feeling crawling around inside of my chest.

So I stole glances. The distance between us feeling too close and too far all at the same time.

Then she shocked me by breaking the silence.

"I wanted to thank you."

I blinked in surprise. "What?"

"I owe you a debt. What you did, making me drink your blood–it probably saved my life." She stopped, turned to look up at me. "If you hadn't given it to me..."

Regan and the others would have killed her. She wouldn't be standing here by my side now.

I'd almost lost her.

I felt my breath catch. The whole time I'd been watching her, I'd wondered if she hated me for making her drink it. Yet now here she was, thanking me for making her do something she still didn't fully understand the consequences of. Something inside me twisted and stabbed. Claws of shame. Claws of guilt.

"You don't owe me anything," I said stiffly. "I'm just glad you survived."

Her green eyes searched mine. "Is that why we're in trouble? Because of your blood?"

She didn't know the half of it.

I ran a hand through my hair. "No. At least, I don't think so. There's more to it than that. Though I did break the rules by giving it to you."

I wanted to shield her from the confrontation that was coming up. I wished I could ask her what she wanted me to do if things went in a certain direction.

My thoughts kept circling back to Regan and each time they did, my fury threatened to overflow. She'd defied me. Gone after Pendragon when they were supposed to work together. I'd known it was coming, but even so, when those three girls had cornered her, it could have turned into a bloodbath.

I wondered if Regan had known how close she'd come to dying that day.

Or how close she still was.

Pendragon had only survived the games because of the precautions I'd taken. Giving her my blood. Asking Visha to watch her back.

That, and her own strength and presence of mind. She hadn't panicked. Once the drugs had cleared from her system, she'd pulled herself together and done everything she'd had to do to survive. Even when it meant killing one of her best friends. She'd passed every test they'd thrown at her and I was proud of her. So fucking proud.

I thought of Coregon. Pendragon and I had that in common now. We'd both killed a friend.

I doubted it would be something we'd fondly reminisce about together.

Visha. Panic struck me. I wondered if she'd told Pendragon the truth about that first day in the training yard. Visha had taken things further than she was supposed to, so I'd had to get Sankara to intervene. Even so, I'd initiated the set-up. If Pendragon ever found out, she'd be furious.

The fact that she was walking here so calmly beside me now, thanking me, must have meant Visha had kept quiet.

I stayed close to her as we approached the headmaster's office.

We stepped inside, and the atmosphere hit me like a wall of ice.

Kim sat behind his desk, his dark robes draped around him. His sharp eyes flicked upwards as we entered and it was as if the weight of all Bloodwing's expectations bore down on me. There was and never had been anything comforting about Headmaster Kim. He was the cold, uncompromising face of highblood authority at Bloodwing.

On the far right stood my uncle. Viktor Drakharrow, the living embodiment of high-blood privilege and familial intimidation. He was the oldest highblood in the room. He glanced my way, his eyes glowing deep and unsettling red. His eyes moved to Pendragon and I felt my skin crawl. I wanted to grab his chin and force his head in the other direction. Nothing about that dirty, disgusting old man should be near her.

I made myself look in the other direction and my eyes fell on Regan. She was seated in a wooden chair to the left of Kim's desk. She looked every bit the spoiled highblood princess, with her pointed chin held high and her mouth fixed in a smug pout. Behind her stood her father, Lord Pansera, a tall man with many of his daughter's features but even less of her charm. His gaze swept over Pendragon as if she were something stuck to the bottom of his boot.

My stomach tightened. I stayed close to Pendragon's side as the door clicked shut behind us.

Headmaster Kim cleared his throat. "I don't believe introductions are required. We are gathered here today to discuss the conduct of Blake Drakharrow's triad during the Consort Games. There are questions regarding the actions of his consorts, specifically the lack of cooperation between them, as well as several broken rules. Consequences must be determined."

My heart was already pounding. Clearly Regan's father was here to act as her repre-sentative to Kim. And ours? Good old Uncle Viktor.

There was no way I wanted Viktor defending Pendragon. I was here for her. I'd speak for her. If there were penalties to be paid, I'd take them upon myself. No one would harm a hair on her head.

Headmaster Kim was turning towards Regan. "Miss Pansera, a great deal of this centers around your conduct so let's begin with you. Would you care to explain your actions during the Games?"

Regan lifted her chin defiantly. "Explain? What's to explain? I did what I had to do," she said, her voice edged with prideful anger. "I wasn't going to sit back and watch while she—" She narrowed her eyes at Pendragon. "—made a mockery of our traditions. She doesn't belong in Blake's triad and she doesn't belong at Bloodwing." She looked over at Viktor. "With all respect, Lord Drakharrow, she never has and I hope the Games have proven this once and for all. She only survived because of me." She shot a glance at Pendragon, her eyes full of poison. "Did I want to cooperate with her? No, of course not! I wasn't about to trust my life to her incompetence."

Pendragon's hands were curled into fists by her side. I could see her shoulders shaking.

Everything Regan said had been lies.

Was Pendragon going to point that out? If she didn't, I would, I decided.

I took a step forward. "With all due respect to Miss Pansera," I said—in other words, none whatsoever. I turned to look at Regan, my eyes holding hers. "I'd be fully sympathetic to her dilemma if I didn't happen to know for a fact that every word out of her mouth was a lie. We *all* know that. We were as good as there. We saw exactly what happened. Miss Pansera—" I saw Regan stiffen a little more each time I used her title and not her first name. "Abandoned my consort and went off without her, leaving her to navigate the first challenge alone. It was only thanks to the selfless actions of Visha Vaidya and Evander Sylvain that my consort made it across at all." Giving Evander any credit was a little rich, but I figured mentioning his name wouldn't hurt. After all, the Sylvains were another powerful highblood family. "And what did Miss Pansera do next? Did she go to Miss Pendragon, apologize, and offer her assistance for the rest of the Games? No. She underhandedly and cowardly enlisted the help of two other consorts to try to murder Miss Pendragon."

Lord Pansera cut me off. "My daughter acted with the strength and resolve of a true highblood," he said, his voice firm. He refused to look at me. "She was placed in a completely untenable situation, paired with an unworthy blightborn girl who should never have been allowed to participate in those Games, let alone serve as a consort to an archon of one of our noblest families. If you ask me, that error is where the real problem lies."

He swept his gaze across the room, from Headmaster Kim to my uncle. "Lord Drakharrow, I understand the dilemma you faced that day in the Keep, with the heads of the other four houses all watching to see how you would react to this strange girl's arrival. But Medra Pendragon, this supposed *dragon rider–*" He fairly spat the words. "–is the reason things went wrong in the first place. She's the reason my daughter almost died. She lured us all in with blightborn trickery. There is nothing noble about her. And as even she admitted that first day, she is useless–for despite what we all may wish, there are *no dragons* and there never will be again. My daughter's triad has been doomed to failure from the moment it was formed, from the moment you allowed the blightborn girl to take up a place here where she does not belong. If you want to ensure the future success of your nephew and my daughter, I insist you cut her loose now. Expunge her from Sangratha." He turned to rest his eyes on Pendragon. "Execution is too good for her, as far as the Pansera family is concerned."

I growled low in my throat. "Watch yourself. If anyone deserves to be cut loose, it's your treacherous daughter."

I scanned the room. "Who requested the Crown of Bones be used on Pendragon?" I looked over at Regan. "It was you, wasn't it? I want you to admit it. You purposely tried to sabotage your fellow consort. You did so repeatedly, over and over. Every act of disloyalty you committed towards Pendragon was an act of disloyalty towards me and my house."

I could only hope Viktor would see it that way, too.

I could hardly stand to look at Regan. We'd grown up together. Our parents had been friends. Now the sight of her filled me with nothing but loathing. Had I really ever let that snake into my bed?

There was a tense, uncomfortable silence as Regan stared back at me, refusing to confess.

"It doesn't matter," Headmaster Kim finally interjected. "It doesn't matter who re-quested its use. The Crown of Bone was used fairly. We were within our rights to allow it. And your consort survived. That's all that matters."

I felt Pendragon tremble at my side. Yes, she'd survived. But what about her friend, Naveen? I knew she had to be thinking about him.

At least now she knew that the Crown of Bone had nothing to do with me. Its use had been cruel and monstrous. Even for fucking highbloods.

Regan's face twisted in frustration. "You think you're better than me, don't you Blake? Why, you're the biggest cheat of all. You used your own blood on her. Do you want to tell everyone about *that*?"

I'd known this was coming.

The air in the room took on a greater chill.

I felt my uncle's gaze hone in on me, razor sharp, even though I knew Marcus must have already told him what I'd done. Still, he stayed silent. I wondered what he was hoping the outcome of this hearing would be exactly. It was evident he had his own objectives in mind as usual.

I glanced down at the flame-haired woman by my side. I longed to wrap my arm around Pendragon's waist and hold her against me, giving her my strength, steadying her.

But I settled for going on the offense. "What of it? It was my right to protect my consort. Even if it was from her co-consort. I did what I had to do and I'd do it again in a heartbeat."

"If there's to be a punishment for what Blake did," Pendragon said, stepping forward, her voice cutting through the tension in the room. "Let it be mine to accept. I only did what was necessary to survive. I was desperate. I didn't want to go up against Regan. I didn't want to hurt anyone. I met with Regan before the Games and asked her to work with me. I truly tried. When she and Gretchen and Quinn came after me, I defended myself. But I tried to show restraint."

I couldn't help it. I chuckled. "You certainly did. Far more than most would have."

And now her restraint might actually pay off. If she'd dared to kill a highblood consort back on that island...

Headmaster Kim glared at me. But I knew he was thinking the same thing. She'd shown more self-control than any highblood in the room would have.

"It wasn't until Regan had no other choice that she agreed to work together," Pendragon continued. "And even then I had a choice. I could have left her alone in that dome to die when she was overwhelmed by the...creature. But I didn't. I helped her fight that monster. I didn't abandon her when I had the chance. Even though I know she'd have abandoned me."

I felt a rush of pride. What she spoke of was mercy. Not a trait typically valued at Bloodwing. Still, I wondered if Lord Pansera understood how close he'd come to losing his daughter because of her own petty selfishness.

I didn't see a thank you forming on his lips though. He wasn't about to stoop to thank a blightborn, no matter what she'd done for his family.

Kim was watching us carefully, his fingers steepled over his desk. "Typically, an archon strengthening a blightborn consort with his blood would not be condoned in the games. But nor would it have been necessary in the first place, for consorts are encouraged to help one another. In this case, many other rules had been broken first. Perhaps the first and foremost, the one which governs consort behavior. I've interviewed a number of Miss Pansera's friends. They've all testified that she was absolutely determined to refuse to assist Miss Pendragon in any way." He glanced at me. "I presume you learned of your consort's defiance beforehand?"

"I did. I learned of it and acted to thwart it," I said.

Kim's eyes flared with something like approval, which surprised me. "Very well. I see no reason to punish Medra Pendragon or Blake Drakharrow for what happened in the Games. Miss Pendragon acted primarily in self-defense. She drank her archon's blood at his command. Unlike Miss Pansera, she deferred to his instructions. She did not seek out an advantage intentionally."

I could feel Pendragon exhale beside me.

But Regan's fate still hung in the air. I wasn't about to let her off the hook so easily.

"Thank you, Headmaster Kim. Your judgment is fair as always," I said calmly. "However, that leaves Miss Pansera's punishment to still be determined. Before you discuss that matter, let me state now, before all of you, that I refuse to accept Miss Pansera as my consort any longer. She betrayed me and my triad. I invoke the Right of Dissolution. I hereby end our betrothal."

Regan's face paled. Her father's eyes darkened with fury.

"Tread carefully, boy," Lord Pansera growled.

"Silence, Pansera." My uncle spoke for the first time. "The *boy* is within his rights."

Part of me was shocked that Viktor wasn't contradicting me, that he wasn't going to try to persuade me not to cut Regan loose.

I leaned forward. "Your daughter betrayed me, Lord Pansera. She defied me."

Lord Pansera slammed his hands down onto the back of Regan's chair. I watched her jump. "You can't just throw my daughter away like she's nothing! My daughter has been loyal to you and to your family..."

"No," I cut him off. "I beg you to say no more about loyalty. Your daughter has no loyalty to anyone but herself and I think you know that. Good luck finding her a new archon."

Regan shot out of her chair, her face contorted with fury. "You can't do this. You don't understand, Blake. Everything I did, I was doing it for you. For *us*! I wanted things to be like before. Don't throw it all away. Not for that blightborn bitch!"

"I'm not," I snapped. "I'm not throwing anything away that's worth having. Nothing but you, Regan."

Her lips quivered in anger.

"Miss Pansera." Headmaster Kim's voice was icy. "Sit back down." He turned his head towards me. "Very well. Blake, if your uncle makes no complaint, I will accept your request." He looked over at Viktor. My uncle gave a slight nod. "Let the betrothal between Blake Drakharrow and Regan Pansera be dissolved. My secretary will notify the Sanctum and have the records adjusted accordingly."

Kim's eyes shifted to Pendragon. "But we are not through with Miss Pansera's hearing. By highblood law, the death penalty may be invoked for her actions in the Games. Miss Pendragon, as the injured party, you may invoke the Right of Retribution. Do you wish to do so?"

Every eye in the room was suddenly on Pendragon.

"I..." she started to say.

But Lord Pansera cut her off. "Absolutely not, Headmaster. Go no further with this, I warn you. What you propose is an outrage. A blightborn cannot decide the fate of a highblood. If you are determined to continue this farce, I will have to demand the establishment of a tribunal."

We all knew what would happen then.

"No tribunal is required for a disciplinary hearing having to do with a triad when all parties attend this academy," Headmaster Kim said coldly. "But on the chance that you later wish to question these proceedings at the highest level, allow me to alter my original question to one that I believe no tribunal would take issue with." He looked over at me. "Blake Drakharrow, as archon of this triad until a few moments ago, the final decision will be left with you. Do you wish to invoke the Right of Retribution for Miss Pansera's actions against both you and your other consort in the Games?"

I stared back at him. If I said yes, Regan would be executed.

I looked down at the woman by my side. Without having to ask, I already knew what she'd want me to say.

CHAPTER 57

MEDRA

"You did the right thing," I said, as we stepped into the hall.

"Let's just get away from here as quickly as possible before I fucking explode," Blake snapped. "*Was* it the right thing? It sure as hell didn't feel like it."

"It was," I insisted. I gulped down a deep breath, thinking of Naveen. Would Regan's death have paid for his? Would it have been sufficient? Or would it simply have started a new feud between Regan's family and Blake's, ultimately leading to more bloodshed, more chaos, more loss of blightborn life? In the end, Regan hadn't chosen Naveen to die in that dome. I had. "It was the right thing for me. I couldn't live with the guilt of another death on my shoulders."

Blake stopped and turned back to look at me. "Even if it was Regan's?" He raised his hand and brushed it against my cheek. To my surprise, I didn't pull away. "She didn't deserve your mercy."

"She'll never believe it was mine. She thinks it was your mercy," I reminded him.

He laughed. "I'll set her straight about that if she dares to come near me." I felt him glance down at me. "In fact, if she comes near you, I want to know about it. If she ever dares to lay a single finger upon you, I'll..."

"You'll what?" I demanded, whirling to face him. "Kill her yourself?"

"Maybe," he said at last. He shrugged. "I don't usually kill women."

"So, she's safe then." I rolled my eyes.

He grinned. "I didn't say Visha had any qualms about it."

I shook my head. "You're incorrigible."

"You love it. Admit it." He grabbed my arm and pulled me into an alcove, leaning back against a stone windowsill and trapping my body between his long legs. "Tell me you love it when I kill for you."

"What the hell is happening here?" I asked, but the words came out half-heartedly. My heart was pounding. He was so very close. So very warm. "I didn't ask you to kill anyone."

He leaned forward, nuzzling his face against mine. "But you could. Ask me, I mean."

I looked down at him, at the smirk playing over his wide mouth, at those beautiful lips. Being around Blake was like dancing on the edge of a blade. Dangerous but intoxicating.

He pulled me closer against him until there was almost no space left between us. "Admit it, Pendragon. Admit that you love it when I get my hands dirty for you."

My mind whirled. "Blake..."

He cut me off, his finger moving to tilt my chin upwards so I had to meet his eyes. "You think I'm joking, but I'm not." His voice turned serious, more raw. "While you were in the Games, I realized something."

I swallowed hard and tried to pull away again. But his hands gripped my waist, not painfully but tight. "Fine. And what was it?"

"That I'd do anything for you," he said simply. "Hurt anyone. Kill anyone."

My breath caught as the words settled over me. He meant it. I knew he did.

I stared down at his chest, then lifted my finger to the triangle of exposed white skin, tracing the top of his dragon tattoos. His body stiffened beneath my touch, goosebumps forming under my fingers.

What the hell was I doing?

"I don't want that," I said softly, finally lifting my head and looking into his eyes. "I don't want you to kill for me."

He was quiet for a moment. Then he pushed his forehead against mine. "It doesn't matter what you want, Pendragon. You'll never have to ask."

My heart raced. My body was responding to him, with or without my permission.

"I've missed you," he whispered again. His breath moved over my skin, warm and familiar.

I shivered. "I've missed you, too," I breathed. "But Blake, I..."

The kiss was like a thunderstorm that had been gathering for far too long. His lips crushed mine, desperate, heated. Lightning flared. Sparks deep in my soul. My blood tingled.

I should have pushed him away. But I didn't. Instead, I wound my hands around his neck, pulling him closer down to me, sliding my hands into his hair, unable to bear the distance between us for another second.

Blake's hands gripped my waist. He pulled me against him, flattening my breasts against his chest. I could feel every inch of him.

He kissed me as if I were air and he couldn't get enough.

He kissed me like wildfire, consuming everything in its path.

He kissed me as though I were the last drop of blood in the world, the only thing that could ever sate his hunger.

Part of me feared his desire. It was as dark and as deep as a void. If I let him, Blake Drakharrow might just swallow me whole. Devour me like a dragon.

His fangs brushed against my lower lip. My breath caught as I slid my tongue over those sharp points, feeling their edge. He was dangerous. But instead of fear, that knowledge was only fueling the tempest inside of me.

Blake growled, the sound vibrating against my mouth. A shiver coursed down my spine. His hands tightened on my waist, as his lips moved down my neck, grazing my skin with his fangs.

For a moment, I thought he might actually bite down, that he might lose control.

For a moment, part of me wanted him to.

"Your uncle is looking for you, Drakharrow," a cool male voice said from behind me.

The moment shattered.

Blake's head jerked up, his lips parting in a feral snarl. "Tanaka." He stood up, pulling away from me with a growl of frustration.

I turned to see Kage leaning against the opposite wall.

Blake gave me one last look, hungry and possessive. "Later, Pendragon."

He stalked off down the corridor.

I watched him go, trying to steady my breathing, my pulse still racing.

"Well, well." Kage pushed himself off the wall and came over to me. "That looked... intense."

"Just how long were you watching?" I asked coldly.

He smiled. "Not long."

The inked curve of his crescent-moon tattoo curled along the side of his muscular neck. I remembered his house motto. *Luna sanguinea surgit.* Blood moon rises.

I started walking towards the First Year dormitory. He fell into step beside me.

"What do you want, Kage?"

"You know he's only going to break your heart, right?"

I glanced at him sharply, caught off guard.

Kage's usual smooth demeanor softened as he looked down at me. "When that happens," he said quietly. "Remember you have other friends."

"Strangely not comforting," I snapped. "Why don't you mind your own business? We went on one date. You don't own me."

"And neither does Blake. I'm glad we're in agreement," Kage said calmly. "Look, I've seen how this goes, Medra. The Drakharrows are only interested in one thing. Power. And trust me, nothing will come between them and what they want, not even you."

I tensed at his words. "Are you really going to claim House Avari is any different? Please. Spare me the speech."

"I never said we were any different. But I'm not pretending to be something I'm not," Kage replied. He met my gaze and held it. "Just be careful. With Blake. With all of this. Can't you feel it in the air? Something is shifting. The balance. Blake's uncle..."

"What?" I demanded, suddenly afraid.

"Lord Drakharrow senses it, too," Kage said slowly. "Something there. On the horizon."

"Senses what?" I demanded. "Why don't I sense anything?"

"Maybe you do," he said softly, looking at me intensely. "Maybe you don't want to admit it, even to yourself."

I looked away. The only thing I was sensing that I didn't want to admit to Kage was feelings for Blake that went way beyond hatred.

"I don't need your warnings, Kage," I finally said, trying to push past him.

He held up his hands, making no attempt to touch me. "Just keep in mind what I've said. In the spirit of friendship."

"Right," I muttered, walking past.

But even when I got back to the First Year tower, his words lingered, sticking in my mind longer than I wanted them to.

CHAPTER 58

BLAKE

The door to the chamber closed with a thud. Viktor stood at the far end of the room, his back to me.

I approached him with caution, well aware that nothing good had ever come from one of our meetings.

"You've been busy," Viktor said, without turning. "Do you even understand what it is you've just done?"

I clenched my jaw. "Getting rid of Regan was the right decision. She made us look like fools. She made us look weak."

"She made you look weak," my uncle countered. "She made you look like a fool."

"She was a blight on House Drakharrow," I said stubbornly. "She took advantage of your kindness, thinking you would allow her to defy me publicly."

"Ah, so that is what you believe." Viktor rubbed his chin. "Lord Pansera is furious. But it's no matter. I have other plans that House Pansera may be worked into."

"I have no doubt about that, Uncle. You always do," I said coolly, determined to stroke his ego.

Viktor turned to face me. There was something else in his eyes tonight. Something dark, something hungry.

"Marcus came to me with surprising news." He closed the distance between us, stopping inches away. "Am I to understand you've solidified your bond with the dragon rider?"

I forced myself to keep my expression neutral. It wouldn't do to look too eager, too pleased with myself.

It also wouldn't do to tell the full truth.

"I have," I lied, my voice steady. "I've fed from her. As I'd already made her drink of me, our bond is now complete."

For a moment, Viktor said nothing, his cold red eyes scanning my face as if searching for any hint of deceit.

Could he tell? Could he see? I wouldn't have risked it if I thought it would be so obvious.

I stood tall, refusing to crack.

I met Viktor's gaze and then I saw it. Just for a moment, but it was enough. Hunger. Lust. But more than that. The fury in those red eyes.

Viktor hadn't expected me to be able to bond with Pendragon. He'd planned for me to fail, planned for Regan to rebel against the triad, for everything to spiral out of control.

And in the ensuing chaos, Viktor would have stepped in and taken Pendragon for himself.

Just as he'd wanted to do but hadn't dared to do that first day in the Black Keep.

He knew more about her than he was letting on. He always had.

"You're a bold man," Viktor said, his voice smooth. "I always knew you had it in you."

"Thank you," I said stiffly, trying to accept the praise I knew to be a lie. "She was a rich gift, as you said. I owe you for it."

"You do. Just as she still owes me her life. Neither of you should forget that." Viktor's hand shot out, gripping my shoulder painfully. "Be careful, Blake. A bonded blightborn mate is a valuable thing. You cannot feed from another now." He smiled slightly. "But then, that's what you've always wanted, isn't it?"

"I don't know what you mean," I said carefully.

He pushed me backwards and I staggered, nearly falling from the force.

"You've never been quite like us, have you, Blake? Not like your brother, Marcus, with his endless appetites."

"If you mean I don't enjoy murdering blightborns for sport, then no, I'm nothing like Marcus," I said coldly. "I take pride in that."

"The shadow of your father," my uncle mused. I knew it wasn't meant as a compliment. "But don't forget that everything you have, everything you are, is because of me. I made you, Blake. You know it. Your mother knows it. I can unmake you just as easily."

I thought of Aenia, of Pendragon. Of my mother's retreat into the Sanctum. I said nothing.

I couldn't afford to play this game fully. Not yet.

"You're only as strong as I allow you to be," Viktor said, still watching me closely. "Don't forget that."

I nodded stiffly. "I won't let you down."

I started to turn away, then decided to risk a change of subject. "Before I go, I wondered if you received the list of selected First Years I had sent over. Selection Day is tomorrow."

"Another school year, over so soon," my uncle said. "What happy, carefree times you all must have in these old halls. And what a year it has been. Yes, I received it. The list was acceptable. You know I trust your judgment." He smiled thinly.

"Thank you, Uncle."

I hoped Pendragon would be happy with my choices. I'd made some of them with her in mind.

"There will need to be a formal celebration, of course," my uncle said, as I turned to go. "We must welcome your bride into our family."

"I'd thought, perhaps over the summer..."

He nodded, waving a hand dismissively. "We'll arrange it. I look forward to spending more time with Miss Pendragon. A fascinating woman, I'm sure. Well, she must be, to have made you so infatuated to the exclusion of all others."

"She is," I said stiffly. And my uncle wouldn't be getting near her if I could help it. I'd done all of this to protect her. But suddenly I wondered if I'd simply dragged her further into the dragon's den.

Would she have been safer with Kage?

I shook the thought away. Never.

I left the room, my mind in tumult as I strode through the academy corridors towards the House Drakharrow tower.

The weight of the lie I'd told my uncle clung to me. The consequences of what I'd done only began to hit me as the cool spring air hit my skin, blowing in off the sea.

I'd told Viktor that I'd already fed from Pendragon.

Feeding from a blightborn mate was not something to be undertaken lightly. Once I'd done so, I would only be able to feed from her. My bond with her would be exclusive.

I'd ended our triad. We were now a pair. Regan was gone, expelled. There would be no returning to that arrangement, no forging of a new triad.

There was only one inevitable next step if I wanted to protect Pendragon from my uncle.

I had to feed from her and soon.

The lie wouldn't hold unless it became truth.

I'd do it the next night, after Selection Day was over.

My throat was suddenly dry as I thought of it. The idea of finally tasting her blood. I'd waited so long for this moment, for the chance to claim her fully. Blood, body, and soul. To taste her, to take her. To fully possess her in every way I could.

The mere thought of her blood stirred a hunger deep inside me. One I'd been repressing since I'd first found her that day.

I'd fed to survive, fed to live. But this would be different. I could almost taste the sweetness in my mouth. I imagined the way the red liquid would flow from her veins, stirring my senses. She would taste like she smelled. No, better. Unimaginably better. I knew it.

A whiff of guilt crept over me. Would she mind? Would she surrender herself to me like I needed her to?

I pushed my doubts aside. I could explain it to her in a way she'd have to accept. She already wanted me. I knew that. I'd make her understand this was good for both of us. Necessary for survival.

Tomorrow night I'd take what was mine. There was no turning back now.

CHAPTER 59

MEDRA

It was the last day of school.

Florence and I walked side by side down the hall towards the Dragon Court. Today was Selection Day. All First Years would be funneled into one of the four houses. Next year most would take up paths they had already selected. A few exceptions had been made for especially gifted students like Florence, who still couldn't make up her mind.

The halls were alive with a hum of activity as students' cheers rang out every few moments. Despite the ones who were no longer with us–the lucky ones who had been sent away, the unlucky who had been sacrificed in Bloodwing's cruel traditions–the overall mood was celebratory. Students were tossing caps and scarves into the air, spring's warmth having finally broken winter's cold grip. The trees lining the cloisters were in full bloom, soft petals swirling in the breeze.

As we passed by groups of laughing and chattering First Years, the air was thick with anxious energy. Selection Day announcements were coming up in a few minutes. The Dragon Court lay ahead, the vast courtyard where our fates would be decided.

"Feels strange, doesn't it?" Florence said softly. She tucked a strand of sleek black hair behind one ear. "We're missing so many, and yet…" She trailed off but I knew what she meant.

"You deserve to be happy," I said firmly. "You worked hard. You made it this far. Naveen would be proud of you."

"It's so unfair that he's not here with us," she said, lowering her voice.

I nodded. "We'll honor him by surviving." I knew that was what he'd want for Florence. I wasn't sure what he'd want for me.

Regardless, I didn't want my friend harboring too much anger towards the highbloods who had done this to Naveen. I wouldn't have Florence risking herself. It was too dangerous.

And what about me? I'd harbor my anger, store it away, save it up. If what Kage had said was true, something was coming. Whatever it was, maybe I could use it to my advantage.

Because it wasn't Regan who was really to blame for what had happened to Naveen. It wasn't even entirely me—though I would hold onto that guilt like a tether for the rest of my days, refusing to let go. The entire highblood way of life was to blame.

I forced my thoughts away from the darkness and scanned the courtyard ahead as more and more students joined the crowd.

Someone punched me on the arm, hard, and I yelped. "Ouch!"

"There you are," Visha smirked. Her short, silvery-white hair caught the sunlight. She'd razored the sides and looked even more badass than usual. She tucked her hands into the pockets of her trousers. "Mind if I join you two? Thought I'd slum it up today."

She laughed as she caught my expression. "Only joking. Who do you take me for? Regan?"

She inclined her head slightly and I saw Regan on the far side of the courtyard. The queen bee of House Drakharrow was standing all alone.

Visha nudged me. I turned my head and saw Quinn, Gretchen, and Larissa. They had their heads together and were whispering while looking over at Regan.

"How the mighty have fallen." Visha drawled.

"If I know Regan, she won't stay fallen for long," I said drily.

"Oh, she'll crawl back up out of the gutters, no doubt," Visha agreed. "It'll take her a while though. And in the meantime, we can all enjoy her suffering."

"Good afternoon, girls." It was Professor Rodriguez. For once his dark hair was neatly combed. There were no patches on the dark brown corduroy jacket he wore either. He looked at me, his gaze softening slightly. "Miss Pendragon, Miss Shen, Miss Vaidya. I wanted to wish you all luck today."

"Thank you, Professor," Florence said, smiling brightly. "I'm looking forward to seeing more of you next year in Intermediate Alchemy."

"Does that mean you've decided on a healer path, Miss Shen?" Rodriguez asked.

"Not exactly, sir," Florence said, blushing.

"Ah. You've received permission to extend your decision?" Rodriguez smiled. "They only do that for exceptional students. Good luck making your final choice next year."

Before Florence could say anything further, a tall figure strode up and slapped Rodriguez on the back with an easy laugh. "There you are, Gabriel. Ready for Summerfell break?"

We eyed Professor Sankara with interest. The highblood teacher had changed up his appearance a bit, letting his normally tightly cropped curly hair grow out a bit. Silver stubble coated his handsome face, giving him a more rugged appearance.

"Not as much as you are, I think," Rodriguez said, looking at Sankara appreciatively. "The beard suits you, Sebastian. Very pirate-y."

Sankara tossed his head back and gave a deep, rumbling laugh. "You like it? Figured I'd try something new. Why not?"

I glanced at Florence and Visha. Were our teachers actually flirting with each other in front of us?

Rodriguez chuckled. "You'll have the students thinking you've gone rogue."

"Let them think what they want," Sankara replied, giving Rodriguez a playful wink before turning to the three of us. "Good luck today, girls."

As the two men walked away, continuing their banter, I noticed something.

"Florence!" I exclaimed. "Are you checking Rodriguez out?"

She flushed prettily. "No! Of course, I wasn't... He's a teacher!'

Visha raised an eyebrow, her violet eyes sparkling with amusement. "Oh, I saw that. You totally were."

Florence groaned. "You're both imagining things."

Visha's grin widened. "Hey, can't say I blame you. Rodriguez is hot. And with Sankara? Even hotter."

I stared at her for a moment before joining Florence in a fit of laughter.

Visha burst out laughing, too, and for a moment, the tension of the day melted away.

Today was going to change everything. But for now, maybe this was enough.

As our laughter faded, I noticed another familiar figure approaching.

Theo Drakharrow's posture was tense, his hands shoved deep into his pockets. He approached slowly, almost shyly, his steps hesitant, as if not sure what kind of reception awaited him.

I felt a tug of sympathy at the sight of Blake's cousin. He'd had a hard year and something about him seemed so forlorn.

"Theo," I said, stepping forward. I wrapped my arms around him briefly before stepping back. "It's good to see you."

He looked startled, but his expression was grateful. "Hey," he said softly, glancing back at Visha and Florence. I took a few steps away from them. "I just wanted to congratulate you. For getting through the Consort Games." He smiled briefly. "Not to mention for getting Regan out of the triad. I know Blake's thrilled."

I still hadn't fully processed that I was no longer connected to Regan in any way. It was just Blake and I now. We were still betrothed. What did this mean for us? What came next?

"Right," I said slowly. "I still can't believe it myself."

Theo nodded, awkwardly shifting from one foot to another.

"It's been a rough year," I said, watching him. "I hope in the new one we can become better friends."

Theo perked up. "I'd like that. You know you'll wind up in House Drakharrow today, right?"

I nodded. "I figured." What other possibility was there really? I just hoped Florence would be assigned to House Drakarrow with me. With her and Theo and Visha, the next year might not be quite so bad.

Theo took a step back, glancing at the growing crowd. "Anyway, I should go. Have a good Summerfell, Medra."

The year had wrapped up so quickly I hadn't even thought about the summer. Florence was planning on staying at Bloodwing with her mother. I figured I'd do the same.

I watched Theo walk away, wondering if I should have asked him to stay. He seemed so alone. I glanced around the courtyard and realized I hadn't seen Blake anywhere.

Vaughn Sabino suddenly appeared at my elbow. His expression was cheerful, but I knew he must have seen me talking to Theo.

"Hey," Vaughn said.

"I was just talking to Theo Drakharrow," I said. No point in hiding it. Before I could stop myself, I decided to ask the question that had been on my mind for a while. "Do you think... after everything... that there might be a future for you and Theo?"

Vaughn's face stilled, the easygoing smile falling away.

"I don't think he had anything to do with what happened to you," I said softly. "Do you?"

Vaughn shook his head. "No. He came to talk to me, you know. After it happened. He swore he'd had nothing to do with it. He looked absolutely miserable."

"What did you say?"

Vaughn was silent for a moment. "I told him to fuck off. That was when I thought my arm might not heal. That I might be kicked out of Bloodwing."

"Oh." Vaughn's reaction was understandable. Even more so when I thought of Naveen. That could easily have been Vaughn. Did he think about that sometimes? "Tough call."

"Yeah." Vaughn sighed. "He's not a bad person. But... He's not good for me. I just need to stay away from highbloods." He grimaced. "I mean, as much as that's feasible considering where we are."

He lowered his voice. "I'm hoping I get assigned to House Orphos. I've talked to Lysander and he seems like a decent sort. He runs his house in a completely different way than any of the others."

"Really?" I asked curiously. "You'll have to tell me more..."

I suddenly realized the buzz of chatter around us was quickly fading.

The crowd quieted as Headmaster Kim stepped up to the podium at the other side of the Dragon Court.

His sharp gaze swept across the gathering of students.

"Welcome to Selection Day. Today, we honor those of you who have made it through your first year at Bloodwing. Today, you discover where you truly belong."

All eyes were on the headmaster.

Beside me, Florence fidgeted slightly, playing with her hair as though to calm herself.

Visha stood up straight, her arms crossed over her chest. The highblood girl had no reason to be anxious. She was an official consort in House Drakharrow. As was I, I realized. Was this really only a formality where I was concerned? As far as I knew, no one had ever been assigned to a house other than the one their archon was in.

A large stone table had been set up beside the podium. Atop it rested the Selection Stone. The weathered stone orb was enchanted every year and imbued with the names of all First Year students as well as their placement assignments. Once a First Year placed their hand upon the stone, it would glow the color of the house to which they'd been assigned. Red for Drakharrow, silver for Avari, purple for Orphos, and white for Mortis.

Headmaster Kim gestured to the stone. "You will come forward when I call your name, one at a time. Place your hand on the stone. Once you have received your house assignment, go and stand next to the dragon for your house. Once we are through, your House Leader will take you to see your new dormitories so that you know where to go at the beginning of the new term. Let us proceed."

I glanced around and saw that sure enough, the four house leaders had arrived. Blake stood at the base of the Inferni dragon statue.

But he wasn't alone.

I squinted slightly as I noticed something small and furry dart around his legs.

I had to suppress a laugh as I realized what was going on.

Neville had somehow managed to follow Blake all the way to the Dragon Court. Now the pup was skittering around Blake's boots, his fluffy tail wagging as if this was the most exciting day of his little life.

Blake's expression had swiftly gone from amused to horrified. He glanced around, his face flushing as he scanned the courtyard, clearly hoping no one had noticed. Then he quickly bent down and scooped up the pup.

I bit my lip, trying to hold back my laughter as Blake, looking guilty as a child caught stealing from a candy store, stuffed the fluffin into the canvas duffel bag he had slung over his shoulder. The pup's head stuck out from the top of the bag, his pointed ears twitching as he surveyed the courtyard, evidently unbothered by his confinement.

Blake's face was still slightly red. I put a hand to my mouth to stop myself from laughing out loud. I didn't think I'd ever seen him this flustered.

His eyes met mine as he scanned the crowd. I caught the faintest hint of a smile tugging at his lips before he turned away again.

Meanwhile, Headmaster Kim was reading through the list of First Year names. He'd already gotten all the way through the Cs.

I shifted back and forth on my feet restlessly, waiting with Florence and Vaughn for our names to be called.

Around us, one by one, students stepped forward to face their future.

Again and again the stone lit up in various colors.

Finally it was my turn.

"Medra Pendragon."

I took a deep breath as the sound of my name rang out around the courtyard. Heads turned toward me.

I approached the Selection Stone, my hand trembling slightly as I raised it over the orb. I lowered it, touching the stone. It pulsed faintly beneath my fingers. I pressed my palm firmly against it, trying not to think of the last time I'd touched a magical object. The Crown of Bone.

The stone glowed. Vibrant red flared to life beneath my palm.

House Drakharrow.

I pulled my hand away and started walking towards the red dragon.

This had always been my fate. Right from the start. I was bound to House Drakharrow. Always had been.

So why did an uneasy feeling stir inside my chest?

The other students made way as I moved to stand beside Blake.

"I wasn't aware that animals were allowed to attend Selection Day," I whispered, tilting my head up to his ear.

He flushed. "Neville wasn't aware there was a rule against it. If one exists, he believes it should be rewritten."

"Neville can't decide who he loves better, you or Florence. I think he thinks you're both his pets and not the other way around," I said with delight. "Or is it that you're cheating? Have you been luring him away from Florence and the First Year Tower with treats?"

Blake shook his head, his lips twitching. "Soon Neville won't have to make such hard decisions about where his home lies. Watch."

Headmaster Kim had reached the surnames beginning with S. He called Vaughn's name.

The orb glowed red the moment Vaughn placed his hand upon it.

"One down," I murmured, bouncing up and down on the heels of my feet. Then I thought of something. I glanced up at Blake. "Did you...?"

He looked down at me. "Hmm?"

"Hmm indeed," I said archly, as Vaughn walked up to us, wearing a disappointed expression.

I patted him on the back. "It won't be that bad," I whispered. "We'll stick together."

He nodded, but I knew this wasn't what he'd wanted.

Had Blake selected Vaughn to try to appease Theo? Or for me?

Florence's name was being called.

She walked slowly up to the orb looking extremely nervous.

She touched her hand to the stone.

Blake's hand slipped into mine. "Don't worry," he whispered.

My heart sped up. I hoped that meant what I thought it did.

Florence's palm met the stone.

The orb glowed silver.

House Avari.

My heart sank.

"What the fuck," Blake muttered.

I glanced at where Kage Tanaka stood by the black stone dragon. He didn't look our way.

Florence's face had fallen the moment she saw the silver glow. I could tell she was trying hard to keep it together as she walked slowly to join the First Years standing around Kage.

"I swear, I didn't know," Blake said in a low voice. "She was on our list. I'll find out how this happened."

"It's all right," I assured him half-heartedly. "There's nothing you can do now."

I was happy to hear he'd tried to select Florence for House Drakharrow for my sake. It would have been nice to be together.

I glanced at Visha standing a little ways away. Then Vaughn.

At least I knew people in House Drakharrow. But Florence was going to be all alone. I knew she was familiar with all of the other First Years. She'd helped most of them over this past year in her role as a warden. But Naveen and Vaughn and I had been her closest friends. In some ways, she'd be starting from scratch.

"There's nothing to say you can't be friends with students in other houses," Blake whispered in my ear.

"There isn't?" I was kind of surprised. "Glad to hear it."

Because my friendship with Florence wasn't going anywhere.

Blake shook his head. "It's just... not common." He was quiet for a moment, then, "We need to meet. Just you and I. Tonight. Find me here, at the Dragon Court, at midnight."

"A clandestine meeting with my new House Leader?" I murmured. "Now that has to be against the rules."

He shot me a boyish grin. "Not as far as I'm aware. The strangest things should be, but aren't."

I looked up at his profile, at the lines of his lips, and felt myself blushing slightly as I remembered our interrupted kiss from the day before.

I knew I'd be there to meet him that night. Rules or no rules.

CHAPTER 60

MEDRA

The Dragon Court was quiet under the silver glow of the moon. Long shadows stretched from the towering statues of the four dragons, their stone scales gleaming in the faint light.

I walked across the courtyard.

A figure moved in the shadows.

Blake stepped out of the darkness. For a moment, I couldn't breathe.

He looked as if he belonged to the world of shadows and moonlight more than to the realm of flesh and blood. His white linen shirt clung to his lean chest and broad shoulders, fitted enough that I was reminded of his strength. He had a black jacket slung casually over one shoulder. As he walked towards me, he tossed the jacket onto a bench, and my heart fluttered wildly in my chest.

He was... impossibly handsome. More beautiful tonight than I'd ever seen him.

"Pendragon," he said. Then more softly, "Medra."

A small smile tugged at my lips. I wanted this. I'd spent so long pretending that I didn't, but now, in the dead of the night, with Blake looking at me like that, all the denials seemed utterly pointless.

When he spoke my name like that, I couldn't hold onto the anger or the hurt. All I felt was the pull. The irresistible tug that had always drawn us together and that seemed even stronger lately. Urging us to be one, no matter how much I fought it.

His hand reached out, brushing against my cheek with surprising gentleness. Before I could think better of it, I leaned into his touch.

He kissed me.

The kiss was hot, urgent, igniting every nerve in my body.

I kissed him back eagerly, my hands reaching up to tug at the collar of his shirt, pulling him closer, as if afraid if I let go, he might disappear back into the shadows.

His hands settled on my hips, strong and possessive.

Time stopped. There was no guilt, no fear. No past, no pain. There was only this. Only him.

Blake deepened the kiss, his tongue sliding between my lips, and my head spun. How many times had I told myself I hated him? But now, all of that seemed to dissolve.

He'd changed. He'd shown that, hadn't he? He'd protected me. I'd seen how much he protected the people he cared about, how much it hurt him when he failed. He had a softer side. Just look at him with Neville.

Maybe, just maybe, we could move past all of the hurt and the bitterness. Regan was out of the picture. It was just the two of us now. Maybe we could find something real. Forge a true partnership. Find something worth fighting for.

Blake pulled back slightly. He slid his hands up my body and I gasped. Then he raised one hand and touched one of my long, red curls. "You're so beautiful, little dragon," he whispered.

His voice was almost reverent. I found myself melting under the intensity of the words.

Never ever had I been drawn to anyone like I was to him.

He kissed my lips, my cheek, the curve of my jaw. I curled my fingers into the fabric of his shirt, pressing my body closer to his.

His lips grazed my neck. "Medra," he whispered, the words soft and tender. "Let me take care of you."

I could feel the strength in him. Raw power tight beneath the controlled exterior. It thrilled me to touch him, to sense that strength, to know it was for me.

His mouth hovered over the pulse point of my neck. I felt a sense of peace, of trust.

Then I felt his fangs.

A sharp pressure. Then a sharp sting as his teeth pierced my skin.

My eyes flew open as pain jolted through me. For a split second I was frozen, too stunned to react.

Then, with all the strength I could muster, I shoved him away.

He stumbled back. For a moment, he looked wounded, confused, as if he couldn't understand why I'd pushed him.

A smear of my blood stained his lips and I felt a wave of fury flood over me.

His hand flew to his mouth and he wiped at the blood.

I pressed a hand to my neck, feeling the droplets from the two small punctures.

"What the hell are you doing, Blake?" My voice trembled with shock and anger. "You were going to feed on me? Without even asking?"

He took a step towards me but I recoiled. I'd been ready to forgive him, to move past everything, and he had tried to claim me–in the worst possible way.

Blake's expression hardened. "I don't need to ask you."

I think that was the moment my heart cracked.

I stared at him. "I beg your pardon? I think I just misheard you."

"You must know this is the next logical step," he insisted. "It's what we're supposed to do."

I shook my head. "The next step? The next step would be... I don't know. A walk. Dinner. More talking, less fighting." I put my hands to my head. "Not you taking my *blood* without asking."

His handsome face flushed.

"Anyhow, don't you have blood brothels for that? Thralls? Willing blightborn? You don't need to do this."

"I don't need a blood brothel. Or a thrall. Not anymore. I only need you."

"Is that supposed to be romantic?" I gave a harsh laugh. "It's not working for me."

"It's the truth. We're bonded. I don't need to ask to take what's mine." His eyes were wild. He was hungry. How long had he gone without blood, I suddenly wondered. I knew he hated to use thralls. When was the last time he had fed? How long could a highblood go without feeding?

"You're insane if you think that's true," I said coldly. "I'm not yours. I am not your property."

He took a step towards me and I held up my hand in warning.

"Just listen," he pleaded. But there was no hint of apology in his voice. "From the moment your lips touched my blood and from the moment mine touched yours, the bond was complete. I can't feed from anyone but you."

"What did you just say?" I stared at him as if I might be able to will fire from my eyes. "From the moment my lips touched your blood?"

He nodded slowly.

"You lied to me." I was shaking with rage. "You said your blood would protect me. You said nothing about it speeding up this bonding process or whatever the hell this is."

"I didn't tell you. I couldn't. I knew you'd say no."

"You're right," I said. "I would have. You lied to me. What you did was a violation. I would never have drunk your blood if I had known that."

"Then you would have died," he said bluntly. "I needed you to trust me. It was part of the process. You can't force the bonding. Or it won't be as strong."

The words crashed down around me.

"Do you really think you would have survived against Regan? Against three high-bloods, without my blood inside you?" He shook his head. "You're strong and you're fast and you're the smartest woman I know. But even you aren't that good. You must have known, you must have sensed what my blood was doing for you."

I said nothing. He was right and I knew it. But he was also deeply, horribly, troublingly wrong. So wrong.

I felt numb. I stared past him, my eyes landing on the black stone dragon of House Avari. A deep crack ran down its side. The tremors. The quakes must have been damaging the stone statues. I wondered if they could be repaired.

The crack called to me. Reflecting the one splitting my heart in two.

"That doesn't excuse it," I said, my voice low. "I deserved a choice. I still do."

"If you don't let me feed, I'll die," he said. "So what's your choice?"

"Die then," I hissed. "Because I won't save you. Not like this."

"I've saved your life, over and over again, Pendragon. I've killed for you. Bled for you. I did it willingly and I'd do it again."

"I never asked you to do any of that," I shouted.

"That's what mates do for one another," he shouted back. "Don't you feel it? This... compulsion? We are bound, you and I."

I shook my head. "I don't know what's real. I don't know if anything I'm feeling is true. If I believe what you're saying, then we weren't bound until you tricked me into taking your blood. So what is this I feel now? Wanting you? It's all a lie."

"It's not a lie," he insisted.

"I thought you'd changed," I interrupted, my voice rising. "I thought maybe we could move past everything that happened this year. The way you treated me. The way you spoke to me. But I was wrong."

"Medra, I..."

'No," I said coldly. "I think I liked it better when it was just Pendragon. Because you don't know me. And I clearly don't know you. You've bullied me, tormented me, humiliated me. I know what you did with Visha. She told me."

He looked taken aback and I felt a surge of satisfaction.

"She told me the truth," I repeated. "You sent her after me that very first day. You, not Regan. You wanted me to fail. I could have died."

"She lost herself to bloodlust. I went and got Sankara as fast as I could," Blake protested. "I didn't want you to fail. I wanted to test your mettle, that's all."

"Sankara. Right. Sankara not you. You could have stepped in at any time if you'd really cared. You could have stopped her, undone what you'd started. But you didn't. You got a teacher to do it instead. And I'm sure you only did that because, what? You were afraid of getting into trouble?"

"No, because even then, I felt something for you," he insisted. "I wasn't supposed to care about you. I never was. But I did. I do. More than you can..."

"I don't care," I cut him off, my voice flat. "I don't care if you cared then. I don't care if you care now. I don't care about any of it." I shook my head. "I don't want you. I don't want this. You think that just because you come from a family, no, an entire culture, of people who manipulate and control one another that you can do that to me with any repercussions? Well, you can't, Blake. I won't let you."

His eyes darkened. "What's done is done."

I stared at him. "What are you saying?"

"I'm saying we're bound, whether you like it or not. I can't undo that, even if I wanted to."

"And you don't," I whispered. "Do you?"

He didn't respond, just took a step towards me.

"We're mates now. Of the highest order. I can't feed from anyone else, even if I wanted to. And your body..." His voice softened, but a dark undertone remained. "Your body will respond to my call. Whether you want it to or not."

My mind reeled. "That's not true. It can't..."

"It is true." Blake cut me off, taking another step closer. "You feel it, don't you? The pull."

"No." My voice was sharp with fear, but a traitorous warmth was spreading through my body, despite my protests.

"I'll have to show you," Blake murmured.

I turned on my heel, my only thought escape.

"Stop," Blake commanded.

I froze. I couldn't move. Couldn't walk. My body was betraying me.

Panic ebbed through me. Invisible chains pulled me back towards him.

I gasped. "What are you doing to me?" I choked out. "You're using thrallweave."

I slammed up my mental wards, trying to shut him out. But there was nothing there. I couldn't feel him in my mind.

Yet my body was clearly under his control.

Blake stepped closer. "I'm not," he whispered, his breath hot against my ear. "This is the bond."

His eyes were dark and hungry. "I'm sorry it has to be this way."

His mouth hovered over my neck. His hand lifted the hair away.

"No," I whispered. I was trapped, caught in a spell I hadn't even known was being worked upon me.

Blake didn't hesitate. He sank his fangs into my neck with sudden force, piercing my skin.

I gasped. The pain was instant, sharp and hot.

I could feel the blood pulsing from my veins into his mouth. My body shuddered.

My breath came in quick, shallow gasps. My mind screamed for me to push him away. But my hands wouldn't move.

The pain began to fade. Something almost like pleasure replacing it.

I lifted my hands, not to throttle him, but to tangle them in his hair. "Blake," I pleaded.

"I feel it, too," he murmured, between pulls. "We can't deny it. We aren't supposed to. It's never been so good. You're mine now. Always."

Blake's fangs were deep in my neck, his lips pressed firmly against my skin as he drank. He wasn't stopping. The pull of my blood called him.

Something was changing. Energy was draining from me. My body, once warm with heat, was beginning to grow cold. I tried to move, tried to shove him off, but my limbs were weak.

"Blake..." I gasped.

He didn't stop. Or he couldn't. His hunger, his need, seemed all-consuming.

His grip on me tightened as he drank deeper, more urgently.

My vision began to blur, the world around me starting to slip away. I felt my body shaking. The ground was trembling.

But it wasn't just me.

The stones of the Dragon Court were shaking.

Suddenly, we were thrown to the ground, Blake's fangs ripping from my neck, as our bodies collided with hard stone. I cried out in pain but my voice was drowned out by the deafening sound of stone erupting around us.

The entire courtyard was vibrating with incredible force.

Blake rose up over me, wrapping his arms around me, and shielding my body with his own. "Stay down," he growled, his voice harsh.

"Get off," I choked out, struggling weakly against him.

But he wouldn't move.

A huge chunk of stone crashed nearby, sending dust and debris swirling into the air.

Then another fell, striking Blake on the head.

I screamed as blood began to trickle from a gash on his forehead, dripping onto me. But still, he didn't move. His breathing was heavy, his muscles tensed as more stone rained down around us.

Amidst the chaos, something caught my eye.

The stones that were falling. Every single one of them was black.

The ground shook again, harder this time.

There was a shuddering roar. I watched Blake's eyes widen.

But I already knew what was happening. Maybe part of me had known all along.

I watched Blake turn his head just in time to see the black dragon's stone shell begin to crumble and the ancient beast beneath begin to move.

Layers of rock slid away from the dragon's body, revealing sleek, midnight-black scales.

It shook its wings free from the debris, unfurling them with a powerful snapping sound.

With another, earth-shattering roar, the black dragon stretched its wings wide, blocking out the moonlight.

The sight was horrifying. Utterly magnificent. Utterly terrifying.

I pushed against Blake. "Move. Blake, move." My voice was hoarse, desperate, and this time, he did as I said.

I scrambled to my feet, my body weak. I shook my head a little and stepped towards the dragon.

He was looking back at me.

The creature was immense. Seeing the skulls had been one thing. This was another.

His wings stretched wide, every inch covered in shimmering black scales, an impenetrable-looking armor.

His eyes were deep-set, reptilian, glowing like embers in the dark.

His head was long, graceful, and crowned with dark, spiraling horns.

He lowered his head slightly and his jaw parted, revealing rows of razor-sharp, white teeth.

My heart raced, but still I took step after step towards the dragon.

Then I heard him speak.

"Thank you for waking me."

I froze. He was speaking in Classical Sangrathan, his mind to mine.

"I didn't wake you," I replied, my voice trembling slightly. "I think perhaps there's been some mistake."

"No mistake." The dragon's head tilted slightly, eyes narrowing as he regarded me. Despite his massive size, there was an elegance to his movements. "You spoke the words. You severed the binding. You brought me back."

"I don't understand..." I began. Then my thoughts flew back to the incantation I had performed in the very same courtyard, months ago. The one I had used to break the soul-binding.

"By blood and breath, by night and sky," I whispered. "The binding of souls I sever."

The dragon inclined his head slightly.

"Let what was trapped be freed to fly,

No longer bound forever.

From heart to soul, from blood to bone,

Let life return where stone has grown.

What's locked away, now shall take flight,

Awakened be the soul tonight," he recited. "Old words. Powerful ones."

"I don't understand," I whispered back. "The ritual. It was meant to end the binding. To set a soul free."

"And it did," the dragon pointed out.

"But I didn't mean...to bring something back."

"Perhaps the pages of your book were stuck together," the dragon growled, voice tinged with amusement at my predicament. "You performed a ritual meant to end a soul binding, yes, and to return a soul to life. And now, I am awake."

The dragon's wings beat slowly, sending gusts of wind through the courtyard that rattled the pebbles and debris and blew my hair back.

My mind raced, frantically trying to remember everything I'd read in Professor Rodriguez's books about dragons.

Dragons weren't mindless beasts. They were intelligent, ancient beings with vast wisdom and power. They lived longer than blightborn. Most could live longer than highbloods. Bonding with one was an almost sacred act and a dangerous one. It required initiation. Bonding was the only way to tether a dragon's loyalty.

I couldn't believe I was actually thinking of attempting it. Not after what Blake had just put me through.

But if I didn't at least try, what would happen to me?

My thoughts scrambled as I sifted through what I could recall about the rituals, the methods. I could feel the dragon's eyes on me, watching my every move with a sort of detached curiosity.

Time was slipping away.

"Nyxaris, Duskdrake of House Avari," I began. My voice was trembling. Would this ancient creature really respect anything I had to say?

"Ah, so you know my name," the dragon rumbled. "And are you of House Avari, young one?"

"No, but I... I need to initiate the bond," I stammered. "I can't let you leave. I'm the only dragon rider in Sangratha." The words sounded absolutely ridiculous as they came out of my mouth.

The dragon must have thought so, too. He snorted, hot puffs of breath washing over me. I flinched.

"Nyxaris of House Avari, you... you are magnificent. Your scales shine like the night itself, glistening with the wisdom of the ages." I wracked my brain, trying to remember the words I had read. Why, oh, why hadn't I devoted more time to those books? "Your beauty... It's like the stars. Each star must quiver as they see your majesty. Bound to you in reverence."

The dragon's eyes narrowed slightly and I could feel his amusement growing, but I pressed on, my voice gaining strength.

"You are the most powerful being this world has ever known. You've endured centuries. Seen empires rise and fall." I had no idea if any of this was true, but it sure seemed possible. "No one else, not even another dragon, could possibly match the depth of your knowledge or the breadth of your courage or the strength of your powerful wings."

Nyxaris let out a low rumble. "Flattery, little one?" The dragon's voice was ripe with amusement. "You think you may charm me into submission?"

My heart raced. "Not just flattery, O Black Nyxaris. Sincerity. I see your greatness. I sense your wisdom. You deserve to be honored, revered... and to have a rider worthy of you. Someone who can carry your legacy forward and stand loyally by your side."

I took another step closer, my eyes locking with the dragon's gaze. "Let me be that rider. I'll be your companion, never your master." Somehow that seemed important to say. "I will never bind you or hold you back." As if I could if I tried. "Together, we can..."

Nyxaris made a low resonant noise. The sound vibrated through the air, shaking the ground I stood on, and I wobbled, throwing my arms out to keep my balance.

It was a laugh, I realized. The dragon was laughing at me.

"Let me stop you there, child. Enough. Do you think I am so easily swayed by flowery words?"

Panic flooded through me. I closed my eyes, searching for the words I had read, the phrases used by riders who came long before me.

I raised my hands, palms up, and sank to my knees, trying one last time. "By blood and breath, by night and sky, I pledge myself to you, Nyxaris of House Avari. Your beauty, your power are unmatched. Let my soul be bound to yours, my life to your flight. Together, we will..."

"Stop." Nyxaris's massive head tilted slightly, his eyes growing brighter and more cold. "Do you not think I have heard these words before, spoken by riders now long dead? Do not waste your breath. I will not fall for it again."

My heart sank. "What do you mean?"

The dragon moved backwards, his wings beating a little faster.

He was getting ready to fly. He'd leave me here behind and never return.

"Nyxaris, please," I begged, my voice cracking slightly. "If you leave, I think they'll kill me. They'll kill me if they think you aren't coming back and that it was my fault. I can't survive without you."

Nyxaris's eyes remained locked on mine, cold and unwavering. "Then, little one, you had best get very good at lying," the dragon growled. "Make them believe I will return, if you wish. But I have no plans to do so."

Something in the dragon's eyes softened as he looked at me.

"You have freed me from a cursed slumber. Restored my soul in an unasked for gift. But make no mistake, that is the only reason you are still kneeling there on the stone. Any other creature, I would have already burned to ash." I felt a shiver go down my spine. "Especially that highblood man skulking behind you," Nyxaris added.

"So you do not consider yourself bound to House Avari?" I asked, trying one last time.

"No. Even if I did, you are not of that house. Are you?"

I shook my head wordlessly.

"Do not mistake this for kindness, little one." The dragon's words held a quiet, terrifying power. "It is simply gratitude. Fleeting as it may be."

Nyxaris gave a final, dismissive glance towards me, and then unfurled his wings fully, beating them against the air with a force that rattled the stones.

Slowly, the dragon's black-scaled body rose up from the courtyard.

My breath hitched as I watched the dragon lift higher and higher, his great wings stirring the air like a storm. The wind was whipping through my hair, pushing me backwards, and yet I couldn't tear my eyes away.

Nyxaris was the most magnificent thing I had ever seen and in a moment, he'd be gone forever.

With another powerful beat of his wings, the black dragon rose up over Bloodwing Academy. As he soared, he roared and the sound echoed across the stones, shaking the walls of the courtyard.

Every student, every professor at Bloodwing would have heard that roar, if they had not already felt the tremors. Many had no doubt rushed to their windows and even now were witnessing the dragon's ascent.

Nyxaris banked sharply, wings catching the wind as he turned in the direction of Veilmar. He flew away from me, across the moonlit sky, his black form slowly becoming nothing but a distant shadow over the city.

For a moment, I stood there, frozen, the courtyard now eerily silent. The wind had settled. Yet I could still feel the echo of the dragon's presence.

The enormity of what had just happened settled into my bones.

I had awakened a dragon.

Finally, I turned around.

Blake stood behind me, his eyes wide, still staring up at the sky where the dragon had vanished. His face was pale, streaked with blood from the wound on his head.

Our eyes met, the weight of everything hanging between us unspoken, too vast for words.

A dragon was free. The world had heard his roar.

There would be no going back.

THE DRAGONS ARE COMING...

Medra's story has just begun.
Will she survive her Second Year at Bloodwing Academy?
Book 2: A Legacy of Dragons will be here in early 2025!
Preorder now on Amazon to be the first to find out what happens next as Medra faces down vampires, dragons, and a fate she never asked for. The tentative release date is February 28—but dragons, as you know, are unpredictable and could show up even sooner...

Also, if this book kept you up at night, filled your soul with slow-burn tension, or made you consider taking up dragon riding yourself, please consider **leaving a review on Amazon or Goodreads**. It helps so much. I'm an indie author, and reviews are my lifeline.

Are you House Drakharrow, Avari, Mortis, or Orphos? Whatever you choose... I'll see you in Year 2!

JOIN MY STREET TEAM: BRIAR'S ROSE COURT

If you'd like to discuss my books, meet other romantasy book lovers, share pictures or quotes about your favorite characters, vote on character names and book titles, get sneak peeks at covers and other art, and enter exclusive giveaways, then I would love to have you over in our private **Rose Court Street Team Facebook group**!

Come join in the fun!

Sign-Up for the Street Team: rosecourt.briarboleyn.com

Also by Briar Boleyn

Blood of a Fae Series

Queen of Roses

Court of Claws

Empress of Fae

Knight of the Goddess

Bloodwing Academy

On Wings of Blood

Book 2 – COMING EARLY 2025

Written as Fenna Edgewood...

The Gardner Girls Series

Masks of Desire (The Gardner Girls' Parents' Story)

Mistakes Not to Make When Avoiding a Rake (Claire's Story)

To All the Earls I've Loved Before (Gwen's Story)

The Seafaring Lady's Guide to Love (Rosalind's Story)

Once Upon a Midwinter's Kiss (Gracie's Story)

The Gardner Girls' Extended Christmas Epilogue (Caroline & John's Story – Available
to Newsletter Subscribers)

Must Love Scandal Series

How to Get Away with Marriage (Hugh's Story)

The Duke Report (Cherry's Story)

A Duke for All Seasons (Lance's Story)

The Bluestocking Beds Her Bride (Fleur & Julia's Story)

Blakeley Manor Series

The Countess's Christmas Groom

Lady Briar Weds the Scot

Kiss Me, My Duke

My So-Called Scoundrel

About the Author

Briar Boleyn is the fantasy romance pen name of USA TODAY bestselling author Fenna Edgewood. Briar rules over a kingdom of feral wildling children with a dark fae prince as her consort. When she isn't busy bringing new worlds to life, she can be found playing RPG video games, watching the birds at her bird feeder and pretending she's Snow White, or being sucked into a captivating book. Her favorite stories are the ones full of danger, magic, and true love.

Find Briar around the web:

https://www.instagram.com/briarboleynauthor/
https://www.bookbub.com/profile/briar-boleyn
https://www.amazon.com/stores/Briar-Boleyn/author/B0BLWFKHWC
https://www.tiktok.com/@authorbriarboleyn

Made in the USA
Las Vegas, NV
03 May 2025

21593062R00301